09/15

PRAIRIE DU CHIEN MEMORIAL LIBRARY

125 S. Wacouta Ave.

Prairie du Chien, WI 53821

(608) 326-6211

Mon/Thur 9-8   Fri 9-5   Sat 9-1

17.⁰⁰ 09/15

Published by Broken E Publishing.

ISBN-13 (Print): 978-1511759076
ISBN-10 (Print): 1511759070
ISBN (ebook): 978-1-943087-02-0

Cover Design by Jenny Zemanek at Seedlings Design Studio

Visit me at teresayea.com

3

CHAPTER 1

AMERICAN GOTHIC

Bloodstains are the hardest to remove.

I scrubbed the floor until my shoulders screamed with pain. Heat from the desk lamp fried my back like a white-hot sun. I studied the brown splatters over my bed and blew an inky strand of hair away from my face. "Eff my life."

After the floor, the wall was next. Not that I was a neat freak or anything, but this stain had to go. This was war: Ava Nolan versus the spot.

As I paused to dab my sweaty temple, it occurred to me I could be doing better things on a Saturday night. In Santa Monica, life was one drunken party after another. There were no parties in Eckhart. Unless you counted the pulse-pounding bingo tournament held every afternoon at the senior center. Most of the locals were in bed long before the ten o'clock evening news.

I had no friends in this fog-choked town. No homework. And thanks to my expulsion from school three months ago, no

5

diploma or future. Scrubbing a sixty-year-old homicide off my bedroom floor was the highlight of my night.

I dunked the brush into the bucket, flinching as my raw knuckles made contact with a brew of bleach and lye. A ribbon of blood trickled down the back of my hand. I wiped the cut on my jeans, slapped the brush to the floor and got back to work. What's a little blood in times of war?

"Just one more."

One more scrub should do it.

A clean slate. We could be happy.

You can't start a new life in a new house with the former occupant still splattered everywhere. My dad bought the abandoned Hopkins' farm at a steal. Sometime during the '50s, Old Man Hopkins slaughtered his entire family before training his shotgun on himself. I got eight-year-old Mary Hopkins' room and judging by the size of the stain, I'd say her short life came to a particularly gruesome end.

Despite the stigma of moving into a murder house, I was determined to make a fresh start. Sure my dad, brother, and I weren't living in the most sanitary surroundings, but here in Eckhart we were hundreds of miles north of Los Angeles and ten years away from memories of my mother.

At the thought of Mother, fear gnawed at my stomach like a persistent rat. I dropped the brush and stared at the bucket.

I saw a bathtub.

6

Filled to the brim with soapy water.

And Mother.

Washing my hair.

Scrubbing my skin pink.

I could never be clean enough, not even when the water turned bloody.

To stem the tide of an impending freak-out, I recited an old childhood chant, invented the day Mother disappeared.

She was dead. The dead couldn't hurt the living.

But as I listened to the wind whistle across the eaves and the incessant mewing of a tomcat, I wasn't so sure anymore.

"Ava." My mother's voice clawed across the black skin of night. *"Ava."*

Lifting my sweater, I pinched my abs until the skin underneath my belly button became red and angry. The pain reminded me of my mother's touch. According to her, I was born rotten and whenever I threw a tantrum, she would dig her nails into my stomach so my dad wouldn't notice the crescent-shaped marks she left behind.

Sometimes she did this when I was already calm—just to make me howl. I believed she was testing me. When I remained unruffled even as blood dribbled down my navel, terror swarmed my mother's face like a cloud of locusts. "You have a dirty soul, my lovely. A wicked heart," she said, dragging me to the bathtub where she'd wash me as white as snow.

I was eight years old when my mother tried to drown me.

Mary Hopkins and I had a lot in common.

I rose to my feet and shook the kinks from my body. Mother was gone; all my resentment over her trying to kill me had long since scabbed and crusted over. The funny thing was, as much as I feared her, I still loved her. Not even an attempted murder, committed in a moment of temporary insanity, could break the bond between mother and daughter. My love was buried deep inside the chambers of my wicked heart.

In need of a breather, I sidestepped a fortress of moving boxes to get to my dressing table. I picked up my iPhone and checked my messages, hoping for a text, an @reply, a Like or comment on my sexy new Instagram selfie.

There were none.

Sighing, I lifted my eyes to the photos clustered around the mirror. While I'd yet to tackle unpacking, I'd spent the better part of this afternoon Scotch-taping each picture with care. In my sophomore Sadie Hawkins portrait, I was perched atop a paper moon and wrapped in the arms of Drake Elliott, the hottest guy in school. My attention traveled to Winter Formal. Homecoming. Senior Prom. I was the star of every event.

Leaning over, I peered at my cell, expecting a text in the space of a second. I did get an email, but it was only the king of Nigeria trying to sell me a diamond mine. Apparently, my friends had forgotten all about me. Maybe my selfie wasn't as epic as my make-out snapshot with my friend Cindy. I needed to top that.

I unwrapped my homecoming crown and, being careful not to bleed on the silver sparkles, propped it on my head. Lounging next to the bloodstain, I stripped off my sweater and struck a pose to show off my lilac push-up bra. I snapped the picture and typed "A Royal Bloody Mess" before posting.

A minute later, my phone dinged. I had ten Likes and five comments.

"Sweet."

"Gross, whose blood?"

"I don't get the crown???"

"Take the bra off!"

"I'll tap that."

"Me too."

The Likes poured in. Giddy from the attention, I typed, *"I killed someone, bitchz!"*

Drake's comment popped up. *"Hot! Let's do it next to the bloodstain."*

Leave it to Drake to post a public booty call. I smiled and replied, *"I'm open."*

Cindy added to the thread, *"We know ur legs are. Narcissistic slut J/K. FYI, the crown is LAME!"*

My smile vanished, especially after her comment garnered more Likes than my picture and some agreement about my sluttiness. I shut off my phone, feeling more lonely and lame than hot and popular.

I flexed my fingers and studied the weeping cut on my hand. "A royal bloody mess," I whispered.

The cat ceased its mewing and hissed at something or someone unseen. Setting my crown gently atop a velvet cushion, I glanced over my shoulder. Something was stirring in the air, an electric ripple that filled me with misgiving. I ran a hand across my forearm and discovered all the hairs standing on end. The ivy rustled against the wrought-iron trellis and somewhere on the lawn...

Footsteps.

Turning around, I listened again. Yes. Footsteps.

Purposeful strides crunching on weeds and nettles.

I crossed to the window to investigate. Beyond the slanted outline of our rickety fence, rows of leafless trees stretched to infinity, remnants of the old apple orchard gone to seed. My breath frosted the single-pane glass like icing.

When the mist evaporated, I realized I had an audience.

A tall figure leaned against the fence post, squinting at the beacon of light from my window. He tucked his hands in his jacket pocket and turned his collar up against the cold. His breath coiled about him like cigarette smoke.

Shouldn't most pervs scurry or hide when caught? This lurker had balls. He never budged.

I pressed my body against cool glass, trying to get a better glimpse at his face. The shadows cloaked his features, smudging out his eyes. Even so, they burned with the fanatical intensity of a traveler on a black pilgrimage. Judging by the way he was staring at me, one would think he'd found his Holy Grail.

His staring problem sent the hackles rising on the back of my neck. What a creep. As I tugged on my sweater, an infusion of revulsion and rage coursed through my bloodstream.

He'd seen me.

Half naked and in a plastic crown, of all things.

He'd probably tell his friends about the new girl at the Hopkins' farm and they'd judge and laugh. When they were done laughing, they'd return to their comfy homes and tidy lives, relieved in the fact that no matter how bad their problems were, at least they weren't as screwed-up as mine.

As if he could read my mind, the stranger raised his hand. Slender fingers curled in the air. If this bargain basement James Dean expected to intimidate or scare me, he had another thing coming. But as I dashed to my brother's room, the memory of those ghostly fingers lingered. Perhaps this stranger was not waving at all, but beckoning me to join him on a dark adventure.

◆

He was a scrawny guy about my age, seventeen, maybe nineteen at the most.

11

Propped against the barn, he looked as pathetic as a scarecrow. Somehow he'd seemed scarier standing outside my bedroom window, a dark prince cloaked in fog and shadow.

His name, we learned after my brother put him in a headlock, was Ben Wolcott.

"I don't get you, Ava." Cam scrubbed the sweat from his buzz cut. "You wanted me to talk to him and here I am"—he kicked Ben in the ribs. Ben groaned and hacked up a string of bloody spittle—"talking."

"Stop it!" I latched on to Cam's brawny forearm and dragged him away from Ben. My brother and I had different definitions when it came to "talking."

"He's had enough, you idiot!"

Cam never knew when to quit. My brother's head, as our dad always said, was filled with missiles instead of brains—and it only took a spark to launch WWIII. As his sister, only I knew how to work the controls, but I wondered if I ever had control in the first place.

Cam cursed under his breath and booted a rusty wheelbarrow instead.

Point made, I drew my corduroy jacket closer to keep my teeth from chattering. Back in Santa Monica, I lived in tank tops and shorts, wore my bikini to the mall. Moving to NorCal was like moving to the North Pole. I was having trouble acclimatizing to Eckhart. One week in this seaside wasteland and I'd not only lost my tan, but was seriously thinking about investing in a whale hunter's jacket.

Fog swirled around the orchard of twisted apple trees. Uphill from the barn, our clapboard farmhouse loomed against a violet sky, all windows dim except for my bedroom where a halogen lamp flickered like a bug zapper. Dad was still asleep. Good thing I had the foresight to use my indoor voice when alerting Cam. Dad would freak at the sight of all this blood, yet this was the same man who thought moving into an *In Cold Blood* crime scene was a good idea. Fortunately, my brother was easier to figure out.

"*Beat him up,*" Cam said, "*No, not too much.* What do you want from me?"

"I never ordered you to beat him up. Don't put words in my mouth."

Cam—probably still smarting over my "idiot" remark—muttered, "I was only doing it for you."

I stepped forward to apologize, but the sentiment knotted around my tongue and left me feeling awkward and embarrassed. Saying sorry usually involved lots of bumbling, and I ended up sounding sarcastic instead of sincere.

Taking Cam by the hand, I dragged him away from Ben. "Remember your police record," I whispered in his ear. "Does it need another assault and battery charge?"

With a grunt, Cam jammed his hands in his pockets.

"Control your temper. For me, okay?" I seized his chin and

forced him to look into my eyes. "Don't be like Mom."

Thanks to our mother, violence flowed through his veins like a genetic disorder. While I tried to fight this flaw in our blood, my twenty-one-year-old brother had all the makings of a sociopath. Dad and I lived in perpetual terror that Cam would kill someone and get put away for life. Murder woes aside, us Nolans were just like every American family.

Cam lowered his head. "Whatever."

Taking this as a sign of agreement, I pecked him on the cheek. "I'm a jerk."

He mustered a grin. "I know."

I looked to the boy wheezing in the weeds and debated calling the police. Negative. Dad's fear of blood took a backseat only to his fear of cops. All the interrogations they put him through after our mother's disappearance really did a number on his nerves.

In the interest of saving Dad another breakdown, I decided to take matters into my own hands. "Did he say anything to you?"

"He says he got the wrong window," Cam said. "He's here to see Professor Nolan."

"Dad?" It was hard acting like a badass when you were having convulsions from the cold, but I was determined to rebuild my defenses. I pulled my tangled black hair into a messy ponytail. "What does he want with Dad?"

Curling his hands into fists, Cam started toward Ben. "I'll find out."

14

I pointed to the horse trough at the far end of the barn. "Go sit over there and let me do the talking."

The thought occurred to me that Ben may have a gun or knife. But instead of fear, a secret thrill shimmied up my spine. Ever since my mother tried to drown me, I'd been a little in love with death.

Lifting a gaudy bangle from Forever 21.

Downing Ecstasy with a shot of vodka.

Driving ninety in Drake Elliott's Ferrari and then pulling over to hump his brains out by the side of the road.

The rush.

The high.

My mother and I had one thing in common: we desired all the things which would destroy us in the end.

Kneeling in front of Ben, I listened to his labored breathing. He lolled his head against the barn and studied me through the puffy slit of a swollen eye. He'd had ample opportunity to run, yet here he remained, which made me wonder if he was a little in love with death, too.

"You can thank me now." I dabbed his nose with my sleeve. His blood stained the corduroy a brilliant shade of red, my favorite color.

"For what?"

"Saving your life."

On impulse, I traced the shattered bridge of his nose.

15

Underneath the blood and bruises, he was all angles and sharp lines. A blade for a nose. Daggers for cheekbones. I could cut myself slapping him in the face. Naturally I was intrigued.

Ben jerked his head away, wanting no part of my nursing. "Humility. Ever heard of it?"

"Humility. What's that? An SAT word?"

He snorted, then winced in pain. "Are you for real?"

"I'm the good cop." I peeked over my shoulder to make sure Cam stayed put. Glowering at us, Cam splashed slimy trough water over his face and proceeded to clean the blood from his knuckles. He could be as mean as a pit bull when riled up, but he was always sweet and loyal to me.

Following my gaze, Ben said, "You should keep your brother on a leash."

Apt words. Little did he know, I was already keeping Cam on a leash. "For someone who's just been beaten into a bloody pulp, you sure have a mouth on you. Hold still…"

As I dabbed his nose again, my sleeve slid up my wrist. Three old scars, reminders of my tenth-grade cutting days, caught the moonlight.

"You like to play with knives?" he asked.

I tugged down my sleeve, feeling as guilty as if *I* were the one caught peeping. "None of your business."

I didn't take a razor blade to my arm because "the physical pain was the only way I could release my emotional pain" or some

16

textbook shit like that. This was an experiment to see how fast I'd heal and the answer was: pretty damn fast. My skin melded back after an hour, a shame, too, since I thought the blood droplets mesmerizing, each one an isolated jewel. I once asked Cam if I could cut him too and he'd shrugged, "Sure, what the hell." Cam healed just as fast and his blood had been just as precious. My brother and I were single-handedly putting Band-Aids out of business while keeping psychiatrists fed.

Ben, probably delirious from his ass-kicking, muttered, "He said you would be…good with a knife. You're exactly who we've been searching for."

"Who the fuck is he?"

He blinked—or winked to be more specific since he only had one working eye. "What did I say?"

"You tell me."

Ben opted for silence. Long, *awkward* silence.

"You said you were here to see my dad," I asked before he got any weirder. "How do you know him?"

"I was in his Occult History class last year," he said, confirming my hunch. Dad taught at UCLA until he was fired for failing to show up for lectures or stumbling in drunk when he did.

That was over a year ago. Why would Ben try to contact Dad now? And during the middle of the night? This guy took stalking to a new level.

"I suppose you followed him all the way up here to talk about your term paper?" I plucked a stray dandelion from the weeds, marveling at the way the moonlight turned the bulb iridescent. "My dad isn't exactly holding office hours from home. You're a long way from LA, friend."

"Eckhart's my hometown." Ben grinned, baring straight teeth coated in blood. "I came to ask him one question. Maybe you can answer it, *Ava*."

Despite our mutual hostility, I liked the way he wrapped his lips around my name. So calm. So cool. No fear. No shame.

"Fine." With Cam watching my back, I didn't see any harm in flirting with danger. "I'll play along."

"Come closer…"

Discarding the dandelion stem, I crawled toward him.

"Closer."

"Don't push it, perv," I said, inching forward until I was practically straddling one of his thighs.

The same tomcat raced through the brambles and the caw of a blackbird echoed through the deserted orchard.

His clothes smelled of grass after the rain. The peppermint sting of his breath scraped my lungs and stirred the hairs on my temple. "Has he found Arabella's Curse yet?"

A chill crawled up my forearm. No longer in a joking mood, I pulled away. "The ruby?"

"You know of it?" Ben asked, black eyes dancing in amusement at the sudden change in my expression.

18

Of course I did. No self-respecting daughter of Professor Mortimer Nolan could escape childhood without hearing about Arabella's Curse, the ruby with the power to resurrect the dead.

Magic.

Immortality.

The power of God.

Dad used to tell the best bedtime stories. There was the one about an ancient set of scrolls that foretold the apocalypse. Or the fable about a sword forged with the venom of a sea serpent that could vanquish the undead.

As a kid I couldn't get enough of Dad's tales of good and evil. Or stop marveling at his collection of macabre artifacts. An elixir brewed from mermaids' scales. An executioner's ax from the days of Henry VIII. His morbid cabinet of mummified cats.

But I wasn't a kid anymore. There was no magic in the world, no prophecy in the stars. The dead stayed dead. My dad, who once loved me most of all, could no longer stand being in the same room with me. And much like Bigfoot or the Loch Ness Monster, Arabella's Curse couldn't possibly exist—especially not in a dump like Eckhart.

"Fairy tales," I said, unable to hide my bitterness. Dad would do better chasing windmills than searching for Arabella's Curse.

The porch light switched on, dousing the overgrown lawn in an eerie wash of green. The screen door slammed and Dad marched down the steps, navy bathrobe flapping like a cape behind him. "What the hell is going on here?"

Cam jogged up the hill, meeting Dad halfway. Their shouting—well, mostly Dad's shouting—cleaved through the whistle of the wind. "She put you up to this, didn't she?"

This was going to be bad.

A drop of blood splattered my forearm. With a strained smile, Ben wiped his nose and collapsed against me.

"Don't discount a good fairy tale," he croaked. "The best ones begin and end in blood."

CHAPTER 2

A PLACE IN THE SUN

Slamming the kitchen door behind us, Dad backhanded me across the face.

I stumbled into the fridge, my ears ringing from the slap. I was underwater. Swimming. Happily swimming.

Meanwhile, on land: Cam called Dad an asshole. Dad whacked Cam upside the head for having the gall to call him an asshole. The gall? He was a scholar after all, licensed to use fancy words when slapping his children around. Quite comical, really. Three Stooges silly. Ha. Ha.

"Keep your voice down!" Dad's eyes shifted to the living room, where we'd deposited a semi-conscious Ben on the sofa.

I probed my throbbing lip and clutched the fridge handle. The orange floor tiles swirled like a kaleidoscope of bad taste. Digging my fingernails into my palm, I reminded myself that I hadn't cried in front of an audience since my mother disappeared, and I wasn't about to start now.

I was a black-hearted bitch, or so, that's what someone scribbled in my yearbook junior year. Okay, the note really called me the "C" word, not that it bothered me. In fact, I invented a motto to show how *much* it didn't bother me:

Black hearts bruised and bled, but never felt pain.

Black hearts couldn't be broken.

It only took a slap for me to realize this motto was utter nonsense. This bitch's black heart was breaking.

Dad turned on the faucet. Tasting blood, I squared my shoulders and stared at the back of his head. His lumpy skull seemed a familiar sight, especially in the kitchen. Before the memory had a chance to stir, he appeared at my side and pressed a wet dish towel to my lip.

A frown tugged on his brows as he turned my face left and right.

In that moment, he resembled the father who used to take me to two-dollar cinemas and whistle along to *Singing in the Rain*. Those were happier days, a childhood when he held my hand while we crossed the street and tried to braid my hair. One day, quite out of the blue, he stopped holding my hand and taking me to old movies. His smiles curdled into grimaces, his compliments into criticisms, his warmth cooled into a nuclear winter.

My dad raked a hand through his hair, causing the fair strands to stick up like tuffs of straw. "I *am* an asshole. You have permission to hate my guts."

22

Dad confused me. Sometimes it seemed he seriously hated me, then there were these rare moments of tenderness. His love was on and off, hot and cold.

In his defense, Dad never struck us unless we deserved it. The last time Dad laid a hand on me was in May, when I'd been expelled a month shy of graduation. He'd gone apeshit after my school board hearing and did a little dance on my face. But later that night, he'd sat by my bedside and caressed my cheek. I didn't dare move or breathe. I was too afraid; if he knew I was awake, he'd stop. In the grand scheme of things, a little pain was worth it—if it meant he'd pay attention to me again.

Laying a shy hand on his arm, I plucked the towel from his grasp. He felt so thin, like he was wasting away. I'd already forgiven him. Screw pride. Fuck dignity. Dad was the sun around which my world orbited, and I'd spent the years since my mother's death chasing after his light.

I am still in the dark.

"I could never hate you, Dad," I said, and waited for him to say the same in return. I could warm myself for another decade on just one kind word from him.

As if my touch repelled him, Dad backed away and I knew, every time he went through these episodes, he was thinking of *her*.

Whenever he looked at me, he saw my mother. We were look-alikes: raven-haired, gray-eyed doppelgangers. Even though their marriage was a collection of screaming matches, it seemed

Dad would've preferred I'd been killed that bleak December night instead of his beloved wife.

Alarmed by our father's strange behavior, Cam stepped forward. "Dad? Dad? What's wrong?"

"I-I have to…" Dad scrambled to his feet. Haunted blue eyes fixed on the splotch of blood on my towel. "See to our guest."

"What was that all about?" Cam asked after Dad vanished through the door.

"You have to treat it so carefully." I dabbed at my lip. The imprints of his fingertips were still warm on my skin. "Handle it like a piece of fine glass. It's so fragile."

"What?"

"His love," I said softly.

Seizing my chin, Cam examined my face. "That bastard shouldn't have hit you."

"Don't call him a bastard."

"Next time, I'll—"

"You'll what? Beat up your own father?"

Cam punched the fridge and howled.

Rolling my eyes, I opened the freezer and fetched an ice tray. "What did the kitchen appliance ever do to you?" I asked, chasing after him with the tray as he hobbled from corner to corner. "This is why you need to re-enroll in anger management. Gandhi never punched a fridge—"

"He didn't have a fridge. *Because he never ate anything!*"

Muffled voices drifted in from the living room. Dumping the ice-wrapped towel into Cam's hands, I tiptoed to the door and cracked it open.

Ben's spindly shadow crept along the wallpaper. "Do you remember me, Professor Nolan?"

Slumped in his favorite armchair, Dad nursed a cup of gin. He seemed more interested in the gin than Ben. "I'm sorry, young man. I can't say I do. What did you say your name was again?"

"Ben Wolcott."

"Wolcott, Wolcott," Dad repeated, tapping a finger along the rim of his glass. "Doesn't ring a bell."

"I was your best student."

Cam tapped me on the shoulder. "What's happening?"

I held up a hand, motioning for silence. It took me a few seconds to discern the reason for Ben's surprise visit.

"He wants to help Dad research his book," I whispered. The same book Dad's been working on for a decade to fill the void in his life after Mother's death. I held my breath, confident Ben's visit was coming to an end. Dad was immensely private about his research and never talked to anyone about his work. Even with all of my snooping and invasive questioning, I still couldn't get Dad to let me help him. There was no way in hell he'd trust a stranger over his own daughter.

"I appreciate your offer, Mr. Wolcott." Clearly disinterested, Dad fumbled for the remote and clicked on the TV. He flipped through channel after channel of static garble only to realize we hadn't hooked up the cable. "But I don't have the money to pay you. I don't even have money for—" Frustrated, he tossed the remote in the couch cushions. "HBO. And trust me, I'd much rather have HBO."

"You won't have to pay me. I'll work for free. I have another job so money isn't an issue."

"I've made my decision."

"Let me prove to you—"

"It's late, Mr. Wolcott," Dad said with a note of finality that sent a smug curl to my lips.

From my vantage point, I watched Ben's shoulders slump in defeat. "I'll see my way out." His footsteps receded as far as the foyer. "Professor Nolan?"

Dad let out an impatient sigh. "What?"

"Out of curiosity." Ben's shadow reappeared on the wall, looping toward Dad with an ungainly gait. "Who do you want to bring back from the dead?"

Dad stood up so abruptly he dropped his drink. I strained to see Dad's expression, but I couldn't do so without revealing myself. "What did you say?"

Standing with his back to the kitchen door, Ben blocked Dad from view. I stared at the back of Ben's head, which was cocked to the side like a chess player planning his next move. "Arabella's Curse is the reason you're in Eckhart, right?"

26

I snorted. *Nice try. You lost this game. My dad has a PhD, which qualifies him as too smart to believe in your bullshit.*

And then, unbelievably, Dad stumbled toward his study. "Come along, Mr. Wolcott," he said, swiping a bottle of brandy from the bar. "We have a lot to talk about."

As Dad disappeared inside, Ben stood in the center of the living room. His eyes traveled from the pile of moving boxes in the corner to the spilled gin on the floor. Bending down on one knee, he picked up the fallen cup, found a crumpled napkin on the coffee table and dabbed at the spill.

"What the—" I watched him clean, totally bewildered. What a freak.

Slapping his hands together, Ben snatched up the remote and switched off the TV. Then he turned around. "The walls have ears," he said.

Rather than shutting the door, I met his stare straight on.

He set the remote on the side table, tweaked it so the angle was perfectly parallel to the July issue of *Smithsonian*. "I'll see you around, Ava."

Gnawing on my lip, I watched him limp inside Dad's study and into my rightful place in the sun. It was so easy for him, wasn't it? He'd never spent years panting for one kind word— only to be rejected at every turn. What did he know of rejection? He'd achieved more with my father in a few minutes than I had my entire life.

27

Ben Wolcott. Give me a break. He was nothing more than a stray dog skulking outside my window. He even moved like a dog, one who'd recently learned how to walk on his hind legs, every step weighed and measured as if he were studying how to be human.

I slammed the door. My split lip had already healed, but I could still taste the blood. I remained with my back turned, so dizzy with rage I was ready to slam my head against the wall until it dawned on me: when it came to my dad that was exactly what I'd been doing. Every day. For ten fucking years.

Perched on the countertop, Cam nursed his hand. He looked up and whistled. "Wow. If looks could kill, I'd already be dead."

"Cam?"

"Yes, sis?"

"See what happens when you take in a stray? They get too comfortable and forget who's master. What that dog needs…" I turned to the window above the sink. My reflection scowled back, pretty features twisted into a sinister likeness of my mother's face. "…is a smack on the snout."

CHAPTER 3

ECKHART HOUSE

I clutched my cell in a white-knuckled death grip. For the first time since our move, I was grateful for Eckhart's crappy reception. It meant Drake Elliott couldn't detect the bitterness in my voice above the static.

"Why wasn't I invited to Cindy's party?" I asked after Drake finished recounting all the fun he and our crew had last Saturday night. "I was free."

"Cindy didn't think you'd be up for the drive," Drake said.

"She's my friend. I would've driven down to LA for her birthday— had I known there was going to be a party." The porch swing creaked. I scraped at a patch of whitewash, biding my time for the question I really wanted answered. "Why didn't *you* tell me?"

I pictured Drake stretching, scrubbing a hand over his face to keep himself awake. It was nearly noon but Drake liked to sleep in late. In high school, he was notorious for stumbling into class well after tardy sweep, if he bothered to show up at all. If I was being honest with myself, it really bothered me that Drake was starting his first semester at USC while I was stuck in a dump like Eckhart. Life was going on without me.

"I was busy figuring out my new classes," he said after a long pause. "Must have slipped my mind."

"Slipped your mind," I repeated. *"Right."*

It was on the tip of my tongue to ask if something happened between Drake and Cindy at that party. I expected Cindy, who always coveted everything I owned, to try to sleep with Drake behind my back. As for Drake, I wondered if he tried very hard to fight off Cindy's advances.

God. What was I so worked up about? Drake wasn't my boyfriend. He was just a friend whose bed I crawled into during those insomniac nights when even the shadows on my wall were out to get me. We had a good arrangement, convenient with none of the messiness and heartache of puppy love.

I held the cell away from my ear. Ben and Dad's laughter echoed down the hall. I drove my nails into my palms.

"I'll see you tomorrow, Professor Nolan," Ben called.

Dad chuckled. "All right, Ben."

What could Ben have possibly said that was so damn funny?

In my ear, Drake droned on and on about Cindy's birthday party.

"Relax, babe," Drake said. "I was too busy missing you the

whole time."

"Yeah right."

The sun played peekaboo with the storm clouds, disappearing altogether by late morning. I hugged my legs to my chest and rubbed some warmth into my freezing limbs. I tried to remember my last encounter with Drake, how he trailed kisses down my back and licked my spine. Even that memory couldn't crowd out the creeping fear that Ben had managed to replace me in my dad's affections.

"Ava?"

"Hmm?"

"You seem distracted lately," Drake began. "What's up?"

"It's this godforsaken place," I said.

"That bad, is it?" Drake sounded amused.

"Eckhart's like purgatory after high school."

The front door creaked open and Ben strolled onto the porch, a messenger bag slung across his shoulder. He halted beside me.

Awkward.

Over the past three weeks, I hadn't spoken more than two words to Ben, or so much as acknowledged his existence. For all my surface indifference, I was acutely aware of his presence as I sensed he was equally aware of mine.

"This town is a dump. The wind blows garbage straight to your doorstep, into your home..." I locked eyes with Ben. "And the trash never leaves."

Ben's expression was cryptic beneath the mask of fading bruises. Then I detected the faintest tick in his jaw. I guess he got the message.

With a curt nod, Ben bounded down the porch and disappeared around the corner.

A car door slammed.

"What are you talking about?" Drake asked.

"Nothing." I stood up and leaned against the porch railing, eager for the next phase of my revenge plans to unfurl. "Listen, Drake, I hear my dad calling. Gotta go."

"Ava?"

Disconnect.

Tossing my cell aside, I waited.

Right on cue, Ben's car engine sputtered and choked. His tires ground against our pebbled driveway. The stench of burnt rubber seared my nostrils.

I rounded the corner just in time to see Ben pop the hood. Leaning against his Chevy's rust-corroded side, I watched him cough and wave away a billow of smoke.

As I inhaled the fumes, my mother's voice rang in my ears.

Destruction is your talent, baby doll. When you grow up, you'll set the world a-burning.

Unable to shake the feeling that I'd fulfilled my mother's crazy prophecy and grown up to become a dick, I was struck with regret.

"Hey…" I scrambled for a non-incriminating way of saying *I know what's wrong with your car—and I can fix it* when Ben finally noticed me. He gave me the foulest I-know-you-are-the-Antichrist glare and I didn't feel so bad about being a dick anymore.

In fact, I embraced it. "Car trouble?"

Ben slammed the hood. The entire car rattled. He looked like he was about to have a stroke. "You did this?" He didn't sound surprised.

"Now, now. How could a little girl like me do this to you? I know next to nothing about cars." Actually, I knew next to nothing until I did an extensive Google search with the key words "How to sabotage a car and make it look like an accident." Not to hog all the credit, Cam helped too.

Ben took a threatening step toward me. I crossed my arms and stood my ground. Since his smackdown, Ben acted as normal as apple pie. And while he'd put up a filter on all the odd things he said that night, I wasn't buying his clean-cut professor's apprentice act. In a way, I saw as much of him as he'd seen of me. There were razor blades under that deceptively wholesome crust.

He studied my face for a long time before speaking. Maybe he was thinking the same thing about me. "Professor Nolan was right about you."

"What does my dad have to do with this?" I shifted from foot to foot. "And what do you mean he was right about me?"

"We've met before, sort of." Ben scratched his chin. "Outside your dad's office at UCLA. You were bringing him lunch."

I scavenged my brain for a memory of meeting a beanpole outside Dad's office and drew a blank. "As if I'd remember a loser like you."

Ben snorted. "Of course you wouldn't. Why should you? Pretty girls like you never notice guys like me, but I remember you."

My lips curled. "Did you like what you saw?"

"You had an interesting face."

I had one unique feature. "Bet you wanted to stick your finger in my chin dimple."

"And risk catching something?"

He rocked back on his heels as I bared my teeth in a scowl. "*Anyway*," he continued. "I asked Professor Nolan who you were. And you know what he said?"

I shrugged. "'Dream on, Mr. Wolcott. My daughter's out of your league?'"

"I believe his exact words were, 'You wouldn't be so infatuated if you knew my Ava's true nature.' I asked him what he meant. Naturally I assumed he was joking. But he just shook his head and said, 'We all have our burdens. My daughter is mine. Don't make her yours.'" Ben leaned closer and whispered in my ear, stressing every malicious syllable. "Now I see why he's ashamed of you."

34

Ben was obviously making this up to get back at me.

Dad would never talk shit about me to a stranger. He had this thing about keeping our dirty laundry in the family, and I could bet my homecoming crown that he didn't consider Ben family.

Besides, Dad was softening. Just last week, he gave me extra cash for a warmer jacket. So put that in your pipe and smoke it, douchebag.

A raindrop splattered the tip of my nose. I glanced up. Storm clouds rolled over the sky, blotting out the sun.

"It's going to rain," I said, my voice more shaky than usual. "Enjoy the walk home."

◆

The rain pounded my windshield in sheets. Even with my headlights on, I couldn't see ten feet ahead of me. With the lack of visibility, I might risk running over Ben, which wouldn't be so bad.

Slowing my speed to a crawl, I peered through the sweep of my windshield wipers.

No sign of Ben. That cretin couldn't have gone far. It was a long trek back to town made longer in this weather.

Ben's parting remarks snaked through my system like venom. In the half hour since his departure, I couldn't seem to go on with my day.

If I was standing, I wanted to sit.

When I sat, I wanted to lie.

I wandered the halls, picking up random objects and sniffing them.

Unable to stomach the guilt, I stomped outside and took a look under his hood. I attempted to repair the damage only to realize that once you took a sledgehammer to an engine it was pretty much trash. To repair what I'd broken would require more money than I could afford to spend. Now Ben's beached Chevy was a rusty brand upon my conscience. Like the Tell-Tale Heart, every time I peeked outside my window, it whispered, "You are a dick."

I cranked up the heater and drummed my fingers against the steering wheel. "Damn him."

With a few carefully chosen words, Ben had forced me to see the bleak reality of my relationship with my father. Dad didn't like me and there was nothing I could do about it.

Believe me, I'd tried.

Over the years, I'd tried on more identities than Cindy tried on boyfriends. I started freshman year as the good girl following the straight-arrow path toward an Ivy League future. When that wasn't enough, I decided popularity was the key. I should've known Dad wouldn't be impressed if I traveled with a flock of It girls or won a cheap tiara. The only time he noticed me was when I was bad, but instead of trying to save me, he seemed willing to stand back and watch me drown.

If only Dad had a set of rules, a guideline for good behavior. If only things were that simple. There was no getting through to him, no crack in the wall he'd built around himself.

Then I remembered Arabella's Curse.

The mere mention of the ruby affected Dad in such a profound way that he'd disregarded his better judgment and opened up his home to a stranger.

The ruby was the key.

Suppose I found it and handed it over to Dad as a gift? What would he think of me then?

You couldn't force someone to love you. But I was going to try.

Swiping the damp hair from my face, I glanced in the rearview mirror. Red-rimmed eyes stared back at me; without my usual heavy coat of mascara, I looked like a twelve year old.

I squinted through the curtain of rain and spotted a Ben-shaped dot trudging beside the grove of twisted apple trees. He glanced over his shoulder, shielding his eyes from my headlights' glare.

Slowing my BMW to a crawl, I flung the passenger door open. Rain poured into the car and soaked the expensive leather seats. "Need a ride?"

"Here to add a 'drive-by' to your to-do-list?" he shouted above the rain.

"Don't tempt me."

Ben marched with his head down.

With the door open, my radio blasted Beethoven—or "Lovely Ludwig Van," as I was fond of calling him—into the storm. Ben, still walking, poked his head up. "Searching for some Ultra-Violence?"

As a film buff, I recognized the *Clockwork Orange* slam. Last Halloween, I dressed up as the main character, Alex, and hit the clubs with my droogs, Cindy and Drake, twirling our canes and howling "Ode to Joy" down Hollywood Boulevard. It was on the tip of my tongue to say *Clockwork O* was one of my all-time favorite movies, but I wasn't going to tell Ben that. It would only affirm his belief that I was a sociopath and not, say, someone with a soft spot for the bad guys.

"I'm not a monster," I said, finally.

"You're just a heartless bitch."

"Those who are heartless…" A lump formed in my throat. "Never mind," I said, reaching for the door.

Ben halted and motioned for me to stop.

I slammed on the brakes.

"What were you going to say?" He tipped his head to the side. "Those who are heartless…"

"Once cared too much." I spoke to my steering wheel, so softly I was sure he couldn't possibly hear me above the storm.

Ben climbed into the passenger seat and shut the door.

"Drive."

♦

The rain subsided to a drizzle but the fog—much like my passenger— was suffocating and depressing.

I inched my BMW up the steep mountain highway. Waves smashed against the jagged cliff's face, spraying white foam as high as the rusted guardrails. "Soooooo I hear you're pre-med," I said. "What kind of doctor do you plan to be?"

Ben stared out the window and shrugged. Oil derricks dotted the coast like silent sentinels watching over Eckhart. By now, I'd grown accustomed to his profile.

"*Okay.*" I puckered my lips and shifted my eyes elsewhere. Someone was taking his license to brood to the limit.

"A cardiac surgeon." He pressed a thumb against the window, blotting out the derricks. "I like the idea of holding someone's heart in my hands."

"Maybe one day you'll bring me back from the dead."

"When you become a doctor, you're required to take the Hippocratic Oath. To never inflict harm on anyone." Ben released his thumb, leaving his fingerprint behind. "Why would I want to unleash you back into the world?"

I rolled my eyes. Funny guy. "Shouldn't you be back at UCLA? The school year's started."

In true buzzkill fashion, he pressed his forehead against the window. "I'm on academic leave."

"For how long?"

His shoulders tensed. "Not long."

"When do you go back?"

"Soon. What about you? Why are you here instead of starting college?"

"Can't go to college without a high school diploma." I trained my eyes on the road. "I was expelled."

His eyebrows raised in surprise. "For what?"

"It was a month before graduation. A couple of my friends thought it would be cool to have a party on the roof of the gym. But somebody had to break into the school and make sure the coast was clear." I scratched my nose. "I volunteered."

"Smart of you."

I shrugged. "I was the most nimble," I said, thinking of all the nights I'd scaled the Elliotts' two-story house to get inside Drake's room. "And I never say no to a dare. It's my thing."

"I didn't know 'crazy' was a thing."

"Badassery is my thing."

He snorted.

Ignoring him, I went on, "You know the Santa Monica Ferris wheel?"

Ben arched an eyebrow. "What about it?"

"Once my friend Cindy dared me to jump from one pod to

the next while the wheel was in mid-spin."

"Oh," Ben said, "your friend wants to kill you."

I sat up proudly. "I jumped three pods without a single injury. I'm hard to kill."

"You thrive like a weed." He paused. "Or a parasite."

"What the hell is your problem?" I whirled on him, spinning the car dangerously close to the guardrail.

Tensing, Ben grabbed the "Oh-Shit" ceiling handle. "Eyes on the road!"

My BMW rolled away from the cliff's edge. His insult hit a little too close to home. In fact, my mother once tucked me into bed and told me a terrifying story about how she tried to abort me with a pair of knitting needles, but I was a stubborn little fetus and just wouldn't die. I "raged to live." It wasn't until middle school, when I learned what an abortion was, that her story made sense. Seriously, the world was lucky I grew up only slightly bitchy and not, say, a rampaging serial killer. This shit will fuck you up.

"About the gym?" Ben asked, steering me back on course.

"I thought I could get away with it." I gripped the wheel until my knuckles turned white. "I almost did. I got all the way to the top of the roof when I found the security guard waiting for me."

"So you think you were set up?" Ben asked.

"Probably. You may find this hard to believe, but I've made my share of enemies."

"You?" Ben fixed me with a wry grin. "*Nooooo*. But if you ask

41

my opinion—"

"I didn't."

"Your 'friend' Cindy ratted you out."

"Cindy?" I considered the possibility. "No way! She *covets* my balls. She and the rest our crew lives vicariously through me. Besides," I brought a hand to my chest, "I believe that deep down people are, like…really good at heart."

"Tell me you did *not* just rip off Anne Frank."

"That's *my* motto. If anything, Anne Frank—whoever she is—ripped me off."

Ben turned to me in disgust. "You didn't just."

"I did."

"You are so vapid!" Ben covered his wet hair with both hands. "Just go…go star in a Sofia Coppola movie!"

"Sofia Coppola movies are existentially deep."

"Style over substance," he muttered.

"Substance done with style." This hater was starting to piss me off. "My friends," I continued, "wish they could cuss out teachers and break into school, but they're too chickenshit to do it themselves. I'm a rock star in their eyes."

"So you took one for the team? How very Christlike of you." Ben massaged his temples. "Let me ask you this: did your friends graduate?"

Every single one. With honors.

I didn't like the direction of this conversation. "Anyway," I said, changing the topic. "Dad moved us to Eckhart right after my expulsion. I guess it all worked out for the best. I'm taking care of him now. He's not well."

"Hmm."

I glowered at him. "What?"

"He doesn't seem sick. A little depressed, perhaps. But from what I can see, he's as healthy as a horse. I don't think he needs to be taken care of."

"That's the thing. He's lost the will to live."

Ben stretched his long legs. "What are you going to do about it?"

"I have enough will to live for both of us."

A deep-throated chuckle. "Now *that* I believe."

With the walls of hostility crumbling between us, I asked: "Where's Arabella's Curse?"

Ben sat up straighter. He frowned, growing silent for a moment as his eyes rested on my profile. "So that's why you offered me a ride," he said finally.

"I don't know what you're talking about. I was on my way to town. So... How much is it worth?"

"It's priceless."

"Everything has a price."

A dark squall clouded Ben's features. I could tell he was debating whether or not to trust me with the information. "Get off the main road and take a left."

I squinted through the fog to the winding path. A sparse litter of trees with pointed leaves flanked the cliff's face. Dust particles swirled through the air like fallout from an atomic bomb.

"What's up there?" I nodded toward the gabled roof of the Victorian mansion on the hill.

"Eckhart House."

◆

Enclosed behind a towering gate and enshrouded in acres of shriveled oak trees, Eckhart House leaned like an old man about to topple into his grave.

I followed Ben's long-legged strides up the incline where our shoes trampled the overgrown weeds. He halted at the gate, waiting for me to catch up.

Zipping up my new whale hunter's jacket, I tugged the fur-lined hood over my head and waddled up beside him.

"You look like an Eskimo in that thing." He whacked me on the arm, back, shoulders, and chest. I think he accidentally punched me in the boob, but I couldn't be certain. I felt nothing through the layers of padding.

"Stop hitting me," I said. "I'm not a piñata."

"Y-you're a b-big m-marshmallow p-puff." His teeth were chattering.

"Cold?" I asked.

He cupped his hands over his mouth and blew. With his damp clothes and rain-matted hair, he was probably in danger of hypothermia. "Shut up."

The sight of his suffering brought joy to my heart. I peered up at the turret. The roof with its patches of missing shingles reminded me of a sickly fish shedding its scales.

I rested my weight against the gate and watched the sepia-tinted fog spiral around the crew of gargoyles perched on the eaves.

"My dad thinks Arabella's Curse is in there?" I asked in a hushed whisper normally reserved for church.

"*We* think," Ben corrected, studying me. He seemed more interested in my reaction than in Eckhart House.

"We think," I repeated. "You mean you don't know for sure?"

"Nobody's actually seen Arabella's Curse for a hundred and thirty years. It's sort of an urban legend around these parts."

Ben jammed his hands into his pockets and stared up at the boarded bay windows. "Charles Eckhart, the man who built this house and founded this town, bought a ruby in the West Indies as a wedding gift for his new bride. She was a local beauty and fifteen years old to his thirty."

"Arabella." A shiver—not from the cold because I was actually quite comfortable in my awesome new jacket— raced through my body.

Ben rubbed his lip, enjoying my discomfort. "Poor Arabella died not long after the wedding."

"How?"

He blinked. "You mean you don't know? You're Dr. Nolan's daughter, after all."

As far as Arabella's Curse was concerned, I knew only the bedtime story basics. It wasn't as if Dad was going to shell out the time to give me a tutorial on resurrection stones. I kicked a pebble and repeated, "How?"

"An unfortunate accident," he said, pointing to the turret. "She hung herself in there. The maid found her dangling from the rafters. She must have underestimated the drop because the rope sliced her throat and—"

I held up a hand. "Okay. I get the picture."

"Charles went a bit mad after that. He sold his lumber mills and barricaded himself in his house. He had no friends, no family. He died all alone..."

All alone.

Sounded like my future.

With the exception of Drake, none of my "friends" had so much as called me. I was just the girl who could always be counted upon for a good time. Did they even consider me a friend? Or was I just a means of entertainment to them? By moving to Eckhart, I had virtually dropped off the face of the earth, and when I ceased to be entertaining, they discarded me as easily as my dad.

All alone.

My throat burned like I'd swallowed crushed glass. I wanted to roar *I'm a human being* and let my cry slice the silence of this desolate hill and echo across space and time.

I was your daughter—not trash you could toss away.

I was your friend—not a train wreck put here to entertain.

I was not a girl you could fuck and never call.

I had dreams and hopes and a heart that could be broken into a million pieces.

Blinking away my tears, I lifted the giant padlock and yanked. Sturdy. Unyielding. "So what happened to the ruby?"

"Rumor has it Charles hid it somewhere in there," Ben said, motioning toward Eckhart House. "Buried it in the walls or under the floors, in his grave, who knows?"

I glanced down at my palm. The padlock had left behind a stream of liquid rust. "Rumor? More of your urban legend? Who lives in Eckhart House now?"

"Nobody. It's been sold and resold over the years. No one has lived in it for long. They say it's haunted."

"Has anyone ever tried looking for this ruby?"

Ben grew pensive. "Of course. A good number of people did after Charles' death. But they weren't very successful."

"Meaning?"

"Arabella's Curse isn't something to be taken lightly," Ben

warned. "Charles bought the ruby at a West Indies plantation auction. That was around the 1880s. But the ruby goes back father than that."

"How far?"

"Its origins are unknown, but it was first reported during the Fall of Constantinople some six hundred years ago. Professor Nolan thinks it's older, far older than we can imagine."

"Then it's more valuable than we can imagine," I whispered.

I was already dreaming about how much money I could make off the sale of the ruby. With enough money, we could move back to LA and leave this shithole. Dad could shove the ruby down the throats of his history department colleagues who made him an academic laughingstock.

All because he had Arabella's Curse.

All because I found it for him.

He'd have no choice but to love me.

Ben heard me and was not amused. "Don't you start getting any ideas. I see that gleam in your eyes. I know what you're thinking. You have no clue what you're getting into."

I laughed at his seriousness. "You don't really believe it can resurrect the dead, do you?"

Silence.

"Well? Do you?"

"I'm not superstitious," he said, "but I've read your dad's research. Nothing good ever happened to anyone who tried to find Arabella's Curse."

"Have you ever tried to find it?"

Ben frowned. "What do you mean?"

I brushed a strand of hair out of my eyes. "You know exactly what I mean. I find it hard to believe you'd know so much and not try to go after it. You can't stand there giving me this 'cursed' spiel and say you've never been tempted."

"I tried." Ben glanced up at Eckhart House. "Once."

Crossing my arms, I snorted. "I guess you failed or else you wouldn't be here now."

Ben whirled on me, black eyes blazing. "Very perceptive."

"And has anything horrible happened to you lately?"

I was unprepared for the effect my question had on him. His shoulders sagged and his sharp features contorted in pain. "Yeah, it did." He shouldered me aside and started for the car. "I met you."

I lingered a moment longer. Eckhart House was enormous, an impenetrable fortress guarding a buried treasure. Assuming Arabella's Curse was indeed real and not the stuff of lore, finding it within Eckhart House was literally like finding a needle in a haystack.

I shook the iron gate. It was as sturdy as the padlock. Scrutinizing the bars, I estimated it to be about twenty feet high, slick and slippery after the rain. A gust of wind caused the bent weather vane on the roof to twirl and creak. I sniffed, detecting kelp, a confirmation that a steep drop to the ocean corralled Eckhart House from the other side.

Tapping a fingernail against the padlock, I filed Ben's story to the back of my mind for future use. Maybe my situation wasn't so bleak after all. It was a long shot and who knows? Someone might've pilfered Eckhart House and absconded with the ruby long ago. But if there was even the slightest chance the ruby was inside...

I glanced over my shoulder for one last look at Eckhart House. "Arabella's Curse." I started back to the car, a new bounce in my step.

CHAPTER 4
AN UNCLE ON THE SIDE

The next morning, Dad joined us for breakfast. I scooted my chair closer to his side and ladled a generous helping of scrambled eggs onto his plate.

Dad accepted the food with a nod of thanks. "I didn't know you cooked."

"Oh, it's just a little something I whipped up at the last minute," I said, gesturing to the fancy spread: steaming stacks of pancakes, scrambled and fried eggs, bacon, sausage, and freshly squeezed orange juice.

Not knowing what would please Dad, I'd decided to make everything in the breakfast food category.

Dad unfurled his napkin. "I still can't believe you did all this."

"I didn't know you could boil water," Cam piped in.

I glared across the table at Cam, who was squeezing a disgusting amount of maple syrup over his mountain of food. "I guess I'm full of surprises."

Dad forked a slice of cantaloupe. "I hope it wasn't too much trouble."

I'd awoken at the crack of dawn to battle gallons of bacon grease. My shoulders felt like lead and I might've torn a ligament whisking those damn pancakes.

"Oh no," I said with a casual wave of my hand. "It was easy."

"I'm impressed." Dad sounded faintly surprised. "Yes. Very impressed."

I lowered my head, hiding my smile. So far this morning's toil had been a success, and I'd managed to lure Dad away from his study.

Too exhausted to nibble on my own food, I watched Dad chat amiably with Cam.

Dad yanked off his wire-rimmed glasses and rubbed his brow. I took his downtrodden appearance as a sign he was making progress with his book.

Meeting Cam's eye from across the table, I mouthed, "Ask him."

Cam shifted in his seat and shoveled another forkful of pancakes into his mouth. We'd agreed last night that Cam would broach the topic.

"Ask him," I mouthed again.

"Ask me what?" Dad sipped his coffee, regarding me over the rim of his mug. "What are you little vipers up to?"

"We're not up to anything, Dad," Cam said.

Dad arched a brow. "Really? Then why do I feel like I'm in the middle of an ambush?" He turned his full attention to me. "Ava?"

Cam had the spine of a jellyfish when it came to verbal confrontations. I sighed. Once again, I was forced to face the firing squad.

"Our cells are dead," I said and waited for the repercussions.

Cam wiped the syrup from his lips. "No service for a week."

Dad picked up the newspaper. "Call the company later. It's probably nothing more than bad reception."

"We already did," I began. "Our bill was past due. They shut off our service."

Dad sipped his coffee. "Check must've gotten lost in the mail."

"Actually..." I locked eyes with Cam. "You never wrote the check."

"Of course I wrote it." Dad scanned the sports section.

"Not according to our bank statement," I said, and immediately wished I hadn't mentioned anything. I gave him the benefit of the doubt. "Maybe you forgot?"

"It completely slipped my mind. I'll get it paid," Dad said, chucking the newspaper on the table and easing himself out of his chair. "Now if there isn't anything else, I have to get back to work."

"Do we have any money to pay it with?" I called after him.

I only had room for numbers in my thoughts, starting with the alarmingly low number in the Nolan family bank account. If that was all we had, we were screwed with a capital S. Forget the cell phone bill—this farmhouse didn't come mortgage free.

Cam kicked my leg under the table. "Shut up…"

Dad whirled around. "Are you calling me a liar? Or you don't think I'm able to handle my own money anymore?"

"That's not what I meant—" I turned to Cam for support, but with his head lowered and arms folded, my brother had withdrawn like usual during our petty family squabbles.

"Instead of wasting your time second-guessing me," Dad continued, "get a job and pay for your own damn cell phone."

"But I'm studying for my GED," I said meekly.

"You're a smart girl, Ava. You know as well as I do that you don't need to study for it," Dad retaliated. "Besides, Ben Wolcott has two jobs and is studying for his MCATs in advance."

"You're comparing me to that loser?!"

"Wolcott has ambition. He has direction. He knows what he wants out of life. And you, my darling, can't even go through high school without getting yourself expelled. So no, I'm not comparing you to him. It would be an insult to him."

I stared at my untouched plate. The fried egg was cold, the yolk gelatinous and disgusting.

"Now are we finished?" Dad asked.

I jammed a fork into my grapefruit.

54

"Are we finished?" Dad repeated, louder this time.

Then the telephone rang.

It rang and rang and rang some more.

"Someone get the goddamn phone!" Dad barked.

At Dad's command, Cam dashed into the hallway at a half jog. He tapped my shoulder a minute later.

"It's for you."

I set down my fork. "Who is it?"

"Some guy from the carpet cleaners," Cam said. "He asked for you."

"Why would I want to talk to him?" I wasn't in the mood for phone calls, let alone warding off some shady telemarketer.

"You better take the call." Cam lowered his voice. "Or this fight could go on forever."

Cam was giving *me* advice? To his credit, there was actually some wisdom behind it.

I took the phone and tiptoed around Dad to get to the hallway.

"Hello?" I said when I was alone.

"Hey little girl," the telemarketer's hillbilly twang spoke in my ear. "Is your carpet dirty?"

"What the f—" My pent-up anger found a vent with the perverted caller. "Listen to me, you sick piece of shit. If you ever call here again, I'll hunt you down, cut out your heart and *eat* it!"

The crank caller exploded into hysterical hyena laughter.

"Temper, temper, Sweet Pea."

I froze, recognizing the voice. Not quite British, not exactly American, but cultured in a freaky cross between the two like the speaker grew up in the cornfields of Iowa but was weaned on *Doctor Who*.

Glancing over my shoulder, I whispered, "Uncle Tav?"

A good-humored chuckle followed. "The one and only."

"You know you're not supposed to call here. What if…" I glanced over my shoulder. "What if Dad had answered?"

"I'm not worried about Morty." Uncle Tav had the creepy phone voice down to an art. At the moment, he could be stroking a cat like Dr. No. "What did you expect me to do? You haven't answered any of my texts or calls for a week. Surely you're not ignoring your dear old Uncle Tav?"

"Old" was the last word I'd use to describe Ian Tavistock, Dad's stepbrother. He was around Dad's age, forty-six, give or take a few years. While Dad was already showing signs of premature wear and tear, Uncle Tav, following a strict regiment of expensive facials, seemed impervious to time.

"I'm not ignoring you, Uncle Tav." I hesitated. "Dad forgot to pay the cell phone bill."

Uncle Tav grew silent.

"How many times did he 'forget'?" he asked finally.

"Just this time. He's been very stressed lately what with losing his job, the move, and the pressure to finish his book."

56

"The same book he's been working on for the past ten years?" Uncle Tav asked.

"Not everyone is as prolific as you."

"True, true."

Like my dad, Uncle Tav was a scholar by trade. Only much more successful. While Dad's small-time university press publications gathered dust in the library, Uncle Tav penned nonfiction bestsellers about trekking through the Amazonian rainforest in search of the lost city of El Dorado and climbing Mount Everest in the midst of a snowstorm. His book about the forensic investigation of a five-hundred-year-old murder mystery in Jamestown, Virginia garnered him a Pulitzer Prize and talks of hosting his own show on the History Channel.

Uncle Tav and Dad hadn't spoken in the decade since my mother's death. In fact, Dad had forbidden us to have anything to do with Uncle Tav.

For Cam, who always had a snide remark about our uncle's flamboyant wardrobe, banishing him from our lives wasn't a problem.

The same could not be said for me.

In ten years, the only time I'd seen Uncle Tav was on TV. But through secret late-night phone calls, emails, and a PO Box set up specifically to receive his gifts from around the world, Uncle Tav had devised a way to be a part of my life against his brother's wishes.

When I was fifteen, I'd asked him why. Why me instead of Cam?

"We all have our favorites," he'd said. "I've just taken a shine to you, Sweet Pea."

Now Uncle Tav was pushing his boundaries.

"...so what does he do all day?" Uncle Tav pressed, his normal good-humored tone curdled by disapproval. "Stare at a blank screen?"

"Sometimes I hear him type."

A sigh of frustration. "I wonder when Morty is going to find another job so he doesn't 'forget' to pay any more bills."

"I've been considering finding a job," I said. "I want to do my part."

"What about school? You're just ten credits shy of a diploma. Have you given a thought as to what college—"

"Dad and I talked about this. The only high school in Eckhart is a dropout factory. Since I only need ten credits, I'll take my GED and take a year off..." I wrinkled my nose. "To work."

"So he wants you to support him while he finishes his book?"

I listened to Uncle Tav curse my dad until he calmed down and said, "If it's money you need, I can wire you within the hour."

"No!" I wanted Uncle Tav to share in my self-pity. I didn't actually think he'd resort to extreme measures. "Dad will find out if there's a paper trail."

"Damn him! I don't care if he knows! I have a mind to come to Eckhart and flay him alive with my riding crop."

Now there's an image.

Uncle Tav owned a riding crop. As far as I knew, he only used it on horses. Just as badassery was my thing, being pervy and inappropriate in the presence of minors was Uncle Tav's thing. They weren't that touchy about that stuff in England. Also, he went to the Willy Wonka school of uncle-ing.

"Please don't make this harder than it is. He doesn't know I still talk to you. If he finds out, he'll disown me. Please don't do this to me."

My desperation softened Uncle Tav. "Okay. But I want to help out, pet. Follow my instructions exactly."

I hesitated. "I don't think—"

"Follow my instructions," Uncle Tav repeated. "Or I will come to Eckhart and your father and I will have a little chat. Do you understand?"

My shoulders slumped in defeat. "I'm listening."

"Good girl. In three days, I want you to go to the post office. I'll have a present waiting for you..."

♦

Uncle Tav's gift had taken a drenching between the post office and my mad dash into the railroad car-shaped diner. I'd come in seeking refuge from the storm and spotted the HIRING sign.

Joe, esteemed owner of Joe's Hideaway, sounded like he gargled with motor oil. "You know anything about waitressing?"

"No, but..." I thought about the bills Dad still hadn't paid despite his promise to "take care of it," which probably explained our malfunctioning Wi-Fi. "I can be trained."

"Have you *ever* had a job before?"

"Well, when you think about it..." My dad was a trust fund kid. Thanks to my dead grandpa, Cam and I were, too. Those days of opulence vanished with the recession. "Life is a job."

He shook his head. "Another philosopher."

As Joe flipped through my application, I gawked at the coarse hair studding his fingers like wooly rings. Every once in a while, he'd glance up, beady-weasel eyes flickering from my damp hair and puffy jacket to the limp cardboard package on the seat next to me.

I picked at the flaky remainders of my blackberry pie and tried not to touch the sticky tabletop or gag at the stench of decades'-old grease from the deep fryer.

He waved his pen at me. "What's with the costume?"

I glanced down. "You mean my jacket?"

"You look like you're going to harpoon a walrus."

"I'm cold." I peeled off my coat anyway.

Joe scratched his beer gut, revealing a yellow pit stain on the side of his shirt. I studied his acne-pitted nose. The man could use a good plastic surgeon. As I debated slipping him Cindy's dad's business card, he stared at my chest, frowned, then scribbled something on my application. Guess he thought the same about me.

"Can you start tonight?"

I blinked. "You mean I got the job?"

"As long as you're not the clumsy type." He slapped my application down on the table. "You break a plate, it comes out of your pay."

"Sweet, how much am I making? Fifteen? Eighteen dollars an hour?" I was willing to start low.

Joe studied me as if I were crazy. "This is a diner, Duchess. Minimum wage plus tips."

"Say *whaaaaat?*" I grimaced. "Is that negotiable?"

"Only the tips. You're cute, you'll do well with the truckers. One more thing, employment is conditional. If Wolcott thinks you're an idiot..."

"*Wolcott?*" He doesn't mean... Please God, not *him*. The world can't be that small.

Joe's attention drifted outside. Rain sluiced down the window, carving grimy streaks in the glass. Wind whipped through the cypresses and sea grass. A tall figure in a hooded black sweatshirt trudged through the sandy muck toward the diner.

Seconds later, the doorbell dinged.

Joe grinned, revealing a chipped dogtooth. "You're late," he called over my shoulder.

"Only by five."

The owner's eyes widened. "Did you walk all the way here?"

"Car trouble."

At the mention of "car trouble," the spiky barb of guilt burrowed deeper into my conscience. Grimacing, I kept my back turned and concentrated on the sound of the whirling fans overhead.

On my half-eaten pie crust.

On the yellow stuffing peeping out of the red vinyl booths.

On anything that could help me mentally prepare for the reckoning to come.

I guess the Fates were out to screw me after all.

"…and the storm blew the power out at home," Ben said, slapping the water from his clothes. "I had to fix it before work. You know how my mom hates the dark."

Joe's roughhewn face softened. "How's your mother?"

"Same as before."

"I'm sorry for that," Joe said sincerely.

Finally Joe gestured to me. "We have a new waitress. This is…" He squinted at my application. "Meet Ava. She's going to take Stephanie's place."

Ben grew silent.

I took a deep breath and turned around. "Hello, Benjamin."

Ben yanked off his hood and wiped the droplets from his face. "*Oh no.* It's you."

"You two know each other?" Joe asked.

Ben shuffled from foot to foot. "Unfortunately."

"What's the matter?" I tilted my head, studying the hard set of his jaw. "You don't seem happy to see me."

"I'm just wondering what I did to deserve this visit," Ben muttered.

"Great." Joe lugged his bulky body out of the booth and patted his pockets for his keys. "Saves the 'getting-to-know-you' chitchat. I've got a long drive to San Francisco tonight. I'll leave you to show her the ropes." He slapped Ben on the back. "Have her prepped and ready for the midnight run."

I narrowed my eyes at Ben while we waited for Joe to wobble away. Might as well make Ben sweat with my menacing stare.

"Spare me the questions," I said when we were finally alone.

Ben rocked back on his heels, regarding me down the tip of his nose. "This is the last place I expected to see you."

I scanned the tacky jukebox and crooked pictures of vanishing Americana gas stations. "Yeah, well, I'd never thought I'd see myself here either."

In the tenth grade, upon the urging of my history teacher, I took the PSAT. To my surprise, my scores qualified me for a National Merit Scholarship. When I rushed home to show my dad, he'd only shrugged and muttered, "You've inherited somebody's brains. Not mine." The next day, as Mr. Olsen passed around the midterm, I put my head down on my desk and took a nap. I flunked U.S. History that year, along with English and Geometry. On a positive note, when Dad was called into my guidance counselor's office because I'd been placed on academic probation, he certainly paid more attention to me then.

As for that perfect score? Only three people knew about it.

"I needed a job…" My voice lost some of its bite. I hadn't thought about the PSAT in a long time, and it struck me as funny that the memory still had the power to hurt me. "…and this was the only place that was hiring."

Out of the corner of my eye, I caught Ben staring at me with pity instead of annoyance. I turned my back and tried to rearrange my face into a stoic mask. When I turned around, I was once again the bitch everybody loved to hate. "Aren't you going to show me around this dump?"

Without preamble, Ben unzipped his hoodie and looped around the counter. He motioned for me to follow.

I lugged Uncle Tav's gift with me, balancing it on my hip.

"Are you a waiter too?" I followed him through the kitchen to the employee break room. Pine cubbyholes lined one wall.

"Not exactly." He pointed to the bottom-most cubbyhole. "This was Stephanie's, now it's yours."

"Lucky me."

I tried to jam my package, without Ben noticing, into the tiny cubbyhole.

"What's in the box?" he asked.

"It's called 'None of your business.'"

As I peeled off my cardigan, Ben rummaged in a locker and handed me my uniform on a hanger. "Steph was just your size."

I held my new uniform—a hideous hybrid between candy striper and bobby socks bimbo—at arm's length. Although the dress smelled clean enough, the florescent lights illuminated a grime-caked collar that no amount of dry cleaning could remove. This Stephanie might've been blessed with a cute little body, but she wasn't known for keeping it clean.

"What's your get-up look like?"

Ben slapped the water out of his jeans. His navy T-shirt clung to his torso. I counted three of his ribs. "You're looking at it."

He walked away, snapping his fingers for me to follow. "Come on."

The soles of my sneakers stuck to the black and white linoleum floor like flypaper. Ben led me to the nearest booth and shoved a half-empty ketchup bottle into my hands. I held the bottle between my thumb and index finger. It was sticky and had a generous splattering of germy fingerprints.

"Rule number one: Always, and I mean always check for empty condiment bottles," Ben said. "If those bottles aren't filled for our All-You-Can-Eat-Onion-Ring-Hour and those truckers start howling at me, I'll have your ass for dinner."

My lips curled into a naughty smile. "I bet you'd like that."

He chucked another squeeze bottle at me.

I caught it one-handed.

Impressed by my deft reflexes, Ben raised an eyebrow. "Refill at every service. That goes for mustard, relish, and napkins. Do I make myself clear?"

I saluted. "Aye. Aye."

Ben scowled. "Familiarize yourself with the menu. We have a daily special. Know it. Study it. I want you to recite it in your sleep."

I flipped open the laminated menu and skimmed through the main courses. Turkey sandwiches. Cheeseburgers. Chicken-fried steak. Easy stuff.

"I think I got it."

Ben narrowed his eyes. "Do you? Do you really?"

I tossed the menu aside. "It's waitressing. Not rocket science."

Ben seized the menu and returned it to its holder. He proceeded to turn all four menus cover side out and positioned the ketchup bottle to the right, mustard to the left. Checking over my shoulder, I surveyed the other booths. Ketchup to the right. Mustard to the left.

"Jesus H. Christ…" I'd already suspected this guy liked all his i's dotted and his ducks in a row. Never knew he was one napkin crease away from becoming the Martha Stewart of Eckhart.

"One more thing." He stepped closer.

I tapped my foot impatiently. "What now?"

"Your attitude."

"What about my attitude?"

"This Beverly Hills Princess act is not going to fly here."

"I'm from Santa Monica—that's *south* of Malibu." I stepped up to Ben and gazed into his black eyes. "Bitch."

"Regular hood rat, I'm sure," he muttered before walking away again. "Please refrain from calling the customers bitches. We've already got a low enough Yelp rating as it is."

At the counter, Ben patted the register. "The zero key on the register sticks. To dislodge it you use the screwdriver—"

"Wait, you never told me what exactly it is you do."

Ben set the screwdriver down and rested his palms against the countertop. A grin spread across his face. In that moment, I understood the true meaning of karma.

"I get to tell you what to do." He paused, and added, "Who's the bitch now?"

♦

Later that night, I sat on the edge of my bed and stared at a rain-soaked teddy bear. Creepy black button eyes stared back at me. The crumpled cardboard box held no note. No letter of instruction.

"Uncle Tav..." I shook my head, perplexed. "You strange, strange man."

I glanced at my laptop, longing for an internet connection so I could email Uncle Tav. Why had he made such a big deal about getting this all-important package to me? With all this buildup, I expected... The keys to his lime-green Lamborghini? Arabella's Curse, perhaps?

Frustrated, I squeezed Teddy's bloated belly. Paper crinkled beneath the surface. Teddy definitely wasn't stuffed with cotton.

I sat back and smiled. "Hello. What's this?"

Hopping to my feet, I yanked open my dresser drawer and rummaged through three layers of underwear until my fingers found the ivory handle of a butterfly knife, a souvenir Uncle Tav picked up from his travels to the Philippines. I hadn't put the knife to much use outside of opening envelopes. Now I finally knew where to stick it.

I flipped Teddy over and parted his matted brown fur. A jagged line of black stitches zigzagged along Teddy's spine. Flipping my knife open, I pressed the blade along the trail. The first three stitches popped. I jammed my hand inside Teddy and fished out a crinkled hundred-dollar bill. And another. And another. And another.

I sat down on my bed and stared at the money on my lap. Three thousand dollars. To pay the bills. To buy groceries. Not a miracle, but an extension from complete destitution. I flopped down on my back and laughed as tears streaked down my cheeks.

Hiccupping, I fanned the money along my belly and stared at the water-damaged ceiling. My body ached all over and I desperately wanted to peel off my dirty uniform and take a shower, but I was too exhausted to move an inch.

I curled onto my side and closed my eyes. Like a child whose prayers had been answered, I whispered, "Thank you, Uncle Tav."

The cash caressed my bare legs. Sinfully. Lovingly. Lulling me to sleep.

The world may fall apart. Everyone, even God may let me down, but my Uncle Tav never would.

CHAPTER 5

A MOTHER'S LULLABY

"Dad!" Twirling my car keys around my index finger, I stomped down the hallway. "I'm off to my new *job*."

I'd only been working for a week and already rubbed everyone at the diner the wrong way. Maybe it was my chin dimple? Or my constant quoting of *Pulp Fiction*—as if jumping behind Ben and screaming "DID I BREAK YOUR CONCENTRATION?" wasn't amusing. I couldn't explain why the staff didn't like me, so I found solace in the words of a wise philosopher: "Haters gonna hate."

The diner was run like a dictatorship. Ben Wolcott, a tyrant of cleanliness. Yesterday, he made me scrape the gunk out of the deep fryer and scrub the stove. Before handing me the toothbrush, he'd said: "ALLOW ME TO RETORT." Using *Pulp Fiction* quotes to make me do my job was just mean.

I picked at the grease stain on my pinstriped skirt, shuddering at the prospect of another night of mopping, bleaching, and the never-ending rearranging of pickle jars by expiration date.

Ben wanted the diner so spotless you could eat off the floor, but why would anybody eat off the floor when there were booths? What did it matter if the pickles were out of order? What kind of a fascist regime was I working in? When I brought this up, my coworkers, the Dodd sisters, stared me down as if I were some dangerous revolutionary.

Whistling the end of "Do You Hear the People Sing?," I knocked on Dad's study. "Do you want me to pick up anything from the grocery? Milk? Bread?"

I nudged the door open. The study was empty.

My attention lingered on Dad's cabinet of curiosities: a glass-enclosed bookshelf crowded with artifacts both morbid and sublime.

A row of human skulls ranging in size from infant to adult.

A Victorian-era windup figurine of a gentleman with a beak and raven wings.

An Egyptian death mask.

There was an empty spot on the shelf, which I assumed was reserved for Arabella's Curse.

"Stay out of there!" Dad jogged down the stairs.

"I wasn't going to—"

In one quick stride, he slammed the door and locked it. He wasn't wearing his angry face, but his mouth had compressed into a thin line of annoyance. "Just don't touch my things when I'm away," he said, pocketing the key.

Like I needed a key. If I really wanted to get into his study, I had bobby pins at my disposal and mad lock-picking skills thanks to Uncle Tav.

I gave Dad a once-over. He was wearing his favorite blazer and carrying a battered suitcase. "Away? Where are you going?"

"San Francisco. There isn't a decent research library in all of Eckhart." Dad snatched his car keys from the ceramic dish in the foyer.

I trailed on his heels. A vacation? Awesome. "Just give me a moment to change and I'll—I'll go with you."

Dad caught my wrist before I could dash up the stairs. "I have enough work on my hands without having to babysit you too."

Babysit? Since when did he ever babysit me? I'd been taking care of myself since I was eight—since my mother left. "Oh, I see…" I swallowed. "How long will you be gone?"

"Just a few days. Call me if you need anything." He opened the front door, then halted. "Oh, and keep an eye on Cam. Make sure he stays out of trouble."

"Dad, wait!" When he turned around, I flung my arms around him. Desperation drove me to it. Or maybe I thought I could detain him in Eckhart if I tackled him like a linebacker.

He stumbled backward, surprised. "Ava," he said, "stop embarrassing yourself."

I closed my eyes, nestling my cheek against the scratchy tweed of his blazer. He smelled good—not of whiskey or gin—but of spearmint aftershave. "I'll miss you."

His arms dangled at his side. "You're too old for this."

"Too old to hug my own father?"

Dad went silent. Seconds later, I sensed his hand hover hesitantly over the small of my back. With a sigh, he gathered me closer and rested his chin on the top of my head.

This was progress. A crack in the stone wall. All these years, Dad gave me designer clothes, a BMW, my own credit card. When all I'd ever wanted—the only thing he'd ever denied me— was a kind word. A kiss.

"You still love me…" Burying my face in his lapel, I slowly went to pieces. "Tell me you love me. Tell me I'm still your little girl."

Dad ran his hand through my hair. His lips brushed my temple. "Helena, my Helena…"

My skin prickled at the mention of my mother's name. This was a first. I knew my resemblance to her bothered him to no end, but he'd never mistaken us this completely before. He held me for a few awkward seconds before prying himself out of my embrace.

I stared up at him through a haze of tears. His face had drained of all color. Dad cleared his throat. "It's only for the weekend," he said, patting my hand. "Now I really must go. The traffic…"

He was gone before I could even say goodbye.

♦

I drove up the hill in tears.

Parking underneath an elm tree, I slammed the door of my new 1980s Nissan Sentra—a recent downgrade from my beloved BMW—and marched to Eckhart House.

I blew my nose in a Kleenex. Dad didn't even say goodbye. He said he'd be back in a few days. "A few days" usually meant Cam and I wouldn't expect to see or hear from him for weeks.

I picked up a fallen branch and dragged it alongside the gate. The air swarmed with dust particles, swallowing the Victorian mansion in a sepia-tinted twilight. There were only minutes of sunlight left in the day. Could I get in and out in time?

On *Antiques Roadshow* the other night, they appraised a woman's bronze cat collection at twenty-five grand. Cats! For a six-hundred-year-old occult ruby, I'd have museums and private collectors throwing money at my feet.

If I found Arabella's Curse, Dad wouldn't be so quick to ditch me again.

I stretched my legs, flexing my hamstrings. The starchy cotton of my uniform brushed against my bare thighs. Tapping my fingers against my leg, I contemplated the climb.

All those late school nights scaling the Elliotts' two-story colonial to Drake's bedroom had honed my agility to rival that of the most nimble cat burglar. The climb was the easy part. Once I reached the top, I'd have to summon all my strength to hop over the sharp spikes—or risk being impaled.

Since my first trip up the hill with Ben, I'd wondered why Dad never visited Eckhart House himself. Now I understood. The jagged landscape issued an uninviting welcome. Gnarled oak groves intertwined like monsters locked in a wrestling match. Swaying weeds infested the lawn, casting ghoulish shadows upon the veranda.

Dad's haunted expression swirled before me. He was more on edge these days. Scared of his own shadow. Terrified of an innocent hug. I rubbed my frozen hands together and peered through the bars. Dad was probably too chickenshit to come up here.

Guess I had to be brave enough for both of us.

He'd called me by my mother's name. Maybe he was going crazy?

Fortunately, I was perfectly sane.

I stripped off my puffy jacket and tossed it to the ground. "H-holy s-shit!" It felt like a freezer up here. Jumping up and down to warm my blood, I tackled the gate and slipped. The iron was as slick as a Popsicle. Wiping my hands on my skirt, I prepped for a second try when I spotted a wrought-iron dome bursting with pomegranate trees. It must have been Charles Eckhart's private pavilion.

Recalling Ben's story, I pictured Arabella Eckhart strolling through the pavilion, the hem of her Victorian gown trailing along the once manicured lawn. I squinted into the darkness, imagining Arabella's elegant fingers brushing the leathery petal of an exotic orchid. She would be humming, gently humming.

Maybe my imagination was playing tricks on me, but I swore I heard—

A woman humming in the distance?

In my earliest memory, my mother used to sing us to sleep with a tone-deaf rendition of *The Last Rose of Summer*. My dreams were anything but sweet when my mother tucked me in.

I ground my palms against my eyes. All I could see was my mother's elfin face, flawless except for the insanity clouding her gray eyes like a film. She'd stare down at me with those same crazed eyes while I lay small and helpless in bed, her blood-red lips mumbling the lyrics.

"Since the lovely are sleeping."

"Go sleep thou with them," I said.

Somewhere in the pavilion, the foliage rustled. The knobby branches rapped against the iron dome like witches' talons. I shivered at the memory of my mother's nails raking my tender skin. Out of habit, I probed my jugular. My pulse was irregular. My breathing shallow and pained— as if scalding bathwater still filled my lungs. I remember how she held me down.

How the water boiled me alive.

How I clawed at her face.

At the sides of the slick porcelain tub.

At the air.

She was dead. Dead for ten years.

The dead couldn't hurt the living.

I licked my lips. "Must be the wind."

The surrounding trees stood absolutely still. Only those in the pavilion shook. Could the wind be that selective?

Whoever or *whatever* was inside seemed angry.

Restless.

Backing away from the gates, I tried to convince myself it was a stray cat or a raccoon. But why was I still hearing her lullaby?

I dashed toward the Nissan. My foot snagged on a jutting root. I broke the fall with my hands, crying out as my knees skidded gravel.

The rustling ceased. Only my frantic breathing punctuated the hilltop's silence.

That thing about being "perfectly sane"? Strike that. I was as crazy as my mother.

The noise did not stay at bay for long. Footsteps crunched on dry grass, softly at first then clipping at a faster pace. Building to a run in my direction.

I scrambled to my feet. The footsteps grew louder and

quicker.

No human could run like this.

I ran. The creature sprinted.

Faster and faster.

It matched my pace. Soon it would scale the gate and jump on my back.

It leaped—

With a yelp, I ducked and covered my head.

The trees behind me exploded in a flurry of black feathers. A murder of crows soared above the tree line and blackened the sky like a storm cloud, circling and cawing over Eckhart House.

♦

I hurried through the front door of Joe's Hideaway, letting in a glacial gust of wind. The tacky kitty-cat wall clock told me I was half an hour late. Squaring my shoulders, I made a beeline for the coffeemaker.

The coffee pot rattled against the lip of my mug. Scalding coffee splattered the back of my hands. Pot and cup crashed to the floor.

"Shit!" I kicked a shard of broken glass and searched for a towel.

Across the diner, someone clucked her tongue. I glanced up. Marlene Dodd stopped wiping her booth and rolled her eyes at her sister Sydney, who was ringing up an order at the cash register.

"Somebody's in trouble," Sydney said in a singsong voice. Whereas Marlene, with her moon face and plump body, was drawn in circles, Syd was all lines and no curves.

Marlene sidled beside her sister. "Just wait till Ben hears about this."

I peered past Syd's twiggy body to the kitchen. "You mean he's not here?"

Strange. Ben was never late. Or sick—germs couldn't infect someone so reprehensible.

Syd glared down her beak nose at me. Unlike Marlene, whose roots were beginning to show under her bad bleach job, Syd still retained her mousy hair color, which she wore in a bird's nest bun impaled by a much gnawed upon No. 2 pencil. "Don't think you can get off that easy. We'll make sure he finds out. Then your ass is grass."

My ass is grass? What's with this town?

"Like I'm scared of him," I muttered.

Ignoring the twits, I wiped the spill in slow circles. Ben Wolcott and his wrath were the least of my worries. The creature lurking behind the gates of Eckhart House was far more frightening than Ben's work detail.

Mother was dead. The police told us so.

A clump of hair, a patch of scalp, and a blood-soaked grave in the Mojave all equaled a dead mother.

I glanced down at my scraped palms and skinned knees. A strange mixture of fear, loathing, and *yearning* caused my hands to tremble anew. If my mother was alive, I wanted to hide from her and hug her at the same time. Despite everything, a part of me still missed her.

When she wasn't tormenting me, we had some good memories. The time she bought Cam all the soccer balls from Sports Chalet and transformed our living room into a giant ball pit was a blast. Almost as fun as the time she picked me up from school in a "borrowed" Porsche and allowed me to drive while propped on her lap. Mother was never normal. During her manic episodes, however, she told me she loved me and how grateful she was I'd been born. It was only during her "down" phases that she tried to kill me.

Love and hate.

Good and bad.

Sometimes the lines weren't so clearly defined.

The Dodd sisters, intimidated by my alpha-girl pheromones, regarded me as some kind of super villain. One life lesson I learned from Mother: every villain was a hero in her own mind.

Marlene and Sydney were at the opposite end of the counter, heads bent in gossip. They probably considered themselves heroes, in which case, they were sadly mistaken. Not to point the arrow in my direction, but heroes were often misunderstood and alone. The Dodd sisters had each other while I'd pretty much spent my life nailing the loneliness and bad rap thing. Plus, the makeup girl at Sephora said I had epic cheekbones, so who were we kidding here? I *am* Batman.

"Willa's coming home in two weeks." Marlene busied herself filling up the ketchup bottles. "Wait till she sees this place. I've already ordered the helium tank and a hundred green balloons."

According to the local gossip mill, Joe's darling daughter Willa was spending part of her summer in San Francisco with her mother. If Willa was as spiteful as the Dodd sisters, I wasn't looking forward to making her acquaintance.

Syd toyed with the rainbow straw dispenser. "Hope Ben's coming."

"It's for Willa! Of course he'll come."

"He's been acting über freaky since his brother's—" Syd slid a finger across her throat and added some gagging sound effects. "—accident."

What happened? Did Ben's brother choke on a chicken bone?

"Willa's worried to death about him," Marlene said. "Can't get him to talk about it, the poor thing."

Scandal involving the saintly Ben Wolcott was too good to be true. I pretended to wipe the counter with my ears trained to their conversation.

"Poor Willa or Poor Ben?"

"I'd hate to be in his shoes. And that drama with his mama. Willa said it was unnatural for him to be so devoted—"

"Well," Syd said, "'a boy's best friend is his mother.'"

The front door swung open and Norman Bates himself slumped in. Ben halted at the threshold, startled by suddenly being the center of attention.

Clearing his throat, he nodded at the Dodd sisters. "Ladies."

"Ben," Syd and Marlene replied in unison. Both wore a pitying look that made me even more curious about this mysterious accident.

Ben walked right past me. His disgusting black Wellingtons left a muddy trail on the floor. Now here was a super villain.

The sisters descended upon him like a couple of noisy hens.

"We were just wondering where you were," Syd said.

Marlene moved in to take his jacket. "You must be freezing. Let me get you a cup of coffee."

Ben held up a hand. "That's really not necessary."

I snorted at Marlene. "I was freezing. Why don't you offer me a cup of coffee?"

Scowling, Syd turned to Ben. "She was late."

Marlene nodded. "A half hour late! And she sat there doing nothing for the other half."

Fixing his full attention on me, Ben arched an eyebrow. "Is that true?"

I gestured to the empty diner. "There's nothing to do. Don't be a..." I traced a square in the air.

Syd, Marlene, and Ben exchanged a long, three-way stare.

Mistaking their silence for confusion, I clarified, "That was from—"

"We know," Marlene said. "We got it the first hundred times you quoted *Pulp Fiction*. There are other movies, Ava, other movies to quote from."

"There is only *one* movie, and I'm going to keep quoting it because of a little thing called 'Freedom of Speech.' If you have a problem with that, *I will strike down upon thee with great vengeance and furious anger.*"

"I'm going to kill her," Syd muttered to Ben. "If you don't do something, that's it. I'm about to get medieval on her rich girl ass."

With a sigh, Ben headed for the kitchen, returning a moment later with a metal bucket and a mop.

"There's mud all over my floor." He dropped the bucket at my feet, sloshing soapy water over my shoes. "When you're done with that, meet me in the bathroom. The toilet's overflowed again and there's shitty water all over the place."

♦

Dropping my last quarter into the pay phone slot, I pressed the receiver to my ear and waited for the first ring. My cell was dead. Not "out of reception" dead or "company turned off our service because we couldn't foot the bill" dead but "won't turn on" dead. Even the iPad in my messenger bag was out of order. Also, I left my whale hunter's jacket at Eckhart House.

Eff my life.

I gazed at the crumbling marquee of Eckhart's only movie theater, The Arcade. Judging from the boarded-up windows, The Arcade hadn't shown a movie in over a decade. Main Street was a ghost town of saltbox storefronts. Like The Arcade, most of the stores had long been abandoned as if the owners left town in the face of an impending apocalypse. At this late hour, with the fog swirling around the trash-littered sidewalks, it wasn't hard to imagine myself as the only person alive on earth.

I was certainly the only one in this town who appreciated a good movie.

The phone rang a fifth time.

"Pick up," I whispered into the mouthpiece.

He wasn't home. He didn't have an answering machine. He was ignoring me.

I glanced behind my shoulder just as the neon sign spelling Joe's Hideaway dimmed one letter at a time.

The glass door swung open. The Dodd sisters trotted out, linked arm and arm like Siamese twins. Ben turned to lock the door.

"It's not possible for one person to be so annoying." Marlene's grating giggles echoed across the deserted streets. "I'll never forget the look on her face when you made her mop the floor."

"She turned beet red like someone was strangling her," Sydney added. "I swear she was going to throw a bitch fit."

"I've never seen this side of you, Ben," Marlene said. "But I like it."

"Suits her right for what she did to your car."

"This is a historic night." Ben tossed his keys in the air and caught them one-handed. His mood had certainly improved. "You've just witnessed the downfall of a queen."

Suddenly Ben's attention flickered in my direction. I slipped behind a curtain of shadows, thankful for the shattered streetlights.

His boastfulness dissipated into worry. "Did you happen to ask her how she hurt her knee?"

"Why should we care?" Syd exchanged looks with her sister. "Why should *you?*"

"I don't." Jamming his hands in his pockets, Ben shrugged. "Her palms were skinned too. She seemed..." He shook his head. "Never mind."

"What?" The sisters edged closer.

"Spooked," he said. "As if she saw something she didn't like."

They walked away, three voices receding into the shadowy parking lot behind Joe's Hideaway.

"Come on! Pick up." Covering my face, I sobbed quietly in the crook of my elbow as the sixth ring hammered against my temple. I was about to slam the receiver when the phone clicked on the seventh ring.

"Uncle Tav?"

"Ava? What are you doing calling this late?"

At the reassuring sound of his voice, I swallowed the lump in my throat. "I just... I wanted to thank you for my gift," I said, remembering the self-satisfied smirks of the Dodd sisters as they watched me mop the floor.

"It's been a long time since you've called and I've been wondering—"

"You were wondering when I might send you another?" Uncle Tav asked. "Isn't that right, Sweet Pea?"

"I called you because I missed you!"

"You certainly took your time."

I racked my brain for a proper explanation. The truth of the matter was: life just got in the way. I'd forgotten about Uncle Tav just as my friends had forgotten me.

"I was waiting for the right time," I rubbed my forehead, "and time slipped away. That doesn't mean I'm not grateful for all you've done. You've always been there for me, even when you're not here. By *here*, I mean, like...physically present. If I hadn't thanked you before, know that I've already thanked you...in my..." Poking myself in the chest, I cringed at my awkward words and pauses. I had a silver tongue when it came to sarcasm, but speaking from the heart was not something I did often, and it showed. Everything that left my mouth sounded like bad movie dialogue. "Uncle Tav? You there?"

Uncle Tav broke the tension with a chuckle. "That was horrible. What *was* that?"

I wrapped the phone cord around my finger. "I was trying to be sincere. Everybody hates me, so I figured if I turned over a new leaf and tried to be nicer…"

"Well, stop trying to be what you're not. It's painful on the ears."

I sniffled, strangely comforted by his logic. The world, with its preoccupation on "good," didn't make sense, but Uncle Tav's vision of the world was a haven for the wicked and misunderstood. "But what am I?"

"Your mother's daughter and a greedy, greedy girl. Own it." He sighed. "I suppose I could find it in my generous, and need I remind you, *forgiving* heart to send you another treat in the mail."

For the first time that night, I smiled. "I knew you'd never let me down. I'll pick up the package in three days?"

"Not so fast. This time I expect payment in return."

My smile vanished. "What is it?"

"You sound as if I'm about to ask for your soul. What good are souls to me when I can have your trust? All I want from you is honesty. You've been keeping something from me, Sweet Pea, and I don't like secrets. Not between family. Not between friends."

I flexed my raw palms, flinching at the pain. More evidence of tonight's failures. "What do you want to know?"

"I fret about my brother from another mother," he said. "We used to be the best of friends and *poof*—without word or explanation, he's cut me off from his life. But I'm tired, Ava, so tired of always being in the dark."

"Me too," I muttered into the mouthpiece. Uncanny. It was like Uncle Tav had carved a peephole into my soul.

"So maybe you can illuminate my curiosity, pet. Toss me a bone about your father and your pockets will never be empty. Are we agreed?"

"Um, sure. Why not?" I tapped my chin dimple. "Let's see. Last week, Dad bought some new socks—"

"The *juicier* the bone," Uncle Tav interrupted, "the fatter Mr. Teddy will be."

Having been instructed by Dad to never trust Uncle Tav, I hesitated. Then it dawned on me: what was so horrible about Uncle Tav anyway? He was a strange man, but not a monster, not a heartless mercenary. If anything, he was as lonely as, well, as me.

"About a month ago..." The deserted shops of Main Street and the shattered window of the ticket booth magnified my loneliness. I needed someone to talk to more than ever. "This asshole came to our house. He claimed to know what Dad's been researching all these years. Have you heard of a ruby called Arabella's Curse?"

Silence.

"Uncle Tav? Are you there?"

Uncle Tav cleared his throat. His voice sounded practiced and strained. "Tell me more…"

CHAPTER 6

THE DOWNFALL OF A QUEEN

Huddled on the floor of the employee break room, I glanced up from my cell.

"Unbelievable!" Ben crossed his skinny arms. "This is a new low. Even for you."

Ben was mad. What else was new?

"I'm still on my break." I texted: MISS U. WHEN R U COMING HOME? Then hit send.

"Correction. You *were* on break. You were supposed to be back a half hour ago."

I tapped my thumb against the screen, waiting for my phone to ding and Dad's avatar to pop up. "So I lost track of time. What's the big deal?"

Actually, I was acutely aware of time. According to my stalker log, Dad left town two days, sixteen hours, and thirty-seven minutes ago.

"While you're hiding back here, Syd and Marlene had to cover your lazy ass." Ben continued, "Of all the irresponsible…"

Blah. Blah. Blah. Maybe Dad never received the twenty messages I left in his inbox? Or he didn't know how to check his inbox? That had to be it. Silly me. Dad wasn't intentionally ignoring me. He was just old.

Ben sighed. "Have you heard a word I just said?"

I tucked my phone in my apron. "What was that?"

He did a face-palm as I heaved myself to my feet.

"Really, Ben…" I dusted off my skirt. "Don't you think it's a little inconsiderate of you hiding back here during the busiest night of the week?"

Shaking my head, I slipped past him and marched to the dining room.

At the counter, Ben pressed an order pad and ballpoint pen into my palm. "Booth 8 is waiting. I know this may be hard for you, but *please* try to be friendly."

Rolling my eyes, I started toward Booth 8 and froze. Instead of the usual batch of truckers, there was a pretty boy bro tonguing his girlfriend. A month ago, Drake Elliott had been tonguing me. What the hell were Drake and Cindy doing here? In Eckhart? In Joe's of all places? Any remaining doubts about Drake's fidelity vanished as I watched him nibble on Cindy's earlobe.

My first impulse was to pounce across the counter and pound some two-timing skulls. Then my arm brushed against my starchy uniform and fury segued into mortification. I was at work. At their mercy. Just the thought of taking their order made me want to keel over.

Fortunately, Drake and Cindy were too busy groping each other to notice their surroundings.

I glanced from side to side. Marlene was flirting with a potbellied trucker. Syd stumbled toward the kitchen, arms loaded with dirty dishes. I stepped backward, trying to appear inconspicuous. Casual. Cool. Yup. I was just one cool chick who forgot something in the bathroom...

Whirling on my heels, I ran smack into Ben.

He caught my shoulders. "Whoa. Whoa. Where do you think you're going?"

"To the bathroom. I need to pee." To illustrate this point, I hopped from foot to foot. "Badly."

"What are you? Six? Hold it in until you've taken Booth 8's order!"

"Studies show its bad for the bladder to hold—"

"Go!"

"Lower your voice!" I glanced uneasily behind my shoulder. Oblivious to the commotion at the counter, Drake nuzzled Cindy's neck.

"Ah, I see." Ben stared past me at Booth 8. "Friends of yours?"

Shushing him, I dragged him into a secluded corner of the

kitchen.

Ben rocked back on his heels. "Shouldn't you go over and catch up?"

"Let me trade with Marlene or Syd. I'll wait any table. I'll wait *all* the tables except that one." I wrinkled my nose in distaste, then added, "Please."

His lips quirked at the corners. "Why ever not?"

"I can't do this."

Ben half pushed, half shoved me to the counter. "If they walk, you're done. Got it?"

Clicking my pen, I fought the urge to stab the ballpoint into his eye and laugh triumphantly over his lifeless body. "How do you sleep at night?"

"I have a long walk home. Thanks to you. I'd say I sleep rather well."

I smoothed down the wrinkles of my pinstriped skirt, crossed myself, and began my trek to social suicide.

Oblivious to my approach, Drake caressed Cindy's inner thigh. She wiggled her miniskirt-clad rump against his crotch. Dude, this is a *family* diner.

"It's about time," Drake said with his back to me. "What do we have to do to get some decent service around here?"

I propped a hand on my hip. "You can stop groping my friend for starters."

Drake froze with his hand wedged between Cindy's legs.

94

Cindy's almond-shaped eyes, raccooned by eyeliner, widened in disbelief. "*Ava?*" She gave me a full body scan. "What the hell are you wearing?"

Typical. Leave it to Cindy to think about wardrobe at a time like this.

Ignoring her, I zeroed in on Drake. "You bastard."

Drake raked a hand through an enviable mane of honey-blond hair. He didn't even have the decency to look me in the eyes. "I know this must look bad—"

"*Must* look bad? Because it looks to me like you're digging for buried treasure under her skirt."

"We drove all this way to visit you," he said, trying to change the subject. "We didn't expect, I mean, we didn't know—"

"We didn't know you worked *here*." Cindy beamed. What was mine was now hers. "So you wait tables now?"

That comment took the 'friend' out of frenemy. Why did I persist in hanging out with girls I wanted to punch in the face?

Drake groaned. "Shut up, Cindy."

I flipped open my order pad. "Yes I do." With all the dignity I could muster, I clicked my pen. "Can I take your order?"

"Ava—" Drake pleaded.

"*Can I take your order?*" Heads turned in our direction. I didn't give a fuck about causing a scene. I whirled around. The moment our eyes met, Ben glanced down and scribbled furiously in his notepad. So much for backup.

"Chili." Drake cleared his throat. "I'll have the chili."

I scribbled down his order; double, triple underlined "chili" until my pen ripped into the carbon paper. "And I guess Cindy's already had my sloppy seconds, so I'll put in your order. Good day."

My insult wiped the smugness off Cindy's face. She slumped back in a huff.

Upon my return, I ripped off my ticket and slapped it on the counter. "They'll both have the chili."

Ben plucked up the ticket and passed it to Karl, the short order cook. "That wasn't so bad now, was it?"

"Go to Hell."

"When I'm around you, I'm already there."

Moments later, two steaming bowls of pre-cooked chili appeared at the order window. As I loaded the food onto serving platters, I contemplated the bubbling chili. It called for spit. Yearned for spit! I cleared my throat and dislodged a sizable chunk of mucus left over from last week's cold when Ben appeared behind me.

"Don't even think about it," he said.

I swallowed the evidence and whirled around, my face the picture of innocence. "Whatever are you talking about?"

Ben narrowed his eyes. "You were going to spit in their food."

"Oh Benjamin." I lifted my serving platter. "You should

know by now I'm saving all my spit for your eye."

Drake and Cindy were in the middle of an intense argument. Cindy had the monopoly on the yelling. "How can you sit there and let her insult me like that?"

Drake's ears turned pink at the tips. "Why do you have to be such a bitch?"

"I'm the bitch? *I'm the bitch?*"

They hushed at my approach.

"Trouble in paradise?" I slammed their order down. Chili sloshed over the ceramic bowl and splattered onto the table.

Drake's big hazel eyes pleaded forgiveness. "We didn't mean to hurt you."

I nodded to Cindy, who arched her eyebrow in challenge. "Speak for yourself."

"Cindy feels terrible too," Drake explained. "We, I mean, me and Cindy, it just happened and it's not as if we—"

I held up a hand. "It's not as if we meant anything to each other. You're absolutely right, Drake. I'm more disappointed than hurt. I thought you had taste. Obviously"—I nodded to Cindy—"I was wrong." I slapped my hands together. "Anyway, here's your dinner. Choke on it."

Cindy's singsong call stopped me from fleeing the scene. "Oh waitress?"

I turned around. "*What?*"

Cindy pushed her bowl away. "I didn't order this. Please take it back and get me something that doesn't look like dog shit."

I batted my eyelashes and smiled. "Then you should've asked your parents to return your face."

"Waitress." Cindy drummed her hot pink nails on the tabletop. "I would like a slice of apple pie. Is that too hard to remember? I know you didn't graduate high school like the rest of us. Maybe I should speak more slowly so you'll understand."

I gave Ben a long-suffering stare over my shoulder. He leaned against the counter. Despite a credible poker face, he clearly relished every minute of my humiliation.

Every part of me wanted to chuck my apron at his feet and say *To hell with this job,* then march back to Booth 8 and shove Cindy's face into the chili. But I was practical to the very end. This was reality. There were no better jobs in Eckhart. There were *no* jobs in Eckhart, period. Long afternoons browsing Craigslist assured me that Joe's was as good as it was ever going to get. I'd entertained the notion that I was somebody, but to Drake and the world, I was easily replaced.

I was nothing.

Sighing, I said, "Give me your plate."

"Here, let me help you…" With a sweep of her arm, the bowl crashed to the floor, splattering the tile and my shoes with chili. "Oopsy, clumsy me."

Specks of scalding chili dribbled down my calves.

Cindy snapped her fingers and Drake got up. "Here's your

tip." She flipped a quarter at my feet. "Buy yourself a new friend. Come on, Drake. Let's get out of this dump."

"Sorry," Drake muttered before trailing after Cindy with his tail dangling between his legs. Two dings of the doorbell and they were gone.

Silence filled Joe's Hideaway, then the whispering began. They sounded like snakes, hissing and clicking their thick tongues.

Blinking back tears, I crouched down and tackled the ceramic shards when footsteps approached. I lifted my head to the sight of Ben's Converses. What was he going to make me do this time? Scrub the floor with a toothbrush?

"All right," I said. "Say it."

"Say what?"

"They walked. I'm fired, right?"

He knelt down and started picking up the broken pieces.

"I'll take care of it," Ben said without meeting my eyes. "Just get yourself cleaned up."

I watched his quick hands work. I expected him to gloat. This, however, I was not expecting.

When I still hadn't moved, Ben nodded to the counter. "Booth 6 is waiting. Onion ring platter. You can't serve them with chili all over your shoes, right?"

I stared at him, dumbfounded.

"Go!"

I scrambled to my feet and took a few hesitant steps before

turning around. Kneeling on one knee, Ben scooped up the chili with a wet dishtowel.

"Thank you," I said.

Ben ceased scrubbing. He didn't move, didn't speak. All I could see was his profile: the long bridge of his nose, the sharp line of his jaw, and his lashes blinking in surprise. Then he shook his head and went back to wiping the chili off the floor.

♦

After work, I drove across town to pick up Cam. My brother couldn't get behind the wheel of a car. He lost his license last year, after his second DUI. Every Saturday night, I chauffeured him to the gym so he could spar in a cage with his unemployed friends.

I swerved to the curb and watched Cam gangsta-shuffle to the car.

"Pull up your pants," I said when he slid into the passenger seat.

"She's a bitchy one tonight." Cam glanced down at my chili-splattered dress and socks. "What happened at work? Someone take a shit on your lap?" He caught my wrist before I could smack him upside the head and planted a sloppy kiss on my cheek.

Pushing him away, I glanced at his T-shirt. "Is that blood?"

Cam clicked his seat belt. "Not my blood." He turned to his side and I got a gander at his puffy eye.

100

"Urgh. Cage fighting. What a stupid waste of time."

"But Ava, I'm good at it. The owner says I could go pro."

"Tomorrow," I said, gunning the engine, "we're hitting Craigslist and finding you a desk job."

"I'd have sponsors and—"

"A desk job that *pays* a salary. All right?"

Cam glanced out the window. "Whatever."

We drove home in silence.

When I pulled closer to our dilapidated farmhouse and the shadowy outline of Drake Elliot's Ferrari materialized in our driveway, I banged my head against the steering wheel. The horn blared. "Eff my life!"

Drake glanced up from his iPhone and hopped off the porch steps.

Cam poked me in the arm. "Chill. It's just Drake." He bolted out of the car. "Yo Elliott! What are you doing here?"

They exchanged a non-lingering bro hug followed by a series of manly fist pumps.

"I want to speak to your sister." Drake peered over Cam's shoulder. "Hey babe."

If I didn't know any better, I'd think Drake was tormented over cheating on me and had neglected to shave or bathe or put on a decent pair of pants. Unfortunately, I knew him far too well. It cost him a lot of money and hours in front of the mirror to look like a poor man's Robert Pattinson.

"Hey Drake!" I slammed the car door loud enough to make the earth rattle. "Sleep with any of my other friends lately?"

Drake stepped toward me. "Can we talk in private? Maybe take a walk?"

"Sure thing. You can start by walking off my porch and out of my sight before I really get angry."

Cam turned from Drake to me. "Is there something going on that I don't know about?"

"Ava's just blowing off some steam," Drake said. "It's nothing." He reached for my arm. I jumped back before he could touch me. "It's over between me and Cindy. I made a mistake."

I shoved him in the chest. "You're not the only one who made a mistake!"

"Is that what all this is about?" Cam appeared relieved. "Look Ava, I know Cindy's your best friend and all, but you can't really blame Drake. Everybody hooks up with Cindy. She's like a rite of passage."

"Or a glory hole," I muttered.

Then I studied my brother. "Wait a minute. What do you mean 'everybody hooks up with Cindy'? Have *you*?"

Cam kicked at a pebble. "I'm a guy, and Cindy can be very—"

"Easy?" I volunteered.

"Seductive," Cam said.

Drake coughed. "I concur."

Too Much Information. As I tried to exorcise the disturbing

102

mental picture from my brain, I caught Drake smirking out of the corner of my eye. Sorry about cheating *my ass*.

"Speaking of hooking up," I said. "Remember the first time we hooked up, Drake? Hopefully you can, because I was buzzed out of my mind from the drink you mixed me."

Drake turned as red as the paint job on his Ferrari. "Lying little…"

Cam's easygoing smile vanished. "You date-raped my sister?" He took a threatening step toward Drake.

Drake held up his hands in self-defense. "Look man, I don't need roofies to get laid! Especially not with her!"

Cam's hands furled and unfurled into fists.

Drake saw he was in hot water, yanked open his driver's side door, and stood behind it like a shield. He pointed at me. "Maybe you should tell him about all the nights you snuck into my room and practically *begged* me to fuck you. *Touch me, Daddy…*"

"Shut up!" I screamed.

"Kiss me, Daddy…"

"Shut up!"

"Love me, Daddy." Drake sneered. His angry face was quite ugly. "Believe me, Bro, your sister is one sick bitch."

I flew at him. Drake seized my wrist before I could claw him across the cheek and gave me a vicious push.

Stumbling backward, I turned to Cam. "What are you standing there for? Get him!"

Instead of charging Drake, my brother stared down at me with an expression that could only be classified as disgust. "It's not true, is it?"

"Of course it's not true!"

In the second it took to set the record straight, the weasel slipped into his Ferrari.

I marched up to Drake. He rolled down the window.

"You have till the count of three to get your bitch-ass the hell off my property," I told him in my most level voice. To look at me, one would think his malicious words had no effect. Inside, I was shaking, steaming, shrinking into nothing. "Or I'll have Cam show you our horse trough. How long do you think you can hold your breath?"

Drake slammed his Ferrari into reverse. Flecks of mud splattered over my legs. He poked his head out the window. "You're a lying whore! And one day everybody's going to know about it."

♦

Sticks and stones may break my bones, but words will never hurt me.

I kicked off my shoes, yanked off my blouse, and shimmied out of my jeans. Shivering in my underwear, I crawled into bed when a glint of silver caught my eye.

104

I picked up my homecoming crown from the vanity table.

The plastic felt lighter and cheaper than it did the night I won with Drake Elliott, the most popular guy in school, standing by my side.

I twirled the crown around and around, leaving a trail of sticky sparkles on my palm. On impulse I propped the crown on my head and wrinkled my nose in the mirror. I pressed a hand to my flat stomach, pinching the flesh there to make sure I hadn't gained any weight.

Taking a step closer, I puffed out my cheeks. Perfect skin. Check.

Widened my smile. Perfect teeth. Check.

I caressed the crescent-shaped scars marring my collarbone like a necklace. A gift from my mother. The scars were surface deep and easily concealed with foundation or a high-collared blouse. Nobody, not even Drake, whose focus usually narrowed in on my boobs and other unmentionable areas, knew about them.

"You've just witnessed the downfall of a queen," I whispered, recalling what Ben had said to the Dodd sisters during my first week at Joe's.

"Royalty at sixteen and now look at you." My reflection blinked back at me. "A loser at seventeen. A nobody. A lying whore."

I ripped off the crown and, out of habit, set it down carefully, almost reverently on the tabletop. Then I surveyed the cluster of photographs taped around the mirror.

Candid snapshots of bonfires under the Santa Monica pier with the Ferris wheel spinning in a neon blur in the background.

Summer pool parties at Cindy's Bel Air mansion.

Soccer games at the park with Drake and Cam.

Winter formal, junior year: Drake and me posed in front of a black and white painting of the New York skyline.

Sadie Hawkins, sophomore year: Drake and me again, this time perched atop of a paper moon.

When I first moved in, I'd taped up each picture with care. Now it just looked cluttered.

I peeled off the nearest photo, crumpled it into a ball, and chucked it in the wastebasket.

The mirror was still too cluttered. I tore off the Sadie Hawkins photo and ripped it into little pieces.

"Stupid memories…"

High school was over, everyone had moved on with their diplomas and their bright, illustrious futures, and I was stuck in Eckhart with neither diploma nor future… pathetically reliving my glory days.

"Stupid! Useless!" I clawed and slashed at the wall, yanking off photos by the handful, tearing them to shreds. "Junk. Junk. Junk!"

I slumped against the table.

There was one more thing I had to do.

I snatched up my homecoming crown and bashed it against the side of the table.

One.

Two.

Three times I bashed it until it began to resemble the cheap hunk of plastic it had always been.

The crown found a new home in the trash.

When I was finished, I lifted my eyes to the bare mirror. My reflection stared back at someone who resembled me. Frazzled hair plastered to her sweaty face. Savage gray eyes. Chest rising and falling as she tried to catch her breath.

"Now you're truly nothing," she said to me, "but now you have nothing to lose."

CHAPTER 7

RUBIES ARE FOREVER

A corroded trash can stood before me. I doused its contents with lighter fluid and contemplated journeying to the tool shed for a second canister when I looked up and saw Ben trekking through a swaying field of lavender.

He halted inches away from the can and bent to retrieve a scrap of photograph from the ground. He studied it, saying nothing.

Ignoring him, I squeezed the last drops of lighter fluid over my precious high school mementos and picked up a box of matches.

I struck the match and watched the flame dance at my fingertips. The scent of sulfur singed my nostrils. Without a second's hesitation, I flicked the match into the can, jumping back as a small mushroom cloud erupted over the rim.

My photographs crackled as they burned.

"Life's full of ups and downs." I watched the old Ava Nolan

roast and dissolve into ashes. Flames licked over the mangled remains of my homecoming crown, melting the plastic and sending plumes of acrid smoke into the sky. "One moment you're queen, the next you're nothing. Lower than nothing. Irrelevant."

I turned to Ben, slowly surfacing from my trance. The fire cast a lambent light over his cheekbones. He watched me instead of the flames. In the distance, the sky rumbled, signaling an impending thunderstorm.

"One day, I'll be queen again," I said.

Ben tugged at the hem of his jacket, which hung too short in the sleeves. When the flames wavered, he looped over to the horse trough and dipped a bucket into the murky water.

"Why are you here?" I asked, hugging my elbows against the chill.

"I left something in your dad's study. He still in San Francisco?"

"Last I checked." I watched him douse the fire, leaving a lowly ember smoldering amongst the ashes. My eyes traveled to his mud-speckled jeans and guilt settled like a stone in the pit of my stomach. "Look, I'm sorry about your car, okay?"

He glanced over one shoulder, then the next. "I didn't say anything."

"Stop rubbing it in my face."

"You're cold." Stripping off his jacket, Ben mumbled, "And delirious."

I shrank away. "Whoa! What are you doing?"

"What do you mean?" Ben draped his jacket around my shoulders.

The wool was still warm from his skin. The faint scent of freshly cut grass lingered in the thin fibers.

A single drop of water splattered on my nose. The skies rumbled. A second raindrop plopped on my arm.

His hands lingered on my shoulder. He stood very close.

I kept my eyes trained carefully on the flannel pattern of his shirt. The diner. Now the jacket. He must have something up his sleeve. "Why are you being so nice to me?"

Ben thought for a minute. "It seemed like it's been a long time since anyone's been nice to you."

Having succeeded in making me feel like dirt, Ben cleared his throat and swatted me on the arm like I was his best buddy. "We'd better get inside," he said, tilting his head to the storm clouds.

I watched his wiry figure walk away, graceful, carefree, and completely unaware he'd knocked my world off its axis.

◆

As Ben searched for his lost things, I wove across Dad's study and cracked a window to air out the stench of cigarettes and sour milk. I switched on the lamp, stirring up a cloud of dust motes.

Dad had left a half-eaten bowl of Cheerios next to his hibernating laptop. Green spots sprouted on top of the curdled milk, reminding me of the mold colony I grew for a fifth grade science project. Wrinkling my nose in disgust, I scooped the bowl into the trash.

Slapping my hands together, I set about picking up all of Dad's discarded pens when my thumb bumped against an overturned picture frame.

I flipped the frame over.

It was my parents' wedding picture, a quickie snapshot of the newlyweds on the steps of Los Angeles City Hall. Their wedding had to be a quick one. You could already see the baby bump that would eventually grow into Cam beneath my mother's simple wedding dress. With her black hair curling lightly at her shoulders and a faint blush coloring her cheek, my mother could almost pass for normal. She was eighteen, looked fifteen—a child bride.

Linked arm in arm with his new bride, Dad beamed at the camera. With the trademarked sag to his shoulders gone, he looked impossibly handsome and carefree.

Uncle Tav loomed behind the newlyweds, totally photobombing the shot. Although the photograph lacked depth of field, I spotted a purple dot—the pocket square—on the breast of his impeccably tailored white suit. Slouched against a pillar, Uncle Tav watched the happy couple with a scowl.

Across the room, Ben picked up an old tartan blanket from

the sofa. "Now where did I leave it?" he muttered to himself. "Where did I leave it?"

I clutched the silver frame, wondering if Dad was purposefully tormenting himself. The last thing he needed was another memento of his unhappy marriage. For Dad's peace of mind, I slipped my parents' wedding photo in the trash. "Find what you're looking for?"

Ben yanked a black extension cord from between the couch cushions and looped it around his hand. "Think so."

Rather strange item to leave behind.

Ben saw me staring. "Lots of power outages in my neck of the woods," he explained. "You never know when you might need an extra jolt."

"Guess not." I studied him suspiciously. "So what do you guys do in here for hours on end?"

"We research. Mostly we read," he said. "Is your pulse racing yet?"

"I can't stand the excitement," I said dryly. "More Arabella's Curse-related research?"

"Something like that." Ben jammed the extension cord into his messenger bag. "I'd better head out."

"Whenever I mention Arabella's Curse, you become evasive. Why is that?" I sank into Dad's leather executive chair and leaned as far back as the creaking springs allowed. "You're the one who took me to Eckhart House."

"I was trying to scare you."

"Now you've intrigued me."

"You mean I've sparked your greed. You wouldn't be so intrigued if you knew…" That familiar tick in his jaw had returned. He made a beeline for the door. "I'm leaving."

"I've been back to Eckhart House," I called.

Ben halted at the threshold. *"What did you say?"*

Something told me I'd pushed all the right buttons. Steepling my fingers, I repeated, "I went back to Eckhart House."

He crossed the study in three quick strides. "How far did you get?"

I twirled around in Dad's chair. "Not far."

Ben spun my seat around and loomed over me like a police examiner. "Goddamn it, Ava! This isn't a game. How far?"

What a shame. So young and already crotchety. Lolling my head back, I stared up at the underside of his jaw. There was a shaving rash on his throat, right over his jugular. As I counted the beat of his pulse, it occurred to me that Ben could benefit from a good old-fashioned screwing. Then he wouldn't be so uptight. Not that I volunteered to do the screwing. After last night's brush with Drake, I'd decided to take a vow of celibacy. Still, the thought triggered a mental picture of my arch-nemesis pinned to Dad's desk, his jeans pooled around his ankles, panting and writhing as I balled him until his liver exploded.

A shiver raced through me and I discovered—to my

114

disgust—that I was incredibly turned on. By Ben Wolcott of all people.

"I didn't get through the front gate." Exhaling a shaky breath, I poked his chest and let my index finger linger over his heart. Ben glanced down in surprise, but didn't brush my hand away. "There was a dog in the yard. A Doberman or something. I didn't chicken out. Next time I'll be prepared."

"There will be no next time." His voice was husky.

I gave him a push with my finger and Ben stumbled away on unsteady legs. "You can't tell me what to do." I stared at his tense back. "For all I know, you want Arabella's Curse for yourself."

"You don't know what Arabella's Curse is. You don't know the half of it."

"Then tell me."

Ben turned around. He studied me for a long time before stripping off his messenger bag and extracting a black three-ring binder. "When I'm done, I want you to forget about Arabella's Curse forever."

"Is this your Arabella's Curse research?" I asked.

"It's your dad's," Ben said, sitting on the edge of the desk. "He's not the most organized person, so I keep it tidy for him."

"Kind of like a secretary."

Slamming the binder on the desk, he flipped to the first laminated page. "Focus! I don't have all day."

I peered down at a colored photocopy of a medieval

illumination. A plump young woman, naked to the waist, was bound to a stake. Wild red hair whipped about her face and dissolved into orange flames. A crowd of leering spectators swarmed around the wooden platform like human-sized rats.

"Looks like an artistic rendition of Hell," I said.

The footnote read: *The Trial and Burning of the Witch Eliza Darrow. Northumberland, England, 1553.*

Ben pointed to the ruby dangling from a silver chain between her bare breasts. It resembled a misshapen pigeon's egg, much cruder than the sleek and polished stone of my expectations. The unknown artist had painted the ruby the color of coagulated blood. In a certain slant of light, the ruby could be mistaken for a hole in Eliza's chest where her heart should've been.

Talking about Arabella's Curse was one thing, but seeing it, even in a crude drawing, made it real. I ignored the gruesome subject matter, my attention locking on the ruby. It was grotesque.

"*Beautiful.*" I caressed the page, breathless from sheer exhilaration. "Arabella's Curse."

Ben studied me, a strange, devious light flickering in his eyes and a trace of a smile on his lips. As soon as he caught me staring, his expression vanished.

"Three hundred years before it acquired its namesake. Back then it was just a gaudy ruby in an age of gaudy rubies."

He leaned in until his arm brushed against mine. "Look closer. Do you see how this area is a lighter shade of red?" he asked, tracing a circle around the ruby's circumference.

I ran a finger along Eliza Darrow's navel, following the trail of red ink. "The ruby's cutting her," I whispered. Not just cutting, *burrowing* into her flesh like a hookworm.

"Whoever gave her that ruby should've had it polished. Maybe he did, most likely he failed," Ben said. "Many have tried, including Charles Eckhart, who hired the best gemologist in San Francisco. All with the same result. Arabella's Curse cannot be cut. Not with a laser or even with a diamond razor. No man can alter its original form."

I snorted. "You can't cut it, but it cuts you. It's like the Chuck Norris of rubies."

Ben laughed. "To put it mildly, yes. At the height of the Byzantine Empire, Arabella's Curse was used as an execution tool. It was strapped to a staff and employed as a makeshift axe." Ben slid a finger across his own throat. "Ear to ear."

I grimaced. "Lovely."

"Legend has it Arabella's Curse is ten shades darker than your average ruby because so many men and women have bled on it over the centuries. It's said to have no core."

"Eliza Darrow's fate didn't end at the stake." Ben turned the page. His breath tickled the nape of my neck. "Look."

I concentrated on the illustrations before me. The pictures told a story, sort of like a medieval comic strip. Except there was nothing comic about it.

After the burning, two pageboys hauled away Eliza Darrow's charred remains and tossed her corpse onto a mule-drawn cart piled high with bodies.

The next image: Eliza's corpse, appearing only singed around the edges, strewn atop a mountain of bodies as two-dimensional gravediggers shoveled quicklime into the pit.

"She spent two days and three nights in a mass grave," Ben whispered in my ear. "And on the third night..."

My eyes traveled to a picture of a naked Eliza, her body now as plump and white as the day she was born, sitting up.

Recalled to life.

"The ruby brought her back from the dead," I said.

"She came back all right," Ben went on. "And she came back angry."

The next illustration was a massacre. Men lying on the ground with their intestines spilling out like rope, women wearing their split throats like ruby chokers, and in the center of this bloodbath: Eliza Darrow, holding the Lord of Northumberland's severed head by the hair.

Ben said, "She could have slashed her way through the entire village."

"How did they stop her?" More importantly, *who* could stop her? It seemed Arabella's Curse had not only brought her back to life, but made Eliza inhumanly strong. Not to mention demonic.

"One of the knight's pages," Ben said. "He took his dead

master's sword and *thwack!* Off with her head!"

The story ended there.

A ruby that could slice off your finger? A ruby that could resurrect the dead? It was a great ghost story, but in the end, it was just that: a story.

"If you're trying to scare me, you've got to do better than a few bad drawings," I said. "You don't even have photographs. No pictures. No proof."

Ben's eyes lighted with mischief. "Who says I don't have pictures? Wait till you see the prize of my collection."

I arched a skeptical eyebrow. "Show me."

"Turn the page."

I flipped to a grainy black and white daguerreotype of a girl, no more than fifteen, with dark tendrils framing her elfin face and eerie gray eyes. She wore a puffed-sleeve, scooped-neck Victorian wedding gown. The ruby dangled beneath her collarbone: as grotesque and misshapen as a tumor, but oh so glorious in my eyes. It was real. Not the stuff of superstitious lore. Not the byproduct of a ghost story. Real.

"Arabella Eckhart on her wedding day," Ben whispered, gauging my reaction.

Under different circumstances, I could sit here all day staring at the ruby, studying its rigid edges, tracing its curves and depressions forever and ever and ever.

But there was something familiar about Arabella Eckhart. I

focused on her face until the old-fashioned hairdo and the lace bridal dress faded away.

If I retrieved my parents' wedding photo from the trash and held my mother's smiling face next to Arabella Eckhart's somber one, I knew what I'd see: an identical match.

Arabella Eckhart hung herself in the turret of Eckhart House when she was fifteen. What if, like Eliza Darrow, the ruby brought her back to life?

She had my mother's face. I thought of the creature lurking behind the gates of Eckhart House humming that familiar lullaby, and black dots swarmed over my eyes. My throat clamped up, and I opened my mouth, gasping for air. Mother's hands wrapped around my esophagus, squeezing, crushing. Phantom water filled my lungs.

I slammed the binder shut and shoved it across the desk.

Forget going back.

Forget the ruby.

Abort the mission.

The cost of facing her again was too great. I wasn't strong. I wasn't ready. I wasn't brave enough, would *never* be brave enough.

"What's wrong?" Ben jumped to his feet.

Burying my face in my hands, I counted to three and tried to breathe. Ben grabbed my shoulder, his strong fingers grounding me to reality. "You look like you've seen a ghost."

I glanced down at my forearm; all the microscopic hairs stood on end. "I'm not sure that I haven't."

CHAPTER 8

DOWN FOR REPAIRS

With ruby-hunting off the agenda, I requested an extra shift at work. On the fifth day of my waitressing marathon, Ben—probably sensing I needed a distraction from my mommy issues—enlisted my help in a project.

"Wrench." Ben held out his hand while I rummaged through the jumbo toolbox. Crouched behind an industrial freezer big enough to keep a human corpse on ice, Ben fiddled with a tangled mass of wires. "Any word from your dad yet?"

"Nope." I handed him the wrench and leaned against the stucco wall, listening to him *clink* away at whatever obstruction was responsible for the short-circuiting fridge. Stacks of frozen hamburger patties shared the kitchen counter alongside giant tubs of vanilla ice cream.

"Think he's got a sugar momma up there?" Ben asked.

"Not funny."

"Bet he's wining and dining some hot college chick."

I kicked his foot.

Ben snickered. After a long pause, his tone turned somber. "I don't know why you try so hard to impress him. He's such a dick to you."

"He's not a dick all of the time."

"And the Nile is just a river in Egypt. Sorry to break it to you, but he kinda is."

"You don't know him like I do. He used to be warm…gentle." I fished a peppermint from my pocket and toyed with the wrapper, trying to conjure up the father who used to fill my head with epic tales of deities, empires, and kings. Ben wouldn't understand. Picking the lint off the peppermint, I popped it in my mouth and said, "I believe in second chances. Dad is in there somewhere, hiding behind a cantankerous drunk."

"Another SAT word." He sounded impressed. "You've been expanding your vocab, Nolan."

I curtsied. "I've been reading erotic fan fiction," I said, rolling the candy from cheek to cheek. "Just finished the naughty Jane Austen series, moving onto Harry Potter slash."

"A little too much information." A muffled chuckle echoed from behind the fridge. "At least you're reading the classics."

Strangely enough, I was enjoying my conversation with Ben— it was a tango in which we both fought to lead. Ben Wolcott kept me on my toes, which was more than I could say for Drake, who usually liked me on my knees.

His elbow made an appearance as he twisted the wrench.

"I've emailed my two-weeks notice to that cantankerous drunk."

"What?" I blinked. "You've quit? But isn't my dad your hero or something? I thought you were content living with your nose up his ass."

"Har Har. Har." Ben tossed a metal doohickey at my feet. "You may believe in second chances, but I don't. I'm not working for anyone who slaps his daughter around."

I stared at the top of his head in disbelief. "Wait a minute, you're saying you quit because of me?"

"Don't flatter yourself. I quit on general principle." A screw bounced off my shoe. "Besides, I got what I wanted out of the job."

I sucked on the swiftly disintegrating mint until it became a shard. "A glowing letter of rec?"

Ben poked his head around the fridge, lips curling into one of those lopsided grins Mr. Darcy gave Lizzie Bennett before he spanked her with his riding crop. "I met you…"

These three little words turned my stomach—and my loins— into mush.

"Which is not by any means a good thing," he corrected. "But my life has never had a dull moment ever since." The lopsided grin gathered symmetry into a teeth-baring smile. There was a chip on his right canine. I stared at it. What would it feel like to run the tip of my tongue under it? Would it cut me like the peppermint shard?

This time I forgot to kick him. Eager to change the subject, I nodded to the enormous rectangular shadow on the wall. "What happened to the second freezer?"

"Broke down." Ben slipped out of view.

"Yeah, but what *happened* to it? Joe hauled it to a junkyard?"

"Gave it to me."

"What does one do with a freezer that big?"

"I'm a carnivore," he said. "I've got a lot of meat."

My turn to snicker.

Ben set the wrench by my feet. "Phillips head."

"Huh?"

"Screwdriver."

"Oh." Absently, I picked at the toolbox. There were four different types of screwdrivers and I had no clue which one he meant.

As I debated between the screwdriver with a red handle and the one with the blue handle, Ben tapped my bare calf.

I jumped in surprise.

"The blue one." Motioning me aside, he plucked the screwdriver from the box along with a pair of needle-nose pliers. I caught a glimpse of a disapproving frown as he disappeared behind the fridge. "What's the matter?"

"Nothing's the matter."

"You look confused."

I *was* confused. My calf burned where he'd touched me and I

126

rubbed it against my other leg, imagining Ben's hand traveling up my thigh and under my skirt…

In addition to freaking me out, Ben's private history lesson had unleashed a few old skeletons from the closet. Sexy skeletons. And okay, naughty Jane Austen had something to do with it too.

"The ice cream's melting," I said, feeling hot, bothered, and screwed up in the head. It was the night we met all over again, except this time, I had the benefit of seeing the chivalrous side to the lurker outside my window. I quite liked him.

"Almost done," he called, sounding completely oblivious to the weird note in my voice.

Another second passed and Ben inched his slender body out from the cramped space and stretched his sore arms. The stretching made his navy blue T-shirt ride up, revealing a swath of taut stomach above the low ride of his Levis. As if possessed by the spirit of a nymphomaniac, my fingers itched. I jammed my hands into my apron pockets to stop myself from groping him. I wanted more than just to touch, I wanted to drop to my knees and press my lips to the hot skin of his abdomen. Kiss it. Lick it.

I glanced up to find Ben staring down at me, brows knotted in question. He stepped around me and swung the freezer door open. An arctic blast cooled my fevered skin.

"Let's get the ice cream back in so it doesn't… " His dark eyes lingered on the slight part of my lips. "Melt."

Ben cleared his throat and turned to the frozen food. For the next few minutes, we transported the ice cream and frozen meat back to the freezer in heavy silence.

When the silence became too pronounced, Ben asked, "How many times have you watched *Pulp Fiction*?"

"Hundreds," I said. "It's my feel-good movie. It restores my faith in the world every time."

"That explains why you are..." His lips twisted into a sideways smirk. "How you are. But hundreds of times? Don't you ever get sick of it?"

"After a while, I don't even see the movie anymore." I flipped the hamburger patty over in my hands, trying to put my strange habits into words. "Any film buff will tell you that repeat viewings are all about trying to rewind something."

"Rewind what?"

"What kind of person you were the first time you watched the movie. Who you were with. You're rewinding..." I handed him the patty and rubbed the numbness from my frozen fingertips. "Happiness."

Ben stepped closer. "And who was with you during your first *Pulp Fiction* viewing?"

For such a direct question, I was unprepared for the break in my voice. "My daddy."

The phone rang.

Ben dumped a gallon of ice cream in my arms and dashed to the counter. A moment later, he poked his head back in the kitchen.

"It's for you."

"Me?" My hands were sticky from the ice cream. I wiped them on a damp dishtowel. "Who is it?"

"'Sweep the Leg Johnny.'"

We were watching *The Karate Kid* on TV during a slow afternoon when Ben pointed to the blonde goon terrorizing Daniel-san and said, "That's Cam." The nickname stuck.

I shot Ben a dirty look and took the phone, making sure he was out of earshot before pressing the receiver to my ear. "Sooooo? How'd it go? Did you 'sweep the leg'?"

"Huh?"

"Never mind."

Ben materialized beside me and snickered. Biting my bottom lip, I shooed him away. "Tell me good news, Mr. Payroll Manager."

Cam's words were slurred with fatigue and tinged with fear. He sniffled. "I'm sorry, Ava."

My shoulders slumped. "You didn't get the job."

"No."

I stifled a disappointed sigh. "That's okay, Cam. We'll try again. There's plenty of—"

"I'm in a lot of trouble…"

"*What is it?* Where are you?"

"I'm in jail."

A bottomless hole opened up on the floor and I fell into it. Cam rambled on and on but I could only pick out a few choice words. *Battery. Assault. Destruction of private property. Ten thousand dollars bail.*

Ten thousand dollars.

I scrubbed my face. Ben leaned against the threshold between kitchen and dining room, watching and listening.

"Stay...stay where you are," I said, once Cam was finished. As if he could go anywhere. "My shift ends in half an hour. I'll come get you."

I slammed the phone down and turned to Ben. "I need to make another call."

Though I half expected Ben to launch into a lecture about how it was unprofessional to use the work phone for personal calls, he threw up his hands in surrender and returned to the kitchen. "I saw nothing. I heard nothing."

Punching in a number I knew by heart, I waited for the ring. The phone clicked.

"Uncle Tav?"

"Why, Sweet Pea?" Startled by my frantic tone, Uncle Tav asked, "What's the matter?"

"I need your help."

He listened patiently as I explained our situation. "Of course I'll *loan* you the money. I'll even make the charges against Cam magically disappear."

My galloping heart slowed to a trot. Shutting my eyes, I collapsed against the counter. "Thank you, Uncle Tav. Thank you. Oh God, I could kiss you!"

"Now tell me," he interrupted. Through the static reception, I could hear the wheels in his head turning, the gears clicking into place. "How is the elusive Mortimer Nolan these days?"

"What?" I stiffened. "What does Dad have anything to do with this?"

"Like you, I'm concerned about my brother. Just because he's cut me off from his life doesn't mean I've severed him from mine. Out of curiosity, how does he sleep at night?"

"Sleep?" I raked a hand through my hair. "Uncle Tav, don't you think that's beside the point?"

"Now Sweet Pea, don't be dense. I asked you a question and I expect a direct answer."

Gnawing on a hangnail, I tried to stall for time. The last thing I wanted to do was answer his pervy question.

"Your brother is waiting..."

"Badly." The sigh I delivered left my soul one ounce thinner. "He sleeps badly."

"Define badly."

"He has nightmares," I said. "I hear him tossing and turning through the walls. He speaks in his sleep. Sometimes he screams."

"Good girl," Uncle Tav pressed. "What does he say?"

"Helena." My mother's name.

131

Uncle Tav was quiet for a long time. "Thank you, Sweet Pea. Check your account. I've already wired the money. Good night."

I felt icky, like I'd just helped Uncle Tav sift though my dad's underwear drawer. "Good night."

A dead tone.

Uncle Tav had already hung up.

◆

Cam slipped past the sliding doors of the Eckhart Police Department with a rumpled blazer tucked under one arm and a bruise on his jaw.

I clutched the steering wheel until my knuckles turned white. The passenger door opened and Cam got in.

"Why did you beat up your interviewer?" I kept my eyes trained ahead as he slid back the passenger seat to accommodate his long legs.

His seat belt clicked.

"Why?" I repeated.

"It's not important," he muttered, tugging at his tie.

"Not important?" I whirled on him. Cam stared sullenly at the glove compartment. One hand picked absently at the crease on his black trousers. His knuckles were scraped in some places, scabbed over in others. "*Not important?* Give me a reason. You mistake the office for a cage? Were you itching to hit someone, you moron? Why?"

Cam slumped in his seat. His breath frosted the window.

His insolence was the final straw. I slapped him across the face with all my might.

Cam scooted away, rubbing his sore jaw.

Pushed past my boiling point, I raised my hand to strike again.

"He laughed at me, okay?" Cam snapped. "He laughed when he saw my resume!"

I lowered my hand. The parking lot was deserted, the black tar slick with drizzle.

"He said his five-year-old son was more qualified and asked if I applied as some sort of joke." Cam wiped his runny nose on the cuff of his dress shirt. "I know we don't have ten grand for bail. I don't know where you got the money... I'm sorry, Ava. I screwed up. I'm always screwing things up."

"How'd you get the bruise?" I asked, to keep him from opening the floodgates. If Cam started bawling, I might lose it, too.

"I kind of..." He lowered his head in shame. "Resisted arrest."

"So they beat you?"

"With batons."

"Fuckers," I muttered under my breath. Scooting closer, I probed him in the ribs. I took him by the chin and examined his jaw. "Did they break anything?"

Cam shrugged off my motherly fussing. "Just my self-esteem."

Besides the bruise, Cam was otherwise unharmed. His indestructibility never ceased to amaze me. Maybe, like Wolverine, his skeleton was made out of adamantium.

"Oh," Cam said, "since my court date hadn't been determined, they told me I couldn't leave town..."

I gunned the engine. The Nissan rumbled and spat out a black plume of exhaust. I cranked up the radio. There was a lot of shit about to hit the fan, and I didn't want to hear it.

Massaging the spot between my eyes, I recited my favorite line from *Gone with the Wind*. "I won't think about it now, I'll think about it tomorrow."

I'd always related to Scarlett O'Hara, mainly because she was unapologetically bitchy and surrounded by an Atlanta full of haters. When I thought about how Scarlett's bitchiness—a personality disorder during peacetime—served as a superpower during the Civil War, I didn't feel so hopeless anymore. Cam and I were going to be all right. Getting through these trying times all depended upon being the best bitch I could be.

As Cam buckled his seat belt, I swiped a Kleenex from the console and scooted closer.

"Blow your nose," I shouted above the blast of cheery music. Cam blew into my hand and I balled up the tissue and chucked it out the window. Littering at a police station was probably a capital offense, but seeing as they went all Rodney King on my brother, they could suck it. "We've got a long drive home."

The music dissolved into a static mess midway into the forest. I switched the radio off, drowning the car in silence. Rows of redwoods loomed like giants against the silver light of the moon.

Cam rested his head against the passenger side window and drew his legs up to his chest. He yawned. "Ava?"

"Shut up, Cam. Go to sleep."

"I can't sleep in all this quiet."

"Suck it up and try."

"Remember the lullaby Mom used to sing when we had trouble sleeping? Can you sing it to me?"

"We? Sing to *you*, you mean." My headlights illuminated a swath of meandering highway. Our mother played favorites. Cam, obviously, was spared a dunking in the bathtub. She never tried to abort him. He even escaped childhood with fond memories. Lucky little shit. "You know I can't carry a tune to save my life."

Cam shifted in his seat, his words drowsy. "Neither could Mom."

I squinted through the darkness and spotted an elk darting between the trees. "Don't mention her again," I said. "Now shut up and let me drive in peace."

Cam ceased speaking. I steered the Nissan around another sharp turn and the elk disappeared. In my peripheral vision, Cam rubbed his jaw.

My brother knew our mother's lullaby didn't sit well with me. How could he be so dense as to bring it up now?

And yet.

Tapping a finger on the steering wheel, I cursed under my breath and tried to remember the lyrics to that stupid song. The only word swarming in my head was *why*?

Why not me?

Why did our mother love him and not me?

Why spare him and not me?

Maybe my mother was right and I was wicked to the core. But what made me so irredeemably bad? Better yet, what, if anything, made me good? Heroic deeds and pretty thoughts? I had none to my name, though I suppose there was one thing that lifted me out of complete wickedness.

Who I loved.

And who loved me.

"Tis the last rose of summer…" My voice, flat and embarrassingly off-key, replaced the silence. *"Left blooming alone. All her lovely companions are faded and gone…"*

Finished with the song, I swiped a sleeve over my tear-streaked cheeks before glancing at Cam. He was asleep, a carefree smile on his lips.

◆

When I moved to Eckhart, I'd Googled "How to sabotage a car and make it look like an accident." After bailing Cam out from jail, I refined my Google search and typed "How to fix a car." Early the next morning, I rolled up my sleeves and got to work. Elbow deep in motor oil, I realized that cars were much like hearts: easy to break, hard to mend.

Once the job was finished, I took a deep breath and picked up the telephone. Clumsy fingers tripped over the buttons as I punched in Ben's number.

He picked up on the third ring.

"I need you to come over right away," I said in my best damsel-in-distress imitation. "It's an emergency!"

"What is it?"

"Get over here now!"

I clicked End Call. That ought to get him moving. Mission accomplished, I raced to the porch and waited. I paced back and forth, nibbled my nails into nubs.

An hour passed.

I waited.

Maybe this was a stupid idea? What if he laughed at me? I shook the kinks from my body. The sooner this was over, the sooner I could settle my debt with Ben.

Two hours and thirty-four minutes later (not that I was counting), I spotted Ben sprinting along the dirt path toward my house.

I flew off the rickety steps and raced midway down the pebbled driveway before my inhibitions caught up with me. Slowing my pace to an aloof strut, I leaned against the back bumper of his broken-down Chevy.

Ben jogged toward me. "I got here as soon as… as soon as…" He bent over, palms braced against knees. "What's wrong? Is it Dr. Nolan?"

Feigning an intense interest in my cuticles, I said, "Still M.I.A., nothing new."

Ben narrowed his eyes. "You're not planning on going back to Eckhart House, are you?"

I grimaced, recalling the eerie singing in the pavilion and the equally freaky resemblance between my mother and a dead Victorian chick. "That ship has sailed."

"Are you dying?"

"Nope."

Ben scrubbed his sweaty face. "Then what's the emergency?"

I tossed him a set of keys.

He caught them one-handed. "What's this?"

"You left them in the ignition."

Ben frowned. "You called me all the way over here to tell me that?" He handed back the keys. "You can keep them as a souvenir. I don't think anyone's going to steal my car. You've made sure of that."

I slid into his Chevy. "Oh, I don't know about that…" Meeting his eye, I stuck the key in the ignition and the engine roared to life.

"Consider your jalopy resurrected," I said, getting out and ushering him inside.

Like a sleepwalker, Ben slipped into the driver's seat. He frowned like he was trying to solve a mental equation—one he couldn't figure out. "Ava, you're—"

I held up a hand before he embarrassed us both. We had a comfortable animosity; the last thing I needed was for Ben to get sappy on me. "The longer you beach your car here, the more my property value goes down."

"Surprising," Ben finished. His stare was intense. "That's all."

"Go away," I said, slamming the door.

I lingered in the driveway until Ben's Chevy shrank into a speck of white against the rolling green hills. Blushing, I trotted back to the porch. For the first time since I moved to Eckhart, my world, while not completely in order, was starting to align.

Then I looked up and my smile vanished.

Cam leaned against the banister. There was a pillow crease on his cheek and a cowlick on the back of his head.

Squaring my shoulders, I ascended the bottom step. "You just get up?"

Cam nodded to the deserted road. "You call that 'a smack on the snout'?"

"Oh shut up, Cam," I said, brushing past him. "What I do is none of your business."

"But *who* you do is my business."

I whirled around. "What the hell is that supposed to mean?" One look at Cam's flustered expression and I put two and two together. "Don't tell me you believe Drake!"

"After he left, I asked around," he said. "All your friends are saying—"

"Ex-friends," I muttered.

"There are rumors. That you sleep around."

"Cindy Park. Melissa Klein. Fatima-What's-Her-Face." I counted my fingers one by one. Then I ran out of fingers. "You dirty little man whore, you're one to talk."

"That's different. I'm a guy!" Cam grimaced. He looked embarrassed to even be having this conversation. "Tell me it's not true."

I started back to the house. "I'm not even going to dignify that with an answer."

"Yes or no?" Cam called.

I stalked up to my brother and poked him in the chest. "I fixed Ben's car so I can fuck him in it. Just what you wanted to hear, right? Strap a chastity belt on me, because hot damn! I just can't keep my legs closed."

"Ava..." Cam tried to take my arm.

With a growl, I shoved him away. "Touch me again and I'll–"

140

A screech of tires diverted my attention to the road.

"Is that...?" Cam began.

I squinted into the horizon, trying to make out the driver of the silver Lexus barreling toward us in a chaotic zigzag. "Dad?"

"Why is he driving like a lunatic?" I asked.

"Maybe he's sauced," Cam suggested. "Hope he saved some for me." He hopped off the porch and waved.

Dad aimed for the driveway, swerving at the last second. His wheels slung gravel and careened into the fence post. Smoke steamed from the hood. The horn blared in a jarring loop.

The door swung open and Dad stumbled out, his dress shirt torn and rumpled. A sickly pallor stretched across his face like a death mask. What the hell happened in San Francisco?

Tottering on his feet, he kicked the splintered fence post. "Who put this here?" he asked before collapsing into the weeds.

CHAPTER 9

ELECTRICITY

Two days after his collapse, I found Dad propped behind his desk, listlessly tapping a pen against a stack of papers. His complexion was as ashen as the day he crashed his car. A few greasy strands of hair fell over his forehead. He didn't look up when I entered.

I set a wooden tray on the edge of his desk.

"I made chicken noodle soup," I said in my most cheerful tone. My eyes darted to the locked windows. The air in the room was thicker than the soup. "It's actually from the can, but I heated it up. Let me clear this stuff out of the way so you can—"

"Leave it."

I shuffled papers out of the way. "Once you take a few sips, you'll be as good as new."

"I don't need—"

"Everybody needs to eat, and you can't in this mess. Let me just tidy up a bit."

Dad seized my wrist. "Leave it!"

The hand detaining my wrist shook with tremors. A heavy weight the shape and color of dread descended upon my heart. "Dad?"

Blinking, Dad dropped my wrist. Under the green glow of his desk lamp, Dad's blue eyes appeared dull and filmed over, like the forever-staring irises of a dead fish.

He snatched back the papers and scattered them haphazardly on his desk, recreating the chaos I'd tried to eradicate.

"There's a method to my madness," he said. "I'd appreciate it if you keep your hands off my things and stay out of my study while I'm away. How did you get in anyway?"

"Ben let me in."

"Bad call on his part," Dad snapped. "I'm going to have a chat with him about who he lets in from now on."

Had he forgotten that Ben no longer worked for him? I shifted awkwardly on my feet. "I was only trying to help."

"Do me a favor." Dad swiveled away and opened his laptop. The blue glare from the screen fell across his face, highlighting every haggard line. "Don't."

I stood by his desk, watching him type a few blurry sentences, delete, and retype.

"We're finished," Dad said with his back to me. "You can take the soup away. I'm not hungry."

Acting on autopilot, I picked up the tray.

144

Such a good daughter. Such an obedient dog.

The spoon rattled against the porcelain bowl. Soup sloshed against the rim.

Instead of leaving I hovered for one desperate moment, mentally pleading for him to reconsider. Dad pounded away at his keyboard.

I sniffed, blinking away my embarrassing tears, waiting for him to turn around and what? Apologize? Not likely. Toss me a bone so I could shake my tail and lick his hand?

Disgusted with myself, I turned to go, but a glint of silver on the edge of the desk caught my eye. I'd been too distracted to notice it before. Now I wondered how I could've missed it.

The picture frame was back in its revered spot between his aluminum pencil holder and a new stack of unopened bills. The first thought he had when he woke up was of *her*. Was that why he found his way back to his study? So he could be alone with her picture?

What did he do when he discovered it missing? Fish it from the garbage out back?

She was the only thing that mattered, right?

More than Cam.

Definitely more than me.

The spoon clanked against the tray as Dad clanked against his keyboard. I peered over his head, watching the same stunted Times New Roman paragraph grow and shrink with every frantic tap of the backspace key.

My pulse throbbed in time with the persistent tapping of the keys. *Tap tap tap. Backspace. Tap tap tap.*

What's the matter, Dad? Blocked? Too much of *her* on your mind? Did you want me to leave so you can be alone with her picture? With your pathetic memories?

I slammed the tray on his desk, dousing every surface with scorching chicken broth. "She's dead!"

Dad recoiled from his seat. "Have you lost your goddamn mind? Look at this mess!"

"Ten years! She's been dead for ten years! She's a corpse!"

His face was a slideshow of one emotion: furious. "Ava, stop—"

"Why can't you see that?" I screamed, backing away so he couldn't strike me. "Don't you understand? She *left* you. She didn't love you. She *never* loved you! But I do and I'm alive!"

Snatching the frame, I clawed off the backing.

Dad lunged at me. "No!"

I darted into a corner. "You can't bring her back to life by staring at this—" I ripped the picture into shreds and scattered them across the floor.

He let out a strangled cry and dropped to his knees, gathering up torn bits of photograph.

"Oh Dad…" I choked the words out. I wished I hadn't seen Dad reduced to this: crawling on all fours like a desperate animal.

146

And yet—goose bumps sprung up along my forearm—the sight was not altogether unfamiliar. Where or when had I seen him like this before?

I cast the eerie feeling away as a memory from a dream. "Dad, get up."

"Get out." His voice was barely above a whisper. His hands trembled again as he grappled with the pieces. "Get out!"

♦

Ben Wolcott lived in a farmhouse so decrepit it should've been bulldozed years ago.

Beaching my Nissan under an umbrella of spiky branches, I stared up at the lopsided house silhouetted against the full moon. A gust of wind rattled the cypresses and rippled across the sea of waist-high grass.

Although Ben never told me his address, he always took the same road after work. Always a left turn, away from the hive of tract homes, shielded from the garish lights and sounds of civilization, and deep inside the dark woods.

From the snippets of gossip gleaned from the Dodd sisters, I was able to piece together a few sad facts about Ben. He lived alone with his mother, who had never fully recovered after the death of her younger son, Jason. Odd that Ben never once mentioned a brother. Then again, maybe I had been so self-absorbed with my own problems that I'd never thought to ask.

Rumors swirled around Ben's elusive mother. She never left her house and kept a clutter of feral cats. She roamed the graveyard at night and slept atop her dead son's tomb to keep him company.

As for Ben, everybody knew he left college and a promising med-school future to take care of her until the day she could take care of herself. But would that day ever come? Just the prospect of squandering the prime of your life in Eckhart was enough to illicit sympathy from even the hardest of hearts. Despite our differences, Ben and I lived parallel lives.

I cut a path through the weeds, chasing the patches of shadows and ducking the swatches of moonlight. As I crept closer, my ears picked up on what sounded like the whirling turbines of an industrial fan emanating from the bowels of the basement.

"That's one heck of an air-conditioning system you've got there," I whispered, peeking into the Wolcott's dimly lit kitchen. Ben was slumped behind a tiny square table, absently raking at his mashed potatoes.

His mother flitted to the fridge. She looked like an actress from a '50s movie. Luxurious chestnut curls. An immaculately made-up face. Shiny red nails. A canary housedress. Definitely too glamorous for a dump like Eckhart. Syd and Marlene were trippin'. This woman was too hot to be crazy.

Shivering in my light jacket, I debated whether to knock.

What would I say? Hey guys, mind if I come in and hang? And while I'm at it, mind if I stay the night? I'm not exactly wanted at home.

Suppose Ben told me to get lost? We weren't sworn enemies anymore, but we weren't exactly best friends either. I didn't think I was in a position to reap sleepover benefits. I could always call Uncle Tav for help, but he was thousands of miles away. I hadn't had much contact with him since his creepy inquiries into Dad's sleeping habits, which was probably for the best. Selling Dad out for money made me feel like a spy-whore.

Short of sleeping in the streets, I had nowhere else to go.

The moon dodged its cloud cover, throwing the outline of an iron trellis, half buried in ivy, in its spotlight. I followed the path of the ivy, noting how it meandered its way to a second-story window.

Grabbing a firm foothold amongst the ivy, I began my silent ascent, feeling only the synchrony of my limbs and the steady beating of my heart. Since I was a kid, I scampered up every tree I could find. Before he was banished from our lives, Uncle Tav used to joke I could climb my way out of Hell on Satan's scaly back. As I grew up and the politics of high school took precedence over those carefree days of dangling on trees like a monkey, I'd forgotten how much I loved the thrill of the climb.

Clambering over the ledge, I sprang to the floor on my hands and knees like a cat with coil springs for paws. When my eyes adjusted to the darkness, I could make out the bulk of a desk, a bookshelf, and the metal frame of a twin bed. No posters or framed photographs decorated the walls.

A hibernating laptop doused the small room in an eerie blue glow. Using this as my light source, I surveyed the contents of Ben's bookshelf: science textbooks, a few hardbacks from the university press with Dr. Mortimer Nolan printed on the spine, and an assortment of well-thumbed sci-fi paperbacks arranged alphabetically by the author's last name. Typical Ben Wolcott anal-retentiveness. I rolled my eyes, remembering how every item in the storage room at Joe's had to be organized according to expiration date. Sometimes I'd rearrange everything, giving pickles with the expiration date Oct. 2018 precedence over the Jan. 2017 jar just to spice things up. Ben would always figure it out and the next day everything would be back in its proper place, order restored.

I ran a finger along the edge of his desk. No dust. Not one speck. I felt self-consciously filthy, like I should decontaminate myself in a chemical shower in order to set foot in this sterile environment. An twenty-year-old boy's room should smell like pizza and sweaty socks, not Lysol. Maybe Ben was not a boy but an alien who slept in an airtight pod?

Just as I was shuffling to the closet for a quick peek, the door opened and the alien stumbled in.

I kept silent, studying his wiry frame outlined against the light from the hallway. With his gawky movements and the hum of the basement generators, I could easily imagine Ben emerging from the hatch of a spaceship, scaring little children with threats of menial labor.

With his back to me, Ben slumped against the door and let out a sigh that made his narrow shoulders shudder.

Somewhere down the hallway, his mother sang "You Are My Sunshine." She had a melodic voice, far more pleasant that my own mother's monotonous drone. Yet, there was a melancholy quality to her song that made me shiver as if someone had trickled an ice cube down my back.

I switched on the halogen lamp.

Jumping at the sound of the click, Ben tried, too late, to wipe his eyes on his sleeve. "What are you doing here?" he croaked.

"I couldn't sleep," I said, sitting on the edge of his desk, "so I'd thought I'd— "

"You thought you'd break into my home?" Ben scrubbed his haggard face. "How did you get in here?"

I shrugged but my eyes shifted to the fluttering curtain.

"Why am I not surprised?" Crossing the room, he slammed the window shut. His fingers dug into the ledge. "Well? What's the story?"

"Would you believe I just dropped by to borrow a cup of sugar?"

Ben silenced me with a no-nonsense stare. "Why are you *really* here, Ava?"

"I got in a fight with my dad," I explained, picking at a spot on his desk where the particleboard had chipped away. "Long story short, he kicked me out."

We both knew I hadn't made one friend in Eckhart. If Ben wanted to fully humiliate me I might as well beat him to the chase. "So I came here...for sanctuary."

"Did you go down the hall or touch anything in the other rooms?"

"Of course not! I'm no thief if that's what you're worried about, and don't flatter yourself into thinking you have something worth stealing."

The tension in his shoulders subsided.

"Do you want me to go?" I asked softly.

Ben turned to the window. Wind lashed against the cypresses. Great forks of lightning streaked the sky. His mother's singing ceased, replaced by the power generator's whir and hum.

"You could've broken your neck," he said.

In response, I took his hand and placed his thumb over my jugular. "See?" I whispered, holding his gaze. "Still in one piece."

"Ava..." Ben flushed. "What are you doing?"

Sounded like something Dad would say. In fact, Ben and his knack for disapproving of everything I did reminded me of Dad in many ways. I drew my arms around him, nuzzling my face against his chest. He stiffened in surprise. I wanted so much for him to reach out and touch me in my loneliness. To desire and love me—if only for just one night.

"Make me feel good." It was not a command, but a plea. I must've sounded so pathetic that Ben gathered me into his arms. A pity hug, I assumed, until he shifted and I felt his hard-on poking me in the stomach.

I pulled away and let my hand wander. Ben hitched in his breath. "I could even blow you if you want," I whispered in his ear and had the satisfaction of feeling his fingers dig into my back.

Ben caught my wrist. "You need a cold shower."

"Only if you join me." I pressed my lips lightly against his. "Your move, Wolcott."

Ben kissed me. Timidly at first, asking for permission. His index finger traced the slope of my neck and rested comfortably on the curve of my shoulder. Encouraged, his kisses grew hungrier and rougher until I broke away for air. My lips were chafed and raw, his bottom lip bleeding.

"Don't tell me you want to slow down now." It sounded like a challenge. Timid Ben had morphed into a beast. "Wrap your legs around me and bite me again."

I followed his orders. He was my supervisor after all.

He lifted me off the desk and we tumbled to the mattress in a tangle of limbs. I yanked Ben's T-shirt over his head and attacked the zipper of his jeans. Ben tried to slip my blouse over my head.

153

Either the neck hole was too small or my head was too big. The blouse snagged on my jaw.

I grimaced in discomfort. "Wait. Let me—"

Ben seized the collar of my blouse. A loud *rip* echoed through the room. My blouse fell away in tatters.

I flopped onto my back, laughing until my sides ached. "I didn't know you had it in you, Wolcott."

His white smile loomed above me. "Me either." He collapsed on top of me, trailing hot kisses down my neck and over the slopes of my boobs. His tongue grazed my belly button as his head traveled lower and lower...

Hooking a finger through my panties, Ben yanked them off and dragged me toward the edge of the bed. His fingers dug into my thighs, prying them apart and draping my legs over his shoulders.

"Ben..." A million doubts whizzed through my mind. I hadn't showered all day. It had been a while since I had sex and since Drake wasn't likely to see me naked, I might have let my grooming habits go. "Are you sure you want...want...to do this?"

With a flick of his tongue, Ben tossed all my concerns out the window.

"Don't tell me Drake never did this to you?" he said, holding me still as I writhed and shivered beneath him.

I propped myself up on my elbow and met his eye across the flat plane of my stomach. "He usually stuffs things into my

154

mouth."

His eyes crinkled into a wicked gleam. "Do you want me to stop?" he asked, planting a kiss on my inner thigh.

In reply, I shoved his head back down. "Get back to work, Wolcott."

The halogen desk lamp flickered and buzzed.

The skies rumbled. Rain pounded the roof and streamed through the rafters. I arched my back and watched our shadows splayed across the bare walls as the room brightened and dimmed.

Brightened and dimmed.

All of a sudden, Ben's body froze. He poked his head up.

"It's okay," I said, assuming he wanted to move on to something more serious. "I have condoms in my jacket pocket. Um, not that I came here thinking we were going to—" *Mental head slap.* "They were left over from… Maybe I should just stop talking?"

Ben wasn't paying attention. His focus was on the lamp.

"What's wrong?"

He pressed a finger to his lips. I held my breath and listened, but all I could hear was the pelting rain mingled with the steady hum of the basement generator. Something about that quavering light bulb had Ben visibly spooked, so much so he'd forgotten his number-one priority: to pleasure me. The muscles in his arm tensed as if by watching the lamp he could will the light to stay on.

The bulb flickered one more time before the light

extinguished altogether. Darkness seeped into the four corners of Ben's bedroom and along with it, a silence so loud it roared.

Wiping his mouth, Ben scrambled off of me. I could hear him scavenging the floor for his discarded clothes.

"What's wrong? What is it?"

The dresser drawer creaked. Ben flicked on a flashlight. He'd already slipped on his T-shirt and was zipping up his jeans.

"Ben?"

Ben bent down to retrieve my clothes. Studying my shredded blouse with a frown, he crossed over to his closet, snatched a dress shirt from the hanger, and handed it to me. "Here. Put this on."

"Would you just tell me what's going on?"

"I have to fix the generator." Without meeting my eye, Ben draped the oversized shirt around my bare shoulders, shoved my arms into its too-long sleeves, and began buttoning.

"What? *Now?* Can't this wait till morning?"

My jacket came next.

"It can't..." In the ghoulish glow cast by the flashlight, his features betrayed a struggle. "You have to leave."

"*What?* What do you mean? I'll just wait here until you're finished."

"It could take all night."

I reached for him. "I don't mind."

Ben rested his forehead against mine. "There are things I

156

can't tell you yet..." The callused pad of his thumb caressed my cheek. "You just have to trust me on this."

"Ben, what is this about? What—"

He yanked me out the door. I stumbled, trying to keep up with Ben's determined pace as he dragged me across the dark hallway and down the stairs.

In the foyer, Ben snatched an umbrella from the bin and pressed the handle into my hand. Looking thoroughly wretched, Ben flung the front door open.

"I'm sorry," he choked.

Rain hammered the muddy road. The wind howled through the night like a cyclone on steroids, snapping off tree branches and telephone wires. He was going to kick me out. Knowing I had nowhere to go. Into *that*?

"I'll walk you to your car," Ben offered.

"Don't bother," I snapped. "In fact, don't call me, don't touch me, don't even *look* at me until you get your priorities in order!"

I dashed into the deluge and ran toward the sanctuary of my Nissan. In my rearview mirror, I spotted Ben standing on the porch behind a curtain of water. He lingered until I steered my car into the road and didn't budge until I'd driven away.

◆

On the shredded screen of The Arcade, Gene Kelly was in love. Splashing through puddles. Twirling around lampposts. Clicking his heels like a smitten fool.

Shortly after breaking in, I'd found a stack of rusty film canisters in the projection room and looped the desiccated strip through the cobweb-covered projector. The projector flickered to life, casting a grainy haze across the vacant auditorium.

Rubbing my red nose on the hem of a ratty blanket, I drew my knees up to my chest and shivered. The wind whistled through the broken windows, turning the theater into a freezer. A drop of rainwater splattered on my bed of tattered seat cushions.

There were worse places to spend the night. I'd rather be in my own bed. Or better yet, in Ben's bed generating body heat. But this was…just as good.

Most people lived their entire lives in comfy homes, their futures following tidy lines. They would never experience the romance of camping out in an abandoned movie theater because they were kicked out and discarded like trash *twice* in one night. I felt sorry for them.

Biting my lower lip to stop my teeth from chattering, I stared at the silver screen.

I had everything I could possibly want. Sanctuary from the storm. A private balcony seat. Spiders to keep me company. Movies. Magic. And Gene Kelly…

Dancing and singing in the rain.

CHAPTER 10

BIZARRE LOVE TRIANGLE

Ben didn't come to work the next day. Or the next. When he failed to show up on the third evening, the gossip mill began to churn.

"You'd think he'd at least help us set up," Marlene called over her shoulder. Poised precariously atop a stepladder, her round rump swayed to and fro as she stapled paper streamers along the ceiling. "Did he look like he had the flu to you?"

Syd inflated a green balloon over a helium tank. Her bony shoulders lifted in a shrug. "All I know is: he'd better be here tonight." She turned to me, thin lips twisting into a smirk. "Right, Ava?"

I'd been absently wiping down tables with my ears attuned to Ben's whereabouts. Now that the tide of suspicion had turned to me, I threw down my towel and glared at Syd. "What makes you think *I* know where he is?"

Marlene climbed down the ladder. "He spends all his time at

your house." She arched an over-plucked eyebrow. "Around you."

"Because he worked for my dad, genius."

"Doing what?" Syd asked.

"Research."

"Hmm," they hummed in unison.

Syd tied the end of a balloon and bunted it in my direction. "Sounds like more than research going on."

I caught the balloon in mid-flight and squeezed. The pop boomed across the empty diner, startling the Dodd sisters.

"I'm done," I said. "Call me when the party's started."

Syd and Marlene exchanged exasperated glances.

"You're coming?" Marlene asked.

Syd was blunter. "You weren't invited."

"I wouldn't miss this for the world," I said.

The preparation for Willa Russell's long-anticipated Welcome Back Party had taken the better part of three days. There were counters to scrub and floors to mop in addition to the horde of long-distance truckers and frazzled families with screaming brats to feed. I'd surprised everyone, including myself, by volunteering to help. I didn't mind putting in the time; actually, I welcomed any escape from another lonely night at The Arcade.

In a way, I was curious about this Willa, whose name popped up in all of the Dodd sisters' conversations. I wanted to see the kind of girl Syd and Marlene called their leader. Plus, I was told

162

there would be cake.

As the minutes ticked by and the first guests trickled in, it became obvious that Ben, if he was going to come at all, was going to be very late.

The drinks consisted of chocolate milk and apricot wine coolers. The music: bubblegum pop meets '50s sock hop. With the exception of the Dodd sisters and myself, everyone was either old enough to qualify for an A.A.R.P. discount or young enough to enter Disneyland on a child's pass. Everyone over eighteen probably fled town right after high school.

Willa and Joe arrived at nine p.m.—late by Eckhart standards. By the time they made their grand entrance, I was swigging my second glass of chocolate milk and making conversation with an elderly woman about my sources of fiber.

The men swatted Joe on the back. The Dodd sisters swarmed around Willa in a flurry of giggles, blocking their queen from view. I was the only one who hadn't moved. I knew I wasn't wanted. In fact, I could walk out the door this very moment and the Dodd sisters would jitterbug across the dance floor. So I was determined to stay at this party, not because I had nowhere to go, but out of spite.

The crowd dispersed and I got my first proper look at Willa. The girl in the flouncy party dress looked nothing like her sloppy father. She was built as delicately as a china cup yet curvy in all the right places. Her skin, even without makeup, was flawless and her features were perfectly symmetrical down to her pert upturned nose and luscious lips. She was Cinderella next to the ugly Dodd sisters. The fairest one of all.

I hated her immediately.

Willa scanned the diner, auburn brows furrowed in a frown. "Where's Ben?" she asked Syd.

Syd motioned to Marlene, who whispered something into Willa's ear. Three pairs of eyes darted in my direction.

I met their stare with a challenging arch of my eyebrow. If I could survive a ten-year friendship with a predatory import-model wannabe like Cindy Park, I could eat these girls for breakfast.

Breaking away from the pack, Willa sashayed toward me.

She hooked a nearby barstool and held out a hand. Her nails were painted the same shade of ballet slipper pink as her dress. "We haven't been introduced. I'm Willa."

I ignored her hand. "I know who you are. What do you want?"

"Ben," she said.

I stirred my chocolate milk. "What about him?"

"You know where he is."

"Do I look like his keeper?"

"Syd and Marlene said you guys are close," she said.

"I hardly know him."

"If you are as…as close as they say, maybe you can tell me what's wrong with him?"

"Nothing that a change in location wouldn't cure." I hopped off the stool. "Now if we're through…"

Willa touched my forearm. Desperate eyes the color of polished sea glass pleaded with me. "He's looking for Arabella's Curse again, isn't he?"

I plopped back down in my seat. She had my full attention. "Has he *always* been looking for it?"

"For as long as I can remember. He read about it in some academic article published by some professor of the occult." Her eyes swept over my face in recognition. "Your dad."

I nodded, confirming the relationship. "Dr. Mortimer Nolan," I said softly. "What did he tell you about Arabella's Curse?" I wanted to know if Ben had ever disclosed the ruby's secret to anyone else.

Willa looked thoughtful. "He said it was valuable."

"Anything else?"

"That's all."

I breathed a sigh of relief. She didn't know about the ruby's paranormal properties. He never told her, but he told me. That meant something, right?

Out of the corner of my eye, I noticed Syd and Marlene circling us like vultures. Willa saw them too. She snapped her fingers and they dispersed.

"Arabella's Curse was going to be his ticket out of here." Willa scowled. "*Ticket out of here.* He couldn't wait until graduation.

165

I remember the day he left for college, how happy he'd been to leave everything behind." Willa snatched a stack of party napkins from the counter and tore them into little pieces. "But he could've been happy here too. Daddy's got him a good job managing the diner. In a few years he could own it. Maybe it wasn't neurosurgery—"

"Cardiovascular," I interrupted. "Ben wanted to be a heart surgeon."

Willa glared at me. "Whatever. Anyway, he's back now and that's what matters."

I bet she was going to make sure Ben stayed put. She was staking her territory, telling me to back off. From what little I'd learned of Ben's history, I was able to fill in the blanks where Willa was concerned. Ben wanted out while Willa couldn't see past Eckhart's town limits. High school sweethearts at cross purposes, yes, but a couple with considerable history nonetheless.

As she talked, I tried to imagine her and Ben together. Holding hands. Making out. Making love. Did they even have sex? Probably bland, vanilla sex. With her fairy-tale princess get-up, I took her for the chaste type of girl who collected Precious Moments figurines and giggled when you mentioned the dirty S-word. She even *looked* like a Precious Moments figurine. One I'd like to smash.

"When did he break up with you?" I asked a bit too gleefully.

Willa blinked, taken aback. "What makes you think we broke

up?"

"That downtrodden look on your face doesn't exactly scream 'I'm in a happy relationship.'"

"A few months after he moved away." Her shoulders sagged. "He drove up to tell me in person. He swore it was the last time he'd ever return to Eckhart, and he would've made good on his promise had it not been for Jason." She turned to the pile of shredded napkin pieces. "I warned Ben not to fill a ten-year-old's mind with those creepy stories, but he didn't see any harm in it."

The mention of Ben's brother set me on edge. I leaned in close enough to inhale Willa's scent. She smelled pink. Like cotton candy. "Tell me more."

"Jason went to Eckhart House and wasn't back in time for dinner."

"How did Jason die?"

"Ben found him lying at the foot of the stairs. His neck…" Her delicate hands flew to her throat. "Broken."

Willa peered at me beneath wet lashes. "He carried Jason home. Back to their mother. She wouldn't believe her son was dead, refused to hold a funeral. Ben buried Jason alone."

"Poor Ben." No wonder he always looked so dejected. I couldn't imagine going through life with the death of my brother weighing on my conscience. Cam got on my nerves sometimes, but if anything should happen to him and I was responsible…

"Why didn't Ben tell me?"

"Why would he?" Willa snapped. "You hardly know him. *Remember?"*

A volley of greetings followed the ding of the doorbell. Ben entered, a silver package tucked under one arm. He'd changed into a button-down shirt and black trousers for the party, but swayed on his feet as he greeted the guests. There were dark circles under his eyes.

"Ben!" Willa ran to him, flinging her arms possessively around his neck. As if it were the most natural thing in the world, she stood on tiptoe and pressed her lips to his.

The kiss went on for a long time. Too long for my liking. I tried looking anywhere else—at the peach-colored napkins, at the balloon-cluttered ceiling, at the syrupy remains of my chocolate milk—but my attention always reverted back to Ben and Willa. All the cake I'd eaten settled like cement in my stomach.

Ben expertly extracted himself from her arms. With a polite smile, he handed her the present. Willa squealed and made a big show of ripping off the wrapping paper.

While Willa flaunted her gift—a pink scarf threaded with silver roses—Ben scanned the diner and our eyes locked.

Only a few yards separated us, but his stupid secrets made it seem like a thousand miles. I wondered if he was reliving our hot and heavy make-out session in his room. Did it mean anything to him? Or was I merely the third wheel, a wrong turn on the road to his predestined happily ever after with Willa?

168

Willa steered Ben toward their mutual friends. Their hands found each other, fingers intertwining.

I couldn't watch anymore.

Grabbing my things, I darted out the back.

♦

"Ava?" Dad poked his head into the hallway. "Ava? Is that you?"

I shut the door and leaned against it for support. It was half past midnight and I longed for the comfort of my bed where I could cry myself to sleep.

"Dad?" I followed the light into the kitchen.

The one thing I was not expecting was my father waiting up for me. I stared in bewilderment at the half-opened containers of margarine and olive oil scattered about the countertop, the dishes piling in the sink. "Are you—are you *cooking*?"

"I had this craving for those grilled cheese and tomato sandwiches your mother used to make," Dad said, rummaging through the drawers for a spatula. "Except it's been a while since I fixed my own meal."

Unable to watch him make a mess, I opened the top drawer and fished out the spatula.

Dad's attention was now on the tomatoes. He held one up against the light bulb, squinting at the skin. "This one's spoiled."

He turned to me as if I held all the answers. "They're all spoiled. Do you think we ought to go to the grocery for a new batch?"

I sighed. How could I stay angry at him when he looked so helpless?

"Here," I said, taking the tomato from him. "All you have to do is cut around the mushy parts. Like this." I showed him. "You can't throw away the whole fruit over a few bad spots."

Dad watched me slice the tomato. "Sounds like something Ian would say."

I stopped cutting and looked up, surprised at this rare mention of Uncle Tav. Did he know about our secret phone calls? Was he baiting me? But something in the absent way Dad was opening and closing the cap on the salt shaker told me he couldn't be that sly. Not tonight. He was barely lucid.

"I didn't know Uncle Tav could cook." A part of me wondered how long we were going to avoid talking about our last fight. Despite the giant elephant in the room, this was the first pleasant conversation we'd had in months.

Dad stood very still, blue eyes fixed on the cracked countertop.

"Dad?" I asked, alarmed. "Dad!"

He blinked and set the saltshaker aside. "Oh yes," he mumbled. "He taught your mother that recipe. She couldn't cook a stitch otherwise. The trick is to add a dash of basil and garlic salt. Such a simple ingredient, but it makes all the difference. Funny thing is: I used to toss my plate in the trash whenever Helena made them specifically because my brother taught her how."

I slathered margarine over two slices of bread and tossed them on the pan. "Why get so worked up? It's just grilled cheese…"

Now I was the one baiting. Sibling rivalry was common, even expected, among stepbrothers, especially when they pursued the same field of study like my dad and Uncle Tav. But what could've transpired ten years ago to carve such an unbridgeable gulf?

Dad rubbed a hand over his eyes. "The better son. The better scholar. Better… Always better…"

"Who said that? No one says that."

"Everything I had, Ian took away. Everyone I loved, they all loved my brother more." Slowly he lifted his head. "Why did you take his money, Ava?"

He knew. With shaking hands, I turned off the stove. "I didn't know what to do."

"So you crawled to him? To *him* of all people, begging for handouts?"

"I never begged. He offered to help."

"Charity! Make no mistake about that." He raked a hand through his hair. "What did he ask for in return?"

I turned my head away. "He didn't ask for anything," I lied. "He's family."

Suddenly I wished I hadn't deceived him. Despite his failures,

Dad had his pride, and I'd unknowingly robbed him of it.

"Were things really so bad that you had to go to him?" Dad buried his head in his hands. "I made quite a mess of it, didn't I? If I hadn't been so obsessed with Ara—"

"Arabella's Curse?"

He turned to me. He looked old and ill, like the day he collapsed in the yard. "I suppose you think it's a lot of silly superstition. Rest assured, I'm not planning to bring anyone back from the dead."

I held back a sigh of relief. "I'm just curious why you want anything to do with a ruby so…"

"Macabre?" He raised his eyebrow in a goofy Charlie Chaplin imitation. "It's kind of what I do, isn't it?"

For one fleeting second, he reminded me of the gentle man from my childhood. But the moment was gone, and all I could see was the frail and defeated shadow that used to be my father.

"I've dedicated my entire life to digging through old burial sites, rifling through houses others believed to be haunted in pursuit of what some of my colleagues in the History Department would call 'the ultimate weird.' I suppose they couldn't understand my fascination. But Ian always understood. We had that much in common. Whatever I found, whatever I published, my brother was always there to top me. But even Ian, with all his money and all his cunning, couldn't get his hands on Arabella's Curse."

"All my life," he continued, "I wanted something that was completely mine. I thought if I could just…*find* the ruby, maybe everyone wouldn't think I was such a failure anymore." Dad shook his head. "I couldn't expect you to understand."

I understood all too well what it felt like to lose your self-respect.

Putting the finishing touches on the sandwiches, I set a plate in front of Dad. "Better eat it before it gets cold."

Dad bit into his sandwich, chewing absently.

"I'm off to bed," I said, speaking to the back of his head. He seemed focused on attacking the crust of his sandwich and piling the discarded remains on his napkin.

"Ava," he called when I was halfway out the door. "Welcome back."

◆

Dressed in an old pair of jeans and a black sweatshirt, my long hair swept back in a ponytail, I surveyed each item on my mattress.

Leather gloves.

Maglite.

Extra AA batteries.

Leather boots were preferable, but the only kind I had in my closet came with a five-inch heel. My trusty black Chucks would

173

have to do.

I slipped each item into an old JanSport backpack. On impulse, I tossed in my cell phone knowing it would just die again.

"That's it…"

After months of inaction, of letting fear of my mother overshadow my ambitions, I was finally taking charge of my destiny. And my dad's.

I was going back to Eckhart House, and I did not intend to return without Arabella's Curse.

Failure meant serving apple pies at minimum wage for the rest of my life while vermin like Drake and Cindy cruised by on their daddies' bank accounts.

Failure meant watching my dad grow sicker and not being able to do a damn thing about it.

Failure meant praying Cam didn't lose control one day and kill someone in a fight.

Failure was not an option.

I was going to find Arabella's Curse or die trying. But if the legends were true and the ruby really could resurrect the dead, dying was also not an option.

Hitching the backpack over one shoulder, I mounted the windowsill and paused. Had I forgotten something? My hand sought the nail-shaped scars along my collarbone, reminders of what my mother was capable of.

I leaped back inside and dashed toward the dresser where I

uncovered my butterfly knife. The ivory handles were yellowed with age and covered with an intricate network of tribal engravings. With a flick of the wrist, I flipped the knife open. The blade gleamed under the scant moonlight, so sharp it hummed.

Chances were I wouldn't need it.

I tucked the knife in my back pocket. Tonight I wasn't leaving anything to chance.

CHAPTER 11

RELIC HUNTER

I heaved myself over the iron spikes, scurried down the gate, and landed on the balls of my feet.

"I'm in."

The wind carried my words into the inky fringe of trees. Crouched on the ground, I lifted my eyes to the towering Victorian ruin.

Breaking and entering into The Arcade had been a practice run. All those nights of climbing into forbidden places had prepared me for Eckhart House. I'd been training for this moment my entire life.

I broke into a run. Right into the mouth of the monster.

Pausing at the veranda, I slipped on my leather gloves and scouted for a way in. Someone had nailed several crooked two-by-fours over the first and second-story windows to keep out trespassers.

I yanked with all my might, trying to dislodge a loose board. It refused to budge. I tried again, cursing myself for forgetting to bring a crowbar.

When that didn't work, I tried the door.

The brass knocker was carved in the shape of a Gorgon's head with writhing snakes for hair. With all the windows barred, I was certain the front door would be locked. But it couldn't hurt to try. Heck, what did I have to lose?

I reached for the knob and had barely touched the thing when the doors creaked open—a ghostly invitation that said, *Come in, Ava. Come in. We've been expecting you.*

♦

My flashlight's beam bounced across the floral wallpaper, stirring the dust motes and transforming the air into a stew of filth.

Circling the grand entryway, I contemplated a curving staircase that narrowed in the middle and broadened at the top like a snake through a bottleneck. I shut my eyes. The twisted geometry drove me mad. The subtle slant of the ceilings and the disproportionate windows and doors all contributed to the nauseating sensation of being tumbled through a carnival funhouse.

I dug out my cell, hoping for an extra source of light. My phone was dead. I glanced at my wristwatch; the time had stopped at 12:05. Time to roll.

Half-jogging up three steps, I made the mistake of glancing down. A dark red stain dotted the lush carpet, pooling into a larger puddle at the foot of the stairs. A shiver shimmied up my spine.

They found him with his neck broken.

I shook Jason's death out of my head. This was no time for discouraging thoughts. I was only psyching myself out of my larger mission. But as I ascended the staircase, I made sure to watch my step.

The west wing converged into a narrow hallway lined with doors—doors that came in all shapes and sizes, details and designs.

Feeling like Alice in Wonderland, I opened an unremarkable door to my right. Fully expecting a linen closet, I was taken aback when I discovered a spacious room fit for a sultan. After a quick walkabout, the room proved as barren of occult rubies as it appeared on first sight.

I moved on to the next: a giant portal with half-naked people guzzling wine and grinding against each other — a reminder of the last party I attended—intricately carved upon its cherry-wood surface. Expecting a ballroom on the other side, I came face to face with a brick wall.

Slowly, methodically, I made my way down the line.

A vacant room.

An equally empty closet.

Rooms piled waist high with broken furniture and tattered paintings of somber dudes with walrus whiskers and pinched-faced crones in black bonnets.

"Ugh!" My frustration escalated with every dead end. And here I thought I could waltz inside and find the ruby on my first trip. Guess I'd been overly optimistic or just led astray by the Indiana Jones movies, which, need I point out, were full of lies.

The west wing veered off into another endless hallway. To the right: a steep flight of stairs built into the wall.

I decided to climb.

The air stank of mothballs and wood rot. Spider webs tickled the back of my neck like lover's fingers.

With each step, Eckhart House creaked and groaned. A shadow scurried on the landing, its tiny claws scraping hardwood.

The third floor mimicked the second: a labyrinth of doors that probably led to nowhere.

Bracing a hand against the wall, I massaged my temples. I felt like a lab rat in a maze—scurrying about with growing haste and no direction. No wonder Arabella's Curse remained unclaimed for centuries. Your run-of-the-mill looter could be trapped for days chasing his own tail.

Logic begged me to abort. It was late and going any further without a blueprint of the house, without a basic plan, was pure pigheaded stupidity. But I kept going. Through the haze of frustration and self-doubt, I saw the ruby burning bright, taunting me with its beauty. *Just one more*, it whispered in my ear. *Open one more door and then you can go home.*

Midway down the third-floor hallway, I halted in front of a macabre work of art: a sea of hands reaching out from the woodwork. The hands reminded me of the medieval illuminations of Eliza Darrow's resurrection and the pile of bodies she left in her wake. Maybe this was a sign?

I pushed the door open and stepped inside.

The room, while grand, was in horrible disrepair. A century of water damage had eroded a skylight in the ceiling and weakened the floor.

I treaded carefully, noting how the floorboards creaked beneath my feet.

A wrought-iron daybed rested against the far wall. On top of the bed: an old feather mattress, a faded tartan blanket, and a pillow.

Someone had been sleeping here. I plucked a long black hair from the blanket and held it at eye level. Fairly recently too.

Bending down until my cheeks grazed the soft linen, I sniffed the pillow and recoiled as my mother's lavender perfume wafted through my nostrils.

I flung open the room's only window and sucked in greedy gulps of air.

"It can't be…" I turned around to face the bed.

Fields of wild lavender covered the rolling hills and cow pastures of Eckhart. Most likely a squatter had brought with him a few sprigs to combat the old house smell. Even as I concocted story after story, I couldn't stop myself from shaking.

I was even hearing things.

An echo of footsteps.

Treading up the same flight of stairs I'd climbed earlier.

Creeping down the hall.

Trailed by the soft hum of a lullaby.

A tune I knew by heart. Images of my scrawny eight-year-old self with her blanket pulled up to her chin as she waited for her mother to tuck her in jumped to the forefront of my memory.

That deliberately loud clip in her step.

The relentless drone of *The Last Rose of Summer.*

My mother had a way of announcing herself before she entered a room.

No. Not my mother. She was dead. I clamped my hands over my ears. "Stop it. STOP IT!"

This wasn't happening. A voice chanted in my head: *Don't let her in. She'll kill you if you let her in. Shut the door! Do it quick. SHUT THE DOOR!*

I bolted toward the door and—

SNAP!

The floorboards cracked and I plunged through a hole. Flailing, I grappled splintered wood, scraping and clawing until I managed to stop myself from sliding. My flashlight rolled past my head and plummeted into the void. A long time passed before I heard the ping of metal against rock.

My life flashed before my eyes. Dad. Cam. Ben. There were so many things I hadn't accomplished. So many things left unsaid. I saw myself lying in a pool of blood, my body decomposing in the pit of Eckhart House for days.

It can't end like this. It *won't* end like this!

Grunting, I floundered for a foothold. My legs dangled uselessly in open air. Summoning all my strength, I hoisted myself up.

The floorboard splintered again.

I froze.

Too terrified to breathe, I watched in horror as a hairline fracture formed at eye level. "Oh shit..."

Another crack radiated from the first.

I reached a hand into the air, straining, like the desperate souls carved in the woodwork, for salvation.

The footsteps halted outside the door.

The humming ceased, amplifying the sound of my hoarse breath and the creak of the boards under my weight.

A feline shadow stretched across the threshold.

I braced myself for the inevitable, expecting my mother to scuttle across the room for the attack.

Nothing happened.

I tried to seize a sturdier handhold, but every movement aggravated my already precarious position.

There was no help. No salvation. No hope.

This was it.

I wasn't ready. I hadn't fulfilled my purpose: I hadn't found Arabella's Curse.

The floorboards splintered in a deafening crack. My screams bounced off the walls of Eckhart House as I plummeted to the ground.

CHAPTER 12

OCCUPATIONAL HAZARDS

Manic laughter echoed through the darkness. My eyelids fluttered. Through the three-layer-deep hole in the ceiling, a female silhouette blotted out the stars. The ruby gleamed above her collarbone, resplendent and red.

My fingers twitched.

Red.

The color of a mother's love.

My head lolled from side to side.

Red.

The beginning and end of my world.

I flexed my left leg—

And screamed.

White circles exploded before my eyes. I drove my fingers into the ground to keep from passing out.

After the pain became somewhat bearable, I yanked off my leather gloves and probed the injury.

185

Slippery blood coated my fingertips.

My hand closed around a jagged wooden stake impaled deep in my thigh. I clamped my eyes shut.

Oh Mother, I've fallen through the rabbit hole and now I don't feel so good.

Gritting my teeth, I wrapped my fingers around the stake—and yanked.

Another shriek ripped through my throat. Howling like a pig at the slaughter, I rolled onto my side and retched.

When the nausea subsided, I stripped off my jacket and tied it around my thigh. The act left me weak and lightheaded.

"Stupid!" I banged my head against the floor. "So fucking stupid!"

Flopping onto my back, I draped an arm over my eyes and sobbed.

I'd been reckless. Now I was going to pay. I came to Eckhart House alone. I had to get out alone.

Summoning the strength to sit upright, I surveyed my surroundings. I was entombed in some dank cellar, no larger than your average home basement, bare except for scattered wood and plaster debris. My fingers raked through soft soil, which probably cushioned the initial impact of my fall.

I squinted into the darkness in search of a window or a set of steps leading to a door. Nothing. I forced myself to stand and hunt for a hidden exit along the wall when something furry scurried across my foot. I lost my balance, crying out as I landed on my wound.

A scaly tail swished against my hand. A squeak in the dark made my skin crawl and then I felt the disgusting sensation of tiny claws climbing up my injured leg, trying to nibble at my improvised bandage. With a yelp, I slapped the rat away.

The waning starlight bounced off its whiskers as it moved in for another bite. I jerked away before it could sink its yellow teeth into the web of my hand.

Panting from the close call, I turned to the shadowy recesses of the basement. A dozen iridescent eyes stared back, watching, waiting. The floor was alive with rats. Hungry rats.

Not yet cold and dead, I was already a giant slab of meat to the vermin.

I slid the butterfly knife from my back pocket and flicked it open. Holding my breath, I listened to the scraping of claws along the floor.

The king rat darted in my direction. In one swift swipe, I stabbed the blade into its plump torso. The creature let out a high-pitched shriek, its tail swished and slapped against my hand, its stumpy legs twitched and convulsed.

I twisted the knife and the legs stopped moving.

Empowered by the kill, I forced myself to stand on my good leg. The rat was still impaled on my knife like grilled meat on a kabob.

Swallowing my disgust, I slid off the carcass and chucked its body at its brethren. "Feast on this!"

The corpse landed with a thud. A chorus of squeals closed in around it.

Wiping the blade on my shirt, I hobbled to the farthest wall and felt along its brick surface. To my immense relief, parts of the brick jutted out like grooves along a mountain.

Securing my makeshift tourniquet, I tilted my head to the hole in the ceiling. The stars above Eckhart gleamed with an incandescent light. A deep longing tugged at my heart. I would give anything to be back outside in the land of the living.

I wedged my shoe in a precarious foothold, sucking in stale air as a fresh spasm of pain bolted through my leg. Pressing my forehead against the rough brick, I stifled my tears and prayed for strength. I hoisted myself upward by an inch. The movement brought on a whole new onslaught of torture, but I kept my eyes on the stars.

When I was child, Uncle Tav told me I could climb out of Hell if I put my mind to it. Little did he know, I was putting his words into practice.

♦

The tweezers, along with the last stray splinter, *plinked* into the metal basin, turning the water bloody. I set the basin on the floor, tipped my head over the side of the bathtub, and vomited. Fortunately, I'd already emptied the contents of my stomach on the floor of Eckhart House. There was nothing left to throw up.

Wiping a string of saliva from my chin, I sank back down and assessed the damage to my leg. Blood oozed from the crater-sized wound and dripped onto the cracked porcelain. My bathroom looked like a murder scene.

The operation was far from over.

I jammed a leather belt in my mouth and bit down.

Taking a deep breath, I doused a cloth with iodine and poised it over my gaping wound.

On the count of three...

CHAPTER 13

JUST A FLESH WOUND

Three days and a bottle of antibiotics later, I was back at work.

I hobbled from booth to booth, serving apple pies and strawberry milkshakes, fried egg sandwiches and baskets of onion rings. I kept the ketchup bottles full, refilled the napkin dispensers, and diligently wiped down my tables while Elvis crooned "Can't Help Falling in Love" from the jukebox.

My leg was killing me.

During a lull in the dinner service, I limped to the bathroom. I slammed the door and braced myself against the sink. My fingers dug into the washstand until my knuckles turned white.

Twisting the tap, I splashed cold water over my face. The water sizzled and steamed against my fevered brow. Panting, I yanked up my skirt. A lone circle of blood stained the new bandages. I peeled away the linen, slowly revealing the ugly gash.

If it was possible, the wound looked even more grotesque than before. While the surface had scabbed over, it never completely stopped bleeding. Angry red streaks radiated from the wound, crisscrossing like snakes down my thigh. I pressed a forefinger against the edge of the scab. Yellow pus oozed from its jagged edges.

Someone rapped on the door.

I jumped.

"Ava?" It was Ben. The concern in his voice rang loud and clear. The doorknob jiggled. "You've been in there for a long time."

I fumbled with the bandages. "Just a minute!"

I did a last-minute check in the crooked mirror above the sink and grimaced. Bloodshot eyes. Sheet-white skin. Who dug the corpse out of her crypt?

Smoothing down my skirt, I opened the door and found myself face to face with Ben. His eyes swept over my pain-drawn features.

Ben pressed a hand against my forehead. The intimate gesture took me by surprise. I gave a half-hearted display of resistance, but the coolness of his palm felt so good that I shut my eyes and let myself sway against him for support.

"You're burning up," Ben said.

"I just caught a bug. I'll ride it out."

He caught my hands in a firm grip and turned them over to study my scraped knuckles and broken nails. "That's some bug. Did it give you that limp too?"

I pried my hands away. "I fell."

"How?"

"Slipped on the driveway." My weak attempt at a smile turned into a grimace. "Damn puddles."

Ben regarded me with a skeptical cock of his brow. "How many times did you slip?"

I edged past him. "I'm going back to work."

"Wait!"

Looking up, I found myself staring into a pair of sad brown eyes.

"Take the night off," he said.

"I'm fine."

"Ava, you are so *far* from fine. Will you please tell me what happened?"

At the tender catch in his voice, I almost caved. I wanted nothing more than to lay my burden at his feet. Tell him about my mother and my almost fatal attempt to find Arabella's Curse. Show him my injury. Ben would know what to do. He'd make the pain go away.

"*Ahem.* Am I interrupting something?" Syd's shrewd eyes darted from Ben to me and the corner of her mouth tucked into a frown.

Scowling, Ben asked, "What is it, Syd?"

"Booth 8—*her* booth—is waiting. Or do you expect me to pick up her slack while you play doctor?"

193

Ben opened his mouth to speak, but I silenced him with a placating hand. "I'll see to Booth 8."

White spots invaded my vision, transforming the dining room into a neon and chrome blur. Gripping the countertop for support, I launched myself into the dining room, stopping short when Willa's freckled face came into focus.

"What are *you* doing here?" I asked.

Willa set her menu down. "I thought it's about time we get to know each other better." One look at my clammy complexion and her smile vanished. "You look like shit."

"Thanks," I said dryly. "Why are you in my booth?"

"Are you sick?" Willa asked.

"Never been healthier." The neon Coca-Cola sign behind her head flickered and swirled in dizzying circles. I swayed from side to side. "I'm sick of people asking if I'm sick."

Willa glanced at the counter, where Ben watched us with his arms folded. She gestured to me in question. Ben answered with an exasperated shrug.

"You can't work like this," Willa insisted. "I'm sure my dad won't mind if you take the night off."

"I can't."

"You can and you will. In fact, I *order* you to take it easy."

I slammed my palms on the tabletop and tried to keep from tipping over. "Let's get one thing straight. I work for Joe. Not you. So you can take your 'order' and shove it up y-your—"

194

I shut my eyes and shook my head. Willa's lips moved, but no sound came out. She looked very peculiar with the corkscrew spirals of her hair twisting and slithering like a halo of serpents.

She clamped her hand over her mouth. Someone turned the sound back on to an underwater channel. "You're bleeding!"

What kind of silliness was she up to? I glanced down at my leg. A small dot of blood had appeared on my skirt. The dot blossomed into a circle the size of a nickel, then a quarter, then a half-dollar.

"This will leave a stain," I said.

I staggered backward. The world tilted.

The pain was unbearable.

My head smacked against the floor and the pain was no more.

♦

A monster with eight eyes and four mouths loomed over me. The haze evaporated. Slowly but surely, the world came into focus. The eight eyes converged into four separate sets belonging to four different faces. Ben. Willa. Syd. Marlene.

I was lying in a crumpled heap next to the employees' cubbyholes. The greasy stench of onion rings stirred up a surge of nausea accompanied by another spasm of white-hot agony. I rolled on my side and groaned.

"Ben?" Willa knelt over me.

I glanced up, startled to find her dabbing my brow with a dish towel wrapped around a handful of ice cubes.

"Ben," she said. "We have to do something."

Ben knelt by my side, brows knotted in a frown. He took my hand.

"We have to take her to a hospital," Willa pressed.

At the mention of the word "hospital," I jerked away from Willa and seized Ben's arm. My nails dug into his skin.

"No!" Visions of an astronomical medical bill swarmed before me. "No hospitals! I'm fine, I'm—" I began shivering so hard my teeth chattered.

"Stubborn and stupid is what you are," I heard Syd mutter over Ben's shoulder.

Willa clamped a restraining hand on my shoulder. Her grip was surprisingly firm for someone so slight. "Syd? Why don't you make yourself useful and get some more ice."

"Hrmph!" But Syd stomped off to the soda fountain to do Willa's bidding.

"What can I do?" Marlene looked to Willa for orders.

"Get the keys from my purse. You can start my car—"

"No!" I tried to push myself into a sitting position. "I said I don't want to... Ben! Ben!"

Ben caught my hands and pulled me into his arms. I leaned my cheek against the hard slope of his shoulder, listening to the steady rise and fall of his breath.

Pushing back my sweat-matted hair, he whispered in my ear like someone gentling a riled-up horse. "We won't do anything you don't want to do. But I want to look at your leg, okay?"

I nodded, giving him my complete trust, and scooted back to let him examine my wound. Ben hiked up my skirt and carefully unraveled the bandages.

"Oh for heaven's sake!" Willa sighed. "She needs to see a real doctor, not a Know-It-All who thinks this is a good time to play doctor."

"She also needs some peace and quiet," Ben muttered. "God knows I do."

In a huff, she crossed her arms and fumed.

As he peeled the last of the bandages away, Ben's face paled to the color of new snow.

Marlene peered over Ben's shoulder. "Sweet merciful Jesus! I think *I'm* going to be sick." One more gander at my wound and she raced to the bathroom and slammed the door. The sound of her muffled vomiting did nothing to calm my already frayed nerves.

Willa crawled over to get a better look. She blanched and muttered to Ben: "How long has she had this? How is she still standing? How is she still alive?"

Ben's jaw hardened. "Syd? Damn it, Syd! Where are you?"

Syd appeared carrying a bucket of ice. "The machine is on the fritz—" The bucket clattered to the ground. "Holy shit. That is the most disgusting—"

"Get Willa's keys!" Ben ordered.

"Oh come on! It's not that bad," I said.

"Not that bad? God!" He scooped me up into his arms and raced to the back door.

I licked my chapped lips. "Is this really necessary? All I need is a really big Band-Aid."

"You're going to the ER. Or I'm going to kill you myself." He growled in my ear. "You went back to Eckhart House, didn't you?"

I didn't reply.

"I hope it was worth it," Ben said.

"It was totally worth it." I shut my eyes and let him carry me through the back alley and into the parking lot where Willa waited in the driver's seat of her black Range Rover Sport. "When I get better, I'm going back prepared."

"*If* you get better."

"I plan to. And you know what else? I've seen it. It was beautiful."

Ben snorted, probably assuming I was speaking out of delirium. "Seen what?"

"I've seen Arabella's Curse..."

CHAPTER 14

THE GIRL WITH NINE LIVES

By the time the nurse came to check my vital signs, I was fiddling with the remote control of my mechanical bed, unable to decide if I wanted to sit or lie.

The nurse, an elderly woman with a salt-and-pepper perm and kind brown eyes, strapped a Velcro band across my arm to check my blood pressure. "How's my little Nine Lives?"

"Nine Lives," as in "Girl with Nine Lives," was my nickname amongst the staff at Eckhart Memorial. I liked the name. It made me sound like a Native American warrior. He Who Wrestles with Bears. She Who Tinkles in Brook. Girl with Nine Lives: a modern medical miracle.

My injury was the worst case the doctors had seen in years. If the wound had festered one day longer, I would've lost the leg. The infection had spread to my bloodstream and the resulting septic shock was severe enough to kill a girl twice my size. Not only had I survived, I'd recovered in less than a week.

I slumped back in bed and sighed. Girl with Nine Lives was bored. "Can I go home now?"

"Not yet. Dr. Kung wants to monitor you for a few more days."

"How many days is a 'few'?"

"A week."

A week! What was I going to do for a week? Great. More money down the drain.

Resigned, I tried to make the most of a bad situation. I cranked the dial on the bed's remote to "sitting." "Did my dad come visit me today?"

The nurse stopped scribbling in her chart and peered at me over the rim of her bifocals. "No, hon."

Maybe that was a blessing. I tried to blot out Dad's last visit. He'd stood awkwardly over my bedside with the same expression he wore the day he found out I'd been expelled. The year wasn't over and I'd managed to screw up again.

"My brother?"

She shook her head. "He came yesterday while you were sleeping."

I cranked the dial and the bed flattened. I stared morosely at the ceiling panels.

Cam didn't like hospitals. The sterile surroundings made him skittish. I bet I wouldn't see him again until discharge day.

Out of curiosity, I asked, "Who drove him home?"

"His pretty little redheaded girlfriend," the nurse said.

With another twist of the remote, I was back to sitting. "He doesn't have a—"

Did she mean *Willa?* What was a fine, upstanding guy like Cam doing with the likes of her? Girl with Nine Lives was not pleased. Girl with Nine Lives did not like this one bit!

My heart monitor spiked. Sensing my distress, the nurse clicked her pen and smoothed down my disheveled hair. Unlike the other nurses, this one had taken a shine to me.

"So no one else?" I tried to sound indifferent, but came off meek and pathetic.

She gave me "the pity look" and patted my arm. "Get some sleep, sweetie," she said, making sure to pry the remote control from my grip and place it on my bedside table. "And I'll sneak you in an extra dish of Jell-O when you wake up."

The door clicked shut.

The silence was suffocating, the loneliness even more so.

I was the Girl with Nine Lives, damn it. Didn't that mean something? Shouldn't I have a throng of stuffed-animal-bearing visitors lined up at the door? I gazed around the empty room, listening to the *beep beep* of my heart monitor. I reached for a Kleenex. At least there was one bright side about being unwanted, unloved, and forgotten: no one could see you cry.

I was blowing my nose when someone rapped on the door. At first, I thought the nurse had returned. The door creaked open

201

and Ben slipped in, a board game tucked under one arm. He studied my tear-streaked face before hooking a chair over to my bedside.

Without speaking, he removed the empty plates from my food tray, propped the tray over my lap, and extracted a battered chessboard from the box.

A lump formed in my throat as I watched him deftly set up the plastic players.

I brushed a tear away from my cheek. I was having trouble speaking. "What makes you think I know how to play?"

He placed the last piece, the black queen next to her king, and looked up. "I just know."

"My Uncle Tav taught me when I was a kid. He was the best, which makes me the best. I'll *own* you."

"I'm pretty good myself. So I guess I'll have to come here every afternoon until one of us wins."

In one swift move, he swiped my bishop. Ben kept his attention on the board. "So where was it?"

"Where was what?"

"Arabella's Curse," he said, scratching a spot behind his ear. "You told me you saw it before you passed out. Did you get close enough to touch it?"

Sucking on my inner cheek, I listened to the drip of my IV. "I suppose I could be persuaded to recount my story if…"

He sat upright, face brightening. "If?"

I moved my knight and captured his castle. "If you tell me why you kicked me out of your room."

Frowning, Ben stared at the board. He slid his queen over two spaces and captured a lowly pawn. "Your move, Nolan."

♦

A week after my discharge, I paid my second visit to the Wolcott residence.

Ben glowered through the crack in his door. Muffling a curse, he unhooked the chain and I opened my mouth.

"It should interest you to know: Willa and Cam have grown quite close. And by 'close,' I mean *sex*. I saw her enter the barn with Cam and exit with hay in her hair. If that bitch thinks she could use my brother to get to me, she's living on a prayer!" On the bright side, this meant she was no longer interested in Ben—or so one could hope. Unless she intended to have them both, in which case I planned to be ON her like hound on a poodle. I paused, tapping my chin as I pondered a more pressing concern. "She's invited me over for dinner tomorrow night. What do you think I should wear?"

Ben stared at me, rubbing his jaw. "You have the wrong address," he said and slammed the door in my face.

Balling both hands into tiny but deadly fists, I pummeled Ben's front door.

Ben reappeared. I gave his left nipple a vicious twist through his T-shirt. "I'm trying to tell you something important and this is the thanks I get? What's wrong with you?"

Absently rubbing his chest, Ben studied the fluidity of my movements around his porch. To see his face, one would think I'd spouted wings. "Your leg!"

I glanced down at the aforementioned leg. According to Dr. Kung, it would require months of physical therapy before I could walk again. I didn't have time for such nonsense. I had things to do, rubies to find. So I took an Advil and called it good. "Ah, yes. It's still stiff, but nothing I can't manage. Give me a few days and I'll climb to the moon and back."

He shook his head in awe. "Amazing..." An eerie light appeared in his eyes. "You're the one, just like he said," he muttered.

"Uh, Ben? You're kind of creeping me out. Aren't you going to interrogate me about Willa and Cam? Don't you care?" I peeked over his shoulder and inhaled the mouthwatering aroma of roasted chicken and sweet potato pie. My stomach growled. "Aren't you going to invite me in for dinner?"

"No," he said flatly. "And no." He reached for the door.

"Ben?" A woman's gentle voice called from the foyer. "Who's there?"

Almost immediately, Ben underwent a visible transformation. His shoulders stiffened, and anxiety radiated off his body in jittery waves.

"Just a pest," Ben called over his shoulder. He hovered near the entrance, blocking my view of his mother. "Consider her gone."

Mrs. Wolcott, the elegant woman I'd only glimpsed through the window, appeared behind her son and placed a placating hand on his arm.

Grudgingly, Ben released the door.

A genuine smile played across Mrs. Wolcott's lipsticked lips. Dressed in a black and white striped blouse and matchstick jeans, she was a dead ringer for Audrey Hepburn. "And what a pretty pest she is."

"We haven't been introduced," I said. "I'm—"

"The Girl with Nine Lives." Mrs. Wolcott's eyes sparkled with merriment. "Ben told me about your accident."

I beamed at Ben. "Yeah, Ma. That's me."

"Did Ben ask you to join us for dinner?" Mrs. Wolcott asked, glancing from her despondent son to me.

"Nope. I don't believe he has."

Ben looked like he was plotting my murder.

"Shame on you, Ben! Where are your manners?" Mrs. Wolcott gave me a long-suffering glance. "Please come in."

"Your mother is positively charming," I whispered as I passed by Ben.

In reply, he kicked the door shut.

I followed closely behind Mrs. Wolcott as she glided through the tidy, albeit tiny, living room.

"Make yourself at home, sweetie." Mrs. Wolcott gestured to the sofa. The rose chintz upholstery was worn, but appeared comfy and gave the place a homey French Country atmosphere. "I have to see about this chicken. And Ben, I need you to set an extra place at the table."

Alone with Ben, I paced around the living room, letting my eyes roam along the cream wallpaper to the narrow staircase. A separate hallway on the first floor trailed off into a shadowy void where a familiar mechanical whirr stirred the air and shook the walls.

I took a tentative step toward the source of the noise.

Ben blocked my path. "Don't make yourself *too* at home."

Peeking over his shoulder, I squinted into the darkness. "Is that your basement? What do you have down there?"

Ben surveyed me with arctic eyes. "Not that it's any of your business, but we have one of those old-fashioned industrial furnaces."

Moving away to inspect the pictures on the mantle, I said, "Better keep an eye on it. It sounds like it's about to explode."

I halted before a photograph of Ben in a cap and gown. He had his arms around his mother and a boy with a mop of disheveled brown hair and mischievous eyes. "You look happy here," I said, studying Ben's goofy smile. "Never seen you happy before. It suits you, Wolcott."

Sensing Ben scrutinizing my every movement, I whirled around to face him. In contrast to his graduation picture, this Ben looked like he carried the weight of the world on his shoulders.

Acting on instinct, I placed a gentle hand on his forearm.

Ben shrugged my hand away. "I should go help with dinner."

"I only meant—"

Before I could finish my sentence, Ben backed away and dashed through the kitchen door.

"I only meant to say I wish I had a graduation photo too," I whispered to the empty room.

A table lamp flickered, casting grotesque shadows along the wall. The furnace growled and grumbled like a monster with indigestion.

"Uh, Ben?" I backed away. "Wait for me!" I scurried into the kitchen.

Mrs. Wolcott welcomed me with a smile, ushering me to a seat at a small circular table. I cast a sidelong glance at Ben, who was busying himself at the counter slicing tomatoes for the salad. His knife hacked against the cutting board in rapid succession.

If Mrs. Wolcott sensed something was amiss, she didn't let on. She handed me a tall glass of pink lemonade and poured another for herself. "Are you planning on returning to school?"

I swished the tart liquid in my mouth and wondered how much Ben had told her about the infamous end to my less than stellar academic career. Ben kept his back turned, but I noticed a deliberate pause in his attack on the vegetables.

"I doubt any high school could contain the likes of me," I answered offhandedly.

Mrs. Wolcott frowned. "I don't understand—" She turned to Ben for an explanation.

Ben swiftly dismembered a head of lettuce. "Ava likes to speak in riddles. She hasn't given a thought to going back to school. Her head is still filled with pipe dreams at the moment."

He failed to mention that he'd filled my head with these pipe dreams.

"Oh," Mrs. Wolcott said. Although she had the grace not to show it, I bet she was already comparing me to her honor student son.

Usually I couldn't care less what people thought about me. But I'd taken an immediate liking to Ben's mother and wanted her approval.

"It just so happens, I've begun studying for my GED," I amended.

Mrs. Wolcott smiled. Apparently that was the right answer.

Ben set down his knife and peered over his shoulder. "You have?"

I leaned back in my chair. "I did more than play chess during my recovery."

"Good." His lips twitched as he set the wooden salad bowl on the table. "There's hope for you yet."

Before Ben could sit down, Mrs. Wolcott motioned him to stop. Ben halted with one hand on the back of his chair, shoulders tensed in alarm.

Mrs. Wolcott frowned. "You forgot to set an extra place."

I turned to Ben in confusion. An extra place? There were only three of us.

Ben shut his eyes. His throat constricted as he attempted to swallow. "Mom...please don't do this now."

Do what now? I turned from mother to son, one the picture of serenity, the other on the verge of a nervous breakdown.

"He might be well enough to join us." Standing up, Mrs. Wolcott yanked open a nearby drawer, producing an extra knife and fork. "The least you can do is check on him."

Ben watched his mother flit about the kitchen, his face contorted into a knot of sadness. Finally he whirled around and stalked out of the kitchen, slamming the door behind him. His angry footsteps receded down the hall.

I shifted uncomfortably in my seat.

"You must excuse Ben," Mrs. Wolcott said. "We have this argument every night. He can be so thoughtless sometimes."

Mrs. Wolcott hummed as she arranged the placemat and utensils on the empty spot to my left. "I can't wait until you meet my Jason. He had a minor accident too, but I'm afraid it's taking him longer to recover."

My heart did a series of painful revolutions against my ribcage as I finally understood why Ben didn't want me within a mile radius of his house or his mother.

She really believed her baby boy was asleep in his room upstairs instead of rotting away in a grave.

And Ben. Poor Ben!

He didn't have the heart to tell his mother there's no cure for a broken neck.

◆

Ben walked me back to my car, saying little as he guided me around a pothole in the road.

I cast a sidelong glance at his tense profile. He'd sat quietly at the dinner table while his mother prattled on and on about Jason. The more she talked, the more Ben paled and cringed, his shoulders hunching inward as if he were trying to crawl inside himself.

Our sneakers made suctioning noises in the mud. I slowed my pace as a raccoon scampered across the road, its beady eyes iridescent in the silver light of the crescent moon. It halted in front of us, wiggling its whiskers before darting into the dense thicket of oaks.

My car was parked on the side of the road, partially shielded by the leafy canopy of a willow tree. Jamming his hands in his jeans pockets, Ben leaned against a moss-covered fence post and waited for me to find my keys.

I dropped my purse on the hood. "How long has she been like this?"

"Ten months, one week, and two days." Ben shrugged and stared at the ground. "Not that I was keeping count. The first days after the funeral were the hardest. I couldn't get her to eat and the only place she would sleep was in a chair by Jason's empty bedside. I was afraid she would harm herself."

"Which is why you left school?" I offered, realizing what an immense sacrifice Ben had made on his mother's behalf. "To watch her."

"To keep her alive." His eyes were clouded with pain. "When I tried to pack away Jason's things, she flew at me."

He rubbed his forearm and flinched at the phantom sting of his mother's nails. "I promised never to touch Jason's room, never to pick up his dirty clothes or even air out his sheets. I should've never agreed to it but it seemed to make her happy, building a shrine to his memory, keeping him frozen in time…"

He glanced up. His features were drawn, tormented. My heart contracted in sympathy.

"It was a lie we both agreed upon," he continued. "Referring to Jason in the present tense, setting an extra place at the table, pretending Jason would wake up and join us as if nothing ever happened."

After a silence that seemed to last an eternity, he said, "Now that you know, this is probably the last I'll see of you."

"What makes you say that?" Did he think I was that superficial? Granted, tonight's dinner with his mother was more than a little unusual. Okay, it was downright creepy, but nothing worth throwing our budding friendship away over.

His lips twisted into a self-deprecating smile. "Most people are freaked out when they meet my mother."

"Was Willa?" I probed, seeing this as the perfect opportunity to piece together the puzzle of his past.

"She would be if she knew."

"You mean you never told her?"

"She knew of my mother's condition. Just not the extent of it. Though I doubt my messed-up family would fit into her perfect little life."

Just like that I knew how their relationship ended. Ben pushed Willa away, as he was determined to push me away, because he wanted to deal with this "problem" alone.

"You can't get rid of me that easily." I had the satisfaction of seeing Ben's eyes widen in surprise. "As far as messed-up families go, I have you beat."

"I doubt that," he said dryly.

I unbuttoned my blouse, stopping just short of revealing my lacy black bra.

"What," he swallowed, eyes never leaving my bare chest. A

212

flush swept up his cheeks. "Are you doing?"

"Trying to make you feel better."

Raking a hand through his hair, Ben choked, "I think it's working."

"I've never shown these to anyone before…"

Ben cleared his throat. "Somehow I doubt that too."

Ignoring the jab to my virtue, I took him by the hand. His palms were sweaty.

"*Now* what are you doing?" he asked.

"They're too small to see—"

"I think you're being too hard on yourself."

"—so you'll have to feel them," I said, guiding his hand to my chest.

"I-I don't think… Maybe we should… Okay."

When I placed his hand just under my neck, Ben frowned in confusion. His thumb brushed the exposed skin of my collarbone, pausing in question as he found the first of many crescent-shaped scars.

"A gift from my mother," I said before he could ask. "She was giving me a bath…"

With my eyes shut, I conjured up the memory of mother's fingers tracing calming circles into my scalp. Those same fingers crawled their way down to my shoulders, wrapping around my neck, choking me, shoving me below the water.

I told Ben about the night my mother tried to drown me, and

how my father, rushing in when he heard my screams, yanked me from the tub.

"She had a dream about me. A nightmare vision of death and destruction I caused simply because I existed. Something had to be done about me." I ended my story with a dismissive laugh. "I was eight years old the night she judged I wasn't fit to live."

"In other words, she tried to kill you because she dreamt that you were going to grow up to be...the Antichrist?" Ben studied my face, a frown pulling at his brows. "And by offing you, she was...saving the world?"

"Hard to believe, huh?"

Ben scratched his chin. "Especially when you're so nice..."

I smacked him upside the head, rained an apocalypse down on his sorry ass in the form of punches. "I'm trying to have a serious conversation here!"

"Sorry, sorry. I couldn't help myself." Laughing for the first time tonight, Ben caught my wrist and pinned my arms to the side. He tweaked my nose. I was not amused. "You have my attention, my little devil spawn."

"Listen up, you insensitive turd," I said. "Nothing about you is too bizarre for me."

Ben ceased laughing. A cloud of shame scuttled across his face.

"We're more similar than you think," I continued. "Crazy mothers."

His hands traveled upward to cup my face. "Battle scars."

"Ambition."

My last response reaped a quizzical arch of his eyebrow. Leaning in, his breath fanned my ear. "Given how we met, don't expect a fairy tale."

I traced the bump on his nose bridge, a lasting reminder of the first time he got on my bad side. Blood at first sight—not exactly the beginning of a healthy relationship. Yet somehow, we'd managed to become friends. If something so fragile could arise out of all that ugliness, perhaps it was possible for love to survive as well.

"You know everything except this..." I planted a soft kiss on the back of his hand.

Ben's fingers intertwined with mine. "Which is?" His voice, while good-humored, was low and guttural.

I leaned in as if I were conferring a great secret. "The best fairy tales begin and end with blood."

Standing on my tiptoes, I pressed my lips firmly against his. This kiss was guaranteed to have no interruptions.

CHAPTER 15

RED HARVEST

I liked having my vanity stroked. Unfortunately, Willa was only interested in stroking my thigh—a small price to pay for use of her premium cable.

She ran a finger along the ugly mass of scar tissue, circling the grotesque crater. One trip inside Eckhart House and I could kiss miniskirts goodbye.

My bare leg twitched. Prying my attention away from the giant flat screen, I glanced over my shoulder at Willa. She was propped against a pile of pink pillows, auburn hair gathered into a thick braid that rested off one shoulder like a coiled snake.

I slapped her hand away. "Hey, hey! Just because you fed me, doesn't mean you get to molest me."

Still scrutinizing my leg, Willa grimaced. "It feels disgusting."

"Nobody's forcing you to touch it."

The mattress shifted under her weight. She poked an index finger into the bright red center of my scar. "Does it hurt?"

I shot her a rueful smile. "Actually, it feels better after your lesbian caress."

This was my third time dining at the Russells', and I'd grown accustomed to Willa and her strange ways.

Willa was definitely weird. She was nineteen and living in a room meant for a nine-year-old. Ballerina pink walls. Frilly lace curtains. Creepy porcelain dolls. The first time I stepped inside her room, I knew this girl was not right in the head. And I didn't need to sit through an entire meal listening to Joe call her "Princess" to tell me that.

No wonder Ben dumped her.

I turned to the wall behind Willa's bed where she'd taped up a hundred photographs of Ben. The more I looked at this shrine to our mutual boyfriend, the more I reconsidered hanging out with Willa. On the other hand, someone had to keep her sexcapades with Cam in check. As the saying goes: keep your friends close, keep your enemies closer.

Another reason, more twisted than the rest, drew me to Willa. My mother's disappearance left a hole in my life that only another mentally unstable girl could fill. I could never tell if Willa liked me or plotted to harm me. Her unpredictability kept me on my toes and in some deranged way, her volatile presence felt like a reunion with my mother.

If I had any control over my impulses, I should've steered clear of Willa. Playing with fire was in my blood and my upbringing ruined me for normal friends. Fortunately, Eckhart, much like the Hell Mouth, had no shortage of psychopaths. I'd picked the prettiest one.

Willa's hand hovered over my scar. "Ever think about getting it removed?"

"Never. I want to keep it as a reminder of how close I came to dying and how I must find the ruby next time."

After my recovery, my adventures inside Eckhart House became legend. The Girl with Nine Lives was a small-town god. Fortunately, this newfound greatness had not inflated my ego in the slightest. The Girl with Nine Lives still cared about the little people. Hence her choice in company…

Willa flopped on her stomach, nudging my shoulder. "I wish I could do something half as exciting."

"Exciting could get you killed."

She was quiet for a moment, smoothing down a crinkle on her comforter. "Exciting will get you *noticed*."

Willa, bless her common little heart, was a fan. Unfortunately, the same could not be said for Dad. He refused to call me "Girl with Nine Lives." Just this morning, he threatened to have me institutionalized if I didn't stop referring to myself in the third person.

Frowning from the memory, I thumbed the remote control. One hundred and fifty channels and I couldn't find a damn thing. "Which channel is FOX?"

"Fifty-five," Willa said. "Why? What's on?"

Around the time Dad threatened to call the asylum on me, I received a text from Uncle Tav. It read: GRL W/ 9 LIVES. WATCH ME @ 9.

"Ryan Seacrest is interviewing my Uncle Tavistock." I flipped through a cooking show, a documentary, a boxing match. "There he is…"

Lounging on the sofa, Uncle Tav was wearing an exquisitely tailored herringbone suit. Instead of a traditional tie, he sported a purple bow tie. He'd just finished talking about the tour for his new book, which would bring him to Los Angeles this coming weekend. The Getty Villa was hosting a gala in honor of his humanitarian contributions to the starving children of the world.

For the next five seconds, we watched a clip of Uncle Tav riding on a donkey through a Brazilian slum, trailed by a sea of barefoot children chanting in Portuguese.

Ryan asked, "Mr. Tavistock, what are they calling you?"

Uncle Tav rubbed a thumb across his lower lip, hesitating a long time before he answered, "God."

"Wow. He makes Seacrest look like a slob." Willa turned to me. "You're *so* lucky to be related to him."

"We're not related. He's my dad's stepbrother."

Willa studied me, then the television. The tide of the interview had turned controversial.

Ryan was flipping through his notes. "Gravedigger. Treasure

hunter. Tomb raider. Those are just some of the unflattering things your critics call you. Are there any truth to these accusations?"

Propping one foot over his knee, Uncle Tav draped an arm over the sofa. "Grave robbing," he said in a perfectly calm and rational tone, "implies the act of stealing. One cannot steal from the dead. Ownership ceases upon expiration."

As I admired Uncle Tav's purple argyle socks, Willa scrutinized my profile. I whirled on her. *"What?"*

"You look just like him," she said, "butt chin and all."

I socked her in the arm. "It does not look like a butt!"

"Okay, okay. Chill out," Willa amended. "I was only making an observation."

"Keep your observations to yourself," I snapped. "I look nothing like him."

I returned to Uncle Tav, who was busy charming his way out of an accusation involving the "accidental" destruction of an eight-hundred-year-old Scottish church in search of lost Viking loot. "The stones were old," he said with a shrug, "Old stones crumble. That's what they do."

"Are you close to your uncle?" Willa pressed.

"We used to be," I said, fingering my chin dimple.

"Used to?"

I cleared my throat. "He got weird."

Willa opened her mouth to speak. I shushed her. Uncle Tav

221

was evading questions about his future project.

"No Ryan, it's a secret. You like secrets, don't you? Of course you do, you naughty man," he said. "Though I'll say one thing: once my project is unleashed onto the world, it won't be something you'll likely forget..."

"But I can't take all the credit. I'd like to thank one very special person who has been helping me all along." The camera zoomed in on Uncle Tav's face. He really was a beautiful man, chiseled by a master artisan, a masterpiece come to life. Devilish eyes bored through the screen. The masterpiece winked. "Hello, Ava."

"Ava?" Willa asked over the closing credits. "What's he talking about?"

I glanced down. I was mangling Willa's goose-down comforter. It all became so clear. The desperate phone calls. Money in exchange for information. Uncle Tav's new project was Arabella's Curse. He'd been using me all along.

Scrambling off the bed, I scavenged the floor for my shoes. A lump formed in my throat. I'd thought Uncle Tav cared about me, but I'd been mistaken. He didn't love me; to him, I was just a tool to be used and discarded.

Well, if Uncle Tav wanted my ruby, he had to beat me to it. The Girl with Nine Lives was nobody's bitch.

Willa followed me around the room as I snatched my backpack off her striped armchair. "Where are you going?"

222

"None of your business." I swiped my tears away and reminded myself that black hearts couldn't be broken.

Instead of taking a hint, Willa buzzed around me like a fly. "You're going back to Eckhart House, aren't you?"

I jammed my foot into one sneaker and bent down to tie the laces. "So what if I am?"

"Ben made me promise if you ever get these crazy ideas in your head that—"

"That you'll what? Stop me?" I assessed her puny frame. Her skin would bruise like a summer peach. Height wise, I had a five-inch advantage over her. "I'd like to see you try."

"Who said anything about stopping you?" She dashed into her closet and returned with a coat. "I'm going with you."

♦

"How many more of these rooms do we have to search?" Willa's whine echoed down the endless hallway of Eckhart House to nestle with the shadows and spiders.

The west wing was all familiar territory to me. We'd been searching a good while. How long exactly? An hour? Three? Five? No clue.

Our cell phones died before we'd reached the front door. The hour and minute hands froze at 1:05 a.m. on Willa's wristwatch. Time had no meaning inside Eckhart House.

"Did you hear me?" Willa scrambled to keep pace with my purposeful gait. "How long do we have to be here?"

I knew it. I knew she would be difficult. "As long as it takes."

"This is insane!" Willa groaned. "We've been at it for hours. Let's call it a night. It's practically morning—"

"We're going to search every room, closet, and dumbwaiter. Rip apart every floorboard. Ax the walls. I will burn this house to the ground if that's what it takes. So I'm going to ask you nicely: Shut up or go home!"

Willa glanced uneasily at the darkness behind us. "Maybe a few more rooms before we call it quits?"

My flashlight's beam flickered off the aged wallpaper. Stopping in her tracks, Willa ran a finger along a maroon smudge on the wall. It flaked away like dried paint. "Ick."

Wiping her hands on the leg of her jeans, Willa motioned for more light. The smudge branched into a handprint. Like two patrons strolling through a museum exhibit on Jack the Ripper, our eyes traveled down the length of the wall.

"Looks like a trail," Willa said, rubbing the goose bumps from her forearm.

"It *is* a trail."

"What's the red stuff?"

"Blood."

"Whose blood?"

The handprint was perfectly preserved. You could see the

whorl of the thumb and the loops on the index finger. I stepped up to the wall and pressed my hand to the print. A perfect match.

"Mine," I said.

Willa stumbled away from me. Was she afraid? Of what? Of little ole me?

A phantom twitch of pain surged through my leg as I recalled my torturous climb out of that basement pit. I'd been determined to get out alive and equally determined to mark my path.

"I didn't have any breadcrumbs handy at the time," I explained, "but plenty of blood. I figured I might as well put all that bleeding to good use."

"You're crazy!" Willa doubled over, wheezing for air with every word.

"Driven," I corrected. Frowning, I stepped toward her. "Willa?"

She ripped open her tote, frantically rooting through the contents. As her legs buckled, I lowered her to the floor and pressed her head between her knees.

"What are you looking for?" I asked, taking the bag from her.

"My...inhaler."

"If I'd known you had asthma, I would've never let you come." I located the inhaler beneath a bottle of hand sanitizer and jammed it in her mouth. For the next few minutes, I waited for Willa's erratic breathing to stabilize. Out of guilt, I thumped her on the back. "Sorry I freaked you out."

Willa lolled her head against the wall, her temples clammy with sweat.

I sighed. One more aborted mission. One more defeat to add to my growing list of failures. Fragile and sickly, Willa would never last the night.

"All right," I said. "We'll go home."

Gripping Willa's elbow a little too roughly, I yanked her to her feet. I bent down to retrieve my flashlight and gather the spilled contents of her bag from the floor. Groping in the dark, I located a half-empty water bottle and uncapped the lid.

Willa watched me unlace the scarf from the wicker handles of her tote.

Sensing her eyes on me, I doused the pink silk with lukewarm water.

"I'm sorry," she began. "I know how much finding Ar—"

I pressed the damp scarf over her nose and mouth. "Tie this like a bandana. It'll keep you from breathing in dust."

Scowling, I walked away.

Dull pain radiated from my left leg. Had I re-injured it and not even noticed? There was only the ruby on my mind, propelling me like a heat-seeking missile past the limits of human endurance.

Like the last time, I'd failed. To keep from beating myself up, I switched gears and focused on a new mission: getting us out of Eckhart House. Uninjured and alive.

Willa lagged behind.

"I think I walked faster when I had a stake impaled in my thigh." I tapped my foot, watching her inch toward me with the speed of a glacier. "Hurry up."

Ignoring her protests, I hitched her arm around my shoulders, forcing her to lean on me for support.

We hobbled a few steps before Willa, glancing over her shoulder, said, "There's a light back there."

"What light?" I muttered absently.

Willa stopped moving, forcing us both to halt. She pointed into the darkness behind us. "A red one."

Slowly, I turned around.

The light at the end of the hall flickered like a pair of mating fireflies. And the color... A brilliant shade of red, a kaleidoscope of light and dark all rolled into one exquisite hue.

My entire universe crashed to a halt. I ceased to think. Ceased to breathe. Ceased to be.

Nothing existed but that resplendent red: the beginning and end of my world.

And then someone injected a jolt of adrenaline into my veins. The world turned. My heart galloped, thrusting like an overworked piston, pumping the blood to my brain.

I expelled a whoosh of pent-up air. "*Oh you beautiful thing!*"

"Ava?" Willa's fingernails sank into my forearm. "Ava! What's gotten into you?"

If the ceiling and walls had collapsed around me, I didn't think I could bear to look away.

The ruby was calling to me. Humming to me.

Three feet.

Five feet.

Ten.

Somewhere around the corner was Arabella's Curse. *My* Arabella's Curse.

As I stepped forward, the red light danced farther away. Where was it coming from? Why did it tease me?

Willa dug her heels in the floor, tugging me in the opposite direction. "I don't like what this house is doing to you. Please, let's get out of here!"

"I have to go to it," I said, eyes never straying from the dazzling phosphorescence.

"Like hell you will!" Willa slammed her palms against my shoulders.

Stumbling backward, I glowered at Willa. "Get out of my way!"

Fear dilated her pupils into big black buttons. Instead of backing down, she pushed me again. "No!"

The light was fading, bobbing out of sight like ephemeral starlight. Didn't she understand? Arabella's Curse was almost gone. If my life depended on it, I couldn't return empty-handed. No time! There was no time!

I saw red: the waning light of my ruby, the fiery snarls of Willa's hair—hair growing out of a head attached to a body planted directly in my way. If I failed, it was her fault. *Her fault.* The bitch.

I seized a handful of those insufferable red curls, yanking her head back. She shrieked.

"If you don't get out of my way…" I pulled her closer until her breath fanned my cheek. I sniffed. I could smell her fear, a stink of sweat and tears. "You will make me *very* angry."

In demonstration, I looped the scarf around her throat like a noose.

Willa gagged.

I tightened the noose. "Do we understand each other?"

A tear trickled down the curve of her freckled cheek.

She nodded.

I uncurled my fingers from her hair and released the scarf. Willa stumbled away and slid to the floor, gasping for air.

A fleeting window of logic jarred my ruby-obsessed train of thought. Shaking my head to clear the fog, I took a guilty step toward her. What did I just do?

She shrank away, shielding her face with her arms.

I knelt down and pressed her inhaler firmly into her palm.

Rubbing her throat, Willa glared at me with murder in her eyes. "You're going to pay for this…"

That might be true, but I was the one with the knife. I handed her my flashlight. "Wait here. I'll come back for you."

CHAPTER 16
HIDE AND SEEK

The moment I reached the third floor, I knew I was in deep shit.

A spasm zipped through my leg like a knife slicing through raw sinew. I probed my thigh with an unsteady hand. Warm blood seeped through my jeans.

"This' could be bad," I said, fumbling my way through the pitch blackness.

The third floor hallway contracted and expanded like an accordion. The ceiling closed down, threatening to squash me like a cockroach.

Another vicious stab of agony raked through my thigh, setting off a fireworks display behind my eyelids.

It would be so easy. To sink to the floor. To fall asleep.

Gritting my teeth, I clawed the peeling wainscoting and willed myself to stay conscious. To *move*. One more step.

At the far end of the hall, the light danced—eluding me by

mere inches. Taunting me with absolution from the pain.

Soon it would be mine.

One more step.

Ava.

The ruby spoke to me. Sang to me.

Ava.

It knew my name. Was that really so surprising? Of course it knew my name. It knew everything about me. We belonged together.

Come to me.

It called. I followed.

The corridor veered off to a single door. Red light glimmered beneath the crack.

Dragging my leg, I slipped inside.

Wooden beams buttressed a ceiling pockmarked with holes. The air reeked of rat droppings.

The barn-sized attic served as a warehouse for discarded antiques. Paintings and statues jostled for space with birdcages and velveteen hatboxes.

The ruby, wherever it was, had lost its glow. But not its voice. Not its haunting song.

Find me.

I yanked away the nearest dustcover, revealing a statue of a Minotaur. His bull face was grotesque, but his sad eyes were human. As a surge of dizziness threatened to topple me, I pressed my fevered brow against his chest. My blood smeared the marble like war paint.

Afraid to make the slightest disturbance in the air current, my fingers curled around the ivory handles of my butterfly knife. I unclasped the safety latch.

Leaving the protective circle of the Minotaur's embrace, I stumbled behind an Oriental dressing screen, knife concealed at my side. Moonbeams bounced off the blade in a blaze of blue light—a holy benediction on my pocket Excalibur. The creak of my footsteps accompanied the *drip drip* of rain through the eroded rafters.

The weather vane squeaked a rusty symphony, transporting me back to another time, another storm.

♦

The Ferris wheel completed its slow rotation on the abandoned Santa Monica pier. Outside my bedroom window, sand dervishes cycled across the beach. A storm had blown out the power and Mother wanted to play hide and seek.

At seven, I was already too old for these childish games.

But Mother would not take no for an answer.

Stumbling across our pitch-black living room, I stubbed my toe against the side table and knocked over a lamp. If I took too long to find her, she'd come hunting for me instead.

On that particular night, I didn't stray far from the balcony doors where the forks of lightning striking the inky Pacific provided sanctuary from the darkness.

Inching along the frosted glass to the kitchen, my fingers bumped against a human hip. Lightning flashed, backlighting the entire balcony in a momentary wash of white. Her face was as serene as the marble bust of a Greek goddess. She stepped forward, seeming to spawn right out of the curtain.

Mother seized my wrist.

I screamed.

When I looked down, my pants were wet. Urine pooled on the plush carpet.

She slipped out of her hiding place, dug her nails into my shoulder blades, and forced me to stare into gray eyes clouded by insanity. She'd neglected to shower or brush her hair. Tonight she smelled like meat left to ripen under the sun. No wonder dogs barked at her wherever she went.

My eyes traveled to her chest. The old scar—remnants of an old car accident—had begun to bleed.

"Peek-a-boo. I found you."

♦

I pressed the pad of my thumb over the edge of my knife. The blade sang.

So did the voice.

Ava.

Ten years later, I was still playing hide and seek. On her turf. On her terms. One could only hope I was too old to pee my pants.

To my right, I snatched away a dustcover. It drifted like an umbrella in the stagnant air. A tattered dressmaker's dummy resided underneath.

Undeterred by another disappointing find, I uncovered a statue of an angel with half her face lopped off.

I tackled another sheet, transforming the attic into a blizzard of floating white.

With every useless piece of junk, my frustration mounted.

Another cheery watercolor landscape of a carnival. A park outing. A holiday by the sea. No ruby. Nothing. Bloody nothing.

I hacked at a painting, blade butchering canvas. Exhausted, I collapsed against a nearby wardrobe in a cold sweat.

Ava.

I whirled around. At the far corner of the attic—

Strung across the neck of a mannequin, enshrouded beneath white linen, and thumping like a beating heart was Arabella's Curse.

I stumbled toward it, tripping over my feet—

Ava.

Hands outstretched. Reaching, straining—

So close.

Almost. Almost. Mine.

"AVA!"

I halted, jarred out of my trance. This voice did not belong. It did not coo or coax. It *howled.*

Downstairs, Willa let out a glass-shattering wail of horror, pain, and despair. Reluctant to take my eyes off the ruby, I tapped the blade against my thigh. Maybe, if I were quick enough, I could snatch Arabella's Curse and rush to Willa in time?

The sound of my name spiraled up the stairs—a cry, almost a prayer, for help.

I rushed to the door.

At the threshold, I paused for one last glance at Arabella's Curse. The room was dark, the glow extinguished. "Damn."

Following the terrible echo of Willa's screams, I raced down the hall. When I reached the staircase, Willa let out one last horrible howl.

I clamped both hands over my ears, trying to hold myself together as the sound of her suffering tore me apart. Please God. Please make it stop. Please let me reach her in time. Please—

Silence. Bleak, suffocating silence.

Panicked, I glanced down. The staircase descended into a black abyss. Bracing myself against the banister, I took the next uncertain step down.

On the third step, my sneakers slipped on something soft and squishy. Whatever it was squealed and scampered down the steps. Losing my balance, I cried out, flailing my arms. The last thing on my mind as I teetered over the void was, *Not again.*

Strong arms looped around my waist and yanked me backward. I felt myself being dragged up the landing where my mysterious rescuer dumped me unceremoniously on my rump.

Through the veil of darkness, I discerned a tall man with broad shoulders tapering down to a lean waist. Crouched on his haunches, he rocked back and forth on the balls of his feet like a restless boy waiting to be entertained.

After a long silence, he glanced down at my hand, which was still clutching my butterfly knife. "Always knew you'd put my gift to good use."

That cultivated voice could only belong to one man.

"Uncle Tav?" Squinting like a mole, I tried to make out the face beneath the shadowy mask. Of all the things I could say at the moment, the only words that escaped my lips were, "What are you doing in Eckhart House?"

He flicked on a flashlight, holding it under his trademark chin dimple. Blessed with the face of a fallen angel, his onyx eyes glimmered with mischief. The eyes of the devil.

"Eckhart House?" Uncle Tav grinned, revealing even white teeth. "*My* house."

CHAPTER 17

ONE MORE BREATH

In one of my earliest memories, Uncle Tav was teaching me how to ride a bike. I'd taken a nasty tumble along the sidewalks of Venice and he'd instantly appeared by my side. After tending to my skinned knee, he bought me a strawberry snow cone and urged me to get back on and try again. And when I'd stomped my foot in protest, Uncle Tav made a promise I'd never forget. "I won't let anything happen to you. Everyone, even God may let you down, but your Uncle Tav never will."

Those days were long gone.

Hobbling down the stairs on one leg was a bitch, but I'd managed to do it without that bastard's help. When I lost my balance on the last step, Uncle Tav caught my elbow.

I dared a glance up.

Dressed in a rugged chambray shirt with the sleeves rolled up, he looked like he'd stepped out of a J. Crew catalog.

Uncle Tav helped me down the stairs. "Really, Ava. You're

tracking blood all over my brand new floor."

"Yeah, well," I muttered, trying to jerk my arm away from his ironclad grip. "Who asked you to buy this house?"

"I bought it for you, Sweet Pea."

I rolled my eyes.

Pointing to a spot on the floor, Uncle Tav proceeded to steer me to it by force. "Now I must insist you sit down while I find your little ginger friend."

Drawing upon the last of my strength, I yanked my arm free. The act sent me reeling. I floundered until my back bumped against the wall.

"I brought Willa into this and I'm going to find her. *Alone*. I don't need your help."

A frown creased his brow.

"Look at you!" He gestured to my leg. Earlier, he'd stanched the bleeding by tying a monogrammed handkerchief around my thigh. "You look like a corpse. How do you propose to carry her once you do find her?"

"W-why..." My tongue stuck to the roof of my mouth. "Why would I need to carry her?"

Uncle Tav held out his hand. "Show me where you left her."

"I'm not going anywhere with you!"

"What do you care about more? Your friend or how much you hate me?"

I sucked on my inner cheek and regarded his hand

240

suspiciously. Why did he always have to be right about everything?

Cursing under my breath, I pointed into the darkness beyond. "I told her to wait for me there."

Uncle Tav wasted no time in dragging me down the hallway. I gritted my teeth, struggling to keep up with his brisk pace. We halted at the sight of Willa's discarded tote.

Uncle Tav picked up the obliterated remains of Willa's inhaler, his expression grim. "Things aren't looking good for your friend."

The gruesome possibilities of Willa's fate flashed before my eyes like a horror movie slide show. Any second I was going to keel over with guilt. I'd tried to strangle her and now—

I couldn't think about this now. I had to do something. Anything.

"Willa?" Her name echoed down the empty corridor.

Silence.

"WILLAAAAAAAAAAAAAAA?" I stumbled blindly into the darkness, groping for the first door to my right. With one hand poised over the knob, I held my breath, praying I'd find her and dreading what condition I'd find her in.

Wrenching the door open, I came face to face with a solid wall. No Willa. My shoulders slumped in relief. As long as I hadn't found her, there was still the faintest hope this was all one big practical joke. Maybe she disappeared out of spite? As soon as I opened the next door, she'd pop out like a jack-in-the-box and holler, "Gotcha."

241

Uncle Tav's surefooted steps trailed on my heels. As much as it pained me to admit it, his presence was a comfort. For tonight anyway, I could pretend Uncle Tav would never let me down.

Midway down the hall, we were making splashing noises with each step. I glanced down. "What the—" My shoes were soaked.

Uncle Tav halted too. The beam of his flashlight circled the floor. We were standing in a swiftly growing puddle.

Afraid to move in case the floor caved again, I peered anxiously over my shoulder. "Uncle Tav?"

He held a finger to his lips, his attention on the floor. "Do you hear that?" he whispered.

In the space of a heartbeat, my ears picked up the sound of water gushing somewhere close by. Someone had left the tap on.

Uncle Tav trudged through the muck, brandishing his flashlight in search of the source of the flood. Sure enough, a murky stream seeped through the bottom crack of the door to our right.

He motioned me over, hesitant to turn the knob. "Maybe you should stay in the hall."

Momentarily forgetting why I was mad at him, I sought his hand. His fingers closed around mine and squeezed in reassurance.

"Open the door," I said, "I'm ready."

A flood of water swamped our feet. I zoned in on the overflowing bathtub where a freckled arm dangled over the rim.

Her dainty charm bracelet clinked against the porcelain side and her red curls bobbed above the water's surface like party streamers.

Shoving me aside, Uncle Tav dashed to the tub and hauled Willa out.

Her lips were puffy; pretty face bloated and blue. Dispensing with modesty, Uncle Tav ripped away her blouse and tipped his mouth to hers.

The faucet roared. The water pouring from tub to tile floor screamed: *Murderer.*

I clamped both hands over my ears.

If I hadn't brought her along...

Murderer.

Left her behind...

Murderer.

With a growl, I lunged for the faucet when a gauzy slip of pink caught my eye. Someone had gone to the trouble of tying Willa's scarf around the brass nozzle as a flourish. I unknotted the scarf.

"*Mother,*" I said, winding the damp silk around my hand.

She wanted us to split up.

The water, the bathtub, this was all a part of her game, and Willa just happened to be collateral damage in her sadistic message to me.

"Breathe," Uncle Tav grunted, pounding Willa in the chest

with a force that could crack her breastbone.

Willa flopped on the aquamarine tiles like a rag doll.

"Breathe, damn you!" A swath of hair fell across his eyes and beads of sweat dotted his brow.

"Breathe, you stubborn little…" Halting abruptly, Uncle Tav collapsed to the floor. Water splashed around him, soaking him from the waist down.

"Why are you stopping?" My voice was surprisingly calm despite the hurricane brewing within. "Do it again."

Panting from exhaustion, Uncle Tav rested his forehead on one knee. "I'm sorry, Sweet Pea."

Sorry? Sorry wouldn't cut it. Sorry wouldn't bring Willa back to life.

"Do it again!"

Uncle Tav only looked at me with that pitying expression people gave you at funerals.

I knelt down beside Willa's lifeless corpse.

No. I couldn't think like that. She wasn't dead. I wouldn't allow her to die. Not while I still had breath in my body.

"If you're not going to do anything, I will!"

Taking Uncle Tav's place, I tilted Willa's chin and spotted the bloody scratches along her collarbone. If, I mean, *when* Willa woke up, she was bound to have scars. Like me.

I brought my mouth to hers, determined to recall her to life.

All it took was one—

One more breath.

CHAPTER 18

VILLAINESS

As I strolled through the hospital with a stash of junk food cradled in my arms and a new bandage tied around my thigh, I wondered if this was how heroes felt on a regular basis. Battle-weary. Slightly anemic. Loopy from painkillers. Glorious. Invincible. Awesome.

I was freaking awesome.

In the corridor, I passed by an orderly who recognized me from my last stay.

"Yo, Girl with Nine Lives! How's the leg?"

"Fantastic!" I high-fived him and continued my victory walk to the ER's waiting room.

Rock star, thy name is Ava.

The room was filled with the hush before an execution. Only the low drone of the television, switched to the local news, punctured the frosty silence.

The Dodd sisters were huddled in the corner. Marlene sobbed

into a crumpled Kleenex. Syd, absently flipping through a tattered issue of *National Geographic*, looked up when I entered and whispered in Marlene's ear.

I shifted uncomfortably on my feet. I'd gone from rock star to shooting-range dummy.

"Twinkie, Marlene?" I asked, waving the plastic package in front of her face by way of a peace offering. Marlene never turned down a Twinkie. Sometimes I'd catch her in the storeroom, scarfing down a whole box before dinner service.

Shooting me a laser beam look of hate, Marlene snatched the Twinkie from my hand and chucked it on the floor. Before I could protest, her foot came down with a *splat*.

The news anchor babbled on. Armed robberies. Gangland shootings. Meth lab explosions. I glanced down at the whipped cream-splattered carpet. Oh the humanity!

"You owe me seventy-five cents," I growled.

Syd quipped in with a colorful description of where she'd like to stick her quarters. I decided to let the seventy-five cents slide in case she made good on her threat.

Limping across the waiting room, I found a seat next to Cam and ripped open a bag of ranch-flavored Corn Nuts with my teeth. Losing copious amounts of blood gave me a wicked case of the munchies. "Did you see that? What the *hell* is their problem?"

Cam kept his eyes on the television. I nudged his shoulder, offering him a dip into my feedbag. He refused with a curt shake of his head.

"Fine. More for me." I shoved a handful into my mouth.

I peeked at my cell. There were no messages from Ben. He wasn't picking up his phone. Daring a glance at the Dodd sisters, I wondered if they'd managed to reach him.

When I looked up, Cam was glowering at me too.

"What?"

"Do you have to chew so loudly?"

I swallowed with a gulp. "I can't help it. They're Corn Nuts."

"You make me sick."

"Okay." I set the Corn Nuts aside. "What's wrong with you?"

He shrugged. "Nothing's wrong." One foot began tapping.

"You've been snapping at me all night!"

"Snapping? No one's snapping."

"Clearly you're upset—"

Cam sprang from his seat and made a beeline to the sisters. Syd snatched her purse away and Cam plopped down next to her. Now all three were glaring at me as if I were vermin.

Need I remind everyone that I *saved* Willa's life? She'd be dead if it weren't for me. Fine way to treat a hero.

The doors swung open and Uncle Tav strolled in, looking more disheveled than I'd ever seen him. He took a seat beside me and hunched forward.

"I've just been talking to Joe Russell." He studied his clasped hands. "Do you want the good news or the bad?"

Dread, which had been trickling in drop by drop, slammed against me like a tsunami. I uncurled my clammy palms. "Start with the good."

"The good news is," Uncle Tav began, plucking a piece of lint off my shoulder, "he's not going to press charges."

A brown paper bag would be handy right now. "Charges? Why would he press charges? Against who?"

"Against you, Sweet Pea. He seems to be under the impression that you tried to drown his daughter."

"Me? I saved her life!"

"Of course you did." Uncle Tav patted my knee. "And it was very noble of you. Unfortunately, Willa has a different story, which, believe me..." A nervous chuckle. "I had a devil of a time convincing her to keep to herself."

"Ungrateful bitch! I'm going to kill her—"

Uncle Tav shook his head and pressed a finger to his lips.

"—with love. I'm going to kill her with love." I sighed. The rage and indignation seeped away. "What did she say?"

"Someone attacked her and tried to drown her." His eyes flickered over my face. "Someone who looked exactly like you."

I saw myself dressed in an orange jumpsuit, pleading my case in court. My mother did it! My supposedly *dead* mother. Somehow I doubt the jury would believe me.

"Rather ludicrous accusation," I said between clenched teeth. "Given that you were with me the whole time."

"Only…"

I buried my face in my hands. "Oh God, what next?"

Glancing around the room, Uncle Tav lowered his voice. "Did you really try to strangle her with her own scarf?"

I shifted my attention to the wall clock. It was 4:15 a.m. and officially the longest night of my life.

"Well?" Uncle Tav pressed. "Did you?"

"Strangled is kind of a harsh word…"

Uncle Tav rubbed the spot between his brows, an action prevalent amongst all the men in my life. "May I ask what could have possessed you to try to choke your friend?"

"Temporary insanity?" I snuck a sidelong glance at Uncle Tav, who, for some strange reason, looked bemused. Dad would be livid. It was a good thing Dad wasn't here. "If that's the good news, I shudder to think what the bad news is."

"You're now unemployed."

I nodded numbly. Given that Uncle Tav had managed to get me out of an attempted murder charge, I guess being fired from the diner was the lesser of two evils. "How did you convince Joe not to press charges?"

"I assured him that I won't press charges against *his* daughter for breaking and entering onto *my* property. Rest assured, Sweet Pea. If they make a move against you, I will strike at them with everything I've got."

He took a lock of my hair and curled it around his finger.

"Do you doubt I'm on your side now?"

"I'm softening."

"As you should..." His attention wandered to the doorway. "There's an angry lad," he said, peering over my shoulders. "Someone you know, my pet?"

I stood up so abruptly I almost knocked the chair over. "Ben!"

Ben did indeed look angry, but maybe... maybe he was just mad at the world? Hopefully, he hadn't run into Joe and I could feed him my version of the story before he heard it from the others.

Seizing my elbow, Ben growled in my ear. "Come with me. We have to talk."

Uncle Tav got up and extended a hand. "Ian Tavistock. And you must be Ben Wolcott, the boy with all the answers."

Ben stared at Uncle Tav's hand a long time before shaking it. "Yeah, hello," he muttered. "Excuse us."

He ended the handshake and dragged me toward the exit.

Uncle Tav rocked back on his heels. "It's been a pleasure," he called after us.

"Care to explain what that was all about?" I asked, trying to keep up with Ben as we slipped past the sliding doors to the ER turnaround.

Shielding my eyes against the bright awning lights, I tried to gauge why Ben was acting like such a freak. "Have you met my uncle before?"

Ignoring my question, Ben nodded at my bandages. "You hurt your leg again."

"Just a flesh wound." I dismissed his concern with a wave of my hand.

"At Eckhart House." It was a statement instead of a question. "But this time you thought you wanted some company?"

I didn't like the way this conversation was going. Surely he didn't believe the rumors? "I never meant any harm, I—"

"Willa almost died!" Seizing my shoulders, he rattled me until my teeth chattered. "And for what? A stupid ruby!"

I pushed against him, kicked him in the shins. "Get your hands off me!"

Releasing me abruptly, Ben braced an arm against the side of a parked ambulance and stared up at the sky. Orange rays streaked the horizon, signaling the breaking of a new dawn.

Glaring at his back, I rubbed my sore arms. "I'm not the vindictive type."

"Right," he muttered. "I'm sure my car—"

"You're never going to let me live that down, are you? I fixed your car! If this is the thanks I get for saving someone's life, I'll never make that mistake again!"

"Saved her life?" Whirling around, Ben wagged a finger in my face. I hoped he knew he was in danger of losing that finger. "She wouldn't be in danger in the first place if you hadn't brought her

253

to Eckhart House! I warned you to stay away!"

"Yeah, and you've certainly 'warned' me a lot, haven't you?"

"What's that supposed to mean?"

"You've put so much effort into keeping me away from Arabella's Curse, I'm starting to think you want it for yourself."

Instead of firing back, Ben took a deep breath and said, "Frederick Nichols."

I blinked. "Huh?"

"If you've done your reading—"

I heaved a sigh of impatience. "Again with the reading! You know what your problem is? You read too much. You plan too much. You talk about leaving Eckhart but you'll probably die here. You know all there is to know about Arabella's Curse but when it comes down to it, you're too chickenshit to go after it!"

"If you'd done your reading," Ben continued, "you'd know Frederick Nichols was a Victorian explorer. The best, in fact. Smarter than the rest. Strong as an ox. Tenacious as a bulldog. He had the financial backing, the best and brightest crew in England, and twenty years of experience exploring the African Congo."

I drummed my fingers against my forearm. "Your point is?"

"For all Sir Frederick had going for him, he perished anyway. The day he signed up to find Arabella's Curse was the day he signed his own death certificate."

Ben stepped toward me. The last time we were this close we had been talking about fairy tales amid kisses and later, we hadn't been talking at all. Now if he came any closer, I could rip out his throat with my teeth.

"What makes you think you'll succeed when he can't?" His lips curdled into a sneer. "A silly little girl like you?"

"Sir Frederick had everything going for him, but he lacked one crucial thing. One secret weapon."

With an insolence that made me want to slap him, Ben said, "And I suppose you know what that secret weapon is. Do tell."

"Me! I wasn't born yet!"

"Christ!" Ben raked a hand through his hair, whipping the front into a cowlick. "You actually believe what you're saying."

I didn't answer, just held his gaze with my own.

"You're insane," he whispered.

"You mistake for insanity what is, in fact, *destiny*. I'm going to find Arabella's Curse and God help you if you try to stop me. Now get out of my way!"

Point made, I shouldered him aside and stomped—like a badass—out of his life.

I didn't need him. Or Cam. I especially didn't need that ungrateful Willa. And her tub of lard father could take that thankless job and shove it up his—

Screw them all! I was Ava Nolan, Rock Star. Except I didn't feel like a rock star. I just felt...alone.

With every step, my mood plummeted until, exhausted, I found myself in the hospital's back alley, sharing my misery with the slimy rain puddles and cockroaches.

I slumped against the side of the dumpster, inhaling the rancid stench of discarded cafeteria food. Ben thinks I have such a black heart. The only cure for a black heart is a red ruby.

"Who needs friends when you have Arabella's Curse?"

To my horror, I began to cry. Great, gut-wrenching sobs I muffled with a hand over my mouth.

At long last, I hiccupped, wiped my nose on my sleeve, and gasped.

Uncle Tav dangled a monogrammed handkerchief in my face. "You still have one friend, Sweet Pea."

♦

Dad was asleep in his favorite armchair, a tartan throw draped across his lap. Orange embers glimmered in the fireplace, smoldering into cinder.

An overturned wine bottle rested on the end table. Merlot dripped on the carpet like blood.

Righting the bottle, I knelt in front of Dad and brushed away the blond wisps spilling over his brow. He dozed quietly, eyes flickering beneath paper-thin lids.

"Dad," I whispered, tapping him lightly on the arm.

A faint smile played across his lips as my face came into focus. "Helena?"

I grimaced. "No, Dad. It's Ava."

"Ava," he repeated, anchoring himself more firmly to reality. "I must have been dreaming."

My attention flickered to the living room archway. "We have a visitor."

Dad ground the heel of his hand against his eyes. "It's too late for guests."

"Or early depending on how you look at it," Uncle Tav said, leaning casually against the threshold.

At the sound of his brother's voice, Dad rose from his chair. His face, already pale to begin with, drained to the color of a corpse. I feared he might topple, but he stayed rooted to the spot.

Uncle Tav took this as an invitation to enter the room. The contrast between the two couldn't be more striking. Uncle Tav, dark and scowling, brimming with the energy and virility of a man half his age, seemed to dwarf my fair and fragile father. Devil and angel.

Dad looked like he was in Hell.

"Dad?" I glanced from one to the other. "Uncle Tav invited me to Malibu for the weekend. Can I go?"

Never once taking his eyes off Uncle Tav, Dad nodded.

Uncle Tav studied Dad for a long time until he found an answer to his question. The answer pleased him. His sculpted lips twitched.

"Hello, Brother," he said, crushing Dad into an embrace. "It's been too long."

CHAPTER 19

CHIN DIMPLES NEVER LIE

The evening gown glided against my bare skin, the satin swishing around my legs like liquid emeralds.

I twisted and turned in front of a triptych of mirrors, feeling like Cinderella after a meeting with her fairy godmother's magic wand. "Hello Gorgeous."

After months of deprivation, this weekend detour to LA was like a fairy tale come true. Credit cards without spending limits. The keys to Uncle Tav's Lamborghini, which was far superior to a cheap ole magic carriage. And a fancy ball—a charity gala honoring Uncle Tav— to cap off the night of my eighteenth birthday.

Eckhart, with its muddy roads and torrential rain, seemed like a dream shrouded in fog. In LA, the forecast promised sunny days and clear blue skies.

I wondered what Ben was doing back home. I hoped he was miserable.

Doing a final preen in front of the mirror, I checked my watch. I had to hurry if I wanted to make my nail appointment. Slipping off the gown, I poked my head out of the dressing room for assistance.

The salesgirl was arranging a multicolored tray of French macarons and humming along with the radio. Standing in my underwear, I beckoned her to the dressing room.

She appeared a moment later wearing her best ready-to-suck-up smile. One glance at my bare thigh and her smile vanished. Only the truly brave or those with a cast-iron stomach could look upon my scar without tossing their cookies.

"I'll take this one," I said, handing her the emerald gown.

I watched, amused, as she tried to hide her disgust.

"I see you selected the *long* gown. Good choice. I'll ring you up at the register." She disappeared in a flurry of yellow skirts.

I finished dressing and extracted Uncle Tav's wallet from my purse. Thumbing through his impressive collection of credit cards, my fingers tripped over a folded square tucked inside the empty cash compartment.

I unfolded the square.

It was a photo strip taken from an old-fashioned booth at the county fair. The back was yellowed with age, the images flaking from being folded several times over. Despite the wear and tear, I had no trouble making out the subjects.

My mother's dark hair was swept into a bouncy sideways

ponytail. Uncle Tav had this grungy Kurt Cobain hair going on.

There were four shots in all. Three of the four consisted of them making silly faces. In the last frame, Uncle Tav appeared to be...

My heart froze. My universe imploded. The birds ceased flying in the sky and dropped dead to the ground.

Tonguing my mother. Or was it the other way around?

Collapsing on the dressing bench, I studied Uncle Tav's chin dimple in the picture. The sushi I'd eaten for lunch sunk to the pit of my stomach. Saliva wasn't the only bodily fluid Uncle Tav exchanged with my mother.

I glanced up from the photo to my reflection. Matching butt chins, just as Willa said.

"This is no good," I whispered to the mirror. "This is no good..."

And I doubled over. The sushi swam up my gut and splashed onto the floor.

Once I'd finished projectile vomiting, I wiped my mouth and strutted out of the dressing room. At the nearest clothing rack, I gathered as many items as I could carry and plopped them on the counter.

Slapping my hands together, I surveyed the boutique in search of more unnecessary crap to buy. To the pile, I added a ridiculously expensive clutch and five pairs of heels. Most of them weren't even my size.

The salesgirl looked like she was about to faint as she scanned my purchases. My bill could feed a third-world country.

I picked up a purple macaron from the silver tray and bit into its creamy center.

"It's okay," I told the salesgirl. "My father's going to pay."

◆

High above the Malibu foothills, the Los Angeles elite assembled in the courtyard of the Getty Villa. I clutched the incriminating photo behind my back and scanned the crowd of elegantly dressed people in search of Uncle Tav.

That bastard was nowhere in sight.

A black and white banner of his face hung from the balcony like a scene right out of *Citizen Kane*. As if I wasn't sick enough of that infernal chin dimple, it was now ten feet tall.

A fleet of flat screens lined the inner walkway, each replaying candid footage of Uncle Tav strutting through a slum with his entourage of chanting street urchins. They had different names for him. Savior. Father. God.

I had a string of names for him too. Liar. Traitor. Home wrecker.

As the string quartet strummed the beginning notes of a waltz, Uncle Tav materialized on the other side of the reflecting pool. With his crisp white tux setting him apart from his black tux counterparts, he looked like the next James Bond.

He stopped to adjust his cufflinks and, scanning the courtyard, beckoned me over.

Cold air stretched the scar tissue on my leg. Coupled with my painful stilettos, the simple task of walking across the courtyard was a slow and arduous odyssey. I felt several pairs of eyes on me and knew people were wondering about Ian Tavistock's gimpy niece.

"The banner is a bit much, isn't it?" Uncle Tav tipped his head to the right. "I'm not sure they captured my good side."

"It's almost as big as your ego." It took every ounce of self-restraint to keep from punching him in the face. Knowing him, he probably had his face insured. "Almost, but not quite."

Slicking a hand over his helmet of gelled hair, he caught sight of my scowl. "Smile, Sweet Pea. Is it that time of the month?"

I slapped the photo against his chest. "Maybe you'd like *this* photo better? You've got a lot of explaining to do!"

He studied the strip, a wistful smile playing across his lips. "This was taken on the day you were conceived. We were in the funhouse after dark and…"

"Okay!" I held up a hand. "Stop explaining!"

"Let's go somewhere private. This is not the place to—"

He tried to take my elbow, but I jerked my arm away. "Can it be you don't want your public to know that you *slept with my mother*?"

The string quartet finished the last movement of the waltz, flooding the entire courtyard with silence punctuated by a few awkward coughs. The whispers. The stares. I was causing a scene. I didn't give a damn. Uncle Tav snapped a finger at the lead violinist, who immediately had his band strumming another song.

"Did my dad know?"

"You'll have to ask him," he said, tucking the photo inside his breast pocket.

"How could you do this to him? Your own brother!"

"And being my brother, he should've kept his hands off what's mine. I loved Helena first and I'll always love her more. We're soul mates."

"I didn't know you two had souls," I muttered. "All right, if you're so sure she loved you back, why did she marry Dad then? Did you think about that?"

"To spite me," he said as if that explained everything. Sadly, knowing my mother, it kind of did. "Morty is the other man and he knows it."

"My dad is blameless!"

"Is he really?" His face lost all trace of amusement. "One day you'll realize your father isn't the saint you think he is."

Teetering on my stilettos, I braced myself against a pillar and pointed to my chin dimple. "So you *are* responsible for this?"

"I am," he said, rocking back on his heels. "And you're welcome."

I gazed up at the banner, mentally replaying the part in *Star Wars* where Darth Vader dropped the paternity bomb and Luke Skywalker made the ugliest face in the history of *ever*. "Is Cam also your...?"

He adjusted the red carnation on his lapel. "Don't insult me."

Of course. Cam didn't have a butt chin. Lucky little shit. "So it's just me?"

"That's right, Sweet Pea." Uncle Tav snagged two flutes of champagne from a passing caterer, took a sip from one and offered me the other. "Happy birthday."

I took the proffered flute; if I gripped the stem any harder I'd have a handful of crushed glass. I wanted to fly at him, claw, kick and bite him, and I wouldn't be satisfied until I drew blood.

But I was eighteen now. As an official adult, I must act accordingly.

With a flick of the wrist, I tossed the champagne in his face and limped away.

♦

I fled the Getty Villa in Uncle Tav's Lamborghini and burned rubber across the freeway to USC. I had a date with Drake Elliott.

Drake's dorm reeked of stale socks. Fast-food wrappers and crushed Coke cans cluttered every inch of his desk. Pacing back and forth, I kicked away a funky pair of boxers.

265

Drake was a filthy pig. Then again, Drake always lived in a human cesspool, and I hadn't cared or noticed before. Living in Ben's obsessively neat world must have ruined me for normal people.

Ben. Oh Ben...

His room smelled like rubbing alcohol, which he used to wipe down the keys of his laptop after every use. Okay, so he was a bit of a freak, but at least I knew he was keeping me safe from germs. The same could not be said for Drake.

Gnawing on my thumbnail, I tried to remind myself that Ben had no claim over me. A few heated kisses on the side of a muddy road didn't make him my boyfriend. Nor should I feel guilty about wanting to feel good.

I halted in front of a poster of a bikini-clad tuner model lounging provocatively on the hood of a hot rod and raked a hand through my hair.

The poster made me miss Ben even more...

Before our vicious fight at the hospital, I had helped Ben tack a poster of the periodic table over his bed. Afterward, we stood together with our heads cocked to the side, admiring our handiwork. The periodic table was his only wall décor.

"Are you purposefully trying to be uncool?" I'd asked.

"What's wrong with it?" He'd glanced from the poster to me. He was in complete earnest. "It glows in the dark so I could study chemistry at night."

I'd rolled my eyes, smiling. "You're hopeless."

"Here…" Wrapping an arm around my waist, Ben whispered in my ear, "Let me tell you about the transition metals…"

There were too many nasty thoughts swirling inside my head. Demons and phantoms, truth and lies, jostling for space inside my skull.

If Ben were here right now, he'd know the right thing to say about the bizarre love triangle between my mother, father, and uncle. Ben could make sense of it all. He might even discover some genetic loophole disproving the dominance of chin dimples.

Ben wasn't here.

And this was a stupid idea.

Maybe I should just go home?

Home to what? Back in Eckhart, I was Public Enemy #1.

Besides, this seemed like a fitting homage to my slut mother.

The rush.

The high.

She and I desired all the things which will destroy us in the end.

Bolting to the open window, I inhaled the delicious aroma of freshly baked pizza from the late-night eatery. Five stories below, I spotted a few dormers in hooded USC sweatshirts and flannel pajama bottoms milling around the brick planters, stuffing their faces with chili dogs and chatting the night away.

My eyes trailed to the sky where the stars glowed weakly

beneath a blanket of LA ozone. In Eckhart, you could see each individual star so clearly you'd think you were living on the moon. I missed the starlight, the pockmarked roads, the farmhouses swallowed by a sea of lavender. I couldn't believe I was thinking this, but I missed Eckhart.

Behind me, someone inserted a room card in the slot. The door swung open. My fingers dug into the ledge, but I didn't turn around.

"Leave the light off," I said. Some things required darkness to get through. In the dark, he could be whoever I wanted him to be. He could be Ben.

"I got your text," Drake said. I could feel his eyes roving over my moonlit silhouette, tracing the slope of my naked back. "I thought it was a joke. But you're really here. It's almost too good to be true."

"What did you tell Cindy?"

"That I was tired and had to get some sleep." It was 1 AM on a Saturday night. College parties didn't kick off until midnight. Cindy must be fuming.

"Are you?" I asked, absently.

"If you meant what you texted, I hope to be."

This was said with such insolence I wanted to turn around and knee him in the balls. Drake was such a douchebag. He only had one thing on his mind. But at least with Drake, I was the one in control.

"If I make a promise," I said, "I always follow through."

I sensed him smile. "Good ole Ava."

He moved to the desk. I could hear him emptying his pockets of keys and wallet, fiddling around on his laptop.

"What are you doing?" I asked.

"Checking my email." He seemed to linger for a long time. "How'd you get in here, anyway?"

My attention was still glued to the sky. If I searched hard enough, I could make out the tip of a crescent moon. The city lights and layers of car exhaust may have blotted out the stars, but the moon...the moon always managed to light up the night.

"Don't tell me you climbed up wearing..." Drake took a swath of satin and felt it between his fingertips. His hot breath fanned my ear. "Wearing this."

"I swiped a spare key in the lobby," I said, neither moving away nor encouraging him.

He traced my spine, settling his hand on my waist.

Enough small talk.

I turned around and Drake stepped back. For lack of anything better to do, Drake practically lived at the gym. The thin cotton of his T-shirt concealed abs so sharp you could grate cheese on them. If nothing else, the sight of Drake naked was a tried and true cure for the blues.

I reached for the hem of his shirt. "Take it off."

"I don't think so." Shaking his head, Drake backed away to

his unmade bed. He snorted at my stunned reaction. "You still think you call the shots, don't you? Last time I saw you, you threatened to have your brother throw me off your porch like yesterday's garbage. What makes you think I'm going to wag my tail every time you snap your fingers?"

I watched him flop down on the mattress. "Isn't that why you're here?"

Drake propped his hands behind his head. "Maybe I want to take you down a notch." His eyes raked over my body, appreciating the way the green satin clung to my curves. "My room, my rules. Take off your dress."

♦

Carrying my heels in one hand, I exited the elevator and stumbled into the lobby. I garnered a few stares from several students checking in for the night. My evening gown, now wrinkled, made me stick out like a sore thumb. My leg was sore, but that was the least of my worries. As I approached the sliding glass doors, I caught sight of my reflection. Runny mascara. Tangled hair. Smeared lipstick. Empty eyes. I looked like Cinderella after the magic wore off.

Vapor lights installed in the brick planters provided a harsh glare. The group of dormers I saw an hour ago had long since dispersed, leaving the turnaround deserted. Hobbling a few more feet, I eased myself down on the edge of the nearest planter and buried my face in my hands.

I didn't know how long I shivered in the cold before the sound of approaching footsteps echoed across the turnaround. I assumed it was a night watchman and waited for him to shoo me away for loitering. The footsteps halted in front of me and the night watchman draped a jacket over my bare shoulders. A white tuxedo jacket with a red carnation.

I glanced up in surprise.

"You may find this hard to believe," Uncle Tav said, brushing off a section of brick with his handkerchief, "but tonight's not the first time a young lady tossed her drink in my face."

He sat down on the opposite end of the rectangular planter.

Drawing his jacket tighter around me, I kept my eyes trained on my scar, showcased in all its grotesque glory by the rip in my gown. "Why are you here?"

"I wanted to make sure you were okay." Uncle Tav frowned at my disheveled appearance. "*Are* you okay?"

I glanced down at my bare feet. They were bruised and cut from the stilettos, dirty from my brief tramp across the damp concrete. "I'm reprehensible."

"Everybody's reprehensible," he said. "Some people are just better at hiding it than others."

"Everybody but Ben," I muttered, waiting for him to retaliate. But Uncle Tav had his eyes on the sky, contemplating the weak

271

starlight over the Los Angeles skyline. Too exhausted to pursue the issue, I filed his words to the back of my mind and let it drop.

"Uncle Tav?" It felt strange calling him that after tonight. He wasn't my uncle anymore. But I couldn't bring myself to call him "father."

"Yes, Sweet Pea?"

"I want to go back to Eckhart." My voice cracked and I wasn't eighteen but an eight-year-old who believed her Uncle Tav would never let her down. "Please take me home."

CHAPTER 20

REPREHENSIBLE PEOPLE

Uncle Tav parked at the curb outside Joe's Hideaway. We arrived just in time to catch the live window show: the Dodd sisters were dancing the night away.

"They look like they're having a good time," Uncle Tav said.

"Horrible, isn't it?" I watched Marlene swing a dishrag over her head and toss it behind the counter. "Probably because I'm gone."

Uncle Tav checked his sideburns in the rearview mirror. I plucked a mascara clump off my eyelashes. He cracked his knuckles. I rubbed my chin dimple. Out of the corner of my eye, I caught him doing the same thing and I stopped immediately.

Unable to stomach the awkward silence, I yanked off my seat belt. Before I could hop out, Uncle Tav touched my shoulder.

"One week," he said, referring to his publicity tour. "I'll be back next Saturday. We'll catch up."

Catch up as in father-daughter bonding? "And do what?"

Uncle Tav slipped on his leather driving gloves. "Fix up my new house for starters. Shake down the foundation for stray rubies."

My lips twitched. "I like the way you think."

"Sweet Pea?" Uncle Tav extended a hand and curled his fingers into a fist. "Am I forgiven?"

I stared at his gloved knuckles. Finally, I bumped my fist against his and said, "I'm softening."

Uncle Tav beamed and cocked his head toward the Dodd sisters. "Now go in there and rain on their parade…"

After Uncle Tav drove away, I jogged to the front door. The music drowned out the ding of the doorbell. My left eye began twitching. One thing I didn't miss about working at Joe's: the '50s playlist.

I strolled across the diner. Marlene ceased dancing and glowered at me. I halted behind her sister, amused at the sight of dour Syd Dodd clapping and bellowing at the top of her lungs.

"So if you don't wanna cry like I dooo…."

Glancing anxiously in my direction, Marlene cleared her throat. "Syd!"

With her eyes closed, Syd was *feeling* the music. *"A-keep away from a…"*

"Runaround Sue," I finished, out-of-sync and off-key.

The music ended. Syd froze and turned around. Her sourpuss face was back. A pity since she didn't look half as vile while singing. "What the hell are you doing here?"

"I come in peace." I held up the dry-cleaning bag containing my old waitress uniform. "Joe wanted me to clean out my cubby."

Two pairs of hostile eyes followed me as I dropped a nickel into the jukebox. "Carry on."

It was good to be back in a town where everybody hated your guts.

A biting breeze swept through the break room. Agitated voices, muffled by the bittersweet whine of jukebox music, echoed down the back alley. Hanging up my uniform, I tiptoed to the door.

One of the voices belonged to Ben. "You conniving little shit!"

Even in his more furious moments, I'd never heard him swear. Something must have set him off. Something big. Holding my breath, I nudged the door open and peeked through the crack.

Pacing back and forth on the wet concrete, Ben's shadow bobbed along the brick wall.

"Don't call me that..." Willa stood in the center of the whirlwind, rubbing her arms against the cold. "There was no harm in it."

"No harm? *No harm?* She could have gone to jail!"

"She did try to choke me!" Willa fired back. "I wasn't making that part up!"

Ben halted in front of her. "And that excuses the fact that you made up everything else?"

My heart did flip-flops. I fought the urge to burst through the door shouting, *Ah ha! I told you I was telling the truth.*

"Who really tried to drown you?" Ben asked.

Willa buried her face in her hands. "I-I don't know."

"But it wasn't Ava?" He glowered down at her. "And you knew it!"

Slowly, almost imperceptibly, she nodded.

"But you had everyone believe that she—"

She reached for him. Ben shouldered her away in disgust.

"You of all people should know she's capable of it," she snapped. "Need I remind you that she broke your nose when you met her?"

"Technically, that was Cam. Ava tried to stop him. Didn't he tell you while you two were in the barn? What's the matter? Too much hay in the ears?"

"How did you know about…" As the answer dawned on her, her face twisted into an ugly pretzel. "That bitch!"

I stiffened in indignation. What was with the personal attacks? It wasn't like I forced her to do the deed with my brother. I merely told Ben what I'd seen.

"Ava may be a lot of things, not all of them pleasant, but at least she never pretends to be something she's not," Ben fired back. "You're the wolf in sheep's clothing."

"Ben!"

"Now I see breaking up with you was the smartest thing I could have done!"

With a shriek, Willa flew at him, slapping and clawing at his face like a banshee. Ben grappled with her, deflecting her blows with a turn of his body. I grimaced as I watched the abuse. For such a petite girl, she was surprisingly strong.

Still, I bet I could take her. I rolled up my sleeves.

Before I had a chance to save the day, Willa shoved Ben in the chest and fled the alley in tears. The screech of tires ripped through the night.

Wow. Ugliest post-breakup breakup *ever*. I shuddered to think what it was like when Ben *actually* broke up with her. I studied the back of Ben's head with new admiration. This guy sure had a high threshold for pain.

Ben rubbed his sore jaw. "How was LA?" he asked, his back still turned. He sounded pretty dignified for someone who just got his ass kicked by a girl.

I hesitated, debating on the best way to sum up my disastrous weekend. As Uncle Tav advised me on the ride back home: whatever happens in LA stays in LA.

"I went shopping, found out my uncle is my father, tossed some champagne in his face. Just another boring weekend."

Ben turned around, eyes flickering over my features like I'd been gone two years instead of two days. "Tavistock, huh? I could have told you that. Chin dimples are a dominant genetic trait. It's just a simple calculation of the Punnett Square."

His nerdy assessment of my current life crisis tore my conscience into shreds. I was no better than the puddle scum beneath our feet.

My shoulders sagged. "What do you get when you cross a bipolar mom with a debonair British uncle?"

"The hybrid uncle-dad."

"I suppose this makes me a daughter-niece."

Ben's brows lifted in amusement. "How do you feel about that?"

"There are no words, only tears on my future therapist's pillow."

"While you're there," Ben added, "ask him what your American dad is doing with a British brother."

"Step-brothers." I wiped my nose on the back of my hand. "Duh."

"Of course." Ben stepped closer. Three long claw marks crisscrossed his right cheek, one deep scratch oozing blood. "About what I said before. I'm sorry. I should never have doubted you." He tucked a strand of hair behind my ear. "I missed you."

I dared a glance up. My voice cracked. "I missed you too."

He attempted a smile but flinched from the pain.

Blinking back my tears, I dabbed at his swollen bottom lip with the sleeve of my jacket. Ben watched me closely. A flush

278

stole across my cheeks and I said quickly, "I did this the first time we met."

A low chuckle. "I remember."

"We're always bleeding around each other."

His lips pressed against my temple. "I hope it doesn't become a habit."

I nestled my cheek against his shoulder, basking in the warm circle of his arms. I was home.

During the long drive back to Eckhart, I'd weighed the consequences of trusting Ben with my secrets. My ten-minute mistake in Drake's dorm needed time to digest. I needed to find the right words and I couldn't find them now.

For the time being, I had another problem keeping me awake at night. Try as I might, this was a mystery I couldn't crack alone. I decided right then and there to take a leap of faith.

"Ben?"

"Hmm?"

"I know who tried to drown Willa," I whispered in his ear. "It's the same person who tried to drown me."

Ben pulled away and studied my face. He frowned. "I thought your mother was dead."

I let out a deep breath. "If only things could be that simple."

♦

"My mother left when I was eight…"

I leaned against the pier railing and watched the waves lap against the barnacle-encrusted pilings. A network of jellyfish bobbed in the inky water like a string of light bulbs.

"She disappeared one week before Christmas. No note. No phone call. Nothing. Didn't even bother to pack her clothes."

Ben bumped his shoulder against mine. "Somehow I doubt you were devastated."

On our brief stroll from Joe's Hideaway to the wharf, I'd regaled Ben with stories of my mother's reign of terror: threatening us with a steak knife one moment, whisking us away from school for a fun-filled day at Disneyland the next. There were no rules where my mother was concerned. It was like living next to a volcano, waiting for it to erupt and wipe out everything you held dear. My mother exploded more often than not.

I turned my back to the ocean. The railroad car silhouette of Joe's Hideaway glowed like a neon mecca compared to the deserted warehouses dotting the wharf.

"Cam was devastated. Sometimes I think he still isn't over it. He was her favorite. As for me… It was the best Christmas present ever."

Ben scrutinized my profile with a frown.

Having spoken too seriously, I broke off into a nervous laugh. "You must think I'm some kind of monster."

"Not a monster. Just not very forgiving. Then again, if my mother tried to drown me, I'd have a hard time forgiving too." He picked at a splinter in the railing and went back to staring at the ocean. "What happened next?"

"Mother often left town for days at a time doing God knows what, so we didn't think anything of it at first."

"Where'd she go?" Ben was a curious one.

"Said she went to a spa to get away from it all." I paused, remembering this weekend's paternity bomb. "Guess she was really boning Uncle Tav in a Motel 6 somewhere."

"Tavistock strikes me more as a Ritz Carlton type of guy," Ben interrupted.

I shot him a dark look. "Anyway, after a week went by and it became obvious she wasn't coming home, Dad filed a missing person report. A month after her disappearance, they found my mother in the desert just off the highway to Vegas." I licked my lips. My tongue stuck to the roof of my mouth. "Or I should say, they found just a few...*parts*."

"Which..." Ben swallowed. "Parts?"

I hoped he had a strong stomach. "A clump of hair, a patch of scalp, and a few..." I swallowed. "Fragments of skull. Blood. Lots and lots of blood. No body." I scrubbed a hand over my face. "The forensics team performed some tests, of course, and the DNA evidence matched. But no body, no autopsy. So what do you think happened?"

Ben blinked in surprise. "Are you asking me?"

"Use that brilliant mind of yours and come up with some theories."

He cupped his hands together and blew warm air into his palms. "Given the evidence, I'd say your mother had an unfortunate run-in while hitchhiking."

"Like she met up with a serial killer truck driver?"

"Happens all the time on the news. He buried her in the Mojave, but not deep enough to keep the coyotes from digging her up."

"That's what the detectives thought," I said. "Frankly, Ben, I thought you had more imagination than that. You must have known what you were doing when you showed me the picture of Arabella Eckhart. I know you've seen my parents' wedding photo. Surely you've noticed the physical resemblance."

Ben straightened to his full height. "I can't deny that I've thought about the possibilities."

"A ruby that could bring the dead back to life," I whispered.

"Whoever possesses the ruby could never die," Ben finished.

I contemplated the chances of being the spawn of a hundred-and thirty-year-old walking corpse. "If they're one and the same, I think I'm going to hang myself like Arabella Eckhart."

Ben said, "Like your mother, I doubt you'd succeed."

"Huh?"

And then, completely without warning or provocation, Ben

pinched my arm.

"OW!" I rubbed my sore bicep and glowered at him.

"Did that hurt?" Ben studied me like a specimen under a microscope.

"Yeah that hurt!"

For a moment, he looked vaguely disappointed, then, just as quickly, his face lit up. "But I bet it'll hurt me more than it hurts you."

I took a threatening step toward him. "Wanna test that theory?"

He dodged my advance with a nimble leap backward. "And I bet if I toss you in there," he said, gesturing to the jellyfish-infested water, "you'll survive it."

It was my turn to back away. If he was planning on tossing me in with the jellyfish, I was taking him with me. "So uh…what's your point?"

"If I fell three stories and landed on my back," he explained, "I'd have a broken back. Or neck. Or legs. I'd be dead or paralyzed…"

"It only…" His tone took on a final note of sadness. "It only took a tumble down the stairs to kill my brother."

"But I *was* injured," I insisted, gesturing to my leg.

"And you recovered from septic shock that would've killed a man twice your size. You could've lost that leg, yet you survived with a scar."

He circled around me. "I would love to examine how the ruby works. If you nick your finger on one of its razor-sharp edges, does it do something to your blood? Invade it, perhaps, like a virus? Let's pretend it does. If Arabella Eckhart never died, if she and your mother are one and the same, then half of what's flowing through her veins flows through yours." Ben rubbed his chin like Sherlock Holmes. "I suppose this includes Cam too, which explains his strength, though I wonder if you inherited all the brains."

I swiped the hair out of my eyes. "You make me sound like a circus freak."

"You're the only one who has even seen Arabella's Curse in over a century," Ben reminded me. "And earlier, you said the color 'called' to you? What did it say?"

I cursed under my breath, berating myself for revealing too much and yet, I had to explain why I tried to choke Willa. It simply boiled down to this: red. I remembered seeing that beautiful light and it was as if nothing and no one in the world mattered. All I wanted was to possess it. I would die for it. Kill for it.

"It, the ruby…" I locked eyes with Ben. "It called my name."

"Because it's part of you." Ben didn't look surprised. In fact, it seemed like he knew the answer from the beginning. "I have no doubt you'll find Arabella's Curse. Chances are the ruby has already found you."

High up on its mountaintop perch, the turret of Eckhart House loomed above a swirling circle of fog. Ben's last words made my forearm prickle. Strangely enough, I couldn't be sure if it was from fear or exhilaration. I didn't relish reuniting with my mother. But the lure of the ruby was too hard to resist. I stared down at my white-knuckled fists. I was primed and ready for action.

"Of course," Ben added with a dismissive laugh. "This is all just speculation. Part of the fun of the ruby's lore. We'll never be able to prove your mother is actually Arabella Eckhart—"

"In order to do that, we'll have to…" My idea was so sick and twisted that I was ashamed of conceiving it.

Ben's dark eyes gleamed. "We'll have to what?" he pressed.

I studied the pier's wooden slats. "Open up Arabella's crypt. If they're one and the same, the crypt should be empty. If not, then we're going to Hell for defiling a poor woman's grave. Actually, we're going to Hell either way."

Having spoken my mind, I dared a glance up at Ben. Instead of disgusted, he looked intrigued. Even hungry.

"Tell me more," he said.

CHAPTER 21

TOMB RAIDERS

Halting at the entrance of Charles Eckhart's private mausoleum, I glanced over my shoulder to make sure Ben hadn't bailed. He stood behind a rusty wheelbarrow crammed with an arsenal of equipment that took some ingenuity to acquire: crowbar, shovel, pickax, and sledgehammer.

With flashlight in hand, Ben consulted the blueprint of the mausoleum he'd sketched on a section of butcher paper.

The mausoleum was located on the periphery of the Eckhart estate, built specifically to house the remains of Arabella, who was denied burial in the churchyard due to her apparent suicide. I swung my eyes to the towering statue of an angel guarding the Eckhart crypt. Weeds swamped the angel's sandaled feet and ivy twined around her arms like ribbons.

Slipping on my leather gloves, I motioned for Ben to wheel in our supplies.

"Before you proceed," Ben stalled, tapping a forefinger

against his blueprint, "perhaps we should review my calculations again. I'm not sure if inserting the crowbar at a sixty-five-degree angle will do it. If we leverage our tools at seventy-five—"

"Seventy-five what?" I squinted at the butcher paper where Ben had drawn a perfect architectural replica of the mausoleum's interior. I think he even incorporated a flow chart.

"Degrees." He frowned and peered closer at his diagram. "Though I see what you mean. Seventy-five does sound sloppy, doesn't it?"

I nodded as if I knew what he was talking about. And so, as the owl hooted into the night, Ben yammered away about Egyptian mathematicians, leverages, and something about finding the hypotenuse of a right triangle.

Concluding his Nobel Prize-worthy lecture on grave robbing, Ben rolled up his plans. "Any questions?"

"I think I got it." I picked up the crowbar. "Let's do this!"

Ben plucked the crowbar from my hands and replaced it with the flashlight. "On second thought, I think I better handle this." He puffed out his chest and strolled inside.

I wedged the wheelbarrow against the door to keep it from slamming shut. "Have you done this before?"

His voice echoed in the darkness. "Nope!"

"You sure? You seem like you know what you're doing," I called back.

"It would seem that way— I need a light!"

I scrambled to the wheelbarrow, mindful not to catch my clothing on the pickax, and joined Ben. The air inside was several degrees cooler than outside.

"What am I? Your caddie?"

Ben patted me on the back. "Sidekick."

"I'm nobody's sidekick." I surveyed the airless vault and shivered. "Imagine being locked in here for all eternity. I'm never going to die."

With his crowbar slung across his shoulder, Ben examined two limestone slabs set flush against the farthest wall. "Famous last words."

He motioned for me to shine my light along the inscription.

"Arabella Eckhart," I read. "Where true hearts lie withered…"

"And fond ones are flown…" Ben traced the elaborately carved stanzas and the engraving of a flock of birds in flight. "Who would inhabit this bleak world alone?"

I stood back and swept a hand toward the tomb. "All yours, Wolcott."

Strictly adhering to the flow chart in his blueprint, Ben jammed the crowbar into the corner of the slab, levering it at a sixty-five-degree angle, and pushed with all his might. He grunted, his color shifting from red to purple. He looked constipated. The stone showed no sign of give.

Squaring his shoulders, Ben blew into his hands and angled

the crowbar at a seventy-five-degree angle. This time I thought he'd rupture a blood vessel. The stone remained firmly in place. All that education and he couldn't even pry open a grave. This did not bode well for our love life.

I shook my head. "Let's hope you don't apply the angle method to boinking."

Ben paused for a moment and said, "Fortunately, you're easier to get into than a crypt."

"Touché."

After he failed a third time, I decided to intervene. While Ben prepped for another go, I selected my tool of choice.

"Stand back!"

Ben stared at the sledgehammer with incredulous eyes. "You're *not* serious."

"You don't tow around a sledgehammer unless you plan to use it."

"This is a historical burial ground! You can't—"

The hammer collided against priceless Italian limestone, lodging a crater-shaped depression. Ignoring the strain on my muscles, I primed for another round. To his credit, or perhaps he feared getting in the way of a girl and her sledgehammer, Ben leapt out of my way.

With an Amazonian war cry, I smashed the slab into smithereens. The limestone crumbled like cheap plaster.

Once the dust cleared, I pointed to the hole in the wall.

"Light please."

Pale and shaken, Ben complied. The flashlight bobbed in the dark, revealing the tip of a mahogany coffin. I kicked away chunks of fallen rock and marched to the wheelbarrow.

"Follow my lead." I handed Ben a shovel and snagged the pickax for myself.

Ben stared at the shovel in a daze. "But my flow chart…"

I rolled my eyes and shoved him forward. "For God's sake! This is grave robbing, not rocket science."

Looping the tip of my pickax through one of the coffin's brass handles, I motioned for Ben to do the same. With a grimace, he jammed the butt of his shovel through the opposite handle.

Ben sighed. "I can't believe I'm doing this…"

"If you break into a crypt, expect to get your hands dirty. Now PULL!"

Despite the coffin's small size, it took us more than three tries and much grunting and swearing before the coffin crashed to the ground in a cloud of splintered wood and dust.

Wasting no time, I hacked at the metal closures with my pickax. When the latch gave way, Ben rammed his shovel into the gap and drove the spade in with his foot.

The lid popped open like an oyster shell.

Ben knelt down beside the coffin, fanning away the residual dust. I joined him, flashlight in hand.

Baby spiders crawled over the moldering satin lining in a

frenzy to escape the bright glare. Instead of a corpse, there was a small parcel wrapped in lace.

"No one home," Ben whispered.

The sight of the empty coffin sent a bolt of fear coursing through my body. I had expected it, but there was still some part of me that hoped I'd been wrong. I felt like a girl who'd just discovered the monster under her bed was not a figment of her imagination, but real—complete with talons and fangs, waiting to lop off her head and suck her blood.

Scooping up the parcel, I peeled away the lace bindings, uncovering a rosewood box with a golden clasp. The box looked familiar. If I could only put my finger on where I'd...

I yelped and flung the box back into the coffin.

With a quizzical tilt of his brow, Ben picked up the box and popped the clasp. The haunting melody of my mother's lullaby filled the crypt. Three mechanical blackbirds suspended on wires circled around a lady dressed in a black Victorian gown.

"My mother's music box," I said, clawing at the scars on my collarbone. "Uncle Tav helped me pick it out at a flea market. She had no ear for music."

My birthday gift to her.

Her message to me.

The birds flapped their wings as *The Last Rose of Summer* played—the soundtrack of all my childhood fears.

With a sweep of my arm, I knocked the music box from

Ben's hand. It clattered to the ground. I picked up the shovel and rammed the spade against the delicate rosewood until the birds dropped dead one by one.

Until the Victorian lady's head toppled from her body.

Until silence, blessed silence filled the house of the Eckhart dead.

Panting, I fixed my gaze on Ben, who was standing next to the open coffin. He bent down and picked up the severed head of the Victorian lady. A frown pulled at his brows as he glanced from my dust-smeared face to the rubble around my feet.

Ben probably thought I was completely insane. And he was right. I wouldn't blame him if he never wanted anything to do with me again.

The shovel slipped from my fingers and clanked to the ground. I stumbled out of the mausoleum and collapsed under the marble angel. Leaning my back against her feet, I shut my eyes. Tall weeds swished against my body, tickling my face.

A moment later, Ben sat down beside me and crossed his legs.

"Find another girl," I said. "A normal girl who likes puppies and would never take a sledgehammer to someone's tomb. Trust me, you'll be happier."

There was a long pause.

Ben scooted closer and draped an arm around my shoulders. "I don't want to be happy." He wiped away a smear of dust from my cheek. "I want to be with you."

CHAPTER 22

SEX, LIES, AND VIDEOTAPE

Swinging a sledgehammer took a lot out of me. After washing the corpse dust from my skin, I collapsed into bed. I'd just about drifted off when a moan echoed through the darkness. I cracked an eye open.

On the other side of the wall separating Cam's bedroom from mine, the bedsprings squeaked.

"Eww." Flopping onto my stomach, I buried my head under the pillow and pretended the wild monkey sex sounds were part of a New Age rainforest soundtrack.

Who Cam slept with was none of my business—as long as it wasn't Willa. Even Cam wasn't that stupid. Actually…

I bolted out of bed in a tangle of sweaty sheets and yanked the curtains apart. Willa's black Range Rover was parked in our driveway.

"Idiot!" I marched to the kitchen.

After what she tried to do to me, she had the audacity to set foot in *my* house and screw *my* brother? Over my dead body!

Retrieving a tin bucket from beneath the sink, I filled it to the brim with cold water and hauled it down the hall to Cam's room.

Shutting my eyes, I kicked the door open like I'd seen on *Cops* and let the water fly. Water splashed against naked flesh.

Willa shrieked like a drowned cat.

The bucket clanked to the floor, but I waited at the threshold, listening to them scramble for their clothes. "Can I open my eyes now?" I called, more concerned about going blind than maintaining my badass creds.

Cam roared, "You're insane!" Frantically zipping on his jeans, he shielded a semi-nude Willa from view. "Get out of my room!"

Shoving him out of my way, I pointed at Willa. "Get that bitch out of my house!"

Willa sat on the edge of the bed, calmly snapping on her bra.

"Hey!" Cam wagged a finger in my face. "You can't talk to my girlfriend like that!"

"Your *girlfriend?*"

Wringing water from her hair, Willa said, "Surprise."

I stepped toward her, ready to maim, when Cam whirled me around by the shoulder. "Leave!"

"She doesn't care about you." I brushed away a stray droplet from the tip of his nose. He jerked his head back. "She threw herself at Ben the moment your back was turned."

Cam's jaw ticked. He looked so lost and hurt that I wanted to give him a hug, but I couldn't show weakness in front of the enemy. I had vermin to exterminate.

"Too bad he wouldn't have her." I turned to Willa, who was slipping on her sodden blouse. "What did he call you again? 'A wolf in sheep's clothing'? Ouch. Doesn't sound very flattering, does it?"

"No, it doesn't." She zipped up her jeans and jammed her feet into silver ballet flats. "Noooo, it doesn't."

Ready for a catfight, I was immensely disappointed when she gathered up her hair and deftly braided the damp strands into a loose ponytail. Maybe I hadn't provoked her enough?

As I scrambled for a word dirtier than "whore," Cam glanced from me to Willa. "Is it true?" he asked her.

Willa hesitated, fingers absently unraveling her braid. "I never meant to hurt you."

Cam stared down at his bare feet.

I strolled to the window where I had a perfect view of the apple orchards enshrouded in fog. My part in my brother's heartbreak was cruel but necessary: to spare him more pain later, he needed to hear the ugly truth now.

"Get out," he told Willa.

She nodded and grabbed her purse. Crossing the room, she touched Cam lightly on the arm. "I'm sorry."

"Get out," he choked.

I waited until Willa shut the door softly behind her. "Oh

Cam...."

Sniffing, he rubbed his jaw.

I smoothed down his rumpled hair as I'd done many times when he was upset. "Girls come and go, but no one will love you as much as your sister."

Cam flinched away from my touch. "You too."

I blinked, surprised by the ice in his voice. "What?"

"You heard me. I want you out too."

"I was only trying to help. You need someone to watch out for—"

Clamping a hand over my wrist, Cam dragged me to the door and shoved me into the hall. "Get out!"

The door slammed in my face. Massaging my sore wrist, I barely had time to regain my bearings when a *tsk tsk* made me whirl around.

Willa folded her arm across her chest. "And you wonder why everyone hates you."

"This is all your fault!"

"*My* fault?"

"You've brainwashed Cam and turned him against me."

"You treat your own brother like a dog. You emasculate him at every opportunity. He has a mind of his own. I bet you didn't know he's planning on moving out."

"Listen to me, you sanctimonious little slut..." Seizing her by the blouse, I slammed her against the wall.

Willa snorted and held up her hand in surrender. "Nice. Going to finish me off? I don't have a scarf this time."

"If I catch you anywhere near my brother, if you hurt a hair on his head, I will rip out your heart and shove it down your throat."

"Very poetic." Willa arched a brow. "A slut, am I?"

I released her. "I call it like I see it."

"All right." She cracked her neck muscles and smoothed down the wrinkles on her blouse. "All right."

I squared my shoulders and pointed to the front door. "Now get out of my h—"

Before I could finish my sentence, Willa pressed her lips forcibly against mine. In that moment, three thoughts raced through my mind.

One: So my scar wasn't the only reason she couldn't keep her hands off my thigh.

Two: Under different circumstances, Willa wasn't a shabby kisser.

Three: She'd just been doing the nasty with my brother. Who knows where her mouth had been?

The last thought made me shove her away. "What the fuck?"

Willa tapped me playfully on the cheek. "I'm just kissing you goodbye."

Smiling at my stunned reaction, Willa shouldered past me. "Good night, Ava."

I listened to her footsteps recede down the hall and waited for the inevitable slamming of the front door. Alone in the dark, I wiped my mouth on my sleeve. "And I thought *I* had issues."

♦

"Is Willa a lesbian?" I propped my chin on top of Ben's shoulder and studied his profile under the glow of the porch light. He'd swapped his contacts after dinner for nerdy black-framed glasses, which gave him an adorable Clark Kent vibe.

"Either that or she forgot to take her meds." Ben flipped a page in his tattered copy of *Moby Dick*. "Now why don't you stop overanalyzing Willa's motives and concentrate on your problem sets. I'm here to help."

The porch swing creaked as I tucked one foot under my knee, my GED practice book completely forgotten on my lap. I glanced up at the moonless sky. A bracing wind swept the waist-high weeds, causing the hairs on my arms to stand on end.

"No, it wasn't a lesbian kiss." There was a storm brewing. I could feel it. "Remember in *Godfather II* when Michael Corleone planted one on Fredo, then offed him the next day? It was that kind of a kiss."

"Willa is not going to *off* you."

"Why not? When I tried to strangle her—not intentionally, mind you—she threatened me. She's up to something. I just wish

300

I knew what it was."

Ben whipped off his glasses and pinched the spot between his eyes. He remained like that for a long time. So long, in fact, that his mother poked her head out the screen door and inquired about his migraine.

Waving his mother away, Ben grabbed *Moby Dick* and flipped to page one. "Here," he said, shoving the tome under my nose. "I want you to read this."

I chewed on my thumbnail. "Why?"

"Your reading comprehension scores suck. Almost as much as your math scores."

"Way to make a girl feel good, douchebag." I snatched my backpack and stood up, but Ben caught my arm and pulled me onto his lap. "For your information, I owned my PSAT. I just can't focus when someone's out to shank me."

"I guarantee no one will shank anyone in Eckhart. Not on my watch."

"There will be a most triumphant shanking. I feel it in my bones."

"I'll start Chapter One," he said, a little too loudly. "You're responsible for Chapter Two. We'll alternate." He gave me a peck on the cheek. His lips migrated to my jaw and traveled over my lips. "You'll like it. You have a lot in common with Captain Ahab."

I licked his bottom lip, worries forgotten. "I have a lot in

301

common with a one-legged sea captain?"

Another sultry kiss. "You'll be surprised."

I slipped my hands beneath the hem of his T-shirt. His stomach was hard, his skin fevered. "I could think of a better activity."

Ben pulled away. "Moby Dick."

My hand snuck lower. "You're telling me."

"No…" Ben removed my hand and pushed me off his lap. "We read first."

"Who needs birth control when I've got you?" I crossed my arms and sat back in a huff. "Why? Why are you doing this?"

"I want you to pass your GEDs. I'm going back to UCLA in the fall and I want you to come with me. I want you to go to college. You're too smart not to."

"Tell that to my dad." I snorted. "He says the only smart thing about me is my mouth."

"Your dad could kiss my ass."

That garnered a smile of appreciation from me.

"Now," Ben continued, "Unless you're happy waitressing until you're fifty and being locked in a ridiculous turf war with Willa for the rest of your life, I suggest you pay attention." He flipped to the first page and slipped his nerd glasses back on. "Chapter One. Call me Ishmael."

I stared at Ben for a moment before scooting beside him. He drew an arm around my shoulder and read, "Some years ago, having little or no money in my purse, and nothing particular to interest me on shore, I thought I would sail about a little and see the watery part of the world."

Nestling my cheek against the starchy wool of his peacoat, I listened to the musical cadence of his voice make an otherwise dull text come alive.

"Ben?" I interrupted.

"Hmm?"

I reached for his hand. Our fingers intertwined. The porch swing rocked back and forth. The night was silent, crackling with electricity; the calm before another thunderstorm. "I'm glad you came to my window."

Ben stopped reading, probably recalling the ass-kicking he received from Cam on my orders. "Some things are worth bleeding for."

♦

Three days later, I joined Willa for lunch at Joe's Hideaway. Across the booth, Willa bit into her hamburger, ordered rare and unappetizingly bloody, while she fiddled with her laptop.

I darted a nervous glance at the stockroom, wondering what was keeping Ben and why we had to be at Joe's on his day off. Apparently, Willa had called him on behalf of her father, who was livid over several missing units of ketchup from today's shipment.

303

Ben, dutiful as always, had suggested we stop by so he could do a quick inventory check.

We'd found Willa seated in the near-empty diner. "Go on, Ben," she'd waved him away. She'd gestured to the seat across from her. "I'll keep Ava company…"

Afternoon rain drummed against the windows, distorting the Coke sign behind Willa into red halos. Marlene's laughter echoed from the stockroom, where she was assisting Ben with the inventory. Syd circled behind us like a hawk, absently wiping down a table here, a booth there.

"I'm waiting." I rapped my fingers on the tabletop. "What is this 'super important thing I simply must see'?"

Willa swallowed her last bite of hamburger and gestured toward my untouched tuna on rye. "You're not eating."

"I'm not hungry."

She dabbed at the corners of her mouth with her napkin. "Trust me, you'll need a full stomach to handle this."

I folded my arms over my chest. "Trying to scare me?"

Willa fluttered her lashes. "Yes."

I snorted, confident that nothing she could do or say could intimidate me. "You'll have to try harder."

Taking a sip from her strawberry milkshake, Willa folded her hands primly in front of her.

"Six months ago, while I was still in San Francisco, we got a one-star Yelp review. 'Horrible service,' it said. 'The waitress, in addition to being a stuck-up skank, obviously didn't know what she was doing.'"

"Poor Syd." I gnawed on my thumbnail. "I hope her feelings weren't hurt."

Willa ignored me. "'She can't even carry a bowl of chili without spilling it on herself.'"

When she was finished, I shrugged. "You thought this would scare me? I've been called worse. What'd you do? Memorize the whole review?"

"I've got lots of free time now that I'm single." Willa typed something on her laptop. "Daddy made me message the reviewer and we got to talking. It seems..." She beamed, baring sharp little teeth. "We have mutual friends."

I sat up straighter. She had my full attention.

"Drake Elliott," she said. "I heard you two used to... I was going to say 'date,' but that wasn't really what you did, was it?" She tapped her chin in mock confusion. "Though I'm thinking of another four-letter word. What could it be? Help me out, Ava. Whisper it in my ear."

I leaned forward and whispered the four-letter word, adding "you" for good measure.

"My new pen pal was right. You are a naughty girl! He also told me another interesting piece of information: seems like you two got *reacquainted* when you went down to LA."

"Drake says a lot of things," I said, trying to appear

indifferent. Inwardly, sirens blared Code Red. "None of them true. Your new pen pal is all talk, and only the gullible or the extremely stupid would believe him. Naturally, someone like you would be duped."

"Of course, I took his story with a grain of salt," she continued. "A week ago, he sent me an email and well, it's hard to describe. You'd better see for yourself."

She whirled her laptop around. A video player dominated the screen.

Ben was nowhere in sight. I could hear him joking about pickles with Marlene in the stockroom.

"Press play," Willa instructed.

The video was dim and grainy, but offered a perfect view of a twin bed with rumpled sheets. Car and band posters plastered the wall. Dirty laundry littered the floor. Then Drake made his cameo. He adjusted the hidden webcam and winked.

Standing with my back to him, I couldn't have seen that wink. I was too busy contemplating the weak Los Angeles starlight.

Drake's lips moved. I didn't need sound to know what he was saying.

Take off your dress.

I stepped into view, fumbling with the straps of my evening gown. There was a brief glitch, then I appeared on screen again. Topless and wearing only a pair of sheer black panties, I joined Drake in bed.

306

"What the…?" To say my sex tape took me by surprise was an understatement, considering we *never* had sex that night. We were close. At the last moment, I chickened out. The night ended with Drake tearing up my gown and my knee colliding with his nuts. So the question begged to be asked: after almost being raped by this piece of shit, how was Drake able to record us having sex? *"What the fuck?"*

As much as I didn't want to, I clicked "Full Screen." There was a close up on my left thigh. There were a lot of close-ups, actually, on parts of my body I didn't want floating around the internet, but my thigh was the ticket.

No scar.

I had a giant scar the night I snuck into his dorm. Speaking of dorms, this one magically morphed into his old bedroom. How many times did he secretly record us doing it? During junior year, I'd had this funny feeling the guys were leering at me. I'd also received a few lewd texts from anonymous numbers. Now I knew why.

"Drake is one heck of a talented filmmaker," Willa said, twirling a strand of hair around her finger. "His little home movie is quite the indie hit with his friends. He's something of a big man on campus now. Thanks to you."

Syd dropped a nickel in the jukebox and twirled around the empty diner, singing a duet with Elvis. *"Wise men say. Why do fools rush in?"*

307

I pressed my palms against the table edge. The table rattled.

"...but don't look so down. Thanks to me and my amazing uploading skills, this video recently went viral. Smile, Ava Nolan. You're famous."

Her smirk vanished; she leaned in and whispered, "Ben was mine. We could have been so happy. And then you moved to town and took him away from me. Now he doesn't love me anymore." A twinge of pain crossed her face. "But he will. Once I show him what a whore you are."

"Take my hand..."

I lifted my eyes to meet hers.

Take my whole life too..."

Red.

"For I can't help..."

All I saw was red. And the color told me:

"Falling in love with you."

This bitch was dead.

I lunged across the table and catapulted myself at Willa, sending a shower of plates to the floor. We tumbled to the ground and rolled.

Just as my fingers clamped around her throat, something struck me in the back of the head and a fireworks display boomed in front of my eyes.

I turned around.

Syd stood behind me holding a steel napkin dispenser. Reeling

308

with pain, I slid off Willa and hurled myself at Syd's legs, sending her careening to the ground. Her bony arms flailed, striking me across the jaw.

"Get off my sister!" Marlene grabbed a clump of my hair and dragged me across the floor. She held me down as Willa kicked me in the ribs. My screams turned into groans.

Ben looped an arm around Willa's waist and heaved her off of me.

Scrambling to my hands and knees, I lunged for Willa again. "I'm going to kill her!"

I collided against Ben, his arms restraining me like a straitjacket. "You'll do no such thing," he growled in my ear. "Nobody will be doing any killing on my watch! Now calm down!"

He turned to Willa, who was huddled next to an overturned chair, massaging her throat. "That goes for you, too!" To Syd, hiding behind Marlene. "And you!"

Ben surveyed the spilled food and broken dishes. "Have you all gone mad?"

Syd pointed at me. "Ava attacked Willa!"

He handed me a napkin to wipe the blood off my face. "Is that true?"

I looked away. My cheeks stung and my every breath felt like a stab with a serrated knife. I probably had a collapsed lung thanks to Willa.

Ben lowered his voice to a whisper. "I don't blame you. I know Willa must have done something to provoke you."

Willa, having overheard Ben's words, cackled like the witch she was.

Ben glowered at her. "You think this is funny?"

"Actually, I do." Willa picked up her laptop and assessed it for damages. "Given all the horrible things she's done to you, you're still determined to see good in her. Even when we all know there's nothing there. Ben Wolcott, always forgiving, always trusting. Ever the optimist."

She slammed her laptop on the table and flipped the screen toward Ben. "Let's see if you'll be so forgiving once you see this. Pull up a chair. Your little angel has something she'd like to show you."

I glanced skittishly at the door. "Come on, Ben," I said, tugging on his sleeve. "She's obviously crazy. We don't have to listen to this."

Ben held up a hand for me to be quiet. He walked toward the laptop, his attention transfixed by the enlarged screen capture of me in a compromising position with Drake.

Willa pressed play.

I shut my eyes and raked my hands through my hair.

Ben watched for less than a second. He clicked "Stop" and exited the video.

Silence filled the diner. I waited for him to say something, but he stood unnaturally still.

"Ben?"

No answer.

"Ben, let's go outside and I'll... I'll explain everything."

With a sweep of his arm, the laptop crashed to the floor. The keyboard shattered. The screen fizzled and faded to black.

I jumped. Even Willa looked startled. Behind me, Syd and Marlene gasped.

"When were you planning to tell me? Or were you planning to tell me at all?"

I took a tentative step toward him like someone approaching an enraged animal. "Despite what this may look like, I never slept with him. Not since you." Hell, I hadn't even slept with Ben yet. I'd been as celibate as a nun ever since I moved to Eckhart, and not by choice.

He whirled around. "Really?" he asked, eyes blazing with betrayal. "Because it sure looks like you fucked him to me."

"That was an old..." There was no flattering way to phrase this. "Sex tape."

"Were you or were you not in his dorm last weekend?"

"Yes, but—"

"Snuck in?" Ben stepped forward until we were nose to nose. "Kissed him? Stripped for him?"

"Yes, but..." Taking a deep breath, I searched for the right words. "Okay, I intended to sleep with him to get back at you."

"Yeah, that makes me feel so much better," he said between clenched teeth.

"I almost went through with it, but I couldn't stop thinking about you."

"You know what…" Ben threw his hands in the air. "I'm done."

Before he could walk, I seized him by the shoulder and whirled him around. "He doctored the video! Watch it again."

He shook his head. "I'm not replaying your porno."

I grabbed his forearm. "Look at my thigh. Look at his room!"

With a growl, he shoved me away. I lost my footing and crashed on my ass. My hand landed on a pile of shattered glass.

I stared at the shard embedded in my palm. Blood welled in the gash, dribbling between my fingers. I yanked the shard from my flesh.

Everyone was staring. Scrubbing a hand over his face, Ben knelt down to help me up.

I scrambled to my feet. "Fuck you, too!"

Clutching my injured hand, I fled the diner.

◆

Wind lashed a shroud of hair in front of my face, blinding me to the road ahead. Not that I knew where I was going. If I continued walking, I might walk off a cliff—straight into the ocean. On and on, I slogged through the mud, ignoring the car honking behind me.

I turned around, shielding my eyes against the headlights. It took a second to register that the car was cobalt blue and vintage in the jalopy sense of the word.

My Nissan slowed to a crawl and Cam rolled down the window.

"Jesus, Ava," he shouted above the pelting rain. "What the hell are you doing walking in the middle of the road? I almost ran you over!"

I walked on, not really knowing my destination. I just knew I wanted to be alone.

"Hey! Hey! You listening to me? What's the matter with you?" He honked again. When I continued to ignore him, Cam parked and got out of the car.

I ran.

He chased after me.

"Have you completely lost your mind?" He whirled me around by the elbow

And then he saw my face— the scratches, the split lip, my right eye swollen shut, the clumps of hair ripped from my scalp— and his expression hardened.

Cam cupped my chin and turned my face this way and that. "What happened to you?"

As he scrutinized my injuries, I noticed his clean-shaven jaw and carefully combed hair. "You're wearing a suit."

"I just came from a job interview," he muttered impatiently. "Tell me what happened to you."

He was also sticking it to the man by driving with two DUIs.

"You look so handsome in a suit. But now you've ruined it." I straightened his rain-soaked tie. When I took my hand away, a smear of blood stained his shirtfront.

I glanced down at my palm and stared at the reopened gash. This injury, out of all the cuts and bruises on my body, was the most painful.

Ben didn't believe me.

He didn't even give me a chance.

The world was against me. Whenever I tried to do the right thing, someone always shot me down. Maybe my mother was right and I shouldn't try at all.

I was born wicked.

Maybe this was the world's way of telling me I should *be* wicked.

Cam took my wrist and examined my bleeding hand. "Who did this?"

I shook my head. To talk about it would be to mention the sex tape—not exactly a conversation I wanted to have with my brother.

He seized my shoulders and rattled me until my teeth chattered. "Tell me!"

Thinking only of my heartbreak, I couldn't understand why he kept badgering me about my stupid hand.

I just wanted him to stop.

To shut up.

"Ben!" My voice sliced across the downpour and echoed across the forest beyond the rutted road. "He pushed me after..." A sob erupted from the back of my throat. "He was so angry and he broke the laptop. Oh God! I should have never... I'm so stupid!"

Cam gathered me in his arms. I clutched his shirtfront and crumbled into bloody, pathetic nothingness.

"Don't worry, Little Sis." His hand traced calming circles on my back. "I'll take care of it. Just like old times. Everything will be all right. Everything and *everyone* in their proper place. I promise.

CHAPTER 23

THE WICKED HEART

Home from his publicity tour, Uncle Tav whisked me back to Eckhart House for a little father-daughter bonding slash ruby hunting. We were tracing my steps back to where I'd last seen Arabella's Curse.

"That *is* a beauty." Uncle Tav dug through my hair to examine the stitches on my scalp. "And she did this with a napkin dispenser?"

"Can we focus?" I shooed him away and smoothed my hair back into place with my bandaged hand. "This is not the time or place to be acting like a pair of chimps."

Shifting my backpack firmly on my shoulder, I resumed walking down the second-floor hallway—the same hallway where I'd abandoned Willa.

Uncle Tav followed close on my heels. "Getting beaten up by two girls isn't the end of the world—"

I whirled around. "They did *not* beat me up! I could've taken

Willa, I was just blindsided by her goons. Next time, I'll be ready."

"Already planning your flanking and deployment maneuvers, I see." He arched a brow. "Ah, well. Our friends at the hospital assured me that if you're admitted to the emergency room a fourth time, you'll qualify for a discount."

The beam of his flashlight bounced across my handprints on the wallpaper. Except for a faint tightening of his jaw, his expression remained indecipherable as he studied my blood trail.

"How badly do you want Arabella's Curse?" he asked softly. "Bad enough to bleed all over my new house?"

"A little blood," I said, "is a small price to pay for—"

"A father's love?" Uncle Tav inclined his head toward me. "Trust me when I say this: Morty isn't worth the effort. You can have my love and I won't expect blood in return. At least not *your* blood."

I rolled my eyes and marched on. "My father is an honorable man!"

"Of course I am," Uncle Tav called after me. "I'm afraid the same could not be said for Morty. May I ask where the incorruptible Professor Nolan is now?"

I flipped him off.

"Where is he, Sweet Pea? What? No answer? I'll tell you where he is. In a strip club in San Francisco, drowning his sorrows in booze and boobs."

"That's because you kidnapped him and left him there!"

"I did no such thing. I merely asked if he wanted to tag along. Nobody put a gun to his head, pet."

"What do you have against my dad, anyway?"

"He married the woman I loved."

I snorted. "I'd say he did you a favor. She made him miserable. Ruined his health. Drove him mad. Dying was the least she could do for her family—and she couldn't even do that right."

"Ava, my pet, you know how much I love you, which is why it pains me to tell you that you're being a bitch to your mother and I will not stand for it."

"You know something, Uncle Tav? I've been trying hard *not* to be a bitch my entire life. Everyone had me convinced that it was a bad thing—a disability I should overcome so I could join the ranks of the good. But who is good? Syd, who brained me with a napkin dispenser? Marlene, who yanked a clump of hair out of my scalp? Ben fucking Wolcott, who branded me a whore on circumstantial evidence? The other day, while Willa was kicking me in the head, I had an epiphany."

"That was billed as a concussion," he said. "Your epiphany required a CAT scan, which set me back seven hundred—"

"That's beside the point!" I increased my pace. I was on a roll. "What if being a bitch and being good were not mutually exclusive? What if being a bitch was part of who I am and the only crime I committed was…being myself? From now on, Uncle Tav, I'm never going to be ashamed of who I am."

Uncle Tav's voice sounded as far away as a drop of water in a well. "That's a very motivational speech, Sweet Pea, but the world is unkind to the wicked."

"Then maybe it's time to change the world." My resolution brought a new bounce to my step. I began making plans. "I'll advertise for new friends. Rally a pack of unapologetically bitchy people who will call me leader. We'll be like evil *Avengers*."

But where would I find these unsavory characters? Was there a real-life equivalent of Arkham Asylum nearby?

Lost in thought, I halted in front of a wall and frowned. Were my eyes playing tricks on me? I smacked a hand against solid plaster. "That's strange. You remember a staircase here, right?"

I was met by silence. I turned around.

Uncle Tav was gone.

"Uncle Tav?" I peered into the darkness of the hallway. Rapping my fingers impatiently against my thigh, I waited for a response. "Helloooooooooooo?"

More silence.

"For Christ's sake!" The man had the attention span of a newborn puppy. This was the third time Uncle Tav had wandered off to explore a new room or study some dusty turn-of-the-century trinket.

"When I find you, I'm going to put you on a leash," I

muttered, marching back the way I came. "Uncle Tav! Where are you? What part of 'we must not split up' did you not understand?"

Out of the darkness, a disembodied voice called, "Marco!"

I whirled around. No one behind me. I turned from side to side like a dog chasing her tail.

I swore I heard—

"Marco!"

Yes. There it was again. I took a tentative step toward the direction of the voice.

It called, "Marco!"

I pressed an ear against the peeling wallpaper and bloody handprints. "Polo?"

"In here!" Uncle Tav called from behind the wall.

"Really, Uncle Tav? This is too much. We're wasting valuable time and I'm *not* leaving without my ruby!" I felt my way along the edge and pushed. The wall wouldn't budge. "I can't get in! Are you trapped?"

"I'm quite comfortable actually."

Shutting my eyes, I counted to three. What was I worried about? Uncle Tav was a seasoned veteran when it came to exploring creepy, run-down places. He could take care of himself.

And yet, why did I still feel like something wasn't right?

"How'd you get back there?"

"I found a trick door." The clanking of metal drowned out his laughter.

I jumped at the racket. "What's that sound?"

"I dropped my sword. There's enough medieval weaponry in here to defend a castle."

His words dissolved into more metal clashing against metal. What was he doing? Dancing around in a suit of armor?

"Is Arabella's Curse in there with you?" I asked between clenched teeth.

"No, Sweet Pea."

"Then come out of there this instant!"

"But there's a fourteenth-century mace—"

"Screw the mace! Don't make me come in there!"

He sighed and I hoped, for his sake, he set down the mace. "Geez, you're as square as that Wolcott lad."

I frowned, puzzled by his comment. He'd met Ben once and only in passing. "How do you know Ben's a square?" When he didn't answer, I knocked. "Hello? Uncle Tav? Did you get distracted by something bright and shiny again?"

Pressing my ear back to the wall, I listened closely and froze.

Uncle Tav wasn't alone.

The other voice in the room belonged to a woman. Raspy. Alluring. Familiar. Chasing me in the dark. Calling me for my nightly bath. Coaxing me into the scalding water.

Don't scream, baby. The hotter the water, the cleaner you'll be.

"Uncle Tav?"

But nothing can clean your filthy soul.

I opened my mouth to scream but could only manage to choke, *"Get out..."*

"Get out!" I smacked my palm against the wall. "Get out! GET OUT!"

There were more noises on the other side:

A shuffle of feet.

A groan.

The thud of a body hitting the ground.

And laughter. In my worst nightmares, there was always that mad laughter ringing through the abyss. I had to get to Uncle Tav. But how? *How?*

With a strangled cry, I clawed the wall, pounded it, kicked it, slammed the butt of my Maglite against it. When that didn't work, I took a running start and rammed it.

Again.

And again.

And again.

Stumbling backward, I clutched my throbbing shoulder and glanced down the undulating hallway. The walls and ceiling constricted and expanded like a snake's belly digesting a tasty morsel.

No way in. There was no way in.

The laughter dissolved into silence.

"What now?" I thumped my forehead against the wall. "What

now?"

As if in answer, the wall sank in.

I stepped inside.

Uncle Tav's flashlight rolled across the floor, its beam glinting off an arsenal of swords, daggers, battle-axes, and crossbows.

I stepped forward, breathing in the musty air. A medieval tapestry hung over a termite-eaten dining table covered with dusty books.

There was no sign of Uncle Tav.

Life-sized knights in tarnished armor flanked a fireplace large enough to roast a deer.

The flashlight on the ground wavered as the room faded to black.

A hand clamped around my ankle.

I screamed.

"Just me, Sweet Pea..."

I switched on my flashlight. Slumped on the floor, Uncle Tav shielded his eyes from the glare.

I rushed to kneel beside him. "You almost gave me a heart attack!" My eyes swept over his ashen complexion and traveled down his body. He was clutching his side. "You're hurt!"

"You may find this hard to believe..." He lifted his hand, revealing a tear in his shirt and a long gash below his ribs. Blood seeped through his fingers.

"Oh God," I gasped, clamping a hand over my mouth.

"But this isn't the first time someone's tried to stab me." Uncle Tav bared his teeth in pain. "She slashed me with a dagger, the little vixen. She always liked to play with knives."

"Lean back." I guided his hand to put more pressure on the wound.

With a trembling finger, Uncle Tav pointed straight ahead. "Then she ran away."

Footprints embedded in the dusty floor led to a hollow alcove: another corridor, another trail.

Discarding my backpack, I slid my butterfly knife from my back pocket. The ivory handle pressed painfully against my bandaged palm. "She?"

"My Helena." His head lolled against the wall and his lips curled into a dreamy smile. "Still alive."

I flipped open my knife. The blade sliced against the syrupy air, singing a song only I could hear. This had to end. Now.

Rising to my feet, I stepped in the direction of the footprints. "Not for long."

◆

The corridor—narrow, dank, and silent—stretched on and on. The walls reeked of mold. Rat droppings littered the ground. Ignoring the stitch in my side and the stiffness in my legs, I raced through the darkness.

This was the same old game of intimidation: my mother's sadistic version of hide-and-seek. But I wasn't so easy to scare anymore. An eerie calm settled over me. We were going to settle things once and for all. This was a game I planned to win.

Rounding the corner, I braced my hands on my knees to catch my breath. My spirit sank as soon as I lifted my head. The corridor snaked into infinity. I tightened my grip around the knife's handle and picked up my pace.

Tonight, Mother...

Tonight...

I was ready.

The corridor petered off to a narrow archway. Swiping away a beard of cobwebs, I stepped into a grand ballroom. Gauzy white curtains fluttered like phantoms in the breeze of a cracked windowpane.

To all appearances, the room was completely empty.

"Come out, come out..." I crept beside the floor-to-ceiling windows, chasing the full moon as it darted in and out of silver storm clouds. "Wherever you are."

Three stories below, a grove of oaks stood like an army of monsters frozen in time. I pressed a thumb to the window, blotting out the twisted trees when a glimmer of red danced across the grimy glass.

I stumbled backward.

The curtains billowed around a womanly shape and flapped

across her face like a bridal veil. Like a sleepwalker, her eyes flickered beneath closed lids. The ruby, lackluster and misshapen, dangled from a silver chain above her breast.

I waited for my mother to make the first move. She stood absolutely still, her arms dangling limply at her sides. The curtains parted and she fell to her knees, lifting her palms up as if conferring a holy benediction.

There was blood on her hands. Uncle Tav's blood.

What kind of wicked woman would shank the man she supposedly loved? This one, obviously. This woman had no heart. No soul. She would've killed me in cold blood a hundred times over and never lost any sleep.

Tightening my grip on the knife, I stepped forward. My heart pounded in my ears. I raised my arm and swung—

"My baby!" She crawled toward me on all fours. "Help me. Please help me!"

Blade in midair, I glanced down at her tangled hair and dirty feet.

This is a trick. Don't believe it.

The moonlight bounced off the slope of her neck, exposing her jugular... Her jugular. Throbbing with life. Begging to be sliced. This could end. One blow.

Strike while you can.

I raised my knife again.

Strike!

"Take it off!" She clawed at her nightgown, razor-sharp nails raking at the skin around the ruby, which was—

My stomach roiled in revulsion. Arabella's Curse was embedded in her flesh like a peach pit.

"It wants more blood. And I give it what it wants. Look what it made me do to my poor Ian. But it's never enough. It's always hungry. Take it off…"

The ruby burrowed deeper with her every attempt to remove it. Blood seeped from the jagged edges of the wound.

I darted a glance at the archway. I should run. Turn and run and never look back. Lowering my knife, I began to back away.

But as much as I wanted to leave, one glance at her tortured face paralyzed me to the spot. The fantasy had worn off—or maybe I had grown up. Beneath the eerie moonlight, she looked more like a heroin addict than the murderess of my nightmares. Should I help her? The woman who tried to drown me?

"Please…" My mother reached out to me with bloodstained fingers. Desperate gray eyes sought mine. Deep lines of pain pleated rose-red lips. "God sent you here to save me."

What if she was telling the truth? That the ruby filled her mind with sinister thoughts? Made her kill to feed its insatiable need for blood? Was I to believe that she, a woman with free will, was nothing more than a human husk to an evil stone?

Ludicrous.

And yet.

It had happened to me. The ruby hijacked my mind, made me try to strangle Willa. Granted, Willa needed strangling, but I was not the murdering type. Not until now anyway.

Covered with blood, the ruby began to shine. With every whimper, cringe, and cry of pain, the ruby thumped like a human heart. It glowed as if *happy*.

As a last-ditch call for escape, I glanced at the panel again, then back at the pathetic woman on the floor. Damn. Damn. Damn.

"Don't touch it!" I sank down to my knees and grasped her by the wrist. Life would be so much easier if The Girl with Nine Lives didn't care about the little people. "You're making it worse!"

"What do I do?" Her voice hinged on panic.

I approached her with the same caution one would a rattlesnake. "Let me."

She caressed my cheek.

I jerked my head away. "Don't touch me."

Her hand dropped to her side. "You've grown up," she said with a strained smile.

It felt like I was staring at my reflection. I blinked. She blinked. My mother, one hundred and thirty years old, didn't look a day over eighteen.

"This would be easier if we didn't talk." I pressed my knife to her wound and looped the silver chain over her neck. If the ruby couldn't be removed, I planned to improvise. "This is going to hurt."

She nodded and pried the neck of her nightgown apart. "I trust you. Just make the pain go away."

Working carefully, I jammed the point of my knife under Arabella's Curse. Fresh blood oozed over my blade. My mother's screams filled the ballroom.

Gritting my teeth, I angled the blade and tugged the chain. The ruby dislodged with a *pop*.

The knife slipped from my hand and clattered to the floor.

Holding the ruby in front of my nose, I watched it twirl on its silver chain. Deprived of its host, Arabella's Curse was once again a crude lump the color of rust, more rock than gem. A year of searching and failing and finally...

Arabella's Curse was mine.

"Mine," I said, frowning at the sight of my fallen mother.

With one hand clasped over her chest, she tried to lift herself off the floor. Her scrawny arm wobbled and she fell flat on her face.

So many times I'd dreamt of this moment. My mother, once strong, now weak, was completely at my mercy.

I set Arabella's Curse on the ground. Taking her gently by the arm, I helped her sit up. I nudged her hand away from the wound. "Let me see."

Where I expected a gaping hole, the skin was white and

smooth. I blinked twice to make sure it wasn't an illusion. "Y-you're not hurt?"

She flung her arms around me, crushing me into an embrace. "I'm brand new."

I let my arms dangle as she cried into my hair. I guess living a century as a slave to a sinister ruby warranted an opening of the floodgates.

My mother nuzzled her face into the crook of my neck. "I've missed you."

In her own troubled way, I knew she was sincere. My hands hovered over her back. If I'd learned anything from her unpredictable behavior, I should've pried her off me and run for dear life.

But here was the sad truth: despite all the shit that went down between us, I still wanted her to be my mother. Ignoring the sirens in my head, I wrapped my arms around her. "I've missed you, too."

We held each other tight. In this small pocket of eternity, Ava Nolan, little girl lost, was finally found.

"The bathtub," she whispered in my ear. "The ruby made me do it. It gave me such horrible dreams. It told me you had a dirty soul. A wicked heart."

A breeze wafted through the crack in the window. I wrinkled my nose. She smelled like a decaying corpse under that heavy mask of lavender perfume

"I was only going to wash you until you were as white as snow. But no matter how hard I scrubbed, you refused to come clean. Your stubbornness turned the water bloody."

I flinched and tried to jerk myself out of her grasp. She pinned me down. She was strong—almost superhuman. Her nails sank into my shoulder, breaching skin and drawing blood.

My eyes darted to the ground.

My knife was gone.

Something was wrong.

Terribly, irrevocably wrong.

"No, Mother…" I began, still searching for the knife. "It was your nails raking against my skin that turned the water bloody."

Her rancid breath stirred the flyaway strands of my hair. "Will you forgive me for all I've done?" She pressed the cold blade against my throat. "Will you forgive me for what I'm about to do?"

I shut my eyes. This couldn't be how it ends. Not at eighteen. At the point of my own knife. By my mother's hand. Not before I had a chance to tell Ben I was sorry. Not before I gave Dad the ruby.

"Mother?"

She caressed my cheek and kissed my temple. "Yes, my lovely?"

"I'm not ready."

She held me like a babe in her arms until I was no longer

afraid. I took a deep breath—my last breath on earth.

With a flick of her wrist—

The blade sliced open my jugular.

I collapsed against my mother, spraying her face with blood.

"Don't be frightened, baby." Her voice sounded far away. "Let me sing you to sleep."

She laid my body on the ground, where I gurgled and convulsed like a fish left to die on land.

Darkness swarmed over the ballroom in a torrent of black feathers and predatory beaks. But in the chaotic flapping of death, there was an incandescent light.

Using my last ounce of strength, I dug my nails into the ground and crawled toward Arabella's Curse.

It was so close. Just one more. One more inch.

I reached for it—

Fingers straining until—

My hand closed over the ruby and its serrated edge punctured my skin.

Mother knelt before me, lips mouthing a tuneless song. Behind her, the shadows edged in, shifting into psychedelic shapes. Angels soared across the ceiling. Tigers crawled along the wall. And the devil broke away from the pack and stumbled toward my mother. He carried a shining sword in one hand.

She cocked her head to the side, unaware of Uncle Tav over her shoulder. He raised the sword and brought it down with a *thwack.*

The shadows had won—claiming me as one of their own. Before I closed my eyes for the final time, I saw red.

A resplendent glow bathing the hallowed walls of Eckhart House.

Red.

The beginning and end of my world.

CHAPTER 24

AVA, BURNING

Flames licked my body.

Scorching my hair into cinders.

Melting my skin like wax.

Fire, fire, everywhere. Lighting me up from the inside out like a human jack-o'-lantern. I opened my mouth and roared.

I was in Hell again. And Hell was that pit in Eckhart House where I'd fallen long ago.

The rats swarmed over me, chewing at the scars on my leg and collarbone, gnawing on my slit throat. But instead of tearing me apart, they were stitching me back together.

One cell at a time.

I rose to my feet. Flexed my arms and legs.

The flames caressed my skin one final time and the rats dispersed.

Above the pit, the stars seared the sky with celestial blue light.

Up was the only way to go.

I found a foothold along the wall and began to climb.

♦

My eyes snapped open and I gasped my first breath of air. I probed my slit throat. My fingers fumbled over smooth skin, lingering over a beating pulse.

A spider scurried across the ceiling, stopping right above me. The bristles on its eight legs stood out as distinctly as though viewed through a telephoto lens. I cocked my head to the side, examining my reflection in the spider's compound eyes. A fine sight I made: a girl lying in a pool of blood.

I sat up and my newly beating heart nearly leaped out of my chest at the sight of my mother's body, minus head, sprawled across my legs. Uttering a soundless yelp of horror, I kicked her corpse away, making sure to avert my extra-sensitive eyes from the bloody stump.

The quiet sound of weeping, magnified tenfold, drew my attention to Uncle Tav. He rocked back and forth, cradling something in his hands. A discarded broadsword rested beside him, its blade slick with blood. When he shifted, my mother's lifeless eyes stared back at me. He brushed away the hair from her cheeks and pressed his lips to her temple.

Feeling like an eavesdropper, I turned away and unfurled my fist. Arabella's Curse was embedded in my palm. As I wiggled my

336

fingers, the ruby's serrated edge tore into my flesh like a set of parasitic teeth. Taking hold of the chain, I yanked the stone from my hand. Blood trickled down my wrist like an army of fire ants. I keeled over, clutching my hand in agony.

Eventually the pain subsided into an ache. The ache into an itch. I twisted my hand this way and that, marveling at the miracle happening before my eyes. Cell by cell, my skin melded back together. No cut. No scar. No pain.

I dared a quick glance at Uncle Tav's back. He was still cradling my mother's severed head, oblivious to the world. Tearing the hem of my blouse, I wrapped the cloth around the ruby and slipped it into my jacket pocket—a necessary precaution in case Uncle Tav got any bright ideas about piecing Mother back together again.

Ruby safely concealed, I crawled toward Uncle Tav and tapped him on the shoulder.

He whirled around and seized my wrist.

Uncle Tav's eyes widened, first in horror, but as he noticed my throat, horror transformed into wonder. "You're alive."

"I'm brand new."

♦

In the medieval room, Uncle Tav stood in front of the giant fireplace, watching the flames engulf the woman he loved.

337

"Uncle Tav?" I tugged on his sleeve.

He rolled a silver lighter over his knuckles like a coin.

The stink of singed hair and burnt human flesh seared my eyes and lungs. I wiped at my runny nose and fought the urge to gag. "We have to go…"

His thumb clicked the lighter, igniting a tiny flame. With another click, the flame vanished. Meanwhile, the makeshift funeral pyre we constructed for my mother's remains roared and crackled like an inferno.

"Uncle Tav! Can we please get going?"

"We could have been happy." The firelight flickered over his face, carving wrinkles around red-rimmed eyes. "You. Me. Her. We could have been a family."

A family? I gave his profile an incredulous once-over. This sounded like a blueprint for the most dysfunctional family ever.

Clutching his injured side, he limped toward the fireplace.

"We could've lived here." His face was pale from blood loss. All his blood was on his clothes. *Our* clothes. We looked like actors in a horror movie. "In Eckhart House. Would you like that, Sweet Pea?"

I held out my hand. "We still can be a family."

As if waking from a dream, Uncle Tav blinked. He gave me the briefest of nods.

"Come on," I urged. "We need to get you to the hospital. You can use my discount."

His fingers linked with mine and he allowed me to lead him away.

For what seemed like an eternity, I steered us through a labyrinth of undulating hallways. Uncle Tav stumbled behind me, click-click-clicking at his lighter.

At long last, I flung open the front door and bounded across the veranda, inhaling a much needed breath of fresh air. The stars above Eckhart burned blue and bright. "It's over."

Slumped against the threshold, Uncle Tav cupped a wavering flame against the wind. He turned to the moth-eaten curtains hanging over the main window. Not trusting the strange light in his eyes, I started toward him in panic.

Uncle Tav held up a hand. I halted.

"I'm beginning to think this was a bad real estate investment," he said, patting the wooden beam. "What do you think, Sweet Pea?"

I nodded, giving him my consent.

He held the lighter under the drapes and the brittle velvet went up in flames.

CHAPTER 25

A SMACK ON THE SNOUT

Three days had come and gone since my return from the dead, and the land of the living had never been more glorious. Or seemed so different. I could, if I focused, see every vein on the underside of a leaf and zone in on the solitary buzz of a bee. I had my finger on the pulse of the world, and the world was a carnival of sensations created especially for me.

The world was my playground.

Wrapped in a towel, I knelt beside the bloodstain. Water dribbled from my hair and splattered on the cookie tin containing Arabella's Curse.

The blood belonged to eight-year-old Mary Hopkins, whose short life came to an end at the barrel of her crazy father's shotgun.

When I was eight, my equally crazy mother tried to drown me. The man who I thought was my father pulled me from the bathtub and saved my life.

At seventeen, I fell through three stories and messed up my leg. The fall didn't kill me, but the wound might have. I survived.

At eighteen, my mother slit my throat and left me to die in a pool of my own blood. This time I did die, but not for long.

I felt along the floorboard, recalling how I'd scrubbed my fingers raw trying to out the damn spot. I could've easily ended up like Mary Hopkins: a forgotten bloodstain on somebody's floor. Logically, I should've died at eight, but I kept getting an extension on life.

Nobody can accuse The Girl with Nine Lives of not living up to her name.

Outside in the hallway, not a creature was stirring, except maybe a fly, which I could hear buzzing over a moldy turkey sandwich in Dad's study. Dad, of course, was in San Francisco on another drinking binge. There was nothing to keep him here—nothing except this.

I dangled Arabella's Curse before my eyes. The ruby's color was darker tonight, a black heart on a silver string.

"Everything your heart desires, Dad," I whispered, staring into the coreless center of this unremarkable stone. "You'll have to love me now…"

My fingers sank into the edge of a plank, testing for give. When the plank wouldn't yield, I dug my nails into the groove. The wood splintered as easily as a toothpick.

Working meticulously, I dropped the ruby back into the box

and tucked it into the hole in the floor. I replaced the plank, kicking a rug over my hiding place. Slapping my hands together, I strolled to the mirror above my vanity table.

I turned my head this way and that. Wrinkled my nose. Puffed out my cheeks. Scowled. Grinned.

I looked the same.

I caressed my collarbone, seeking the scars left behind by my mother's nails. My fingers glided across flawless skin. Taking a step back, I lifted the hem of my towel and ran a hand across my thigh. The crater-shaped scar had been wiped clean. My leg was as smooth as the day I was born.

"Who are you?" My breath misted the mirror. "*What* are you?"

♦

The screech of tires diverted my attention away from the mirror. I dashed to the window just in time to see Willa's Range Rover weaving erratically along the twisted road.

"She's gotta be kidding."

Casting the eerie changes in my body aside for future contemplation, I tugged on a wrinkled T-shirt and scrambled into a pair of jeans. Once decent, I stomped into Cam's room and grabbed his baseball bat. Willa brought out the hood in me.

I bounded off the porch just as Willa, swerving abruptly,

missed the driveway completely and beached her Range Rover on my front lawn. Tinted windows concealed the devious little tramp, but I could still hear the wild thumping of her heart. I held my breath and listened. One heartbeat diverged into two.

Willa was not alone.

Ah. So she brought Syd along to bludgeon me with more napkin dispensers. *Excellent.* The more the merrier.

Launching myself at the Range Rover, I swung the bat against the driver's side mirror, lobbing it onto the dewy grass.

Willa flung the door open, waving her arms for a cease-fire. "Put down the bat, you psychotic bitch! I'm not here to start a war with you!"

My bare toes dug into the grass as I pointed the bat at her face. "Then why are you here?"

Her eyes were the size of half-dollars. "You have to help me!"

"Help you?" I snorted. "Why should I help you? I'm about to hit a home run...with your head."

Willa stumbled around to the passenger side and yanked the door open.

"Cam!" My eyes traveled over his blood-splattered T-shirt. I dropped the bat and hurried to his side.

"Where are you hurt?" I patted his stomach and chest, trying to find a cut, a gash, a bullet wound, anything. The blood had to have come from somewhere. But where? "Did you get into another fight? There's blood on your knuckles. Is it yours?"

344

Cam flinched, his vacant eyes locked on the leather dashboard. I shook his shoulders. "Is that your blood? Yes or no?"

Cam gave the slightest of nods that told me absolutely jack shit.

"Is that a yes or a no? Throw me a freaking bone here!"

His left hand clawed into his denim-clad leg, while his right hand remained clamped in a fist so tight that blood vessels twined through his forearm like ropes.

"Damn it! Why won't you answer me?"

I hooked his arm over my shoulder and turned to Willa. "Help me get him inside."

She grabbed the other arm and together we hoisted Cam from the car and lugged him up the front porch.

In the bathroom, I flipped the toilet lid and motioned for Willa to sit Cam down. Swiping a washcloth from the towel rack, I hurried to the sink.

"He came to my house like this." Willa knelt beside Cam. "Almost woke my dad up. I had to take him somewhere."

"Why didn't you take him to the hospital?"

"He's not hurt. He wanted to come here," Willa replied. "To you."

In the mirror above the sink, I saw Willa plant a kiss on Cam's temple. I averted my eyes and concentrated on soaking the washcloth in hot water.

"Go on." Willa brushed Cam's sweat-matted hair off his

forehead. "You can say anything. There's nothing to be afraid of."

"Yes. Out with it," I snapped. "And if you tell me it's bar fight, so help me God."

Cam lowered his head and wept.

I rolled my eyes. *"Christ."*

"Smooth, Ava. Very smooth," Willa said, patting Cam on the back. "Ever heard of a thing called 'tact'? You have the sensitivity of a bulldozer."

"Why don't you shut that hole in your face!" I switched off the tap and tried to reason with my brother. "Now Cam, next time you lose a bet at pool and feel the need to pound a few skulls, think of what Gandhi would do if he lost at pool."

Willa snorted. "Why the hell would Gandhi play pool?"

"Why is your mouth still moving?" I wrung the washcloth of excess water. "Are you listening, Cam? The nonviolent answer is always the right answer."

It was Willa's turn to roll her eyes. "This coming from someone who came at me with a baseball bat…"

Ignoring her, I knelt in front of my brother and dabbed erratically at his scraped knuckles. The sound of his bawling was like a nail driving into my brain. "Enough with the sobbing! You're embarrassing me!"

Cam cried harder.

I pried his left hand away from his leg, but the right hand remained stubbornly clenched in a fist. "I can't clean the blood off if you... Damn it!"

"Let me do it!" Willa snatched at the washcloth.

I slapped her hand away. "Like hell you will! You've stopped being useful long ago, so do us both a favor and throw yourself out with the garb—"

"Smack." Cam choked.

We both hushed up.

"Smack?" Willa frowned and turned to me.

I pressed a finger to my lips.

"That dog needs..." Cam wiped his runny nose on the back of his hand. "Smack...on..." His shoulders heaved one more ragged sob. "Snout."

"Smack on the snout? Smack on the snout?" Willa repeated. "Do you suppose he drove home drunk and ran over a dog? That would explain the blood on his shirt—"

"Shut up, shut up, shut up! I'm trying to think." I screwed my eyes shut and massaged my temples.

Smack on snout? Why did that phrase seem so familiar?

"What that dog needs," I repeated under my breath. "What that dog needs is a smack on the..."

I froze.

The night Ben and I first met. I'd been eavesdropping behind the kitchen door, my lip still throbbing from Dad's backhand. Dad had rejected me, but had accepted Ben and his hokey story of a cursed ruby with open arms. Seething with resentment, I'd

347

turned to Cam: *See what happens when you take in a stray. They get too comfortable and forget who's master. What that dog needs is a smack on the...*

"Snout," I whispered.

Another memory trailed in the wake of the first. I was walking down the road in the pouring rain, too distraught over Ben dumping me over my sex tape with Drake to notice my battered appearance. But Cam had noticed. He demanded to know who was responsible for the gash on my hand. Of all the people who'd hurt me that day, I'd spoken only one name: Ben.

"Oh God, Cam... *What did you do?*"

What did *I* do?

Cam lifted his head and all my fears were confirmed.

"He hurt you," Cam said. "I was only going to teach him a lesson. T-t-things went too far."

I lost my balance and plopped down on the bathroom tiles.

"An eye for an eye," Cam went on. "That's what you've always told me. He hurt your hand and I..."

He unfurled his fist.

Willa gasped. She turned her head away and retched.

I stared at the severed thumb in his palm. It reminded me of a plastic Halloween gag—except there was nothing funny about this little surprise. This was a real thumb and real blood. Ben's thumb. Ben's blood.

Ben once told me he planned to enter medical school after

college. He wanted to become a heart surgeon.

"I like the idea of holding someone's heart in my hands," he'd explained on our first drive to Eckhart House. I'd thought these were pretty lofty ambitions for someone who'd just taken academic leave to live in Eckhart for the unforeseeable future. But if anybody could do it, it had to be Ben. Meticulous and dexterous, not to mention an über science geek, he was definitely going to climb higher than the rest of us.

It's going to be pretty hard performing heart surgery now...without a thumb. I guess the joke's on him. Ha. Ha.

Willa, now recovered, wiped her mouth on her sleeve. "Where is he?" Her voice was an underwater echo.

"Woods by his house," Cam said.

Through the wall, underneath my bedroom floor, Arabella's Curse rattled in its tin coffin, thumping in time to my heartbeat.

"Is he still alive?" Willa pressed.

Cam whimpered. "I don't know."

"Well, which is it? Dead or alive?"

"I don't know!"

She looked to me for assistance, but I couldn't speak a word. My attention was riveted on my brother's throat. That *monster's* throat.

I turned my head from side to side, cracking my tense neck muscles.

Free me.

Grinding the heel of my palm against my eyes, I tried to drive out the relentless beat of the ruby. It would be so easy—

Love me.

To reach out and—

Feed me.

Crush his esophagus like a plastic cup.

"What are you doing?" Willa shrieked.

I blinked. She was staring at me. They were both staring at me.

"Freak," Willa muttered.

Little by little, the haze dispersed. Like an out-of-body-experience, I saw my hand suspended midway to Cam's throat. Shame seeped in. What was wrong with me? Was I really going to strangle my own brother?

If Cam was a monster, it was because I made him that way. How many times had I encouraged, even exploited, his explosive temper for personal gain? I trained my hotheaded brother like an attack dog, and now I was angry at him for doing his job.

I was the monster. I had to make it right.

My hand changed directions. I snatched Ben's severed thumb and pressed it into Willa's palm. She turned green and looked like she was going to faint.

"Put it on ice. Take it to the emergency room." I rose to my feet.

Her panicked eyes followed me to the doorway. "Where are you going?"

"To find Ben." Then I remembered my brother and turned around. "I just washed Cam's favorite sweater. It's on the top left drawer of his dresser. The green one with black stripes. Get it for him, will you? He's shivering."

Willa swallowed. "Okay."

I nodded. "I'll see you at the hospital."

"Ava, wait!" Willa reached into her pocket and tossed me a set of keys, which I caught one-handed. I arched a brow in question, but saw no trace of malice in her face. Only urgency and a shared purpose. "My car is faster," she said. "Hurry."

♦

The forest loomed under a colorless sky as I darted between the trees.

My sneakers slapped against the hard-packed dirt.

Branches clawed at my arms and snagged at my clothing.

The headlights of Willa's Range Rover—abandoned on the side of the road—doused the woods in an eerie flood of light.

I could've run off the face of the earth and had enough momentum to leap over the moon, but I halted in a clearing of ancient redwoods and listened.

A symphony of nocturnal noises assaulted my ears.

The hoot of an owl.

The swoosh of a possum's tail against a cluster of branches.

The scrape of a salamander's claws as it scampered up a tree trunk.

And slicing through the garbled static, beating weakly, but beating nonetheless, was the sound of a human heart.

CHAPTER 26

HEROES AND COWARDS

In the hospital waiting room, I drummed my fingers over a beat-up chessboard. A week ago, I was told I'd only have to wait five minutes before I could see Ben. Now they were still giving me the five-minute lie, and like a lovesick sucker, I was buying it.

I glowered at the wall clock. Five minutes segued into an hour and five minutes. Not that I was counting.

The receptionist behind the counter had her eyes trained on the flat screen mounted on the wall.

"Can I see him now?" I asked.

Without taking her eyes off the television, the receptionist replied, "Friends and family only."

"I'm a friend."

"Or so you think," she muttered.

"What?"

The receptionist pressed a finger to her lips and nodded to the TV. "Skylar's about to tell Aiden he's not her baby's daddy."

I turned to the flat screen where a woman with overflowing cleavage was locked in a screaming match with a man with biceps bigger than my head. "Yes he is," I said absently, "Now about my wait time—"

"What are you talking about? She's been sleeping with Aiden's evil twin, A.J., who's Baby Zooey's real father."

"Wrong! You missed yesterday's episode." I pointed to the television. Even though I had more pressing matters on my mind, I hated being contradicted. "Aiden *is* A.J. He'd been suffering from split personalities ever since his escape from that Iraqi POW camp—"

I stopped myself just in time. The fact that I knew this much about the Aiden/Skylar/A.J. love triangle meant I'd been waiting in this tiny room *way* too long.

Slumping in my chair, I crossed my arms petulantly over my chest. "It's been more than five minutes."

"Hmph." The receptionist shoved a handful of Corn Nuts in her mouth. The crunching grated on my nerves. Who knew Corn Nuts could be so annoying?

Sighing, I reached for my GED practice book. As I attacked a set of compound fractions, my thoughts trailed to Ben. He'd be so proud once I told him I'd finally signed up for the test. I flipped to the "Reading Comprehension" section, but the print blurred in a forest of black and white.

I opened my eyes and tried to focus on the passage before me.

"Call me Ishmael," I read, my lips moving along with the words. "Some years ago, having little or no money in my purse, and nothing particular to interest me on shore, I thought I would sail about a little…"

Just as Ben predicted, I became slowly drawn to Captain Ahab, who, in my opinion, was a rock star. Much like me. The fact that he walked with a limp only made him all the more relatable. He was a simple man with a simple goal. But his crew called him crazy and tried to sabotage him at every turn. They didn't know what it was like to want something so badly you'd give your life for it. Ahab had his white whale. I had my ruby.

"… and see the watery parts of the world." I slammed my GED book shut and assessed the casualty count in my own goals. With Willa almost drowned, Uncle Tav shanked, and at least one rat killed in my relentless pursuit of Arabella's Curse, I wondered if it was all worth it.

Whenever I was at the end of my rope, I used to believe all my problems would be solved once I found Arabella's Curse. Now I had Arabella's Curse and it wasn't doing me any damn good. The ruby could mend your broken bones and bring you back from the dead, but it did nothing to mend a broken heart.

The last time I saw Ben, he was strapped to a gurney and being wheeled into surgery. Due to my quick thinking and even quicker driving, the doctors were able to reattach his thumb and stop most of the internal bleeding, but the damage to his hand was permanent. Ben would make a passable hitchhiker, but he could kiss his dreams of becoming a surgeon goodbye.

I may be the girl with nine lives, but right now, I was a black cat in the lives of others. Everyone I'd befriended or loved ended up in the emergency room. My friendship was racking up a body count.

Ben never did finish reading *Moby Dick*. Judging by the way the receptionist guarded the trauma ward like a bouncer at a nightclub, I might have to read the rest of the book alone.

Just as I was wondering if Captain Ahab's story ended with a happily ever after, the doors swung open and Uncle Tav limped toward me with the assistance of a mahogany cane. The cane, in combination with a daring purple blazer and black cashmere scarf, made him look like a cross between Willy Wonka and Mr. Peanut. If I hadn't seen him fall apart with my own eyes, I'd have taken him for a man without a care in the world.

"What are you doing here?" I asked as he drew closer.

He patted me on the head. "Visiting," he said, moving past me to the reception window.

Winking at the giggling receptionist, Uncle Tav took the clipboard and scribbled his name.

I peeked over his shoulder at the sign-in sheet. "Visiting who?"

"Our unfortunate Mr. Wolcott," he said, matter-of-factly. "Is that a chess set? Do you mind if I borrow it?"

Without waiting for my answer, he swiped the box from under my arm.

"Here you go, Mr. Tavistock," the receptionist said, handing him an orange wristband. "You can go straight in."

"Wait, wait!" My mind was reeling. "How do you know Ben?"

In response, he lifted his arm and poked at his side. "We met while I was getting my stitches removed. We got to talking. Come to think of it, I did most of the talking. The lad couldn't really talk, what with all the tubing up his nose and down his throat. Nasty business, that. Ah well." He shrugged. "Better not get hurt again, Sweet Pea, because I gave Wolcott your hospital discount."

I bit my lower lip. I guess it was the least we could do considering Ben was in the hospital because of Cam, and Cam put Ben in the hospital because of me.

"How'd he look?" I asked.

"His hand pains him terribly and he can't move his, you know." He wiggled his thumb and sighed. "What a tragedy! The boy's crippled for life. He can't adjust the settings on his bed, can't work a remote, can't thumb wrestle, can't bite his thumb if he wanted to try out for *Romeo and Juliet*, can't watch Thumb Wars on YouTube without going into post-traumatic shock, can't hitchhike..."

My eyes watered. "He can still hitchhike."

"Ah, there, there, pet." He tipped my chin up and brushed away a tear with his thumb. "Not everyone heals as fast as you.

357

But he'll heal. Just give him time."

I wiped my nose on my sleeve. "W-what do you guys talk about?"

"Oh, this and that." Uncle Tav scratched his nose and studied the titanium skull on the pommel of his cane. "His mother mostly. I check in on her now and then."

"You go to his house? You just met him!"

"Sure, I pick up his mother's groceries since she's not fit to drive to town. I check the power generators out back and make sure the meat in his freezer doesn't spoil."

He smiled at my expression. "Don't look so shocked. I would do any of these things for someone in need, but in Wolcott's case, well, I can't help taking a shine to the lad."

Picking up the chess set, Uncle Tav sidestepped past me. "Now, if you'll excuse me, I don't want to keep Wolcott waiting."

I touched his arm. "I've been waiting too. Did he... Did he say anything about me?"

"Oh believe me, Sweet Pea," Uncle Tav said. "He had plenty to say about you."

"Huh?"

Uncle Tav regarded me beneath furrowed brows. "The doghouse is a lonely place, isn't it?"

I kicked at an imaginary spot on the industrial carpet.

He tapped my cheek affectionately. "I'll put in a good word for you."

"If you can remind him how I saved his life, I'll be very grate—"

Before I could finish my sentence, Uncle Tav took me by the shoulders and physically moved me aside like a chess piece. Giving my head a final pat, he limped away.

I poked my head through the double doors. "Do you see Ben often?" I called after him.

Uncle Tav raised a hand, but didn't turn around. "Not often!"

With my mind in a whirlwind, I slumped against the reception counter, trying to make sense of it all. Why was Uncle Tav acting so strange? And why did he keep patting me on the head?

"Do you know?" I asked the receptionist.

She brought a finger to her lips and shot me a dirty look.

"Yeah, yeah, I know. Shut up, right?" I glanced down at the sign-in sheet, spotting Uncle Tav's pointy signature. Absently, I flipped to yesterday's page and scanned down the list of names. I didn't expect to find anything interesting, but there, in the same pointy scrawl: *Ian Tavistock*.

I flipped to the day before yesterday.

Ian Tavistock.

And the day before that.

Ian Tavistock.

◆

During the thumb-severing crisis, Dad had been out of town. Again. When he finally came home a week later, he was all: "Why didn't anybody call me?"

Okay.

So.

I called him. Uncle Tav called him. Willa—who didn't even *know* him—took a picture of the thumb and sent it to him, which wasn't weird or anything.

Once I filled him in on the nitty-gritty, Dad didn't take the news of Cam's latest felony well. I studied the vein bulging on his forehead and wondered if this might not be the best time to remind him to watch his blood pressure.

"Stupid idiot!" Dad glowered at my brother. "What were you thinking?"

Huddled on the edge of the sofa, Cam kept his eyes fixed on his shoes. "I-I wasn't thinking..."

"You got that right!" Dad paced back and forth, his rage growing with every step.

I glanced at the cookie box on my lap. The ruby rapped against its tin coffin like a bird pecking its way out. I patted the lid and peeked through my lashes to see if Cam or Dad noticed the anticipation lighting me up like a paper lantern. I might as well have been a fly on the wall for all the attention they paid me.

"What kind of sick person cuts off someone's thumb?"

Cam buried his face in his hands. "It seemed like a good idea at the time."

"You're lucky Wolcott hasn't spoken to the police. If he does... *When* he does, you're looking at a felony. You're looking at time. We have no money. We can't buy his silence. I can't do a damn thing for you. You've screwed yourself! You've screwed your family!"

Cam cringed. "I'm sorry..."

"Sorry? You're sorry? Sorry won't keep you out of jail!"

"But it's been a week." Cam wiped his nose on his sleeve. "And he hasn't said anything to anybody. If he doesn't talk now, he won't talk ever."

Dad halted in front of Cam. "You sound sure."

"Pretty sure." Cam sat up straighter.

"*Pretty* sure?" Dad cocked his head to the side.

Cam attempted a weak smile.

Dad backhanded Cam across the face. The sound of the smack echoed across the study.

I gasped.

"Worthless."

Smack.

Cam shielded his head against the rain of blows.

Smack Smack.

"Moron!"

"Stop it!" I rushed into the fray. "Stop it!"

Kneeling beside Cam, I assessed his face for damage. He flinched away, hugged his brawny arms around himself, and rocked back and forth. Other than a redder than usual flush on his cheek, Cam didn't seem to be hurt. At least not physically.

I whirled on our father. "You didn't need to hit him! He said he was sorry!"

Dad flung open the window, letting in some much needed ventilation. "He's always sorry. Who ends up cleaning up the mess? Me!"

It was on the tip of my tongue to say, *Actually, Dad...it's usually been me. You were out of town.* I kept my mouth shut.

"As for you," he said, pointing at me. "Where were you when all this was happening?"

"Let's just say..." I thought about the knife slicing through my throat like warm butter and the flames roasting me alive. "I went to Hell and back."

I picked up the cookie tin and held it out to him. "I got you a gift while I was there."

"What's this?"

"The answer to all our problems."

Shaking his head skeptically, Dad sat on the edge of his desk. "I'm not in the mood for riddles." He took the box anyway and studied it with a frown.

The desk lamp flickered as he turned the box around and around. His index finger rested on the hook-shaped clasp and my

362

heart skipped a beat.

"Open it…" I urged.

Unhooking the clasp, his thumb inched the lid open—

I watched him with bated breath. It was finally going to happen. All my blood, sweat, and toil had led up to this moment. Once he saw the ruby, we could start over again. We could be happy. Our broken family could be brand new.

With the lid only midway open, Dad shut it with a *click*. His fingers drummed against the tin.

My heart lurched to a stop.

"Ava?" Dad studied me with a strange expression. "You're Ben's friend."

"Yeah, I guess." I watched him play with the clasp. What did this have to do with anything?

"Good friends?"

"Uh-huh." Sweat trickled down the back of my neck. It was getting hot in here. Maybe he should've opened the window all the way. "Aren't you going to…" I mimed the opening of the box. "No hurry or anything."

Absently, Dad lifted the lid again—

I raked my nails on my denim-clad thighs.

The lid slammed shut. "More than just friends?"

What the hell? Why was he so interested in my relationship with Ben all of a sudden? Didn't he realize what he held in his hands? I willed myself not to scream "OPEN THE DAMN

BOX!" at the top of my lungs.

I fidgeted like a heroin addict on withdrawal. "We had a thing. I can tell you all about it after you open my present."

"*Had* a thing?" Dad pressed. "Why past tense?"

"We had a falling out, okay? We sort of...broke up."

"Over what?"

I'd rather go back to Hell and join my mother in an eternal game of hide-and-seek than tell my father about the sex tape. What was a nice way of saying "none of your business"?

"No matter," Dad said. And to my horror, he set the box down on his ink blotter. "Once you make up—"

"It's not that easy." Last time I'd checked, Ben was taking great pains to avoid me.

Dad dashed away my doubts with a wave of his hand. "Nonsense. Young people break up and make up all the time. Once things are rosy again, maybe you can, I dunno...talk to him?"

I glanced at Cam, who ducked his head. He couldn't even look me in the eye.

As my preoccupation with the ruby dissipated, I became aware of the turn in our conversation. "And what exactly..." I licked my lips. "What do you want me to say to Ben?"

"There was no harm done, right?" He attempted a strained smile. "So why name names?"

The bile rose in my throat. "No harm done? He's still in the hospital."

"But he'll recover."

"He lost a thumb."

"And you told me the doctors were able to reattach it."

"He won't forget."

"I don't expect him to forget." Dad knelt before me. "I just want his..."

"Silence?" Now I really did feel sick. I looked around for the trash can.

He tucked a strand of hair behind my ear. "I'm not asking for much."

"No." I shook my head. He was supposed to open the box and tell me he was wrong about me. Tell me he loved me. I'd gone through a lot of shit to give him Arabella's Curse. I was tapped out. We weren't having this conversation. "No. No. No. I won't do it."

"But Ava—"

"You don't understand! I've already done enough to Ben. I can't... This is like salting the wound. He'll hate me forever. I won't. I won't. No!"

Seeing how skittish I'd become, Dad placed a gentle hand behind my neck and pressed his forehead against mine. "Listen, Ava. Listen to me! If Ben goes to the police, your brother goes to jail. And what did I always tell you?"

I let out a ragged breath. "Watch after Cam."

"Because the idiot can't look out for himself."

Cam sunk lower in his seat, his Adam's apple bobbing up and down as he struggled to keep his tears at bay. His crying would only enrage Dad.

"But what about Ben?" I asked. "You're his friend too. He looked up to you."

Dad sighed. "What happened to Wolcott was…unfortunate. And don't think I wouldn't have done everything in my power to help him out if the situation were different. But you have to remember, Ava. He's not family." He clasped my hands. "Cam is. We're family. We have to look out for each other."

Family? Strange hearing that word from Dad's lips. I turned to Cam, who had returned to rocking back and forth, reduced to a whimpering puppy by Dad's callous words.

I stared down at my pleading father. The rose-colored lenses were cracked, the illusion dashed. In that moment, I saw Dad as he really was: a coward.

There was just one more thing I had to know. "When are you planning to visit Ben?"

Passing a hand over his tired face, Dad said, "I just got back from my trip."

"Will you visit Ben in the hospital?"

Dad hesitated. I thought about Uncle Tav, who barely knew Ben, visiting every single day and my fury grew.

"Will you?" I repeated stonily.

"I don't want to disturb him. Given the circumstances—"

I stood up in a daze. "I'm tired." As tired as anyone who'd been fighting a battle only to realize the cause wasn't worth fighting for.

Dad seized my arm. "But we're not finished."

I jerked my arm away. "I am. I-I need to…" I needed to get out of that room. I needed air. I needed to get away from him. "I need to get to bed."

"Sleep on it." Dad rose to his feet. "We'll talk in the morning, yes?"

I did not respond.

Tapping Cam on the shoulder, I motioned for him to come with me. Cam sniffled and looped around Dad to join me at the door.

At the threshold, I turned around. Dad stood in the middle of his study. With his sweater half-tucked into his trousers and blond hair a disheveled mess, he resembled a scarecrow destined for the trash heap. I used to believe my father was made of steel; tonight I saw he was made of straw.

His eyes flickered over my face hopefully. "You've changed your mind?"

"Yes." I said sadly, "I've changed my mind."

I strolled to his desk and snatched up the tin box.

CHAPTER 27

RUBY RED REDEMPTION

Squinting up at Ben's bedroom window, I blew hot air into my frozen palms. No movement. No light. It looked like Ben wasn't home—or so he would have me believe.

Released from the hospital just two days ago, Ben was in no condition to be gallivanting around town. The only place he could be was in bed.

Through the perpetual whirl of the Wolcott's industrial-strength power generator and the static garble of their television set, I could hear two human heartbeats.

The first floor light switched on and a vacuum cleaner roared to life. Edging myself into the shadows of a nearby juniper bush, I watched Mrs. Wolcott hoover the living room.

Whereas his mother's heartbeat was as steady as a metronome despite her aerobic vacuuming, Ben's heart galloped at an erratic tempo. Either he was on a treadmill or something was wrong. Very wrong.

I snatched up a handful of grit and heaved. Pebbles pelted the windowpane like BBs, and yet still no sign of movement from within. The most obvious scenario: Ben was still avoiding me. Perhaps indefinitely. Maybe I should respect his wishes and give him some space? Who knows? Given enough time, Ben might want to speak to me again. I tended to forget that some people's hearts were as cryptic as a crossword puzzle. While my sledgehammer approach may have worked on granite tombs, I needed patience when mending relationships. To earn Ben's forgiveness, I needed blueprints.

Hoisting my backpack over my shoulders, I closed my eyes and attempted my first foray into patience. An owl hooted into the night while I fidgeted on my feet. On the whole, I'd say I was doing rather well with this…this waiting around. Yup. I could do this with my hands tied behind my back until Ben came around and—

Screw patience.

I launched myself at the ivy-covered trellis and scampered up the side of the wall as soundlessly as a lizard.

At the top, I peered through the latched window. Ben was lying on his back, staring at the glow-in-the-dark periodic table tacked over his bed. The poster bathed his face in blue and purple hues and cast an eerie glow across his bare torso. His injured right hand, encased in the kind of metal contraption you'd see in a sci-fi movie, rested over his bandaged midriff. Sometime during his hospital stay, the nurses had shaved his head so they could stitch up the gash on his scalp.

I rapped my knuckles against the pane, but Ben ignored me. Left with no choice, I slipped one hand under the window's edge and heaved. The latch splintered from the sill.

"Would you believe," I said, clambering over the ledge and landing nimbly on my feet. "I just dropped by to borrow a cup of sugar?"

My lame joke collided with a wall of silence.

I cleared my throat. "This was the only way I could get you to see me."

Shifting awkwardly on my feet, I waited for Ben to order me to leave. He kept his eyes stubbornly trained on the periodic table, his face an indecipherable mask beneath the bruises and a split lip.

"Are you...are you well?" I asked, kneeling by his bedside.

Ben turned away from me. I touched his bony shoulder. His skin was hot and clammy.

Gripped by alarm, I flipped him forcibly on his back and felt his forehead. He was burning up. "Why didn't you call me?"

Ben grunted and tried to roll away again, but my hand on his shoulder nailed him to the mattress.

"Why didn't you call anyone? Why didn't you ask for help?" Angry tears spilled down my cheeks as I saw the way he was cradling his hand. He'd been like this for two days, suffering in unimaginable agony. Suffering alone.

371

"Are you taking anything for the pain?"

"Oxycontin," he choked.

My eyes swept over his bare nightstand. "Where's the bottle?"

"In the…" Violent shivers raked his emaciated body. "Tra…trash."

I crawled to the wastebasket and fished out the orange bottle. I didn't need to count the pills to know that all of them were still there.

"Why are you doing this to yourself?" I rattled the bottle in his face and fought the urge to force-feed him every single one of those pills.

His dark eyes clouded in pain, but in the haze, there was a defiant light. "So I won't f-f-for…forget."

I set the pill bottle back on the nightstand. When I'd hurt my leg, I wanted to keep the scar so I would always remember how close I'd come to failing and how I must never repeat the same mistakes again. Ben refused to take his pills for the same reason: I'd hurt him once and he'd forgiven me only to pay for it later. Like me, he would never make the same mistake twice.

Fumbling with my backpack's zipper, I took out the tin box. My hands trembled as I lifted Arabella's Curse out by its silver chain.

Although it must have caused him unbearable pain, Ben sat up, his eyes widening at the sight of the ruby. "How did you—"

Taking hold of his injured hand, I eased off the metal brace.

As I unraveled the layers of bandages, Ben sucked in his breath and looked like he was about to pass out from the pain, but he didn't protest or try to snatch his hand away.

The damage to his hand sickened my stomach. Cam had not only sliced off Ben's thumb, but he'd also taken pains to break every single one of Ben's fingers. It would've been kinder to cut off the entire hand rather than reset the broken bones.

"It won't hurt anymore," I said, pressing the ruby's serrated edge to the pad of his forefinger. "I promise."

Fed by blood, Arabella's Curse glowed, casting a lovely red light over the halogens and transition metals on the periodic table. I studied the light, knowing that a few seconds was all it took for the ruby to work its magic.

Setting the ruby on the nightstand, I turned to Ben.

The bruises and cuts on his face had already vanished. Ben unraveled his bandages and probed his ribs. The broken bones had mended.

He turned his once-injured hand this way and that, flexing his fingers one by one. His eyes flickered over me and a frown tugged at his brows.

I'd seen that same strange expression on his face before, eons ago, when I'd fixed his car and handed him the keys. He'd looked lost that day, like I'd knocked his world out of alignment and taken something very important away from him.

I had an entire speech prepared for the reasons I did what I did and why he should find it within his heart to forgive me.

Dispensing with words entirely, I laid my head on Ben's lap.

The rest was up to him.

Ben remained motionless, and I could only wonder what might be going through his head. I'd been so naïve, believing I could climb into his room uninvited, fix his injuries, and expect to be forgiven.

In the basement, the power generator purred.

In the kitchen, Mrs. Wolcott hummed a happy tune as she rinsed the dishes in the sink, her heartbeat as steady and strong as her son's.

I sensed his hand hover over me.

My body tensed. I held my breath and waited for him to push me off and tell me to get the hell out of his room and out of his life.

And then, quite unexpectedly, his hand rested gently on top of my head and his fingers combed through my tangled hair.

His thumb—the one Cam had cut off—caressed my cheek, wiping my tears away.

I closed my eyes, afraid to open them in case this was all a dream, and smiled.

◆

When I woke up in the morning, someone had clicked the

374

mute button on the world.

Something was missing. This I knew even before I opened my eyes.

Stifling a yawn, my sleep-addled brain deduced the source of the quiet as the absence of the monotonous buzz of the Wolcott's power generator.

That must be it. The power generator had finally short-circuited.

My lips curled into a wicked smile as memories of last night came flooding in with the weak splotches of sunshine. Ben's breath hot against my neck, his lips traveling down the flat slope of my stomach. His hand on my thigh, marveling at the smooth skin where a monstrous scar used to be. His face buried in my hair, whispering my name.

I rolled over, the sheets tangling around my bare legs, ready to pounce on a sleeping Ben for seconds. No, wait... Another wicked grin. Thirds.

I rolled over to an empty mattress.

Ben was gone.

Rubbing the sleep from my eyes, I told myself not to overreact. Ben was always so anal about keeping the power running that he'd probably gone down to the basement with toolbox in hand.

Swinging my legs to the ground, I picked my panties up off the floor and slipped them on. But it was while I was scooping up the rest of my clothing that my eyes lighted on Ben's nightstand and my blood turned to ice.

There were three things missing that morning.

The sound of the Wolcott's power generator.

Ben.

And Arabella's Curse.

CHAPTER 28

TWO HEARTS BEATING

I stumbled down the stairs, pausing midway to make sure I hadn't slipped on my blouse inside out. Taking a deep breath, I willed the blood to stop pounding in my ears and listened.

The sound of two human heartbeats calmed my overactive imagination.

Of course Ben hadn't left me. Knowing his inquisitive nature, he probably wanted to examine Arabella's Curse more closely and had gone to another room of the house so as not to wake me.

Mrs. Wolcott's heartbeat came from the kitchen. The second beat originated from the basement and could only belong to Ben.

Having never been invited on a formal house tour, I assumed Ben had his basement decked out like Dr. Frankenstein's laboratory and was putting Arabella's Curse through a series of scientific experiments as we speak.

The savory aroma of frying bacon wafted through the living room and crowded out the rest of the morning's residual paranoia.

I raced down the remaining steps and burst into the kitchen.

Mrs. Wolcott, looking like a model ripped from the pages of a '50s *Vogue* with her red shirtdress and black peep-toe pumps, was humming "Oh, What a Beautiful Morning" over the stove.

She was alone.

Halting shyly on the threshold, I did a last-minute smooth down of my wild sex hair. When I'd been with Drake, I was in the window after midnight and out the window by sunrise. I didn't usually stick around for breakfast with his parents. Talk about your awkward moments.

"Good morning, Ava." Mrs. Wolcott smiled over her shoulder. "Will you set the table? You remember where we keep the silverware?"

"I... Ah... Sure."

Wasn't she going to ask me what I was doing spending the night in her son's room? Or if we used condoms? Then again, maybe I should be jumping for joy that she was oblivious to everything except breakfast.

Like a sleepwalker, I went to the first drawer and fumbled with the forks.

"Four places?" I remembered how she'd freaked when Ben had forgotten to set a place for his brother Jason.

Mrs. Wolcott piled a plate high with fried eggs, bacon, and grilled tomatoes while simultaneously setting a kettle on the stove to boil. "Just three."

Three? Well, it *had* been a long time since I'd last seen Ben's mother. Maybe she was cured of her creepy delusions that Jason still lived.

"Dig in." She set a plate in front of me. "I'm only having coffee."

I hesitated before sitting down. "Shouldn't we wait for Ben?"

"Ben won't be joining us, but he asked me to take good care of you and feed you well. He said you may be distraught when you woke up this morning."

I dropped my fork.

She tipped her head to study the sudden change in my expression, and the filmy glaze over her eyes dispelled any notions I had about Mrs. Wolcott being cured of her insanity. "But you're not distraught, are you, dear?"

I most certainly was distraught. In a moment, I was going to freak the fuck out.

Licking my lips, I tried to keep my voice steady. "What else did he say?"

"That he's sorry and hopes you'll understand."

"Where did he go?"

"You know my Ben. He's always out and about. Never a word to me."

Flipping on the faucet, Mrs. Wolcott rinsed the frying pan and hummed. I stumbled out of the chair and dashed to the window. Ben's Chevy was parked in the driveway.

"But his car's still here…"

Nothing made sense. Ben couldn't be gone. Two hearts. There were two heartbeats inside the house. I could hear them thumping. Or was it my own heart stampeding like a herd of wild elephants?

"He got a ride from a friend," Mrs. Wolcott said matter-of-factly.

"Friend?" I watched Mrs. Wolcott squirt a generous amount of green apple-scented dish soap onto a sponge and attack the frying pan. How could she still care about the cleanliness of her kitchen when my world was falling apart? "What did this *friend* look like?"

"He was beautiful. Almost perfect…" She turned a slender hand under the water. "Like he was carved from granite by Michelangelo's chisel."

I tapped my chin dimple. "Did he have one of these?"

"Deep as the Grand Canyon."

Mrs. Wolcott lowered her voice in a conspiratorial whisper. "Between you and me, I never cared for the man. His manners were impeccable, but it's his eyes I didn't trust. Black as the devil. Felt like he saw into my soul and wanted a piece of it."

"'Never cared?' You mean to say you've seen this…this man hanging around Ben more than once?"

"Too often for my liking." Mrs. Wolcott returned to her dishes. "Boy goes off to college and makes the strangest friends."

That was over a year ago. Ben and Uncle Tav had known each other for over a year! I recalled their stiff handshake in the hospital waiting room and how they'd taken extra precautions to appear as strangers.

Gripping the countertop, I clamped my eyes shut.

It was all a lie.

It was Ben who took me to Eckhart House. Ben who fed me bits and pieces of ruby lore. Ben who showed me the sixteenth-century illustrations of the witch Eliza Darrow's burning and resurrection.

What about the picture of Arabella Eckhart on her wedding day? Surely, Arabella's uncanny resemblance to my mother hadn't escaped Ben's notice. He'd already made the connection long before he came to my doorstep under the pretext of helping my dad with his book when the only person he wanted to see, the only person of interest to him was…

Me.

"I find it hard to believe that you would know so much about Arabella's Curse and not try to go after it."

"I tried." Ben glanced up at Eckhart House. "Once."

"I guess you failed or else you wouldn't be here now."

If at first you don't succeed, find someone who can.

He knew I had the ruby in my blood. He knew I could handle myself against my mother, Arabella Eckhart.

He'd seen how much I had to prove, how much I needed to

impress my dad.

Like a matchmaker between a girl and her destiny, all Ben needed to do was plant the seed. Cultivate my obsession. Make me want the ruby as badly as he did.

Ben never intended to keep me away from Eckhart House. Quite the opposite: he needed me to do all the dirty work while he sat back and reaped the ruby.

But for what purpose? Money? So Uncle Tav could pay him a handsome reward? Ben didn't strike me as the greedy type. So what could he possibly want with Arabella's Curse?

The shriek of the kettle drew me back to the reality of the Wolcott's tidy kitchen.

Mrs. Wolcott touched me lightly on the arm. "Excuse me, dear…"

I watched her take the kettle off the burner, my eyes boring into the pleats of her red skirt.

Three place settings.

One for me.

One for her.

And the other place at the table?

"I should've never agreed to it but it seemed to make her happy, building a shrine to his memory, keeping Jason frozen in time."

Jason.

His death drove his mother mad, and it fell to Ben to take care of her.

All the clues were there: Ben's many sick days from work, the excuses, the excessive lengths to which he would go to protect his privacy.

Even our first kiss had been tinged with his strange behavior. Memories of that night flashed before my eyes. Shunned from home, cold and alone, I'd climbed into his window looking for sanctuary.

The storm had blown out the electricity…

"I have to fix the generator."

"What? Now? Couldn't this wait till morning?"

"It can't," he choked. *In the ghoulish light cast by the flashlight, his features betrayed a struggle. "There are things I can't tell you yet…"*

Nothing could stand in the way of Ben and that bloody power generator. Judging by the way he practically threw me out of his house, you'd think keeping the generator running was a matter of life or death.

Mrs. Wolcott switched off the fire. In the absence of the screeching kettle, the twin heartbeats popped back on my radar.

Now the generator was dead. Both Ben and Uncle Tav were gone and my ruby with them. But before Ben left Eckhart for good, he had a son's promise to fulfill.

My fingernails dug into the granite countertop as I felt myself sinking…sinking…

I knew now why Ben wanted Arabella's Curse.

The second heartbeat sounded closer now.

Lub. Dub.

And stronger.

Lub. Dub.

Slowly, ever so slowly, the door creaked open. I willed myself to turn around.

Mrs. Wolcott's smile broadened as a little boy stumbled toward us like a marionette learning to walk for the first time without strings. His eyes were black and lifeless; his skin slack and a sickening gray. He cocked his head to the side, not focusing on anyone or anything in particular.

His mother drew him into her arms, oblivious to the stench of formaldehyde seeping through Jason's pores. Happily humming, she plucked the icicles out of his hair and rubbed at his frostbitten fingers, waiting for him to thaw. "Are you hungry, baby?"

Jason looked to me and nodded.

"Why Ava..." Mrs. Wolcott studied me, genuine concern creasing her brow. "You don't look at all well. Do sit down and eat something. Maybe later, you and Jason could play."

CHAPTER 29

SIN IS A BLOODSTAIN

Light from Dad's study doused the hallway in a flood of yellow. Pausing outside the door, I pressed my forehead against the wall and listened to the sound of bristles scraping against carpet.

Was Dad *cleaning*? At midnight? Stranger things had been known to happen. Like Ben keeping his brother's corpse on ice for an entire year and resurrecting him with the ruby he stole from me. Clutching my stomach, I had a flashback to this morning. I'd fled from the kitchen and retched into Mrs. Wolcott's rosebushes. Let's just say, I didn't stay for breakfast.

Yup.

Ben really *screwed* me, both literally and figuratively. Not that I was bitter or planning to castrate him with my butterfly knife or anything.

I peeled my forehead from the wall and peeked through the crack in the door. Dad was on all fours, dragging a brush back and forth over a red wine stain. As much as I longed for a gargle of mouthwash and a good cry in the shower, my feet carried me into the study. With the windows shut, the room reeked of alcohol and lye.

"Dad?"

Scrub. Scrub. Scrub.

Either he hadn't heard me or was giving me the silent treatment for refusing to help Cam. If he kept this up, he was going to scrape a hole in the carpet. Us Nolans sure have a thing for clean floors.

"Dad?" I cleared my throat. "Uh, Dad? I think you already made that stain your bitch."

Scrub. Scrub. Scrub.

"Dad?"

My eyes swept over the collection of empty gin and vodka bottles on his desk. There was probably more alcohol in his bloodstream than on the floor.

"Fine! Don't answer me. I've been through too much crap today to deal with your bullshit too!"

He tightened his grip on the brush and I got a gruesome gander at his raw knuckles. Anger segued into alarm.

"Dad!" My hand hovered over his shoulder. I'd barely touched him when Dad whirled around, took one look at my face, and yelped in terror.

With my smudged mascara, eyes red from weeping, and crazy

Medusa locks, I knew I wasn't a treat to look at, but *geez*, I didn't warrant this kind of reaction.

"Helena?" His voice teetered on a scream.

"Um, *noooooo*." Frankly, this "I'm not my mother" mix-up was getting old. I tapped my chest. "Me Ava." And poked him on the shoulder. "You drunk."

Instead of snapping him back to reality, my touch set him off.

"Stay away from me!" Shoving me away, he scrambled behind his desk. The bucket clattered to the floor, dousing the carpet and my shoes with soapy water.

"What's the matter with you?" I shrieked, watching him grope for his swivel chair and heave himself to his feet.

Clawing ineffectually at his desk drawer, he muttered, "You're supposed to be dead. You're dead—" He yanked the drawer open and withdrew a gun.

Dad fumbled with the revolver's chamber and tried to cock it open. The revolver looked like a tarnished relic from the Old West. Dad couldn't have purchased it from a modern gun dealer or even one of the many pawn shops around Eckhart, which only dealt in run-of-the-mill firearms. This gun belonged in a museum, and the only person I knew who could procure such a rare and valuable artifact was—

I glanced at the coffee table. An extra wineglass sat untouched next to a folded handkerchief with the initials I.T. stitched in the corner.

Dad had a visitor this morning.

"Did Uncle Tav give you the gun? What did he say to you? What did he *do* to you?"

Maybe Uncle Tav slipped something in his drink. Whatever transpired between the two had pushed Dad over the edge of sanity, and now I had to clean up the mess.

Oh Uncle Tav. Just wait until I get my hands on you!

Shaking from rage, I stepped forward.

Dad backed into his bookshelf. "Stay away. Stay away. *Stay away!*" He groped for a handful of bullets stashed in his desk drawer, but his hands shook so violently that the bullets *plinked* against the tabletop and rolled onto the floor.

With a heavy heart, I watched his clumsy fingers scramble for the remaining bullets.

My mother, headless, burnt to ashes, was no longer a threat. Now my most immediate concern was my father trying to shoot me in the face. What a life.

Holding my hands up to show I meant him no harm, I approached him cautiously. Before Dad could chamber the first bullet, I seized his wrists. He uttered a cry of pain as I pried the gun away and held it behind my back.

"No. No. No." He pushed and kicked at me, his eyes shifting around the study like a trapped animal. "You're dead. Why? Why won't you leave me alone?"

"Listen to me," I said. "I'm not Helena. I'm your daughter,

Ava, not your wife. Your wife is dead. She left us when I was eight and got herself killed hitchhiking—"

"No body."

At first it sounded like he was saying "nobody'. Then it dawned on me that he meant "no *body*."

"No body. No body. They never found a body..."

"Coyotes, remember? The police said a shallow grave was bound to attract animals—"

"It was *not* a shallow grave!"

"Of course it was," I lied, determined to uphold the original reports. Something told me this wasn't the time to mention my many run-ins with my supposedly dead mother.

Taking him gently by the elbow, I steered him into the swivel chair.

"Now why don't you sit down." I sounded eerily like Mrs. Wolcott. "And I'll brew us a nice strong pot of coffee. Would you like that?"

"Not a shallow grave," Dad repeated.

"Sandwiches," I said, ignoring him. "How does grilled cheese and tomato sound? I'll even cut off the crust. Just the way you like it."

"No body. Not a shallow grave."

Dad was starting to creep me out. "What are you talking about?"

Haunted eyes bored into mine. "I buried her deep."

◆

I staggered to the couch and plopped down. Too much. First Ben and his twisted secrets and now this? Too much devastation in one day makes Ava a very unhappy girl.

"Ava, Ava." Dad's voice broke. "I've disappointed you, haven't I?"

What an odd thing to say at a time like this. Disappointed? Get in line. Who *hasn't* disappointed me? Cam. Willa. Uncle Tav. Ben. Now Dad was going for his second—no, third round.

It occurred to me that I seriously needed a vacation from these people. A normal life. That was what I needed. I should be applying to colleges and prepping for Grad Nite instead of listening to my father's murder confession.

Dad slumped in his desk chair like he was shrinking into nothing. At the moment, he didn't look like he could beat me at arm-wrestling, much less take down my freakishly strong and impossible-to-kill mother.

"It was *you?*" Shock and disgust made my tongue especially thick. "You killed her?"

"We were having an argument." Dad plucked a stray bullet from his ink blotter and absently rolled it between his thumb and forefinger. "Do you remember?"

I nodded.

I was there.

The night my mother disappeared, I was barricaded in my

390

room with my face buried in the pillow. The waves crashed against the pier pilings, the wind howled through the sand dunes, and my parents screamed at each other in the kitchen.

They'd argued over everything back then: my mother's erratic behavior, how she'd disappear for days at a time without a word, how she tried to drown me in the bathtub.

But tonight, their fighting was especially vicious and they snarled like a pair of killer hounds.

As the plates crashed to the floor, I clamped my eyes shut and hummed "Deck the Halls." I thought about how Cam was enjoying soccer camp and about Christmas and the shiny presents under the tree in the living room.

Most of my gifts were from Uncle Tav.

My parent's argument was about Uncle Tav.

"You're still sleeping with him, aren't you?"

"Deck the halls with boughs of holly…"

"Every chance I get!"

"Fa la la la la…"

"Cheating bitch!"

"…la la la la."

There followed an ear-splitting crash. I held my breath, listening to the shuffle of feet and the roar of a car engine in the driveway below.

When I stepped into the kitchen the next morning, Dad was on his hands and knees, scrubbing a spotless tile floor.

I'd glanced down the hall to my parents' bedroom. The door was shut. My eyes watered from the stench of bleach. "Where's Mom?"

Dad ignored me.

Scrub. Scrub. Scrub.

"Dad?"

Dunking his brush in the bucket, he gave me a cursory glance over his shoulder. Dark circles fringed his eyes. He looked like he hadn't slept all night.

"She's left us." His eyes rested on my chin dimple. A dark squall clouded his face. He turned around and resumed scrubbing. "Go back to bed."

A week later, when my mother still hadn't returned home, Dad went to the police and reported his wife missing.

"You look so much like her..." Dad's voice sliced across the ten-year gap, dragging me back to the present. "Same nose, same lips, same infuriating smile. Same eyes. Watching. Always watching. Every time I turn around, you're there. *She's* there. Even when I sleep. *Especially* when I sleep. Your face. Her face. In my dreams."

Picking up another stray bullet, he added. "You remind me of Ian too."

"You knew. All this time... You *knew* I wasn't your daughter?"

"Not always. Not until she told me that very night. Though I should have known before. Chin dimples—"

"Never lie." I tried to laugh it off, but the laugh dissolved into the beginnings of a sob. I shifted my eyes away and counted to ten. "When you pulled me out of that tub…"

"I loved you then," he said softly. "Because you were mine."

"And now?"

Dad arranged the bullets in a tidy line. "You're Ian's."

I nodded. All in the family, right? And I wasn't family. Everything I'd been fighting for had been for nothing. Even if I'd given him Arabella's Curse, he still wouldn't love me. I was a living, breathing reminder of his place in his brother's shadow.

As for what he did to my mother: the very idea that Dad even *thought* he killed her was hard to swallow. Arabella's Curse practically made her invincible. Yet he'd managed to knock her out and cart her body to the Mojave Desert for burial. The whole thing didn't make sense, unless…

"Dad, remember all those weekends Mom used to disappear? Where did she go?"

"I found a receipt for Joe's Hideaway in her purse once." He set the last bullet down and rubbed his eyes. "And a ticket stub from The Arcade in her pocket."

"Eckhart." My heart skipped a beat. "She came to Eckhart?"

Dad nodded.

My mother used to lie about feeling fatigued and needing some time off at a secluded spa to rejuvenate. I'd always thought she was full of shit, but now I saw that in her own twisted way, she was telling the truth. She did leave us to rejuvenate and she returned to us stronger, keener, and twice as insane. In fact, the night she tried to drown me occurred a few days after her return from one of these mysterious trips.

Arabella's Curse.

All roads led back to the ruby, which I now knew she kept at Eckhart House. With this realization, a frightening new possibility seized me, and I touched my throat, searching for the fatal cut that ended my life. Even though my fingers probed solid skin, my fears were far from alleviated.

What if one cut just wasn't enough? A ruby that could resurrect the dead and revive the sick sounded like a miracle. But miracles came with a price. Suppose one cut from Arabella's Curse left one inextricably bound to the ruby and as dependent upon it as an addict on crack?

A phantom prickle of pain shot through my thigh, and I kneaded my leg. The scar couldn't have returned. It was all in my head.

And yet, the morbid truth was staring me straight in the face. My mother needed the ruby to stay strong.

To stay alive.

If that were the case, what in God's name was going to happen to me?

I didn't have the ruby anymore, didn't even know where it

was. Uncle Tav and Ben could have run off to opposite ends of the earth for all I knew. How much time did I have? Years, perhaps? Months? Maybe only a few days? Without the ruby, I was nothing more than a walking corpse living on borrowed time.

I needed to know, needed to understand—for my own sake—my mother's supposed "murder" at my father's hands. How could she have let it happen? And how could I prevent the same fate from overtaking me?

"Tell me," I blurted out, trying to keep my hysteria at bay. "Tell me everything…"

Dad rubbed at his spindly arms and closed his eyes. When he opened them again, he was a million miles away, staring straight ahead as if he could see the events of that horrible night flickering in the space between us like an old home movie.

"We were in the kitchen. She told me she was leaving that night. To Eckhart. To Ian. And I…I tried to stop her."

"She hit me." He caressed his cheek in memory. "And I pushed her. Hard. Too hard." He took a deep breath, his voice cracking under the strain of guilt. "She tripped and her head slammed against the countertop. Her skull cracked. It was a faint sound, like the cracking of an eggshell. When I got to her, there was blood. So much blood. Pooling beneath her head, seeping between the cracks in the tiles… Red, red everywhere I looked."

"I-I felt her pulse." His hand trembled in midair as if he could reach through the years and erase his sins. "Nothing. No heartbeat. Not even a flutter of breath. I was so sure I'd killed my wife and then—"

He shuddered violently.

"And then?" I pressed.

"Her eyes." He wagged two fingers back and forth. "Flickered beneath her lids. One by one, her fingers stirred. The breath that fluttered between her lips smelled like the wine she drank for dinner. Sweet. Begging for a kiss."

Raking a hand through his hair, he turned to me, haggard face pleading for understanding. "I didn't know how any of this was possible. How she could be so very *dead* one moment and then waken as if from a deep sleep. But I didn't want her to wake up."

He cupped his ear. "A voice whispered, 'When she wakes, she'll go to Ian and leave you all alone. Who would love you then?'

"… I grabbed a steak knife from the counter and pressed it to her throat, right over her jugular. The skin was tender, velvet soft, and warm. And when I hesitated, the voice assured me, 'There is no sin.' I-I listened to the voice."

Dad returned to sorting the bullets into groups of six. "But there is sin, Ava. Don't you see? Sin is a bloodstain you can't remove. Sin is…" He swallowed and the bullets scattered across the ink blotter.

Rising from my place on the couch, I went to him. He did not flinch or protest when I touched his shoulder, but placed his hand

396

on top my mine and slowly went to pieces.

I gave him his time, waiting until he stopped weeping to ask, "Do you believe in second chances?"

Dad wiped his nose on his sleeve and sniffled. "I used to. A long time ago."

"I still do. Dad, I—"

"I think," he interrupted, turning his attention to the haphazard collection of lead on his desk, "I think I may take you up on that cup of coffee."

I stared at the top of his disheveled hair, at the tremor in his hands as he picked up a bullet and began the slow process of lining them in a row again. "Okay, I, um... Sandwiches too?"

He nodded absently, his attention fixed on the third bullet on the left, which he couldn't make stand upright with the rest. "I'd like that."

I set the gun on the edge of his desk. "I'll get started right away."

I began walking toward the door.

"Ava?"

I turned around.

Dad looked up from his project. "You're different from your mother," he said softly. "I know that now. You have a heart. A good heart."

"Let's not get insulting." Before he had a chance to reply, I darted from the study and raced to the kitchen, smiling through my tears.

Working with the speed and agility of many nights slinging orders at Joe's Hideaway, I gathered the bread, cheese, and margarine and had the coffee on drip in less than five minutes. I got out the cutting board, selected a knife from the holder, and began to hum. There were a handful of song choices, but I was hopelessly tone deaf and the melody resembled *The Last Rose of Summer.*

The blade sliced through the tomato, squishing a pulpy glob of seeds over my fingers. The old tomcat meandered through the rose bushes and the wind whistled through the eves.

I reached for the other tomato.

The knife clanked against the plastic cutting board.

The coffee dripped into an overflowing pot.

My content humming filled the farmhouse, drifting through the empty rooms and dark hallway—

Drifting, drifting into Dad's study—

Where the *bang* of a gunshot cut off my song.

The tomcat screeched and scampered through the brambles. Staring at my pale reflection in the window over the sink, I waited for my ears to stop ringing.

I glanced down at the cutting board. The knife had slipped and sliced the top of my thumb—almost to the bone. Blood dripped from the wound and onto the tomato slices.

There was no pain. Not yet. My thumb would heal quickly,

but the pain would come later.

Dragging myself to the sink, I stuck my hand under the faucet and watched my blood swirl down the drain, turning the water red.

CHAPTER 30

THE LAST ROSE OF SUMMER

"Cam moved out yesterday—and don't get me started on how many boxes I had to carry..." I stopped blabbering and stared at Dad's headstone. The granite was still wet from this morning's drizzle, and the mound of dirt above his freshly dug plot had turned to mud. A few green shoots had already sprouted. In a matter of time, Dad's grave would be submerged in a sea of tall grass and lavender like the untended plots of his neighbors.

"Who knew he had so much *stuff*? It wasn't easy, what with him fussing about breaking his new Ikea plates, like he isn't going to eat takeout everyday in Vegas anyway..."

Residual raindrops dribbled off the sprawling branches of a chestnut tree and splattered on my shoulder as I studied each block letter of my Dad's name.

"He's got a trainer now, matches booked. In a year, he'll probably go pro." I chatted away in an unpremeditated rush. "I can't say I approve of this mixed martial arts thing, but at least he's found something he's good at and you'd have to agree, nobody's better at beating the shit out of people than Cam. You ought to be proud of him. I know I am."

Fog swirled around the headstones and shrouded the feet of a stone angel with broken wings. I shivered and clutched a bouquet of yellow roses closer to my chest. The roses were from Mrs. Wolcott's garden.

On my final trip back to Ben's house, I'd peered through the window into the Wolcotts' deserted kitchen. I'd looped around the porch, sidestepping a discarded baseball in the driveway. Ben's Chevy was gone. I'd listened for signs of life, but all I could hear were the clinking seashells on the wind chime.

Mother and son had left Eckhart.

Mrs. Wolcott couldn't exactly re-enroll Jason back into his fifth grade class. His teachers and friends would start to ask questions. Lots of questions.

Ben—wherever the hell he was—had probably sent for them to join him. Soon they'd be together again: a family.

In the meantime, my father was dead, my brother was gone, and I was alone. So much for my dreams of family.

My eyes swept over the hilly slopes of Eckhart's only cemetery. A rickety gate guarded the dead from the meandering one-lane highway.

Dad's headstone was plain, utilitarian—all Cam and I could afford. But I'd fought to bury him under the umbrella of the chestnut tree where he'd have shade from the sun and shelter from the rain.

I set the roses atop Dad's grave, thinking about Ben and his family. He'd saved his at the cost of mine. If Ben hadn't absconded with Arabella's Curse, I could've—

Could've, should've, would've.

There was no changing the past. Not when Dad had been buried for three weeks. Even if I had Arabella's Curse in my possession and felt so inclined to grab a shovel from the caretaker's shed, there might be nothing left of my father to resurrect.

Besides, miracles could only go so far. Could the ruby scrape Dad's brains off the wall and shove them back through the hole in his head?

Even if I had Ben's foresight and refrigeration unit, who said Dad wanted to come back? Death was his choice, his absolution for a decade of guilt. And as painful as it was to admit, Dad had given up on life long ago.

"Cam's still mad at you. For leaving us like this. He, um…" I brushed an errant leaf off the top of Dad's headstone. "H-he didn't take your death well."

I pinched the spot where I'd cut my thumb when the gun went off. The wound had healed, leaving no scar, but the gash itself had taken approximately five minutes and thirty-two seconds to heal—about the time it took for me to dash into the

403

study and find Dad sprawled across his desk, his blood soaking an unopened envelope, rendering the contents unreadable.

The letter was the second notice of foreclosure. There would be no third.

Cam was not the only one moving out. The farmhouse, briefly Nolan-owned, now belonged to the bank. My bags were packed, the old Nissan filled with gas for tomorrow's long drive to LA, where a rented room in a one-story Santa Monica bungalow awaited me. I'd found the listing on Craigslist and emailed the woman, Erin, a twenty-something ER nurse, and we got to chatting. She sounded sweet. Motherly. We immediately hit it off.

The rent was a little on the steep side, but the bungalow was walking distance from Santa Monica College, where I'd enrolled after passing my GEDs.

In the days following Dad's suicide, I'd been busy making funeral arrangements, securing a place to live, finding a part-time job, and taking care of school stuff. I didn't have time to mourn.

As the whirlwind of the past three weeks finally died down, I wanted to scream, wail, beat my fist upon the dirt. Fuck you, Dad. You coward! You poor excuse for a man! Why did you leave me? Without a roof over my head or money in my pocket. Without even a proper goodbye. Couldn't you have tried? Just a little? For me? For Cam?

Fuck. You.

"Willa's gone to Vegas too." I stood perfectly still. "She and Cam are moving in together. I hope they don't get drunk and elope. The last thing I need is Willa for a sister-in-law. You probably never met her, but trust me when I say this: never has a bigger bitch walked the face of the earth. She, ah, she..."

The tears flowed fast and hot. I wiped them on my sleeve as I recalled the morning of the move, made all the more uncomfortable by Willa's presence. I'd avoided her all morning and she'd seemed equally adept at tiptoeing around lampshades and end tables, leaving a room as soon as I entered it, and blending in with the wallpaper. The only words she'd spoken to me all morning were, "Do we have more packing tape?"

I was glad to be rid of her. I'd just finished stacking the last of Cam's boxes into the rented U-Haul when Willa approached me with a plate of homemade brownies.

"I took down the video," she said. "Ava, I—"

Shaking her head, she shoved the plate of brownies into my hands and hopped into the passenger seat beside Cam. It wasn't until the U-Haul was a speck of orange in the distance that I glanced down, frowning, at the brownies. Each square was meticulously lathered with mint frosting and generously sprinkled with grated chocolate.

"They were delicious," I told Dad now, "so sweet, so moist, a-and..." My voice cracked, but I forced myself to continue. "If there was rat poison baked in, I couldn't even taste it."

"Syd and Marlene came by later that night with a peace offering of Corn Nuts and Twinkies," I continued. "Between you and me, Dad, I think they're trying to kill me slowly, or maybe Syd's just riddled with guilt over braining me with that napkin dispenser."

"I don't get people sometimes." I sank to the grass, hugged my knees to my chest, and sobbed. A flock of ravens loitering on the nearby gate filled the cemetery with a chorus of caws. "As soon as you have someone all figured out, they like to switch it up on you until you're all confused and don't know how to think or how to feel. Until you don't even know who you are anymore."

Wiping my nose on my sleeve, I peered through my tears at a pair of black patent leather shoes. The tip of a polished mahogany cane slammed into the weeds.

I shielded my eyes against the sight of Uncle Tav's big, beautiful head eclipsing the sun.

"Shit."

♦

"Hello, Sweet Pea."

Uncle Tav bent down to help me up. He held a bouquet of blood-red roses.

Ignoring his hand, I hoisted myself to my feet and dusted the grass from my bottom. "What do you want?"

"To see my brother." He gestured to Dad's grave. "And you."

His tone sounded solemn enough, but I knew better than to fall for that trick again.

I eyed his navy blazer and purple pocket square in scorn. "Not exactly dressed for mourning, are you? What's the matter with black? Blends too well with your soul?"

"I have a feeling you're not happy to see me."

"Go with the feeling." I gave my jeans one final smack. "How dare you show your face here! You're lucky I don't have my knife on me."

"I deserve that," he said softly.

"You killed my father."

"Sweet Pea..." He shook his head sadly. "He killed *himself*."

"You gave him the gun."

"He pulled the trigger—"

"You planted the seed in his mind. You drove him mad!"

"What nonsense! Me? Planting seeds..." Laughing off my accusation, Uncle Tav flicked a piece of lint from his sleeve. "My dear, the truth of the matter is: your 'father,' as you still insist upon calling him, was a very troubled man. He chose his own fate."

He placed the bouquet of roses on Dad's grave. "May you finally find some peace, dear brother," he whispered and planted a kiss on the top of the headstone.

Urgh! There was no point. He would never admit to his part

407

in Dad's death, just as he'd never admit to his breakdown the night he beheaded my mother.

"One more thing," I said, after he'd finished.

Uncle Tav raised his eyebrows. "Yes?"

I nodded to his cane. "May I see it?"

"Of course." He handed the cane over.

I studied the silver skull pommel and ran a finger along the polished mahogany. "Still having trouble walking?"

"My stab wound healed long ago," he said absently. "It's more of a fashion accessory now."

"Good." I slammed the cane down over my knee and snapped it in half. Uncle Tav blanched as I handed back the pitiful remains of his metrosexual walking stick.

He studied the splintered ends. "You have your mother's temper."

I kicked a stray rock out of my way and poked him in the chest. "How much money did you two cretins get for my ruby? Six figures? Seven? How'd you split it? Fifty-fifty? Seventy-thirty? As if you needed the extra money, you dick!"

With perfectly calibrated frankness, he replied, "I don't have Arabella's Curse, Sweet Pea."

"Of course you don't, you sold it."

"That was the plan," he countered. "Unfortunately, our mutual friend had other plans."

"You're so full of shit!"

His lips curled in amusement, but his black eyes burned with devil's fire. "How good would you say you are at chess?"

"Uncle Tav, that's hardly here or there—"

"On a scale of one to ten?"

"You taught me how to play," I said. "So ten?"

"Have you ever beaten Wolcott?"

I recalled all the grueling chess matches with Ben in the weeks following my accident. They had one of two outcomes: stalemate or my shameful defeat.

"No...never." For the first time, I considered the possibility that Uncle Tav might be telling the truth. Ben was smart. That was a given. But was he cunning enough, not to mention *ballsy* enough, to deceive someone as ruthless and well-connected as Uncle Tav?

The more I thought about it, the more I realized that a guy who would attempt to cheat death by bringing his brother back to life was ballsy enough to do anything.

"Word of advice, Sweet Pea. Never trust someone *that* good at chess."

"Wait, you mean to tell me..."

"Wolcott has the ruby," he said, matter-of-factly.

I scrutinized his face for the slightest hint of bullshitting. "Let me get this straight: Ben stole the ruby from *you* that you had him steal from *me*?!"

Uncle Tav uttered a long-suffering sigh. "Boys can be so

fickle!"

"You don't even seem angry," I observed.

"I don't believe in getting angry," he said. "And something tells me neither do you. One of the many things we have in common, pet."

"We share the same blood. That's about it."

"And the same enemy..."

"What do you want?" I asked bluntly.

"Not to put too fine a point on it," he said, "I want the lad's head on a pike."

"And what do you want *me* to do?"

Uncle Tav glanced down at the splintered ends of his cane and then back up at me. "Do what you do best."

Team up with Uncle Tav to make Ben pay? Team up to steal Arabella's Curse back? The idea had merit, but one critical flaw.

"Ben's disappeared off the face of the earth. He could be living in a foxhole in China for all we know. Plus..." I wrinkled my nose in disgust. "I don't like you. What makes you think I'll help you? What makes you think I want anything to do with you?"

Dropping his broken cane on the ground, Uncle Tav took a step toward me. "It's come to my attention that there's an unflattering video of you on the internet. Made by one Drake Elliott."

Tilting his head, he noted the effect his words had on me, and his mouth quirked into a smile. He took my hand and pressed a key in my palm. A car key.

"What the hell is this?"

"I wish I could've given you his Ferrari," Uncle Tav interrupted, "but after Mr. Elliott drove it off a cliff, it's in no condition for my girl." With a sigh, his long fingers swept the air. "An unfortunate accident…"

"Accident?" A sickening premonition bubbled like tar in my gut.

"Sharp curve, shoddy breaks. He really shouldn't have been speeding," he said with a tragic lift of his shoulder. "Live fast, die young and leave a good-looking corpse. Right, Sweet Pea?"

The key slipped into the weeds. I stumbled to the chestnut tree and braced myself against the trunk. The rough bark scratched my cheek. A cold sweat erupted over my skin. I furled and unfurled my hands. My palms were sweaty, the lines steeped in dirt and imaginary blood. Drake's blood.

I wanted to make Drake suffer, but I didn't want or ask for this.

His hand gripped my shoulder. I stiffened and opened my eyes. The ravens had flown, leaving the gate bare.

"Do you doubt I'm on your side now?" Uncle Tav whispered in my ear. "It must be hard. To be so alone. Be my daughter, Ava." He slipped a handkerchief from his breast pocket and dangled it in front of my face. "Remember, God may let you down, but your father never will."

As I studied the monogram initials, the irony of my situation struck me like a thunderclap. I'd spent half the year trying to find a ruby so my father would love me. My father was dead, replaced by another, who also expected, wait for it...

A ruby in exchange for love.

I'd literally *died* for that ruby, and now Uncle Tav wanted another quest. Another blood-splattered sequel.

One more. Just one more. Greedy, greedy man.

I felt very tired. So very tired. And so fucking sick of Arabella's Curse.

A chuckle escaped my lips. I braced my hands on my knees, laughing until my sides ached.

Uncle Tav frowned. "What's so funny?"

"What's it all for?" I hiccupped. "What's it all for?"

"Sweet Pea?" Uncle Tav sounded genuinely concerned.

"We're all reprehensible. That's what you taught me. Some people are just better at hiding it than others, but you don't try to hide it at all." I pushed his hand away. "I don't need your handkerchief, Uncle Tav. I don't need a father, either. I'm eighteen now. It's about time I stand on my own."

Uncle Tav's chiseled features drew in pain. "But don't you want to be a family?"

"Not if there's strings attached." I continued. "You're going to have to find Arabella's Curse and Ben without me. I'm done."

I backed away.

"Sweet Pea!"

"I'm done."

Ducking my head, I hurried past the other grave markers, not daring to look back.

"Sweet Pea, please…please don't leave me."

The gate creaked as I exited the cemetery and slipped behind the wheel of my Nissan. In the rearview mirror, I saw him standing amongst the headstones.

"Goodbye, Uncle Tav." I pulled into the highway and the lonely figure vanished from my mirror—and my life—forever.

♦

I packed through the night, unable to sleep in a house where my dad's blood still stained the floors. After loading the last moving box into the backseat, I did a quick walkabout of the farmhouse, visiting every empty room except for Dad's study.

With a heavy heart, I entered my bedroom. I ran a finger along the top of my vanity table and touched the remnants of the photographs I'd taped around the mirror.

My hand froze in midair.

There was a sound outside.

Of footsteps on the dry grass bed.

I closed my eyes and listened. There were two heartbeats. The first belonged to me, the second—

I crossed over to the window and spotted an amorphous shadow bobbing along the grove of twisted apple trees. The gate creaked open and Ben stepped out of the darkness like a specter stepping in from another world.

Halting right under my window, he jammed his hands in his jeans' pockets and tipped his head back to look up at me. Just like the night we met. Except this time, Cam wasn't around to beat him up.

I backed away and stood in the middle of my bedroom. What the hell did Ben want from me? I owed him nothing, least of all an audience.

Raking a hand through my hair, I debated hiding inside until he got the hint. After about five minutes passed, I stalked back to the window. Ben was still there. Guess he didn't get the hint.

"Shit..." Heaving the world's deepest sigh, I stomped out of my room and jogged down the stairs. I'd already had one confrontation today. Bring on round two.

I slipped out the kitchen door and stepped onto the lawn. The night air brought with it the scent of lavender and a hint of the ocean. Ben waited for me in the shadow of an elm tree.

We stared at each other for a long time, neither speaking nor moving.

"You let your hair grow," I said, noting the dark strands curling over the collar of his jacket. The last time I'd seen him, his head had been shaved to accommodate the stitches required to close the gash on his scalp.

"And you've cut yours," Ben said softly.

His clothes fit better where they used to hang off his scrawny body and he walked taller, as if he'd finally grown comfortable with his height. He was still pale, however, and the circles under his eyes gave him a sinister-sexy appearance—a dark prince cloaked in shadow.

"You look very handsome, Ben," I said.

At my comment, sadness rippled across his face. "I heard you passed your GEDs."

I nodded, adding, "With flying colors."

His smile was weighted with regret. "And you've enrolled in college?"

"Yes. I think I might go pre-law. I've been told I have a big mouth." I took a tentative step toward him and he did the same, his shoes crushing the fallen leaves. "How's your mother?"

"Happy."

Another step closer and I was standing in the middle of the yard. "And your brother?"

Unfazed by my question, Ben answered, "Thawing."

He closed the gap between us until we were mere inches from touching.

"Is he happy?" I asked.

Ben took a long time to reply. Finally, he walked right past me and slumped against the fence post. "No."

"Is he having trouble adjusting?"

"We've enrolled him in school, but he has no friends. The other children avoid him." He sank to the ground and gathered his legs to his chest. "There's a rusty jungle gym at the corner of the playground where he'll sit for the entire recess bouncing a red ball. Over and over again. The color…fascinates him."

"Red." I probed my throat. The beginning and end of Jason Wolcott's world.

Ben glanced up at the silvery leaves of the elm. "The world is too loud for him. All he wants to do is stay inside—in the dark— with his eyes closed and headphones over his ears. Last week, he asked me, 'Why?'"

"Why?" I sat down next to him.

"'Why did you wake me up? I was having the most beautiful dream.'" His Adam's apple bobbed up and down. "You have every right to hate me, Ava. But I need you to know why I—"

"I already know. You wanted your family back." And that was something I understood only too well. I plucked a dandelion from the ground and twirled it around by the stem. "For what it's worth, I don't hate you."

Ben turned to me. Tormented brown eyes searched my face. "You don't?"

Discarding the dandelion, I reached into my jacket pocket and withdrew my butterfly knife. He stiffened, eyes flickering over the tense line of my arm. I flipped the knife open and ran a thumb along the flat of the blade.

"If you had tried to visit me yesterday or even earlier this morning, this knife would've found a nice home in your kneecap. Fortunately, you've caught me during a transitional period, so I'm not going to stab you—much as you deserve it. My stabbing days are over. I'm an Ava transformed."

"I like the new Ava Nolan." Ben rubbed his eyes. "Especially when she talks in the third person."

I socked him on the shoulder. "Listen up: you've made my Uncle Tav very angry..."

"I know." He buried his face between his knees. The dark side must be a sucky place. "Tavistock...eff my life."

I pressed the knife into his palm and closed his fingers over the ivory handle. "I have a feeling you'll need this more than I do."

He nodded in resignation. "I have something for you, too." His hand disappeared inside his pocket and reappeared with a tiny tin box. "This belongs to you," he said, popping the clasp.

"No, stop..." I pressed a hand over the lid.

A frown pleated his brow. "Don't you want your ruby back?"

"The color red has lost its appeal. Keep it, Wolcott. The Curse is all yours."

"I suppose I deserve that." Ben tucked the box back in his pocket, then tentatively scooted closer. "I guess this means goodbye?"

I bit my lower lip and nodded. "All dark adventures must come to an end."

"Forever?"

The rush. The high. I used to desire all the things that would destroy me in the end. I no longer wanted to dance with death.

"You're bad for me, Wolcott. It's time I walk in the light and you just...you don't belong," I said and had the displeasure of watching his heart break.

He slid a finger down the bridge of my nose and traced the angle of my jaw. His thumb brushed away the tears on my cheek. His next question was a plea. "But don't you want to be with me?"

"I do." I planted a soft kiss on his lips—our last kiss. Our fairy tale began with blood; it would not end the same way. "But I'd rather be happy."

ABOUT THE AUTHOR

Born and raised in sunny Southern California, Teresa Yea prefers the shade because that's how she rolls. She is a UCLA graduate, a science geek by degree, bookworm at heart. *The Witch of Blackbird Pond* is her favorite novel and her crush on Nat Eaton is challenged only by her love for Jamie Fraser. A major movie buff, she has no qualms quoting *Pulp Fiction* and annoying you to no end. She can usually be found singing *Phantom of the Opera* in the car with dramatic hand gestures. Do not underestimate her petite stature for she is a feisty girl who is not afraid to head-butt people in the face. She is also very silly, but her secret evil is revealed only in her novels. Talking about herself in the third person is weird.

Sign up for my newsletter for VIP access to exclusive excerpts, the latest scoop on new releases, giveaways, and cover reveals.

Hang with me at teresayea.com.

Chat with me on Twitter. Musicals and movies are all ice-breaking topics. Better yet, if you tweet me the lyrics to *Phantom*, we're already BFFs: @teresayea.

Follow my Facebook. Warning, I do 'Like' back with a vengeance: Facebook.com/teresayeawriter.

Follow my foodie, fashion, and nail polish-hoarding shenanigans on Instagram: @teresayea.

ACKNOWLEDGEMENTS

A million thanks and endless gratitude to the following people, without whom this book could never be written:

My husband, Eric, who had enough faith in me to suggest I take the leap into writing and supported me through a decade of artistic highs and lows. You are my love, my rock, my everything.

My parents, Steve and Connie, for supporting my career switch from doctor to writer and not kicking me out of the house.

My brother, Oscar, for putting up with my extremely loud typing.

My in-laws, Joy and Craig, for their unshakeable belief, enthusiasm, and support.

All these wonderful writers who have left their expert footprints on this manuscript: Sarah Glenn Marsh, Ami Allen Vath, Heidi Lang, Rhiann Wynn-Nolet, Kristina Perez, and Stephanie Garber.

Christa Heschke for tirelessly fighting in my corner and championing my writing to the end.

Elizabeth Briggs, my pitch-wars mentor and indie publishing spirit guide.

My eagle-eyed copy editor, Stephanie Parent.

My cover artist extraordinaire, Jenny Zemanek.

And all my readers. Thank you.

THANK YOU

If you've enjoyed BLACK HEART, RED RUBY, please consider leaving a review. Reviews help bring others to my work and I'd really appreciate your opinion, even if all you say is "a good book to read while pooping" because, seriously, people have to find *something* to read when nature calls and with your help that book could be this one.

Need something twisted to tide you over before the next WICKED JEWEL adventure? Turn the page to read the first chapter of LOVE IN A TIME OF MONSTERS.

An excerpt from LOVE IN A TIME OF MONSTERS

He has a monster problem
Scotland, 1867. When Rob Stevenson's brother is killed—and eaten—in the forest outside their estate, Rob's sheltered world is shattered by a monster infestation. Determined to keep his village safe, Rob's first duty as laird involves hiring a professional hunter.

She kills monsters
The sole survivor of a massacre in the Congo, Catriona Mornay is rumored to have lost her mind in the jungle. In Edinburgh's gas-lit streets, Cat's skill as a hunter is unmatched. Her reputation as a killer of unnatural creatures, legendary.

Two worlds collide
Faced with a rising body count, Rob takes a chance on Cat, hoping that somewhere inside this tortured yet charismatic girl is the hero he's been searching for. But in this shadow realm of secrets, lies, and underworld crime, their lives overlap in more ways than one. And in an age where harpies flock the sky and serpents rule the sea, it's even possible for a boy and his hunter to fall in love.

But can their love survive in a time of monsters?

Scotland, 1867

That blasted dog was at it again.

Sniffing the soil.

Snarling at the air.

Howling loud enough to wake the dead.

"Virgil!" Rob sprinted after his brother's Border Collie. The pup had been dodgy all morning. "Virgil, get back here!"

Rob started off strong and fast, but he was no match for Virgil's agility. By the time he crested the last hill, Rob doubled over, palms against knees, wheezing. "Bad dog," he reprimanded the thatch of thistle sprouting between his boots. "I'll flay you alive! See if I won't!"

Massaging the stitch in his side, Rob squinted through the haze. Virgil had receded into a black and white dot on a field of green.

The drizzle stung his cheeks and seeped through his hunting jacket. Rob was used to the foul Highland weather, but he didn't want to spend his birthday catching pneumonia and smelling like wet tweed. He stifled a cough, longing for the warmth of his father's library and the shelves of leather-bound books. He would've been content turning seventeen while reading about shooting if it weren't for Alec dragging him outside and shoving a rifle into his scrawny arms.

Kill something.

Be a man.

These were his brother's orders—the laird's orders. How could he possibly disobey?

He lurched down the hill and into a glen.

Whipping off his cap, Rob collapsed against a spire of rock protruding from the valley like a towering monolith. The rock dug into his backside, a small discomfort when his entire body hummed with pain. He wiped cold drizzle from his brow and glanced up. A fortress of intimidating black brier and evergreens loomed before him, barring entrance to the dark woods where the fae, gremlins, and evil spirits walked in the spaces between the trees.

In the distance, Virgil scouted the forest line, ears perked and fur standing on end. Rob stripped off his rifle as Virgil snarled at the moss-covered trunks.

"Slacking, are we?" Alec's voice boomed in his ear. A hand with big blunt fingers descended upon his shoulder. His brother's smile was a white crescent against a swarthy face. Rob shrugged the hand away, feeling pale and insignificant so close to Alec—a rabbit next to a bear.

Rob nodded to Virgil. "What the devil is wrong with him?"

"He's just primed and ready to take down a stag."

"He's a Border Collie," Rob muttered. "They herd sheep."

"I ought to have Virgil herd you." Alec ruffled Rob's helmet of carefully pomaded hair. "England has made you soft."

Rob slicked his hair back, making sure each white-blond strand was in place. He got the same treatment at Eton, except the chaps there did more than muss up his hair. They dribbled ink on his dress shirts, pissed on his pillow, made him lick the horseshit off their boots. Boarding school life descended into a special circle of Hell when they discovered the sonnet penned on the edge of his Latin conjugations. They wrote a poem about him that day. It was called "Faggy Rob" and spawned a nickname he'd rather forget. Though it should be noted their poem was horrendously spelled and blatantly disregarded iambic pentameter.

Dashing the unpleasant memory away, Rob nodded to the string of dead grouse pinned to Alec's side. "I think we've shot enough poultry to feed the entire estate."

"No, brother. *I* shot the poultry. *You've* yet to shoot a thing. We're not turning back until you've hit something." Alec scrubbed his jaw, fingers scraping thick black stubble. Another week or two and Alec would look like Blackbeard.

Rob palmed his own smooth cheeks. He'd tried growing a mustache once. A year later, he was still trying. "I did hit something."

"Empty air." Splotches of sunlight glinted off the sapphire ring on Alec's pinky. Rob shuddered at the unimaginable horrors "Faggy Rob" would've endured if he wore a ring like that to Eton—a treatment his big brother would never know.

He remembered hiding in the shadows outside his father's bedroom as the laird lectured Alec about his birthright. The sapphire, along with their land, was a gift from Bonnie Prince Charlie to the first Earl of Balfour, their great-great-grandfather. Father wore it until the crofters dragged his body from the loch.

Now it was Alec's turn, and the ring fit as if the gold had been forged for his finger. No surprise. Alec was born to lead, while Rob, born last, born sickly, was destined for smaller things.

"Up!" Alec looped a hand under his elbow and yanked him to his feet. "We've got to shape you up before you set foot on that ship, and you haven't given me much time." His bushy brows furrowed as he scrutinized Rob's slender frame. "Five years is a long time to be away from home. Who will look after you if you have a relapse?"

"I haven't been ill in years and well you know it." Rob brushed the wrinkles left by Alec's hand. He'd only just returned from England and was already suffocating beneath his brother's fretting. With both parents dead, Alec was mother and father to Rob and their sister Waverley, but sometimes Alec could be a right tyrant. Rob's commission from the Royal Geographical Society, finalized right after graduation, couldn't come as a more welcomed escape.

The West Indies.

His mind swirled with accounts of the old captains' logs. Of white sand beaches and palm fronds swaying on a distant shore. Rob's heart drummed with excitement. In a week's time, he'd leave his brother's shadow and finally be able to walk in the sun.

"I don't see why I need to learn how to shoot." Rob propped his rifle—a hand-me-down from Alec's enormous collection—against the boulder. "Collecting and cataloging insects is hardly a treacherous activity."

"Not treacherous?" Alec shouted above the incessant barking of his Border Collie. Virgil scrambled back to his master and nudged Alec's thigh with his snout. "Tell that to Hugh Mornay. He sailed to Africa collecting beetles and butterflies, just like you. Where is he now?"

Rob stiffened at the mention of the infamous scientist. "Mornay *used* to study insects."

But in Mornay's final days, his interests had changed to creatures of a different nature. Rob was still in school when he read the headlines of the ill-fated Mornay expedition and the ghost ship docking in Liverpool with only one survivor.

"We're living in a time of monsters." Alec picked up the rifle and shoved it into Rob's unwilling hands. "Take care of yourself. I won't always be there to protect you."

"'A time of monsters' is actually a falsity," Rob hitched the gun over his shoulder, "a bastardization of Mornay's lecture at the Society of Unnatural Creatures." He recited the transcript by heart. "Monsters have lived in the shadow of man since the dawn of creation. Now their numbers are multiplying. The height of our empire is also the golden age of monsters."

"How stimulating." Alec rolled his eyes. "Race you to the woods?"

"What race? You always win." Shoving his hands in his pockets, Rob attempted to kick a pebble and missed.

Coordination was not his forte. "This better not take all day."

"It's only as long as you make it." Alec slapped his thigh and whistled for Virgil. "Come on, boy!"

Virgil circled his master's legs. With a low-throated growl, the Border Collie darted into the brambles.

"Virgil!" Alec jogged after his dog and halted in front of the tree line. "What do you suppose has gotten into him?"

"That's what I've been trying to tell you all morning." Rob stared past his brother's broad back to the briers straining to reach the sky. Even in daylight, the forest was suffused in darkness.

Rob listened for rustling, heard nothing. The villagers called the divide between forest and glen "The Gates of Hell." Cheery lot, the local folk. He'd never been one to believe in superstitious rot. Now, he couldn't help but wonder if Virgil had stumbled into another realm.

Good riddance. He and the dog never got on anyway. "It's a sign we should go home."

"What's that?" Alec whistled. "Virgil! Stop playing games!"

"I said, maybe we should call it a day."

Fingers drumming against his leg, Alec hollered into the dark woods, "Virgil! Come back, boy! Virgil!" His voice bounced off the neighboring crags. He turned around, forehead wrinkled in worry. "He's never like this, Rob. Never..."

"He may be sick. Rabid. You might have to consider the

possibility of…well," Rob paused, nodding to his brother's rifle, "putting him down."

His words hung in the air with the drizzle—cold, wet, and portentous. Alec blanched and Rob wished his physician, Dr. Jekyll's, bedside manners had rubbed off on him.

Alec's jaw tensed. "I'm going after him."

"Shall I go with you?" Rob offered, even though the prospect of wandering the forest in the damp was not exactly inviting. *Please say no. Please say no.* He coughed into his fist, drawing a hacking fit out of a tickle.

Alec swatted him on the back until Rob cleared his throat. "I won't be about a minute. Just…" He seized the loose ends of Rob's wool scarf and knotted it. "Take care of yourself."

Rob chewed on his inner cheek to keep from grinning. Being the family invalid had its advantages. "I'll just wait here."

With a nod, Alec whirled on his heels and slipped inside the forest.

"That was easy." Rob found a comfortable spot in the grass.

Plucking a leather journal from his breast pocket, Rob turned to the page he'd been working on before Alec dragged him outside. He tapped the pencil's tip on his tongue, tasting lead, as he tried to recall the song he'd invented to accompany the fireside story he'd made up for Waverley. His sister had requested a tale about buccaneers and buried gold.

He scribbled a few lines, scratched them out, then wrote:

Fifteen men on a dead man's chest.

Rob leaned against the boulder and stared at the sky. The sun peeked through shifting grey clouds, casting a radiant light on his pages. As Rob set to work, his chills and aches seeped away. It no longer mattered that he was fragile, thin, prone to coughs and fevers. In letters he was a titan. A king confined to a pointy line of scrawl.

Rob burned through ten pages when the *boom* of a gunshot snapped the lead off his pencil. Birds exploded from the canopy, cawing, screeching, flapping in chaotic zigzags.

BOOM!

Rob flinched, shoulders bucking against the boulder.

A second shot?

Seafaring dreams of schooners and maroons quite dashed, Rob scrambled to his feet. His notebook tumbled to the grass. The first serpent of trepidation slithered inside his stomach.

Knees knocking together like a newborn calf's, he stumbled to the fae woods and halted at the line where the green grass ceased growing. Rob glanced over his shoulder. Should he run back for help? Would he have enough time?

BOOM!

Three shots?

Christ, Alec. How many times are you going to shoot the poor mutt?

He got his answer when the third shot gave way to screams.

♦

His rifle landed in the soft peat bed. Rob knelt and scooped up the gun with trembling hands.

The screams, cut short long before he summoned the courage to venture into the woods, echoed in his head. Never before had he heard a man—or another human being for that matter—make such a desperate sound. It reminded him of the same high-pitched shrieks the piglets made when the farmers took them to slaughter.

Rob forced himself to move.

Kill something.

Be a man.

His boots trampled across mushy leaves. A droplet splashed on the back of his hand. Rob glanced at the sky. Scant light diffused through the canopy, turning early morning into darkest night. The forest creaked and groaned like a set of moldering bones.

"What am I doing here?"

He was no man. No brave hunter. Alec was all of those things and more. Alec was trying to teach him how to hunt and he'd refused to listen.

He wished he had. Oh God, he wished he had. Now Alec had ceased to scream.

A twig snapped.

Whirling around, Rob aimed his rifle at a wild hare. The hare glared across the barrel, whiskers twitching.

Rob lowered his rifle and the hare darted through the underbrush. If he couldn't scare a rabbit, what made him think he could take down a—

These are glorious times, gentlemen...

As Hugh Mornay's words rang in his ears, Rob willed himself not to jump to conclusions.

A golden age of monsters.

Every phenomenon under the sun could be explained coolly, logically, with the aid of reason.

My blood is singing.

Rob trekked on. Alec was laird. The best shot. Never sick a day in his life.

He was going to bring Alec home.

The forest hushed to an unnatural quiet save for his harsh breathing and the crunch of leaves beneath his boots.

His lips moved soundlessly, "Fifteen men on a dead man's chest..."

Fifteen dead.

The newsprint of that year-old article swirled before him. Cold statistics drummed up by reporters who had never been there.

15 May 1866.

Fifteen lost to the jungle, including Hugh Mornay, never to see the light of day.

The rest slaughtered on board ship. The deck stained with blood. The bodies in the hull, ripped to pieces. One survivor. A girl gone mad.

As he entered a clearing, Rob wrinkled his nose. The reek of carrion pervaded the air. Flies swarmed and buzzed in a black cloud.

Covering his nose, Rob peered around a fallen trunk and recoiled at the sight of a dead ewe, her fleece stained with blood and dirt. The carcass was missing several crucial parts, notably her head and foreleg.

She had been ripped apart.

He stumbled to the nearest tree and retched. This was not how he'd expected to spend his birthday, hacking up this morning's porridge. Wiping his mouth, Rob stared at the maggots squirming inside the ewe's decapitated stump. He recalled the hushed conversations between Alec and his housekeeper in the days after Rob's return. The tenants were complaining about wolves making off with their livestock. The McBains' rooster. The Abernathys' heifer. Two or three sheep from the Callahans' flock.

Click.

Rob surveyed the gaps between the trees.

Click.

He thought he heard a faint rasp and rustle of leaves. Except there was no wind. The air was heavy with the stench of death.

The calm before the storm.

Then the storm struck.

Saplings snapped and bent like an archer's bow.

A shadow yawned across the clearing.

Rob raised his rifle. The barrel bobbed in the air. As his index finger grasped for the trigger, the rifle tumbled to the ground.

"Useless. So bloody useless." His hand hovered above the rifle, slender and white, no calluses except for the writer's bump on his index finger. These were not the hands of a hunter. As this morning's lesson sadly demonstrated, he couldn't hit the hide of a cow.

Rob grabbed the gun. A newspaper article flashed through his mind and the most inopportune questions bombarded him. The sole survivor. Hugh Mornay's daughter.

Catriona.

Gone mad after months on board with a monster. How did she manage to live when the others perished?

The blurry newsprint came into focus: *Found under a pile of corpses.*

The last of the branches snapped and a swarming blackness encroached upon the clearing. In a blind panic, he forgot about the gun and leaped over the trunk.

Landing next to the sheep carcass, he wiggled as close to the dirty fleece as he could stand. Broken branches snagged his shirt and scraped his stomach. Bile rose in his throat. If he lived through this, he was going to scrub his skin with lye.

Catriona. He'd thought of her often. In the dark of his dormitory at Eton and under crisp sheets. He fantasized about meeting her one day. What would she look like? A Greek goddess, obviously.

Catriona.

Rob recited her name like an incantation; he'd never dreamed the day would come when he would call upon this goddess for guidance. Seizing the ewe by a leg, he crawled under it and gagged soundlessly in the dirt.

Something pounced in the air and landed at the exact spot where he'd stood seconds before. Its shadow stretched and slithered over him. It sniffed the air like a wolf, but when he expected it to growl, it made a *clicking* sound much like the transmission of Morse Code.

Click. Click. Click.

With a final sniff, the creature began to move.

The crush of leaves echoed through his ear. It crawled with remarkable stealth and perched upon the log. Rob squeezed his eyes shut. A maggot plopped on his wrist and wriggled on his skin. He sensed the creature's eyes boring down on the top of his head, felt a blast of hot air as it opened its mouth. A foulness beyond measure sliced through the stench of the sheep.

Click. Click. Click.

Another nasty little worm tumbled down the back of his neck

and squirmed along the base of his spine. He clawed the dirt, grounded his cheek more firmly against the forest floor.

An eternity passed.

The creature waited and it occurred to Rob this entity, this *monster* was a devious thing.

It was studying him, trying to determine if he was indeed dead. *It* waited for him to slip up.

A plump maggot writhed between his fingers. He formed a fist, squishing the maggot into pulp. The creature crouched forward and sniffed the carcass.

Rob stifled a scream. If he moved or breathed, he was as good as dead. Just like Catriona Mornay, Rob felt his mind disintegrating, descending into madness—mathematical equations, sonnets, sonatas unraveling like a spool of yarn.

The air pressure shifted again. The ground trembled. The creature sprang off the log.

Rob dared to crack open an eye. The *thing* scrambled up a trunk like a lizard and leaped.

Tree after tree bowed under its weight. Shielding his eyes from the shower of debris, Rob caught the sunlight glimmering off the creature's armored back.

Black plating.

A foreleg three times the size of a horse's.

Talons.

The creature disappeared into the leaves, absorbed into the

pores of the forest.

Stiff and dazed, Rob crawled from under the carcass.

A whimper greeted him. He lifted his head. "Virgil!"

Breaking into a smile of sheer relief, he flung his arms around that blasted pup. If Virgil was unharmed, surely Alec must not be far behind.

"Where's Alec, boy?" He scratched the dog behind the ear. The fur was slick and sticky. He glanced down at his blood-smeared palms. Rob scanned the forest, searching for his brother. "Where—"

Virgil held something in his mouth: a hand with big blunt fingers.

Rob's smile vanished. His bottom smacked the earth with a *thud*. Virgil dropped the severed hand and whimpered. Trotting toward Rob, the pup buried his blood-smeared muzzle in his new master's side.

A gust of wind stirred the canopy, casting dapples of daylight over his brother's sapphire ring. Rob tilted his head at the section of sky. The clouds dispersed and the sun blazed, glorious and bright, the beginning of a new day.

And somewhere in the distant treetops, the creature lifted its head to the sun and screeched.

Made in the USA
Lexington, KY
15 August 2015